Angela Lambert was born in 1940 and educated at a boarding-school in Sussex and at St Hilda's College, Oxford, where she read PPE. She then worked for a cabinet minister before becoming a journalist in 1969. After this she was a television reporter with ITN and Thames Television for seventeen years until she joined the newly launched *Independent* in 1988. She now writes interviews for the *Daily Mail.* Angela Lambert has three grown-up children and five grandchildren, and lives with her partner Tony Price in London and France. *Kiss and Kin* is her fifth novel.

Also by Angela Lambert

LOVE AMONG THE SINGLE CLASSES
NO TALKING AFTER LIGHTS
A RATHER ENGLISH MARRIAGE
THE CONSTANT MISTRESS

non-fiction
UNIQUE SOULS: THE INDIAN SUMMER OF THE
BRITISH ARISTOCRACY 1939: THE LAST OF PEACE

KISS AND KIN

Angela Lambert

BLACK SWAN

KISS AND KIN
A BLACK SWAN BOOK: 0 552 99736 6

Originally published in Great Britain by Bantam Press,
a division of Transworld Publishers Ltd

PRINTING HISTORY
Bantam Press edition published 1997
Black Swan edition published 1998

Set in 11/12pt Melior by Falcon Oast Graphic Art

Black Swan Books are published by Transworld Publishers Ltd,
61–63 Uxbridge Road, London W5 5SA,
in Australia by Transworld Publishers (Australia) Pty Ltd,
15–25 Helles Avenue, Moorebank, NSW 2170
and in New Zealand by Transworld Publishers (NZ) Ltd,
3 William Pickering Drive, Albany, Auckland.

Reproduced, printed and bound in Great Britain by
Cox & Wyman Ltd, Reading, Berks.

Dedicated with love and thanks to our friends,
Mary and Tom Moore and Kato,
not forgetting Boot.

Acknowledgements

Many friends have helped me to get the factual details in this book right, believing as I do that if you can trust the facts you are more likely to believe the fiction.

Dr David Fleming searched for authentic and suitable words from his collection of madrigals and faxed them over to France within hours of my request. Peter Gray and Barry Peters gave me details of local Cercles des Oiseaux, as well as railway stations in L'Aveyron. Becky Stockland (Mrs Antony Gurton) checked the libretto for the last act of *Carmen*, while Oliver Tims of the English National Opera verified the version used in Jonathan Miller's production at the Coliseum in September 1995 and sent the relevant words.

Dr Ela Wright (Mrs Peter Beer) went to a good deal of trouble to research the exact electroconvulsive therapy (ECT) treatment administered to men whose minds were damaged in the Second World War.

Hilary Taylor (Mrs Spud Taylor) drew my attention to several literary parallels which the reader should be left to discover, or not – it will make no difference to the understanding of the novel. It gave Hilary and me pleasure to work them out.

Nicholas Faith answered several questions about the precise nomenclature of the public rooms in the Reform Club, the hours at which it served drinks and the services it provided. Philip Howard was equally helpful with similar questions about the Garrick Club.

Dr Peter Jones of Newcastle University acted as a one-man research library, always ready to leap to my aid no matter how tiresome or obscure my questions, while also sustaining me with daily faxes.

M. Daniel Mazelier and his expertise kept me writing in the middle of a meadow in France when a less tolerant and sympathetic computer doctor would have given up.

My children, Carolyn Butler, Jonathan Lambert and Marianne Vizinczey Lambert were, as usual, supportive of my efforts and disconcertingly perceptive about my short-comings. Most of their suggestions have been incorporated and without them, the finished book would have been much more embarrassing.

To all these people, for their invisible help which greatly improved and enriched parts of this book that my own knowledge could not reach, my thanks.

As always, Tony Price was the first to read and criticize every paragraph and every page. His patience, generosity and indulgence are beyond praise.

Angela Lambert
Groléjac, France, September 1995 - July 1996

Dramatis Personae
The action takes place during a week in late September 1995

The Gaunt Family:
OLIVER GAUNT 60, (b. 1935) retired and living in France; md. 1959 to
CLARISSA JANE GAUNT née Sullivan, 59 (b. 1936);
their children:
JENNIFER CAPEL née Gaunt 33, (b. 1962) md. Roderick Capel 1982
PHILOMENA GAUNT 33, Jennifer's twin, (b. 1962) unmd. barrister
PATRICK GAUNT 25, (b. 1970) bachelor living in France; estate agent.
OLIVER's college friends:
   Mark Ellacott 60, married to Belinda;
   Ben Vulliamy 60, md. to Mona, 56;
   Matthew Vulliamy 33, their son, a fringe theatre director;
   Thomas Ormerod 61, (unmd.);
   Peregrine (Perry) Horsfall 60, former Army colleague of Oliver's.
JENNIFER's colleagues in publishing:
   Thorwald Gustavsson, her boss at Thorensen and Markworth;
   Marion 38, publishing PR and Jenny's friend.

The Capel Family:
HARRIET CAPEL née Jervis 55, (b. 1940) md. 1958, now widow of
GEORGE RODERICK DONAGHUE CAPEL (b. 1923, d. Easter 1995);
their children:
RODERICK CAPEL 36, (b. 1959) (nicknamed Roddy, Rodders or Rods) banker; married in 1982 to Jennifer née Gaunt;

JULIAN DONAGHUE CAPEL 33, (b. 1963) (nicknamed Jules) unemployed.

Jennifer and Roderick's children:

HUGO GEORGE DONAGHUE CAPEL 9, (b. 23 September 1985) nicknamed Huge (by his parents) and Huggy (by the Gaunts);

EMILY JANE HARRIET CAPEL 6, (B. 1989);

AMANDA MARY CAPEL 3, (b. 1992).

Ulrike Johansson 19, the Capels' Swedish au pair girl.

Victoria 19, Ulrike's French friend, a neighbouring au pair girl.

Alfonso (Fonzi) Aurelio 29, a waiter; Julian's Spanish lover.

Catriona Stevenson 28, banker having an office affair with Roderick.

Dodo (Dorothy) Ballard 90, (b. 1905) former nanny to George Capel and to his sons Roderick and Julian; now Harriet's companion in Dorset.

Mrs Peters, local woman who cleans for Harriet and helps with Dodo.

Chapter One

Harriet Capel had never experienced the damp and disordered sensations of adultery, summed up for her by the picture of Deborah Kerr and Burt Lancaster (still in their bathing suits) grippingly entwined on the seashore, lapped by playful and ambiguous fronds of foam. Sex had never really been Harriet's idea of fun. She was that rare creature, a natural and contented puritan, who thought far too many people in the late twentieth century mistook procreation for recreation. The laying down of genes and founding of families were no longer the inevitable consequence of sex but a matter of choice. To Harriet, this seemed all wrong.

Thanks to her late husband's prudence and a well-constructed Will she was, at fifty-five, a comfortably-off widow. Harriet had been a good wife to George. As a child she had been dutifully affectionate towards her parents and as a mother she loved her two sons, who were now grown up; loved them a great deal. She was fond of her friends, of course she was. She adored Dodo, the family's old nanny. But she had never been *in love*, not least because the whole idea of surrendering to uncontrollable emotion was alien to her temperament. Secretly Harriet was afraid of strong feelings in herself and others. Romantic love often seemed like a rather immature sort of play-acting, deliberately embarked on so as to stir things up and make life more exciting.

It was late September and Harriet Capel was packing. She had just finished reading the latest Iris Murdoch novel, investigating what happened when passion hurled the most unlikely characters into one another's path. She wondered

11

why all these people expected to fall in love? Why should it be assumed that this flash of lightning, driving them temporarily insane with mutual desire, was the proper foundation on which to build a future? Harriet thought: people are selfish and unscrupulous when they are in love and often behave in a thoroughly embarrassing way. Secrets, confessions, scenes, recriminations – and yet ten years later, when it's all died down and they've rearranged themselves, they don't really seem any happier than before. I'd much rather have self-control and peace of mind.

Packing freed her mind to wander while her hands efficiently folded, tucked, smoothed and arranged shoes, clothes and gifts neatly in the case. Shoes go in first, as a rule. Harriet packed two pairs: the taupe high-heeled ones (such a beautiful word, *taupe*: funny that it should mean mole in French and moles are a velvety black, while the colour taupe is a subtle sort of lilac-beige) and flat dark brown brogues in which she could walk everywhere and visit a dozen exhibitions without her feet hurting. Instead of slippers she packed ballet pumps, size 4½ because the soft leather soon stretched to fit her size 5 feet. Tights, three pairs: one light and two dark brown, rolled into soft lumps and stuffed inside the shoes. From her top right-hand drawer she took two white bras, size 36C, one black, same size, and seven pairs of cotton pants, white. These were wedged tightly into the suitcase.

Next she folded her best dress and interleaved it with tissue paper. She had bought it at Oxfam for £15 but the label said Valentino and it was beautifully cut from soft olive green wool with finely finished double seams. The matching leather belt was hand-stitched and brass-buckled. Carefully she folded more tissue paper inside two crêpe silk blouses, one taupe and one grey, two short-sleeved lambswool jumpers in corn yellow and turquoise blue, size 14, and one dark brown and one dark grey skirt, size 12 because Jaeger always sized their garments one down, presumably to make women feel slimmer. A marled dark brown jacket from Jaeger matched both skirts and a black raincoat completed her outfits for the week. She travelled light.

Harriet was preparing to visit her elder son Roderick in

London, where he lived with his family. Being a rational woman without a trace of vanity she packed no make-up or jewellery, no pills or medicines, no mementoes from which she was never separated, no special pillow without which she could not sleep, not a prayer book or Bible; no photographs; no books. Everything fitted into one medium-sized suitcase. She was going to her grandson's tenth birthday party, a family event that combined duty and pleasure. It wouldn't be smart and no glamorous clothes were needed. Not that she possessed any.

On top of the chest of drawers was a pile of gift-wrapped packages, presents for the grandchildren. These would make a firm top layer. She laid them down in a neat interlocking grid, tightened the diagonal webbing straps and double-locked the case. She could prevaricate no longer. Time to go upstairs and say goodbye to Dodo. 'Run along now to Nanny!' George would say to the boys, a sad echo of the countless times his mother must have said it to him. Time for Harriet to run along too. She crossed the top landing to Dodo's bedroom, knocked, and went in.

'Hattie, if you don't start soon you'll be late. Come here, give me a kiss and be off!'

Dodo's mahogany chest of drawers was dominated by a formal wedding portrait in a silver frame, flanked by a pair of christening photographs. Harriet, a young bride in a stiff white dress, a trailing bouquet clutched in her white-gloved hands, stood beside the sturdy thirty-five-year-old figure of her newly wedded husband. There they were again in the left-hand picture, this time with added infant in a long lace robe; on the right, Harriet and George with second infant, same robe, and a scowling small boy at knee-level wearing a Davy Crockett hat with a ringed furry tail. Harriet remembered having to bribe Roddy to behave in church by letting him wear this incongruous but much-loved hat.

There were framed snapshots of George himself, looking remarkably like his two sons, photographed at the same stages of boyhood and often in the same places – as a laughing baby on a tartan rug spread out on the front lawn, a toddler propped up on a pony in the back meadow, a serious boy crouching beside a rock pool on the family's

13

favourite beach. All three wore swimming trunks or shorts and Aertex shirts, crumpled socks and open sandals. Their eyes were darkened by the overhead sun into frowning triangular shadows, symbols of vision like the kohl-rimmed eyes in Egyptian hieroglyphs. The earliest pictures were soft sepia with deckled edges while the rest, taken some forty years later, were in colour. These three males – George and his sons Roderick and Julian – had been Dodo's life's work.

Standing on her bedside table was the last photograph ever taken of George. Harriet remembered coming in to the drawing room one bright February morning eight months ago as he sat by the bay window reading the newspaper, a vase of brilliant daffodils behind him.

'Oh, darling,' she had exclaimed, 'the *light*! Hang on a minute . . .' and she had gone to fetch her camera. At the time George, though thin and drawn, had seemed perfectly healthy; no inkling of his shockingly imminent death. One long, purple-veined hand was raised to ward off the unflattering image. Harriet put the picture down and sighed.

'You mustn't think about death all the time, Hattie. It's unhealthy and morbid.'

'I do try not to, Dodo.'

'Try harder. It's been nearly six months now. Enjoy London and don't worry about me. I shall still be here when you get back.'

Her husband had died without giving her a chance to say goodbye and since then, Harriet had found it increasingly difficult to part from people. She dreaded leaving Dodo. More than seventy years ago Dorothy Ballard, a square-faced, square-bodied village girl, had entered the Capel household as nursery maid to the infant George. Forty years later she took over the care of his two sons. She had been the prop and stay of the family for seventy-two years. Even now, despite her great age, she remained essential to them all – though chiefly, since George's dramatically sudden death, to his widow, Harriet. A combination of good luck, good health, iron will and the knowledge that she was still useful had enabled Dodo to survive. Her body was crooked and frail but her mind, at ninety, functioned remarkably well.

14

Dodo's philosophy was based on discipline, kindness and duty. She had never in her life used words like phobia or post-traumatic stress disorder but she understood Harriet's problem perfectly. Wise enough to know that it is better to articulate fears than to deny them, Dodo said, '*Go*, Hattie dear, I promise you I won't die. I'm not ready to die by a long way.'

'How do you know?'

'I want to finish my book, and it's nearly four hundred pages long. Mrs Peters will come in every day to cook and keep an eye on me – for goodness' sake, that it should have come to that! It's time you were off, Hattie. Goodbye, my dear. Enjoy yourself. Say goodbye. Give me a kiss. There. Good girl.'

The time, the present. Harriet Capel, driving up from Dorset to London, was tense with a nervous excitement that for the first time almost outweighed her sorrow. She was sad because since George's death a mild but pervasive sadness had become her normal state of mind. She was nervous because she was not used to doing all the driving herself and knew – George was forever telling her so – that she was not a natural driver. She forced herself to concentrate. There was a narrow lane with a tricky curve coming up, an accident blackspot. George always approached it at a crawl and had never failed to tell her that she must, too. Harriet dropped her speed to twenty miles an hour and craned through the overarching foliage to peer round the corner. Nothing coming. She accelerated. Only six miles to the motorway.

As she negotiated the narrow country lanes Harriet thought: this is not the moment to get upset about the family quarrel. Change down . . . change up . . . concentrate. Once she had reached the motorway she could switch her driving to automatic, more or less. 'You should look in your rearview mirror every fifteen seconds,' George always said. 'Constant vigilance. Every fifteen seconds.' She was tense because next Saturday would be Hugo's tenth birthday. He was the oldest grandchild and the only boy, and the family gathering to celebrate the occasion was highly unusual because of the feud with the Gaunts. Their daughter Jennifer had married Harriet and George's first son.

Her real reason for driving to London with a load of presents in the boot was not Hugo's birthday, which he could celebrate perfectly well without her, but the fact that ever since George's death, Harriet had felt it was time to make peace. Time had never lessened her husband's dislike of Roddy's mother-in-law Clarissa, and as long as George was alive the quarrel was stoked by his pride and the other side's obstinacy. Each family had become unrecognizably distorted. George saw Clarissa Gaunt as a woman besotted with arrogance and prejudice, her husband henpecked and ineffectual. Clarissa pictured George as a roaring, red-faced, bulbous-eyed, bucolic farmer and Harriet as a timid little country mouse. Each side created a caricature and super-imposed it upon the other. Given such exaggeration, even reasonable behaviour – let alone an overture towards peace – was impossible.

Their children, newly-married, optimistic and happy, had made one early attempt at reconciliation but it failed. From then on Roddy and Jennifer, impatient with barbed glances and stubborn silences, had refused to take sides. Thinking it would be simplest if their parents-in-law never met, they had divided up the children's birthdays, christenings and Christmases in strict rotation between the two sets of grandparents. Thus the situation had remained until George's death in April. The Gaunts had lived in the south of France – the Aveyron – since long before their daughter's marriage and Harriet hardly knew them. They had not come to the funeral, though Oliver had written a formal note of condolence. There was not a great deal he could say; no affectionate anecdotes to evoke George, no shared memories with which to comfort her. It had been a civil note, ending, 'We are both thinking of you, with every sympathy . . .' but Clarissa had not added her name.

This feud, justified as it may have been thirteen years ago, had gone on absurdly long. Harriet's first independent decision after becoming a widow was to put an end to the quarrel before it could harm their mutually beloved grand-children. After talking it over with Dodo, she had written to

Roderick. She had been reflecting, her letter said, and thought it would not be disloyal to George's memory to state the obvious: it was high time all that old business was forgotten. Hugo's tenth birthday was a golden opportunity to make peace. Could Roddy invite his parents-in-law over for a week and perhaps, without George's unforgiving presence, they might be reconciled?

Roddy had responded gratefully to this suggestion so here she was, in late September, setting off to see not only her two sons and three grandchildren, but the older Gaunts as well. At the last minute, however, her daughter-in-law Jenny had rung to say that Clarissa was indispensable at rehearsals for some amateur French musical evening which unfortunately coincided with Hugo's birthday. True or not, Oliver was a start and it was probably better that he came alone. Clarissa, although far from the caricature George had come to believe in, was a woman of firm old-fashioned convictions and Harriet was easily intimidated by phrases like 'It's *preposterous* to imagine . . .' or 'I don't suppose for a *moment* . . .' Harriet had never been that certain of anything in her life. She was glad that she would only have to encounter Roddy's father-in-law in Camberwell tonight.

The four prospective parents-in-law had met for the first time at a restaurant some weeks before the wedding. The ostensible reason was to discuss arrangements for the big day but really it was to take the measure of one another; see if their children were making a promising marriage, check out the genes. George had done most of the talking, though Roddy's future mother-in-law was not easily silenced and her crisp voice had interrupted more than once. The men competed to pay the bill at the end of dinner and George had won, to Clarissa's exasperation.

'You really shouldn't!' she had protested. 'Olly, you *shouldn't* have let him!'

Harriet had noticed then how much Clarissa disliked having to say thank you. She would rather be the benevolent giver, putting others in her debt. It had been a prickly evening. Harriet Capel and Oliver Gaunt had glanced at each other complicitly once or twice before concentrating

17

on the food and giving their spouses mute support. She vaguely recalled Oliver, who had seemed composed if secretive, his face immobile. He had nice hair: dark grey and springy, like iron filings. She would have thought him too subtle a man to be married to a woman like Clarissa, yet they had seemed content. He did not frown or mutter irritably at her bossiness. Harriet herself had long ago learned to suppress her responses to George in public. These were the stratagems by which marriages survived, when marriages had to.

After that dinner everything seemed to have gone splendidly. The entire clan had gathered for the wedding thirteen years ago. The young couple were to be married from the Capels' house in Dorset because the alternative – asking everyone to the Gaunts' place in south-west France – was not practical, whatever Clarissa said. Harriet and Clarissa had co-operated amicably over the catering and the flowers; Jennifer had looked touchingly young and happy; all the omens had seemed good.

The great set-pieces of an English country wedding do not change. It is not a day for eccentricity, which often signals a bad start. Brides who marry in white jeans trailing wild flowers are seldom stayers. The sun had shone – thinly, but it shone – as Jennifer and her father passed under the wooden gateway and stood in the porch of the village church while her twin sister, Philomena, settled the circle of rosebuds more firmly on her lacquered hair. Inside, the two families were seated expectantly in the left- and right-hand pews. The ushers stood at the back of the church, duty done for the time being, everyone correctly arrayed. Roderick and his younger brother Julian, impeccable, ramrod straight, stood at the front. The organ blared its sonorous chords, filling every breath of air in the church with its strong, resounding music. This is perhaps the moment of highest emotion during the wedding service; the moment for Young Lochinvar, the all or nothing pause before commitment and the sacrament begin.

Unbearably strung-up, thinking herself secure under cover of that great noise, Clarissa – who had to say something or burst – leaned across to her sister and hissed: 'Bit *off*, don't you think' – she pronounced it *orf* – 'when the best man's obviously a *queer*?'

At that precise moment the organ had stopped, and a hush descended like motes of dust from the organ loft. In that silence, her remark was audible to everyone in the first half dozen rows. Julian, then aged nineteen, standing beside his brother with his fist clenched over the ring in his pocket, heard it too. An almost imperceptible tremor shivered through him down to the tails of his morning suit and his young ears deepened from translucent pink to crimson. The back of Roderick's neck blushed in anger and sympathy. For half a minute the words seemed to echo and reverberate around the church. George stiffened and went purple. Harriet, afraid he would storm out, laid a calming hand on his arm. Patrick Gaunt, only twelve years old, threw an anguished glance at his mother but at the same moment a rustle at the back of the church announced his sister's entrance in the aisle. A few seconds' pause, and the organ roared the triumphant opening bars of the Wedding March.

After the wedding service, George's anger did not subside. Standing in the receiving line, he boiled with rage. His dark face creased into a heavy frown, his handshake harsh, he bent forward stiffly to kiss each gushing female relative. Harriet was tense, trying by her own immobility to prevent him from exploding into a great shout of denunciation against the condescending woman who stood not two paces away, agreeing with all and sundry that her daughter had looked *quite lovely*.

Harriet and Roddy had changed the *placement* at the lunch that followed, switching the name cards around so as to put George beside Jennifer with her twin sister Philomena on his other side. Philomena had been in the porch when Clarissa's remark was uttered, and no-one had yet told her of it. She chattered away nervously but innocently to George throughout lunch. She was only twenty; he could not hold her responsible for her mother's behaviour. Between the two flushed and pretty young girls his demeanour softened; he ate his way through the four course meal and held his peace during the speeches. But afterwards, as he stood surrounded by a knot of local farmer friends waiting for the young married pair to change into going-away clothes, his self-control, undermined by drink and Harriet's momentary absence, had cracked.

'Long as the young heifer doesn't turn out as big a cow as her mother,' he said.

The man beside him sniggered doubtfully.

'Look at her,' George had continued, gesturing towards Clarissa, holding court in a crowd of Jennifer's young friends waiting to catch the bouquet. 'Tits like udders and a mouth like a slurry-pit.'

George could not have known that Philomena was standing directly behind him. She gave a small involuntary cry and he turned to see her face aghast, suffused by a rush of blood. Even then, had he mumbled an apology all might have been well, but in his embarrassment George merely said, 'Little pitchers have big ears.' She choked and stumbled away, forfeiting – just a few moments later – her twin sister's joyful descent of the stairs, her smile like a tiara, the final family embraces and laughter as guests ran after the car for a few yards.

'Where's Philly?' Clarissa had said, gazing around distractedly. 'Someone call Philly!'

But Philomena, all tears and vomit in the small downstairs lavatory, could not hear.

Since then there had been no apology on either side. George had come to hate the Gaunts, chiefly because of Clarissa's remark but also from shame at his own. Philomena told no-one except her father what she had heard. Oliver, schooled in secrecy, told no-one else. But the knowledge made him disinclined to urge his wife to apologize and Harriet, who remained unaware of George's unforgivable crudity, could not cite it as proof that both sides were in the wrong. The rift widened and the quarrel gaped like an unhealed wound between the two families. When the young came to visit in Dorset, the Gaunts' names were never spoken. When they went to France, the Capels were never mentioned. But Harriet didn't hate Oliver or Clarissa. How could she? She hardly knew them.

Both sides were devoted grandparents. The birth, first of Hugo and then his sisters, Emily and little Amanda, gave the usual pleasure to the older generation, their own immortality ensured and made flesh, their looks and characteristics mirrored in miniature. They took it in turns to invite Jennifer, Roderick and their fervent brood at Christmas. Harriet would have liked a huge family celebration; an extra-large tree; with the kitchen table added on to the dining table to make one immensely long one, a dozen or fifteen people all sitting down together. The old stone farmhouse could have accommodated them all, at a squeeze. It had six bedrooms, though one was permanently occupied by Dodo, who remained spry all through her seventies and eighties. Another upstairs room had been made into George's study, about which he was very territorial – no question of converting *that* into a bedroom, even temporarily. There were still only two bathrooms, plus the loo with a basin downstairs, but that was plenty since the big family Christmas that embraced children, in-laws, stray friends and neglected relatives had never happened.

Harriet had spent most of the years since her two sons had left home looking after George and Dodo. They kept her busy. She was not bored, but it was a life of routine rather than variety. Her pleasures were reading, studying Russian, writing letters to the grandchildren full of drawings and jokes, tending Dodo and the garden. George, splenetic with frustration at the rapid onset of age, had ceased to be a pleasure to himself or anyone else. Their sons were distant, preoccupied, not good at keeping in touch. Harriet had known long before Clarissa spat it out that Julian was gay. Such an inaccurate word – *gay*. Julian usually sounded miserable.

Heavy traffic almost immobilized her from Putney onwards. 'Come early,' Jennifer had said. 'You'll miss the worst of the traffic that way and you could have tea with the children. I won't tell them you're coming. They'll be thrilled!' *Would* they be thrilled, Harriet wondered. They were dear children but very little seemed to *thrill* them. When they came to stay with her and she showed them tadpoles in the pond or foals staggering beside their mothers they didn't seem thrilled. At Easter she had suggested they might like to draw rare early violets picked from the woods

21

or the lavender-blue irises unfolding day by day, jerkily, the most unexpected petals straightening out next, but they had said, 'Oh Granny . . . *must* we?' and Hugo had asked sensibly why they couldn't just take a photograph every day. He reminded her of Roddy as a boy, quiet and self-effacing, and like Roddy at the same age, just beginning to stutter.

That was the last time the children had seen their grandfather. George had died the following week. Suddenly, with no warning, dead of a heart attack. She had been in the garden, came indoors to make tea for George and Dodo and herself, went in to the drawing room and there he was, the paper still dangling from his engorged hand, his face blue, mouth agape, yellow teeth bared, tongue lolling. 'Marvellous way to go . . .' some of their older friends had said wistfully but it had been a great shock to her, the suddenness. She had tried several times to remember her last words to him, or his to her, but no fragment came back. She didn't think they had spoken at lunch-time, could not remember a glance exchanged. When did I last smile at my husband, she asked herself, and could not recall having smiled for weeks. I serviced him; fed him and laundered his clothes, stopped him drinking too much brandy at night, parcelled out his pills. A trained nurse would have been warmer and kinder than I was. I never even said goodbye. I should have kissed him and said, 'I'm just going into the garden for half an hour or so, darling. I'll check the cold frame to see how your broad beans are coming along. See if I can find some tulips for the drawing room.' As far as she could remember she had said nothing. It was guilt rather than grief that made Harriet sad.

The traffic lights changed; her lane crawled forward but she had to wait for a second change of lights. The man in the car to her left was picking his nose and talking on a mobile phone. George would have said something contemptuous about plebs or vile modern manners. Harriet checked her face in the mirror. She raised her eyebrows and wetted one finger before running it along their sleek curves and smoothing the creases in her forehead. Driving was strenuous. George would have set off earlier, or later.

Do I miss George? she asked herself. It was a puzzle she

22

was trying to resolve. The honest answer was, she did, but after living beside him for thirty-seven years this was not surprising. He had become her other half, almost literally. It was like having a Siamese twin surgically removed. Her unconscious mind behaved as though he were still there and instructed her senses to respond accordingly. She would walk into the drawing room and see him sitting in the usual chair, paper in hand: exactly as he had been when she found him dead. It was not a hallucination but a sensory apparition that gave him body and weight, smell and texture. He was not yet a memory but a disconcerting presence. The habits would pass: the everyday arithmetic of making three cups of tea would soon be corrected to two: one for Dodo and one for herself. Missing him implied something far weightier than habit: sorrow, grief, mourning, loss. She knew, secretly, that she was not sad that George was dead. He had once told her that she had a splinter of ice in her heart and she had been shocked by the accuracy of the image. Did that mean she had never loved him? Harriet, she thought, this is pointless. He was the man of your life; the father of your children; you were never unfaithful to him nor, touch wood, he to you . . . what else is love if not that? The man behind hooted. She jerked the car into first gear and it juddered forward.

People who have never fallen in love are regarded as unfortunate, even emotionally crippled, for having been deprived of one of life's great experiences. Yet there is no need to feel sorry for them. Abstinence has its own pleasures and there are many compensations – a quiet mind, for instance; a lack of emotional melodrama – for those who have never suffered the violent pangs of romantic love.

Oliver Gaunt sat quietly in a narrow window-seat watching the green Kent fields sweep past. It was his first trip on Eurostar. Clarissa had driven him to Rodez to catch the TGV; five hours later he was in Paris with time to spend a couple of hours in the Pompidou Centre before boarding the gleaming bullet-nosed train at Gare du Nord. It was years since she had let him come to London by himself.

'*I* can take Jennifer and Philly shopping,' she had always

23

insisted, 'pick up some things I need from Peter Jones or John Lewis – *no* point in your coming along too. It only doubles the cost and you end up being *thoroughly* superfluous. After all, who do you still know in London who'd want to *see* you?' She had no idea, poor old girl, how rude she sounded. She would have died rather than hurt his feelings. It was just that she lifted the top off her head and spoke the words she found there, with no mitigating tact. Blisteringly honest, Clarissa. Better that than the reverse. To Oliver, whose working life had been spent in a world of duplicity, his wife's truthfulness was a refuge and a source of secret amusement rather than offence. Nevertheless, he blessed the fortunate timing of two concerts scheduled to be given the following weekend by a group of amateur singers, the Cercle des Oiseaux Aveyronnais, of whom Clarissa was an enthusiastic member. She felt she could not let them down – 'I've got a *big* voice you see, Olly; they *need* me!' and for once had decided not to accompany him. 'We *saw* the dear children in *August*, after all!'

He looked forward to spending some time with both his daughters and with his old college friends Mark Ellacott, Tom Ormerod and Ben Vulliamy. He would enjoy a lunch or an evening at the Reform with any of them. He hadn't seen the chaps for years; probably not since the disastrous wedding in 1982. The combination of her madrigals with his hint that he could do with a health check ('Be a good idea to pop in to see my consultant at King Edward VII Hospital,') in London had forced her reluctant consent. There was no consultant and no health check, but after more than thirty-five years of marriage Oliver knew which buttons to push to get his way with his wife.

In truth he needed a break from her oppressive presence. Clarissa had always been a strong-minded woman. In late middle-age she was overbearing, intolerant and humourless – but she ran the place like clockwork, catering for summer guests with impeccable efficiency. They were two of her favourite French words . . . *impeccable* and *efficace* . . . and she enunciated them with three-syllabled clarity. *Im-peccable*, she would say, surveying a freshly laid table or a double bedroom faultlessly prepared for guests.

24

They called them guests, as though they were old friends, but in fact most visitors paid to stay with the Gaunts, whose address, along with a photograph of their wisteria-clad *manoir*, was listed in a directory of private homes offering 'hospitality' at nearly the same cost as a four-star hotel. The idea appealed to certain categories of tourist and brought in what Clarissa laughingly described as 'pin-money'. Few 'guests' paid a return visit, but they enabled Clarissa to preserve the illusion of running a grand establishment like the one into which she had been born in 1936.

Thanks to the guests they could afford to employ a rota of two or three French girls from the village, a cook, and a man to look after the kitchen garden that featured prominently in the brochure. Clarissa herself did little if any housework and only put the finishing touches to the food – a few nasturtium flowers scattered over a salad; finely shredded leaves of fresh pungent basil; a gleaming circle of prunes – these were the things people commented on and she would acknowledge their compliments with a gracious smile. The exquisite meals were prepared and cooked by the 'staff'. Candelabra-lit five course dinners gave her the excuse to drink a good deal of wine, also paid for by the guests. Recently she had been drinking at least a bottle a night, disguising the effect in public behind a façade of extreme condescension, berating Oliver afterwards in private before falling into a deep, sonorous sleep.

It was years since Oliver had felt desire, either for his wife or for the hotly perfumed American women who often clung to his glance from beneath downcast, iridescent eyelids. Occasionally – reminded that it was her birthday or the anniversary of the day they met, the day they got engaged or the day they married – he would make love to her. These occasions gave Clarissa more satisfaction than Oliver but he assumed that middle-aged atrophy was the pattern of most people's marriages. He didn't hate Clarissa and it was unrealistic, after thirty-six years, to expect to love her. All the same, he was delighted to be getting away for a week.

Harriet's room on the top floor of the tall Camberwell house had been made ready with flowers on the chest of drawers,

25

a selection of new glossy magazines on the bedside table and – a tactful gesture this; she must remember to thank Jennifer – a photograph of George, resplendent with *bonhomie* beneath a paper crown, taken several years ago at Christmas. She had her own small bathroom with a pile of folded towels and two new cakes of soap. Placing her hairbrush and sponge bag on the shelf beside the basin, she washed her hands with the sweet-smelling soap and tidied her hair in the mirror. She had supposed that one or two of the children would be on hand to watch her unpack and rummage for their presents but other than the distant sounds of television, there was no sign of them.

In the basement kitchen she found two young women – Jennifer's au pair and a French girl – preparing dinner, while at the far end of the room the two older children were absorbed in front of a video.

'What are you watching?' Harriet asked, running the palm of her hand over Emily's shiny fair hair.

'*Mrs Doubtf-f-fire*,' said Hugo and turned his head briefly to acknowledge her presence. '. . . Oh, hello Granny. It's a v-v-video.' He turned back. Harriet, who knew that today's children were obsessed with television much as she herself, fifty years ago, had always had her nose in a book, stifled her disappointment. The au pair asked solicitously, 'Would you like a cup of tea?'

'What time will Mummy be home?' said Emily.

'Where's Amanda?' asked Hugo.

'Children, do you want the tomatoes peeled or not peeled?' enquired the French girl. Imagine being *asked*, their grandmother thought. George had never asked the boys' opinion of anything, not even when they were grown-up. Consultation and family democracy was never the name of the game. He *told* them what to do – and me, too. *And* we did it.

Harriet had forgotten how hard it was to unravel words when four people all talk at once. Ulrike saved her from confusion.

'I hope your room was OK? Would you like some tea? Mummy will be back early tonight for Granny – at about seven. Amanda is playing next door with Toby. I must to collect her in ten minutes. I will first finish the pudding. In Sweden we never peel tomatoes. Hugo, it's time you did your schoolwork, OK?'

'I would rather do it later,' said Hugo. 'So I can see the end of this at the same time as Emily, or she'll tell me what happens and sp-sp-spoil it.'

'Too bad!' answered the au pair briskly, 'Up to your room. Do the work first!' Harriet thought – good for her. She copes well.

Emily's eyes had not moved from the screen. Harriet had a moment of misgiving about her present – Roderick's own childhood copy of *The Faber Book of Children's Verse* – but she told herself that all children loved to hear poems read aloud. She could read them to sleep every night during the week she was here. That would keep her occupied for the first half hour after Roderick got home: she assumed that was timed for the children's bedtime. He and Jennifer needed time to unwind and discuss their day in private. That sort of thing was important in a marriage. She wondered if Oliver Gaunt was staying too, and whether *he* realized the need for a young couple to spend time alone with one another, even in the midst of a busy household.

'Is the children's grandfather staying here?' she asked Ulrike.

'Grandy's not staying with us,' said Emily, looking round for the first time. '*I* wanted him to, but we couldn't have him *and* you.'

Harriet laughed. 'Emily! Darling, that's terribly rude!'

'No it's not. I *like* Grandy. Only we haven't got enough bedrooms. I told Mummy you could *share* one but she said no. Sometimes Daddy sleeps in yours but he can't this week, can he?'

A thorn of anxiety snagged at this remark but Harriet ignored it.

'Come and see what Granny's got for you.'

'Oliver Gaunt,' he announced to the porter at the Reform Club. 'I have booked a room for a few days.'

'Mr Gaunt, sir. We were expecting you.' The porter

27

unhooked a key and leaned out of his cubby-hole to hand it to Oliver, eyeing his luggage.

'Do you need a hand with that case, sir?'

'Just tell me which floor I'm on. I'll make my own way.'

'We've put you on the top floor, overlooking St James's Park. It's the quiet side. You know the form, sir – breakfast and so on. Which newspaper would you like with your early-morning tea?'

'The *Independent*.' It made a break from Clarissa's weekly *Telegraph* and *Sud-Ouest*.

'Very good, sir. I hope you enjoy your stay. If you want any theatre tickets, we can usually get hold of them for you. Or' . . . he hesitated fractionally, significantly . . . 'anything else.'

'Thank you. I'm mainly here on family business.'

'Very good, sir,' the porter said again.

From the window of his room Oliver could see the time by Big Ben. It was ten to eight. He rinsed his face and neck, slapped something from Roger et Gallet round his freshly shaved chin and put on his town jacket. He dug out from his case the black-bordered white casket of Chanel No. 5 bought at the duty free shop in Paris for Jennifer (he had bought a different scent for her twin sister Philomena, with whom he had arranged to lunch tomorrow) and the litre bottle of Johnny Walker Black Label for Roderick. Clarissa's voice rang in his ears: 'Typical! You're so *unimaginative*, Oliver!' Unconsciously he sketched a shrug.

As he got out of the taxi in front of the Capels' pale yellow brick house in Camberwell, Oliver looked up at the bay window, a three-sided glass box that jutted out from the front wall several feet above street level. The curtains had not yet been drawn and he could look straight into the brightly lit drawing room, where people (he saw only their disembodied heads) were already standing about and talking. He gave the cab-driver a ten pound note, whose value he mentally translated from its equivalent in French francs, pocketed the change and climbed the seven or eight steps to the front door. He rang the bell and, as he waited, glanced idly through the window to his left. What happened next

28

took a matter of seconds . . . time enough for a bomb to go off or a man to be hanged, or fall in love.

A slender middle-aged woman wearing a sort of loose softly-coloured blouse stood by the windows with her back to the street. The dark glass acted as a mirror, so that if he shifted focus he could see his own features superimposed on hers. In a perception as rapid and permanent as a flash photograph, her profile was imprinted on Oliver's memory. Her nose was slightly aquiline, but rather than impairing her beauty, it gave her face character and originality. Her eyebrows slanted sharply upwards; her eyes were deep-set within arched sockets and her cheekbones curving, almost pointed. Her mouth was small and although quite narrow, in repose its corners tilted upwards in a faint smile.

The woman's expression was one of touching optimism such as is often seen in the young but rarely in the middle-aged. In the next instant the reason for the optimism became clear, as someone proffered a glass of champagne from a tray. The woman took a step forward and the blouse outlined her figure for a moment, revealing her to be full-breasted within its concealing folds. She smiled her thanks as the waitress moved away and bending over the glass, inserted the tip of her tongue into the effervescent liquid. Her tongue was as clean and pointed as a cat's. Oliver felt like a Peeping Tom, as though she were doing something much more private and erotic than sipping champagne. He shivered.

The intensity of his gaze must have disturbed her for she turned and looked at him directly through the intervening glass pane. She gave him a smile of recognition, as though welcoming him to the warm family gathering. For a moment they stood, he on the outside in the cooling autumn evening, she inside in the warmth, motionless amid the swirl and chatter of the party, two strangers smiling rapturously at one another. Oliver felt the blood drain from his face and an answering flush rose in hers. Dry-mouthed, tachycardic, he thought, good grief, I am falling in love!

The woman's attention was distracted by a little girl and she glanced down into the child's uplifted gaze. Just then the front door opened and Oliver found himself looking into

29

the beaming faces of his daughter and son-in-law. He wished briefly that Clarissa were there to sail majestically ahead of him, booming greetings and inclining her florid, powdery cheek for a peck. There were shrieks from the hall as two of his grandchildren scurried past their parents and collided with him at knee-level.

'*Grandy!*'

'L-l-look, Mum, he's h-here! G-g-grandpa Olly!'

'Push off, infants. Hallo, Oliver. You made it then. Good trip?'

'Hallo Daddy. Gosh you look well! Come on in. *Five minutes*, darlings, then . . .'

He had forgotten how very much Jennifer resembled her mother. Clarissa was twenty-three when they married and Jennifer was by now in her early thirties but she had the same queenly manner, the same upright posture and long limbs. He was moved more by the memory of his wife as she once was, before her body and features became coarse, than by the elegance and maturity of his daughter. Jennifer enfolded him in a childishly tight embrace.

'Daddy! Welcome! *Great* to see you! What's in that bag?'

'The wrong thing, probably – I can never remember what you like.'

Jennifer peered into the bag.

'Chanel No. 5 – oh look, clever *thing*! You haven't forgotten at all. Goody!'

He caught Roderick's eye above her bent head and winked. Straight-faced, his son-in-law mimed an exaggerated, eye-rolling sigh of relief.

'Johnny Walker Black Label any good to you?'

'Can always use it. Come in, Oliver. My mother's here – first outing since my father died at Easter – very sudden, yes, poor old Dad. Well, well. Oh, and we've asked a few of your friends round. Surprise. Brace yourself.'

In the instant before he could greet the friends — who, catching sight of him, started making incoherent staccato noises and grinning like maniacs – Oliver glimpsed the woman who had been standing by the window. She was seated now, the child – it was of course, he realized, his middle grandchild, Emily – on her lap. The silvery hair pulled back from her face glimmered under the light. She glanced lovingly at Emily and catching his eye again, returned a faint abstracted smile. In that isolated moment just before his friends surged forward to claim him, Oliver Gaunt felt like a man alone in a gallery looking at a great work of art, and realized with a seismic shock that he had indeed fallen in love.

Chapter Two

The voice of Roderick, his son-in-law, cut through his stupefaction.

'Champagne?' he invited. 'Not up to your standard, I daresay, but it's quite decent stuff. Mumm. Don't overlook the pun.'

Oliver had never liked champagne.

'Mind if I kick off with a Scotch?' he asked. 'Hadn't expected quite such a gathering. Need to get my bearings.' He grinned. 'By the way, who . . .?'

But Roderick had already gone in search of a whisky glass.

Oliver had not yet set foot inside the drawing room. He stood in the doorway surrounded by his three oldest friends – Mark, Ben and Thomas – their eyes bright with memories of the time when they were young together, impatient to reclaim that intimacy.

'I say old man – bit bloody foreign, that jacket!'

'Face gone a funny foreign colour too . . .'

'—one more layer and I'd call it *swarthy*.'

'What've you done with Clarissa?' (for courtesy's sake).

He looked into their open English faces and saw change. Ben had put on weight; he looked dangerously high-coloured. Mark in particular had aged. His face was grey, with deep lines gouged from nose to chin. His ears, eyebrows and nose sprouted coarse hairs. Only Tom looked much the same as in their college days, still the neat, dapper, puckish figure he had always been. They parted to let Roderick hand Oliver his whisky and closed up again, roaring like young men, punching each other, stepping back to gesticulate, reassured that nothing had changed between the four of them. Ben shouted with laughter. 'The old jokes are the best!' he gasped. 'And the cow – you remember the *cow*?'

'Christ, we were an irresponsible lot when you look back – one car, three bicycles, a college oar and a *cow*!'

Oliver gestured towards the woman he had seen from the front door. She sat in the chair by the window, reading now to Emily who nestled in her lap. He plucked at Mark's sleeve.

'Mark, here a minute!' he whispered urgently. 'That woman over there – by the window – sitting down – do you know who she is?'

'Harriet Capel. Come off it old chap: not *that* long since you were here! You must remember her: Roderick's mother . . .'

Oliver's heart fell like a stone into a long dark well. Mark added, as though there were any doubt: '. . . she's the other grandmother to your three youngsters.'

'Harriet *Capel*,' Oliver said, his voice hollow. He had seen her too soon and learned her name too late. 'We're co-grandparents, of course. Just as well I checked.'

'Wish *I'd* got grandchildren. Can't get my son to breed. In *our* day you couldn't stop us. That boy over there – he's got the look of you. Spotted it at once. Come on then: tell us about life in Provence?'

'Not Provence,' Oliver said. 'West of Provence, the Aveyron. Between Rodez and Albi. You must come and visit us, you and Belinda.'

His son-in-law was at his side again. 'How's your glass? Like a top-up? Everything OK?'

'Thanks,' Oliver answered. 'I ought to go and make overtures to Harriet.'

He left the noisy group and walked towards her with leaden steps. If it were a play, a lone spotlight would encircle him; in a film, portentous music would drum softly, like rain, on the sound-track. But in real life, no-one noticed. Only in his ears the sounds of the party grew dim as he approached, cleaving through the laughter and gossip, leaving it in his wake, creating a silence. He stood above her looking down.

'Harriet? It seems a long time. It *is* a long time. So stupid. You look quite wonderful.'

'Oliver! I saw you through the window! How *lovely* that you could make it! Yes, it's been *ages*.'

She extended her face upwards at a slight angle. 'Sorry I can't get up. Emily's rather anchored me to this chair.'

Oliver bent to kiss Harriet on each soft cheek. She smelled faintly of some old-fashioned soap or toilet water. He lifted her hand to his lips, the hand not clasping the child. Emily giggled.

'Do it to me too, Grandy.'

He took the chubby little paw and kissed that too; then remembered.

'Sorry about George. Frightfully sorry. Out of the blue, I gather . . .?'

'Thank you for your nice letter.'

'We couldn't make it to the funeral . . .'

'Don't worry. I quite understood.'

Of course she would understand. Clarissa had all but ruined Jennifer's wedding; nobody would have risked it happening again at poor old George's funeral.

'What are you reading?'

'Granny brought me the book, it's my present.'

'Poems for Emily. *The Faber Book of Children's Verse*.'

'Which poem were you reading?'

'Brown penny, brown penny, looped in my hair,' said Emily.

'Do I know that one?'

As he took the book from Harriet their eyes met. Her gaze was guileless and unconcerned. How could she not know? His own heart thundered, going through its paces in double-quick time. To calm himself he read out loud,

> '*O love is the crooked thing,*
> *There is nobody wise enough*
> *To find out all that is in it,*
> *For he would be thinking of love*
> *Till the stars had run away*

34

And the shadows eaten the moon.
Ah, penny, brown penny, brown penny,
One could not begin it too soon.'

'Yeats,' Harriet said. 'I've always loved Yeats, ever since I did him at school. *Long* ago.'

'I did Yeats too,' Oliver answered. 'It seems like last year. Time . . .' His voice trailed away. He sensed someone approaching and turned to see Benjamin, who had known him ever since he was that same clever schoolboy memorizing Yeats.

Ben looked at him quizzically. 'Steady on, old man. You've gone dead white. Not going to faint, are you? Something up?'

Oliver took one pace back from Harriet. 'No,' he said. 'No, nothing wrong.'

Roderick arrived. 'Nine o'clock, Em. Time for bed,' he said. 'Don't move, Mother. She can go up by herself.'

Oliver said, 'Shall I take her?'

'You're the star guests. Can't have you disappearing.'

Oliver recalled his social obligations. With an effort, he grinned at Roderick.

'Ben . . . Tom . . . Mark . . . we haven't got together in years. Whose idea was it?'

'Jennifer's. Come and say hallo to Belinda and Mona. Mustn't forget the wives.'

Oliver looked back at Harriet and touched her shoulder. 'We'll talk later.'

'Granny, Granny . . . *you* take me to bed,' the child urged. Oliver followed his son-in-law towards the centre of the room. A new babel of questions surrounded him.

Ben was urging Mona forward. She had once been ravishing, 'all legs and lipstick'. Not any more, poor old girl; giggly now on champagne, she'd become matronly and stayed girlish, an unfortunate combination. But she was still a dear.

'*Mona!*' he said, bending to kiss her.

During dinner Harriet was at the far end of the table on Roderick's right, with Tom beside her. Oliver had been placed at the head of the table, his daughter next to him, Mona on the other side. When Ulrike, the au pair, cleared away the plates and brought more food from the far end of the kitchen, Tom got up to help, aiming a joke at Harriet about being a New Man. Tom was not married and with a lightning bolt of jealousy Oliver thought, perhaps this party was staged to bring them together, now that her husband was dead? Lover's fears already trapped him; nothing was as safe or straightforward as it seemed.

Dinner was fragmented and disorganized by comparison with the perfect order of Clarissa's table at home but this enabled Oliver to concentrate on Harriet, who was absorbed in talking to her son. He watched her grave, attentive profile until he realized he should be paying similar attention to his daughter.

'So, Jenny: how are you? Children are looking well. Emily's a clever girl.'

'I must *talk* to you, Daddy,' said Jennifer with significant emphasis. 'Not tomorrow – you're lunching with Philly aren't you? Sorry she couldn't make it tonight. Busy busy busy. How about after work: could you meet me for a drink?'

'What time do you finish? Come to the club at, mm, shall we say seven? Is everything, you know, all *right*?'

'No, not all right; not all right *at all.*'

His daughter turned to Ben, the neighbour on her left, and switched into flirtatious small talk, teasing him by calling him *Uncle* Ben. For an instant Oliver caught Harriet's eye. Their glance spanned the table, shimmering in the candle-light. Two evenings are going on simultaneously, he thought. One is happening to Harriet and me and the other – agreeable and banal – is happening to everyone else. The person making polite small talk and smiling at my friends – *that* Oliver surveys this table, these people, and wonders why they don't notice that I am swept aloft like a man in a Montgolfier balloon. His train of thought was interrupted by Mona shouting a question.

'*Oliver!* You must be getting as deaf as Ben. I said: *how's Clarissa*?'

At the end of the evening Oliver had planned to take a taxi back to the Reform but Jenny overruled him.

'I insist, Daddy – absolutely *insist* . . .' adding *sotto voce*, 'I must *talk* to you.'

In the good fellowship of arranging to meet his friends again, Oliver had no chance to speak to Harriet. She stood at the back of the group that escorted him noisily to the front door, denying him the opportunity to touch her. He glanced at her and she raised her hand, palm towards him, fingers splayed. A salute, a promise, a surrender, a farewell? Her hair gleamed under the light, a silver penumbra around her unsmiling face. He noticed how dark, how very dark her eyes were, the pupils dilated. Oliver, trained to decode faces, knew that this dilation was an involuntary sign of sexual desire and could not conceal an exultant smile.

As Jennifer opened the passenger door Oliver asked, 'How long is Harriet staying with you?'

'About a week – not more, I hope. Why?' Without waiting for his answer she closed the car door and walked round to the other side. As soon as her seat-belt was buckled she rushed on: 'How do we *look*?'

He didn't understand.

'Me and Roderick?'

'Fine, I thought. Lovely evening.'

'You didn't notice anything wrong?'

He felt alarm. Clarissa always accused him of insensitivity about his daughters.

'The food was delicious. Wasn't it? I didn't see anything wrong.'

'Oh, Daddy – not the food. Didn't you *notice*? Roderick and I didn't address a single word to each other all evening; we didn't even *look* at each other. We've hardly spoken this *week* except to exchange essential information.'

'Darling, I am sorry. It'll pass. All marriages go through phases.'

'I know that, Daddy. We've been married thirteen years now. This isn't a *phase*, it's "*I want out*".'

The lights of the oncoming traffic were dazzling although it was after midnight and the overhead street lamps shone into his face.

'You know he's got a *mistress*?' she went on. 'Don't say anything to him yet. He doesn't know I know. The bitch had the nerve to ring me two weeks ago. "Your husband Roderick Capel and I are in love," she said, dead cool. "We

have been lovers since the beginning of this year. I'm going to be fair to you, *once*, by warning you – in case you thought it was just another office thing, that I intend to marry him."
What the hell could I say? I didn't even know who she *was*. And what did she mean by "*just another*"? How many *more* have there been?'

Her father frowned. Women never fathom the secrets of men's sexuality, he reflected. Most men will fuck when and wherever they can and not even Women's Lib has taught my clever daughters that. He said, 'I had no idea. Listen my darling, I don't want to sound unsympathetic but I've been up since five. Could we discuss this tomorrow?'

He caught the involuntary slump of her shoulders and knew he had let her down.

'Sorry,' she said flatly. 'Yes of course. By the way, Philly knows all about it. You don't have to be discreet.'

She reached across to squeeze his hand. The lights, the lights, mine eyes dazzle . . .

Roderick and his mother stood at the top of the steps waving off the last guests. As the front door closed, before Harriet could excuse herself and go up to bed, he said explosively, 'Bloody, *bloody* woman!'

'Roddy – darling – who?'

'My fucking *wife*. Treats me like a drinks trolley. Doesn't even do the cooking: the au pair and her French friend did that. But Jennifer? Not a word or a smile all evening. Didn't you notice? Lady sodding Bountiful to everyone but me.'

'Calm down. Come and sit here. Pour yourself a nightcap first. Tell me.'

'I've had enough. I'm at the end of my tether. We'll have to divorce. I know Mandy's only three but I won't lose touch with my children – and I'll insist on your having access to them as well. But this can't go on.'

'Roddy – it's very late, you're tired. We've all had a good deal to drink, I daresay. Things are never as bad in the morning.'

'In the cold light of day they look worse. It's a charade, Mother. This house, the dinner, her kissing the children

38

good night for the benefit of our guests – aaahh – aren't they adorable? – it's a *pantomime*.'

Roderick poured another brandy. How will he get to work tomorrow, his mother thought, he's working up to a dreadful hangover. Roddy closed his eyes as the sweet fumes and burning flavour permeated his senses.

'Better!' he said.

She smiled. 'You look like Daddy. Do you remember him and his precious Camus? How he always said it was the best brandy in the world? The *fuss* he made; the ceremony!'

Her son closed his eyes in irritation and gave a small unconscious shake of the head. All right, Harriet thought; if we must, we will talk about you and Jenny. She leaned towards him.

'Every marriage goes through stages.'

'Maybe. But at times like tonight I hate her. Those must be the saddest words in the English language: *I hate my wife*. I can't carry on like this for the next thirty years.'

'The children?'

'Of course I love *them*. But already Hugo's starting to stutter. He's perfectly well aware that something's wrong. Did you ever hate Father?'

She knew the question required a truthful answer.

'Not hate, exactly. I disliked him pretty thoroughly sometimes. He was quite an overbearing man. But I adapted. I learned to retreat – into the garden, books, my study and of course the great panacea was always you and Julian.'

'Yes: and look at the result. I'm married and miserable as hell and Julian is gay and miserable as hell. Father dominated us all. Luckily for me he died fairly young.'

'Seventy-two.'

'I was afraid he'd be one of those old men who live to be ninety, holding the family in thrall beneath his palsied but still iron fist.'

Harriet leaned back in the wing chair and closed her eyes. You try to get it right, she thought, and still you fail. I thought I was sacrificing my own happiness for my sons and now it seems I sacrificed it for nothing. Yet I loved George in the end.

'In the end I loved your father. If you hang on, the person

you married inevitably becomes the man, or woman, of your life. You'll find you come to love her again (and I remember, even if *you* don't, a time when you loved Jennifer very much) if only because you *know* her better than anyone else. Perfect love – perfect happiness – perfect people – there's no such thing. But happy children: now that you *can* achieve.'

Roderick drained his tumbler and banged it down on the polished table. 'Don't preach at me, Mother. I've got enough on my plate.'

She saw her son's anger in his crimson cheek and the tension of his tall body. She leaned over to put a hand on his arm.

'Darling, I'm here for a whole week. Let me buy you lunch tomorrow?'

'Not tomorrow, I'm booked. I have to leave for work at six. I'll shove a note under your door before I go, OK?'

'All right. Sorry. Poor old Roddy.'

They heard a car door slam in the street.

'That'll be her,' said Roderick. 'She'll be suspicious if she catches me talking to you. Mind if I go upstairs? Night . . .' They parted with a brief embrace.

It was nearly midnight by the time Jennifer dropped her father outside his club in Pall Mall but Oliver was not ready to sleep. He needed to think about Harriet, absorb the shock of their collision, conjure up her image in his mind's eye, plot how they would spend time together – already he had jettisoned all other plans. Going upstairs to the Gallery for a last drink he found a club servant collecting empty glasses and two or three old men dozing.

'Am I too late for a nightcap?' he asked.

'No, sir. What'll it be?'

'Double Scotch. Water. No ice.'

The man proffered a round tray with a glass of whisky, a jug of water and a docket to be signed. Oliver, who had already drunk a good deal, felt exhilarated and confiding.

'It's Tom, isn't it?' he asked.

'Bill, sir.'

'Bill then. Ever been in love, Bill?'

'Yes, sir.'

'I'm in love now, Bill.'

'The name's Walter, sir. Very good,' the man said impassively.

'Thought you said it was Bill just now. You think it's good, Walter, to be in love?'

'The bill was for you to sign. Thank you, sir.'

'I hope you're right. It's too late to take it back now.'

'Thank you, sir.'

'Don't go, Walter. I need to talk to someone.' The old man put the tray down on a nearby table and Oliver glanced at the surrounding club members, all of whom seemed to be dozing and one or two snoring rhythmically.

'Don't mind them, sir, they've been asleep for hours and most of them's deaf as it is. You a married man, sir?'

'Yes. Don't keep calling me sir, I'm not used to it. My name is Oliver Gaunt.'

'Is there a Mrs Gaunt living?'

'Yes, I'm afraid there is.'

'In that case I wouldn't recommend it, sir, Mr Gaunt. Wives don't like it. I'd sleep it off if I was you.'

'I don't think it'll be that simple.'

Oliver took another gulp of whisky and the old man watched. His veined hands swept repetitively across the front of his white apron, brushing it down and flattening it as though trying to obliterate his masculinity – or Oliver's.

'Might I ask a question, sir?'

'Fire away.'

'This'd be a *young* lady, would it?'

'No, not so young. My age, or nearly.'

'Ah. She's not what you might call a *professional* lady?'

'Certainly not.'

'Mm-hm.' Walter paused. 'That makes it worse, I reckon. Known the lady long?'

'More than ten years.'

'Ah.'

'Now suddenly everything's changed. Could I have another whisky, Walter?'

'Yes, sir.' Walter made no attempt to move. He and Oliver

41

stood transfixed. Suddenly one of the sleepers snorted loudly, waking himself up.

'Walter! Walter!' he called querulously. Walter said, 'Coming, sir.' To Oliver he added, 'I'd forget about her if you can, Mr Gaunt. It'll only lead to trouble. Take it nice and slowly up the stairs. Good night, sir.'

Harriet woke to the whispering and pattering feet of children and a muffled explosion of shushes. She sat up in bed and called out, 'Did I hear a little mouse rustling?' There was a splash of giggles and Amanda and Emily scurried into the room and hurled themselves across her bed. Behind them in the doorway stood Hugo in his pyjamas. She addressed him gravely: 'Who *are* these mice? Have we *met* them before?' He stooped to pick up a piece of paper.

'There's s-s-something for you, Granny. Looks like Daddy's writing.'

'Clever boy. Bring it here.'

She opened the envelope and read, '*I'll try to get away by six, though I may have to go back to work afterwards. Meet me at Corney and Barrow – it's a wine bar. Take a tube to Moorgate and ask when you're at street level. It's opposite. R.*'

Her grandchildren crowded round: Hugo, Emily and almost-baby Amanda.

'Who wants a story?' she asked. They scrambled up on to the bed, leaning close and squabbling, quietening down as she began: 'Once upon a time there was a tiny fairy Queen, no bigger than a pebble – hardly any bigger than this stone here, in Grandy's signet ring: can you all see? She had a carriage drawn by a team of—'

'Fleas!' shouted Emily.

'No, not even as big as fleas. Atoms. They were as small as atoms. Her carriage was made out of half of a nut – not a walnut. A hazelnut. Do you know how small that is?'

Amanda, too young to understand, cuddled closer. Hugo said, 'Was it as big as my thumbnail?' and showed her his ragged, bitten thumb.

'Yes,' Harriet said, ignoring the chewed nail. 'Look, every-one: her carriage was as big as Hugo's thumbnail.'

42

'Ugh!' said Emily.

'The wheels of the coach were as thin as spiders' legs . . .'

'I like spiders!' said Hugo.

'I hate them!' said Emily.

'. . . and the windows were made of grasshoppers' wings, all shimmery like water, in lots of colours. The reins were as fine as spiders' webs and her whip was made of gossamer.' She paused to remember, stroking Amanda's hair, itself as fine as corn-silk. 'Her coachman was a gnat . . . who knows what a gnat is?'

'Is it like a midge, like you get in Scotland?' asked Hugo.

'*Good*, Hugo: yes, a gnat is like a midge. A tiny, tiny insect. And so the Queen of the Fairies rode through the night in this coach, drawn by her atomies, into people's heads and made them dream nice dreams. That's called their time out of mind.'

They pushed and interrupted, jostling one another to tell her their dreams.

'Come *on* Amanda; we'll be late taking 'Ugo and Emily to school!' Ulrike said patiently, as she had done every morning since term started three weeks ago. The toddler scrubbed at her milk-teeth and dribbled spit and bubbles of toothpaste onto the rim of the basin, then pouted her rosy lips upwards to be dabbed dry. Five minutes later, steering pushchairs side by side along the crowded south London pavement, Ulrike observed to her friend Victoria, the au pair from next door, 'And we thought we were here to improve our English, meet some English boys and see the country! We're not house guests, we're underpaid nannies.'

'It's forbidden by the Home Office, but who makes attention of rules in *this* country?' Victoria, being French, was accustomed to obeying rules.

'We could have stayed at home and worked in a kindergarten . . .'

'It's worse for me. Betty's at home all day, nothing is OK for her. She won't even go downstairs to answer the door *malgré* she's only reading fashion magazines, but *I* have to do it. If the telephone rings I must say, "This is the Linton residence." Pretending to be a *grande-bourgeoise*! *Poof*! At least Jennifer goes out to work and leaves you in peace,' said Victoria sullenly.

'She *has* to work – she must, to earn my wages – and the new nanny's, if she finds another one. They all leave because they don't like to work for her but *she* won't stay at home but she wants a more interesting life.' Ulrike lowered her voice and the Capel children pricked up their sharp ears. 'She is *bored* by her children.'

'We're not b-b-*boring*, Ulrike,' said Hugo.

'*I* don't think you are, sweetheart, no. Not a bit.'

Ulrike was fond of Hugo and Emily and especially fond of Amanda. Their parents' self-centredness outraged her good Swedish sense of the care and duties owed to children. 'Look – there's our bus, isn't it? Can you read the number?'

The two young women and five children raced towards the bus stop, pushchairs swerving wildly. The driver waited for them to catch up and grinned as the children clambered aboard. 'Easy does it. Weakest goes to the wall. There's a good lass. *Up*-si-daisy.'

'One and two halves to Rockingham Primary, please,' said Ulrike.

The Capels rarely did the school run themselves. Roderick left home for the bank soon after six and on the few occasions when Jennifer did take her children to school she was already in smart office clothes, in an office frame of mind, doing her best to ignore the questions and information that clamoured for her attention.

'Mummy, there's a girl in my class who . . . Mummy, my teacher says, could you remember to send me to school with . . . Mummy, *must* I do gym? The teacher makes us . . .'

Too preoccupied with her own problems to listen, Jennifer failed to recognize how much her children's concerns resembled her own: the woman in the office *who* . . . the employer who insisted *that* . . .

The three Capel children loved their parents but they *liked* Ulrike better because she paid attention to what they told her and gave proper answers. When children can't make adults listen they repeat themselves patiently, in a desperate attempt to get them to concentrate. When that

44

fails they are either slapped by their parents or reduced to tears of frustration ... a scene played out thousands of times a day on every street, in every supermarket. In due course both generations get older and it's the grown-up children who pay their parents less and less attention. Then it is their turn to repeat themselves; beg for affection and demand sympathy. In the last resort they weep, which makes the children complain that their agèd parents have become such a *bore*. Yet sometimes neglectful parents are rewarded with the most dutiful offspring, while those who have been conscientious are abandoned in old age because their children have been made arrogant and callous by years of parental devotion.

By quarter to nine Ulrike had taken the children off to school and Jennifer lolled across the kitchen table scanning the newspaper. She looked flayed and haggard without make-up ... no, thought Harriet, that's unfair: she looked unhappy. Under her scrutiny, Jennifer glanced up.

'You OK? More coffee? Sorry – this is my quiet fifteen minutes before I start the morning rush.'

'I'm fine darling – you go ahead. I thought I'd take it easy today.'

'You ought to go and see the thing at the National Portrait Gallery. Young British portrait painters. Simply terrific. You'll love it. *And* it's free. Leicester Square tube. Go to the Oval and get a Zones One and Two day-ticket – better still, week's season. Cheapest and quickest way to get about these days. Tube's quite safe. Look for Northern Line, north-bound, and get out at *Leicester Square*.'

Harriet, who was quite familiar with the tube map of London, had planned to go to the National Gallery and look at some of her favourite Dutch painters whose serene interiors – ochre and brown, black-and-white tiles, aproned housemaids plucking game under the watchful eye of a cat – invoked a lost world of order and calm. She smiled and said, 'Good idea,' wondering whether to add, 'Is everything all *right*, Jenny?' but decided it was too soon. She went upstairs to dress.

Oliver had woken to the six o'clock chimes of Big Ben tolling clearly through the misty London air. For a moment he thought it was the news on the BBC World Service, seven o'clock local time in France. His head was thick and his bladder full of alcohol. He climbed out of bed, put on his tartan dressing-gown and padded to the end of the corridor. Back in the narrow bed he lay open-eyed, remembering Harriet. I have to see her today, he thought; I have to see her every day. She's here for a week. I have to see her at least seven times. When does Jennifer go to work? She must have left by ten. I'll ring at ten. He stared at the ceiling until the porter pushed his newspaper under the door. He hunted through the Entertainments section for things Harriet might enjoy.

The dining room at the Reform was deathly quiet. A dozen tables were occupied by solitary figures engrossed in newspapers and marmalade. One or two were women, to Oliver's surprise. Now that he had made up his mind to telephone Harriet at ten he was calm. He decided to allow himself the luxury of a shave and haircut and set off through the sharp autumnal morning, sunlight falling like a fresh coat of paint on the stuccoed mid-Victorian façades.

He walked to the end of Pall Mall and paused at the top of the Duke of York's steps – wide, shallow, and deserted – to look over St James's Park. The trees stood in urban order beyond the lines of traffic streaming down The Mall. He would stroll with Harriet through the park, along the same paths he had often taken on briefing visits to London, paths considered safe from microphones or over-attentive strangers in the days when espionage was more to do with people than electronic devices. That had been his skill, calculating a man's character and hence his next move, nudging him in your direction away from his old allegiances, paying him with his own breathless anticipation of a new start in life, his fantasies of freedom with another woman. These were at least as important as depositing cash in dodgy bank accounts. The sums were surprisingly modest in any case. To people schooled by the postwar austerities of central Europe, £100 in hard currency seemed a fortune. Cold War was the wrong word; the courage and resourcefulness required were not cold simply because the victories they won were usually invisible, the deaths trivial, the girls soon discarded. Oliver turned back and headed for Jermyn Street.

At quarter to ten Jennifer called up the stairs, 'Harriet? I'm late – want a lift? If you do I'm leaving *now*.'

Harriet came down to find her daughter-in-law, business-like in a beige suit, standing by the front door frowning over a list in her Filofax. It was headed ***Don't Forget!***

They sat motionless amid the fumes of traffic approaching Waterloo Bridge. Harriet wondered again whether to broach the subject of Roddy and last night's disclosures. The silence lengthened. Jennifer stared ahead, tapped her fingers on the steering wheel, sighed with exasperation and muttered under her breath, 'Get *on* with it, you oaf – *move.*'

It hardly seemed the best moment, Harriet decided. Instead she said soothingly, 'The children are doing *so* well. Amanda is a honey – and Emily's getting more and more like you.'

'Do you think?' said Jennifer.

'They do you great credit. You both . . .' (*both* is all right, surely?) '. . . both lead such busy lives. It isn't ever easy to bring up happy children.' She refrained from adding, 'least of all when two parents work' or even 'in a big city'.

'Hugo's starting to stutter.'

'Roddy stuttered, too. It's a phase.'

'Why must everything be a sodding *phase*?' snapped Jennifer, adding contritely, 'Sorry. I daresay you're right.

'OK if I drop you here? I'm going to the NCP in St Martin's Lane – Christ, my meeting's at 10.30, I'll – must go – 'bye Harriet!' She dropped her outside Charing Cross station and Harriet headed for Landseer's monumental lions in Trafalgar Square. I need to sit down by the fountains and *think*, she told herself.

By quarter to ten Oliver was spruce and freshly shaven, smelling faintly of eau de cologne. He went to his room and scrutinized the result, disciplining himself to wait for Big Ben to chime before he could embark on the fearful joy of telephoning Harriet. He buffed his toe-caps, scanned the paper. Just before ten o'clock the telephone on his bedside table shrilled. He snatched it up.

'Oliver?' said the emphatic voice of his wife. 'Is that *you*? It's *me*. I thought you would have *rung* by now. Is everything all *right*? How was the journey? Is Eurostar worth the extra money?'

Clarissa could not be hurried or she would suspect something and cross-question him further. Woodenly, he took her hour by hour through the time they had spent apart and again hour by hour though the day in prospect. He detailed the guests, the food, the grandchildren, Jennifer's dress. He described his room at the Reform, the weather. Then he had to go through the whole ordeal again, this time with the events of her day. Fifteen minutes later, after a string of repetitions, she wound down. '. . . and *don't* forget my Liberty lawn, and the curtain material from Sandersons. You've got the sample. Shall I look up the number? Don't forget to have your hair cut. *Daddy* always went to *Trumper's*.' Finally, skittishly, 'Do you *love* me, Olly?'

As soon as he had put the telephone down he dialled the Camberwell number, hearing Big Ben chime the quarter as he did so.

'Hallo? No, they both went out. I don't know . . . maybe about ten minutes ago? Together, in Jennifer's car. Who did you want to talk to? Granny . . . Mrs Capel did not say where she was going. No, nor when she would be back. Shall I give her a message? It is Mr Gaunt, yes? I will tell her you called. Bye-bye. Oh, thank you. I am glad you enjoyed it. 'Bye.'

Chapter Three

Harriet Capel had married at eighteen, destined for marriage from the moment she was born. Her parents could not have imagined any other future for a girl. In the late Fifties, at a finishing school outside Paris, she had learned the rules of *placement* at diplomatic dinners, the royal family trees of Europe and the hierarchy of bishops both Catholic and Anglican, which she classed with complex fractions and the height of the Himalayas. None were peaks she herself was ever likely to scale but they gave her a sense of proportion. She was chaperoned to the Opéra with half a dozen others, initiating a lifelong passion; and to a number of couture houses, which put her off fashion for ever.

  Harriet was quite fortunate in her marriage. Never, or not on her side, a love match, to a remarkable extent it had become a marriage of minds. George had read Greats at Oxford immediately after the war; although he was a farmer and a countryman born and bred and returned to the same three hundred Dorset acres, he was neither a fool nor a rustic philistine. He had chosen Harriet for her delicate looks and beautiful manners and within a few weeks of their marriage found himself deeply in love with her as well. She thought herself uneducated, never having got beyond O Levels at school, but her unschooled intelligence was an unexpected bonus. He encouraged her to progress from Jane Austen and *The Tatler & Bystander* to Edith Wharton and Henry James and from there to Lawrence Durrell, Angus Wilson and Iris Murdoch. In turn she taught him to love opera.

The Capels subscribed to *Country Life* but also to *The New Statesman* and, when that turned into a magazine for social workers, *The Listener*. When *The Listener* ceased publication they switched to *The London Review of Books*. They went to Glyndebourne or the Royal Opera House two or three times a year and were life members of the London Library. 'Two hundred quid looks a lot of money now,' George had said in 1961, 'but in twenty years' time we'll look back and think, what a bargain.' Although the Capels were very far from the country bumpkins of Clarissa's imagination, feminism reached Harriet like the sounds of a distant battle in another country of which she knew little. As a result she made George very happy – and he was not an easy man to please.

In the early years, Harriet occasionally found country life lonely and like-minded people rare. George said, 'It's lucky that we always have so much to discuss but all the same, it would be better if you had a friend. Surely you miss having someone else to – you know, chatter away with? Whatever it is women do ... gossip, give advice, talk about wombs and babies. No don't look like that, Hattie, I'm joking. Anything, as long as it's not your husband.'

'I've always got Dodo,' Harriet said, 'or your mother.' Secretly, he was relieved. Isolation welded their marriage more solidly. When the boys went off to public school she started to read even more. Four or five books a week were delivered in regular parcels from St James's Square, and as regularly returned. Harriet learned to cherish her own quiet company.

The Open University, when eventually she applied, was manna in the desert of her supposed ignorance. She started with the Arts Foundation Course which took a year but was obligatory before she was allowed to specialize. Designed to impart basic cultural signposts in painting, music, literature and history, she found it easy. Next she chose *Modern English Fiction from Thomas Hardy to Angus Wilson*, and sailed through that in half the prescribed time, getting excellent marks for her essays. After this she ventured further back, studying *Shakespeare and the Metaphysical Poets*, combining them with *England Under the Tudors and Stuarts*. She learned as much as she wished without bothering to complete either degree course. This was just practice for the real thing, learning to concentrate for hours on end, how to structure and pace essays.

Harriet took a long time to decide on her degree subject. Literature and history were not demanding enough. Sociology or politics did not interest her, nor related courses like anthropology or geography. She wanted nothing that might be infected by jargon, the modern jargon that twisted facts and blurred judgement lest anyone could be offended. Yet the obduracy of pure fact would not suit her either: Science and mathematics were not her bent. Languages might be nearer the mark. She toyed with the idea of Greek and Latin, or Sanskrit or Chinese, but the Open University did not cater for such esoteric areas of learning. The ideal combination of intellectual rigour with literary and historical bounty, she eventually concluded, would be Russian. Harriet applied to do a course entitled *Pre-Soviet Russia from Catherine the Great to the Last Czar*, and was accepted. *It is assumed*, said the letter from her course-tutor glibly, *that you have a working knowledge of the language*. She had not, which meant deferring the course until she had learned at least a smattering of Russian.

It was, however, the year in which Roddy happened to be taking Russian O Level. They sat together at a slatted garden table during the long light evenings of the spring and heat-wave summer of 1976 and he revised by guiding her through the Cyrillic alphabet and the rudiments of grammar until she had reached a point from which she could go on to learn by herself. Roddy got an A in Russian as a result.

Two years later Harriet sat A Level Russian, and passed. Competent in the lovely, intractable language and with a knack for translating, she could at last, with a dictionary beside her for occasional reference, read Russian literature in the original. Everything she had studied hitherto had been mere slog compared to what she now discovered, guided by the Open University syllabus. To escape her senile mother-in-law's ceaseless chatter, which was like listening to the thought-processes of a mouse on a tread-wheel, Harriet took over an upstairs bedroom. She placed

51

her desk in the window overlooking a great swathe of fields and coppices. Each time she lifted her head the light, the weather, the crops or the season had changed. Every time she lowered it she was back with the vast panoramas of Russian military history, the plots and counter-plots of Russian princes and Georgian counts, overseen by the unblinking eye of the Russian Orthodox clergy. The pitch and swell of Russia enthralled her. When she tackled its literary summit, Pushkin's *Eugene Onegin*, she realized what else had been missing from her life. In the year of her fortieth birthday, Harriet finally understood what it meant never to have known love, neither passionate sexual love nor the glorious ungovernable love of the heart.

Four years later – it was by now 1983, the year after Roderick and Jennifer's marriage – she got an Open University First. She had not done it to compete with George (who was in any case dismissive) but for her own enlightenment and private satisfaction. No-one outside the family knew. She never boasted that she could speak Russian. Yet after this their neighbours, who had sometimes thought her stand-offish in the past, began to add that she was a blue-stocking. She could not disguise the fact that her learning had changed the way she thought and spoke. Men seated beside her at dinner would tell their curious wives, when they asked afterwards, 'What did you make of her?' that Harriet was 'deep'. They meant she intimidated them.

'Didn't you find her dull?' the wives might persist.

'No, not exactly dull. Hard to know what to call it. She's . . . deep.'

They nearly always omitted to say that she also presented a thrilling sexual challenge or that they were stirred by the idea of upsetting that cool composure. Then they would look at George – good old George! – and think, no, better not.

Cleaning ladies and shopkeepers – barometers of village opinion and gossip – never had a bad word to say against her. Harriet embroidered hassocks for the church's fund-raising efforts although she declined the flower-arranging rota; she turned up at the annual village fête, baked for the cake stall, bought from the tombola, applauded her sons and, in due course, grandchildren perched on donkeys or competing in egg-and-spoon races. After nearly forty years, having been fully accepted as George Capel's quiet, clever wife, she became his widow.

George, and the few debs' delights whose kisses had preceded his, were still the sum total of Harriet's sexual experience. She had sometimes wondered – as George's tree-trunk of a body heaved and lumbered around her in bed – whether they were doing it right. When men paid her compliments she thought they were teasing and she had no idea how to flirt herself, so she had never been able to compare his sexual technique with anyone else's. Harriet assumed that all men did what George did, in which case she was not missing much. Since the Capels were well-known in Dorset, having farmed there for two centuries, any misdemeanour would soon have been reported back to her in-laws. Those who said ominously in the early days of their marriage, 'She's far too pretty for old George! She'll soon look elsewhere!' were forced to concede that they had misjudged her.

Harriet sat on a bench at one side of Trafalgar Square. She loved the excitement of being in the centre, the beating heart of London. She had always particularly loved Landseer's four great lions, that noble monument to a vanished Empire. She used to gaze wistfully at them as a débutante, going from one chaperoned dance to another in the back of her parents' elderly Daimler. You couldn't get to the Ritz or the Savoy – scene of so many identical dances – without circling Trafalgar Square. As they drove round it she would fidget with her white gloves and picture herself and some laughing debs' delight, clambering up to sit on a lion's back and shout at London. She had never done it, of course. She was far too obedient and conventional for that. Now, at fifty-five, she was still obedient and conventional. Well, she'd had her Russian; a good marriage, a beautiful old house, two sons. A husband. Dodo. That was a fair ration, in an unfair world.

Tourists and children wandered past scattering seed from 50 pence packets and taking photographs – dozens of which would include her. When they scrutinized them back home in that first eager moment of curiosity, nobody would ever notice her, a slight woman in a tweed coat. No-one would think: *she* looks on the verge of something momentous.

The intensity of Oliver's gaze had been disconcerting. She had been aware of him from the moment he arrived – from the moment their eyes had met through the window. When at last she had looked straight into his eyes there was something almost threatening about his manner. She sensed that at any moment he might utter a great shout or execute some wild, embarrassing movement, unable to control his inner turbulence. Although he was charming with his grandchildren and courteously attentive to his daughter, when he looked at *her* she felt ill at ease. Harriet wondered, do I wish George were here? – for in the past, whenever some man's too-powerful stare was directed at her, she had only to move closer to George and glance up at him for the man to look away again.

Her thoughts reached the true centre of their spiral. Do I want Oliver to look at me like that; do I know what it means and do I desire the consequences? A motor bike backfired and the sky above Trafalgar Square was noisy with the clatter of pigeons' wings rising in panic; a swarm of birds, a plague. Their sickly smell, intensified by the wheeling simultaneous movement, filled her with nausea and she was further disgusted by the grubby feathers that settled on her coat. Harriet stood up, picked off the wisps and headed for the National Gallery.

In his room at the Reform Club Oliver was trying to calculate where, in the whole of London, Harriet might be. She had set off with Jennifer, who worked for a publishing company in St Martin's Lane, so at this moment she might be only a few hundred yards away. Intelligent anticipation was the clue or failing that, comparisons with similar behaviour. Where would *Clarissa* have gone? Clarissa would head at once for Peter Jones and after an hour and several hundred pounds would window-shop along Sloane Street towards the department stores of Knightsbridge. Several hundred pounds after that she would meet a girlfriend for lunch in a nearby restaurant. But that was not what Harriet would do.

He returned to his starting point and re-thought: where would *I* go? Were it not for Harriet, he would probably enjoy a gentle morning in the Club reading the papers, hoping to see someone he knew, before setting off in plenty of time to meet Philly for lunch at the place she had booked near Aldwych. Suddenly Oliver recalled a fragment of conversation over dinner.

'While you're here you *must* go to the NPG,' Jennifer had enthused, 'National Portrait Gallery. There's a marvellous show on there. Young British portrait painters. They're fantastic. You know where it is, Daddy, don't you? Behind the National Gallery.'

'NG?' he had said, and she grinned.

'Oh *do* go and see it, you *must*. It's walking distance from the Reform and it's free. I went in my lunch-hour last week and it was so good, I went back a second time.' If she had praised the exhibition to him it was more than probable that she had told Harriet to go there as well. It seemed a better bet than Peter Jones. Oliver set off purposefully along Pall Mall.

Roderick sat in a vast marble and glass tower, twenty-four storeys high, each floor of which was an open-plan office. The environment was entirely dominated by pale beige and grey computers that, if he took his contact lenses out, would look like boulders tumbled across a beach, their edges rubbed smooth by the sea. Each held a tranquil blue pool that trembled slightly as though reflecting the sky. The people staring intently into every screen were surrounded by a web of wires like fishing nets, bigger ones like trailing seaweed, linked to fax machines and telephones. These screens in turn were overlooked by much bigger suspended screens covered with tumbling, leap-frogging, constantly changing waves of figures. This was his working environment; Roderick was used to it. The only personal object on his area of curving communal desk was a framed school photograph of Hugo and Emily. He had heard that the real reason for taking these colour pictures every year was to ensure that, if a child disappeared or was found murdered, the police had a recent, full-face portrait to circulate to the

press. Emily smiled confidently into the camera but Hugo –
he noticed for the first time – wore an apprehensive smile.
Already Hugo looked like a victim.

The telephone rang and he picked it up. 'Five-three-
seven-two Capel!' he barked.

A cajoling voice said, 'Don't look, Rods. It's me-ee.'

It was impossible to hold a private conversation any-
where in this teeming public space so when Roderick and
Catriona wanted to talk, it was safest to do so by telephone.
Her voice had a soft, interrogative hiss.

'How was it, last night? Was she OK?'

He hunched his shoulders and whispered fiercely. 'No –
she was bloody, as usual. Sweetness and light to everyone
except me. Listen, darling, can't talk now. Lunch still on?'

'Yes, but gotta make it quick. Usual place?'

'Sandwich bar by Moorgate?'

'Yup. One o'clock. See you. Wait for me.'

Sotto voce, Roderick murmured, 'I'm waiting, sweetheart
– that's what I'm famous for. I can hold on for as long as you
want.'

Catriona's rich gurgle travelled down the telephone line
and, breaking their rule, he looked up to see her a few desks
away grinning conspiratorially into the mouthpiece. The
man beside him said, 'Watch it Rodders . . .' but Roderick
was saved by the shrilling of another of the phones on his
desk. 'Capel!' he barked.

The lofty, richly scented rooms of the National Gallery
surrounded Harriet with the familiar contrast of space and
detail. The floor beneath her feet smelled of polish
and the dark red leather of the buttoned couches
gleamed. Occasionally she had to ask one of the attendants:
'Where are the Vermeers? Where will I find the
Gainsboroughs? Do you know where the perspective box
has gone?' The paintings had been re-hung since her last
visit so she had the added pleasure of coming upon many of
them unexpectedly. She circled slowly, enjoying the pale
turquoise and salmon pinks of the Italian saints' robes that
fell in heavy angular folds like ballgowns. The proffered
infant was plump and serene, protected by a modestly

56

exultant Virgin and the aged Joseph. Harriet moved through tall doors, surmounted with Roman numerals, one high room visible beyond the next and the next in ever-diminishing size, each perspective culminating in a majestic painting. A sense of well-being filled her. She felt like Mary in the Annunciation: transfigured, weightless, soaring above the earth and the possible. The mundane slipped away.

A few streets away, still the same morning; noon. Jennifer's meeting had broken up. As she was about to leave the room Thorwald, her boss, detained her.

'Jennifer? Could you spare five minutes?'

Blast him, thought Jennifer: of course I can spare five minutes. All my time is his, he pays me to be at his disposal. She said demurely, 'Yes of course . . . now?' and followed him into his office. Its walls were lined with framed original book jackets and witty or complicit letters from grateful authors. The plate-glass windows overlooked St Martin's Lane in both directions, surveying the miniature figures fourteen floors down, scurrying to avoid toy cars.

'Any *particular* reason why you couldn't make it on time for this morning's meeting?' asked Thorwald with apparent casualness.

Jennifer thought, how about these? I gave dinner for ten last night, after which I had a hangover; I have three children to get off to school; my mother-in-law is staying with me; and at the moment I hate my husband, not least because he's having an affair. Also, as it happens, I started the curse on Saturday and I can feel my womb draining heavily, dragging me down with its bloody ache. All these have shattered my equilibrium in a way that you, an effortlessly dominant male – provided with your warm bath, your clean shirt, your hot coffee and your executive car by a succession of efficient menials – have never known. But one doesn't say these things to an employer, so she merely answered, 'Sorry, Thorwald . . .' and tried an appealingly frank smile. He did not smile back.

He formed his long white fingers into a steeple, flexed it twice and crossed his legs. 'These things are best said quickly,' he began. 'As you know, Jennifer . . .'

She thought, stop there. I know every sentence that

follows. The only thing I don't know is the size of my pay-off. Will you give me three months, six, or a year to go away quietly and not blab to *The Bookseller*, the literary journals or the bi-monthly meetings of Women in Publishing? Will you allow me the dignity of seeming to resign to spend more time with my family, or is it to be an open sacking? Am I to go now, today, or at the end of the week? Her heart beat fast as his dry Scandinavian voice droned on. Unconsciously, Jennifer picked at the corner of her thumb-nail until a bead of blood sprang. She sucked her thumb.

'Today is Monday. If we gave you till the end of the week to clear up outstanding business would that seem fair, hmm?' he concluded, mock-conciliatory.

What have I got to lose? Jennifer thought. Might as well march out of here with my head held high. Might even give him something to think about, bony Icelander! She leaned forward from the leather swivel chair and placed her clenched fist on his desk.

'You're not *asking* me, Thorwald, you are quite clearly *telling* me that I'm fired because I came *late* to a meeting. I was the *only* woman in that room this morning with a family. *They too* make claims upon my time. I warn you, I shall take my case to an industrial tribunal. I am sick of being discriminated against by men – and for that matter by child-less women – who know *nothing* of the pressures of the *real world*: which means, the world *outside* this office. There is more to life than Thorenson and Markworth, you know!'

'No, Jennifer,' he said steadily. 'You are not being fired for a single incident of lateness. You are being fired, if I must spell it out, for incompetence, idleness, and a sloppy attitude to your duties here. You are being fired because not one of your titles has made the best-seller list in the last eighteen months, nor anywhere near it. You are being fired because you are habitually late and I cannot be expected to pay you the same salary as your colleagues if you work shorter hours and accomplish less. By all means put your case to an industrial tribunal. But if you do, I shall produce details of your work which will make it very difficult for you to find another job in publishing, much less receive compensation. Is that clear?'

58

'In that case I should prefer to leave *today*,' Jennifer said, her cheeks mottled crimson. She clenched her jaw to stop her voice trembling. 'But before I leave and just to make sure that you understand *I too* have a case to put to that tribunal, I'd like to say a couple of things. First of all, I have been nurturing two or three young authors whose work, I am confident, will bear fruit in the next year or two – when no doubt my successor will take the credit. But that isn't really the point. It's this, Thorwald. Every other female executive here is childless or has just one child. Who do you suppose will read the books of the future? Who will run the offices? What will happen to your market? Where will they come from, the next generation of booklovers? Think about *that*!'

'Thank you for your advice. And now, if you don't mind' – he shot his cuff and glanced at a stainless-steel chronometer – 'I have another meeting before lunch.'

'Another sacking, I suppose?' She had gone too far.

'An extremely promising young graduate wrote me such a good letter that I decided to take a look at her.' He opened the connecting door and asked his secretary, 'Has Miss Rhanjani arrived yet for her interview?'

'Yes, Thorwald. She's waiting in reception.'

'Please ask her to come in.'

Jennifer swept through the doorway in a heady gust of Chanel No. 5, muttering gracelessly, 'Goodbye.'

It was all she could do not to stick her tongue out. She would have done, had she been sure that the back of her skirt was not blood-stained. She needed to get to the loo fast.

Good old Jenny, thought her father: she's quite right. These portraits are wonderful: I am almost more absorbed in them than in searching for Harriet. He had already circled slowly twice, but as there were only forty pictures in the exhibition he could not prolong his scrutiny much longer. It was nearly noon. He was due to meet Philomena at one. Oliver decided to tour the upper floors in case she was there, knowing already that his pursuit was in vain. She could be anywhere in London, miles away. She probably had a dental appointment or was meeting a friend. It was pre-posterous to suppose he could find one person in a city of nine million. He had made an intelligent guess and it had been wrong. After lunch he would telephone Camberwell again and leave a message.

He climbed the staircase, glanced at a room of indifferent royal portraits, and got as far as the Tudor kings on the top floor. He was searching for Harriet as she had looked last night . . . a slender woman in a grey shirt. Several lone middle-aged women caught his eye with a demure smile of guarded response and Oliver realized that most of them would accept an invitation to a drink or lunch. He was not in pursuit of any middle-aged woman but of one in particular, the mother of his son-in-law, grandmother to the same grandchildren: the woman with whom he had fallen in love.

After half an hour he resigned himself to the fact that she was not there and made his way down three flights to the ground floor. He hesitated, wondering whether to buy a postcard or two. Yes, why not send a few to his French neighbours? Nice people. It would please them. As he emerged from the gift shop four minutes later, Harriet swirled through the revolving doors of the National Portrait Gallery.

The blood drained from Oliver's face, his mouth dried, throat thickened. He could not speak or call her name. He blocked her path and stretched both hands towards her.

'Goodness, Oliver! *You're* here!' she said. She leaned forward, proffering her cheek for a formal kiss.

Oliver folded her in his arms. 'Oh Harriet. I've looked everywhere for you.'

She disengaged herself. 'Well, now you've found me.'

He had no control over the smile that spread across his face as the colour gradually returned. He smiled like an idiot, like an angel. It is so simple, he thought. Here she is and all will be well. There is no time like the present.

'Could we go and sit in Trafalgar Square for a few moments? Or would you prefer a drink somewhere?'

She laughed. 'I've just come from Trafalgar Square and it's a bit early for me to start drinking. Why don't we have a look at this portrait exhibition? Jennifer told me to go and see it.'

60

'She told me as well.'

They were rooted to the spot upon which they had met. Around them people ebbed and flowed, parted and vanished through the revolving doors. Oliver was about to jettison the lunch appointment with his daughter when Harriet said, 'Wait ... I've just remembered ... you're having lunch with Philomena, aren't you? Jenny told me. You haven't got time. Let's – I don't know – we could walk along Charing Cross Road for a bit until you find a taxi.'

'I'll do anything you want. I would even stand my daughter up. I love you, Harriet.'

He took her arm and steered her unsteadily into the busy street.

Chapter Four

Oliver handed the taxi driver a five pound note and, still breathing hard from haste and astonishment at having bumped into Harriet (not *bumped into*; having searched for and miraculously found Harriet), descended a flight of steps to the restaurant Philly had chosen. In the last few years he had become sufficiently French to wonder why gloom and discomfort should be regarded as desirable adjuncts to a meal. In France, above all in the light and air-loving bit of south-western France where he lived, nobody would patronize a restaurant whose décor consisted of lavatorial white tiles, with shiny floors that were a threat to the hurrying feet of waiters and diners and subdued lighting that made it difficult to decipher the menu. But in Covent Garden privacy was more important than comfort. These clients preferred lighting so discreet that they could hardly be recognized across the room and acoustics which allowed them to flirt or talk business without being overheard.

'Miss Gaunt is already here,' said the waiter, leading him to where Philly sat under a tiny spotlight, engrossed in a sheaf of papers. Oliver pitied his daughter – pitied her because he was late, thus exposing her to the humiliation of having to wait alone; because she was so busy that she must bring work to a restaurant in case she had a few spare minutes; above all because, at thirty-three, she was not married and not even, as far as he knew, in love. *Oh Harriet!* he thought. Putting that name and her image resolutely aside, Oliver prepared to concentrate on his daughter.

Filled with a throb of affection for his solemn child (older by only twenty minutes than her twin sister yet always, even in babyhood, the grave and responsible one) Oliver leaned over to kiss her cheek. Philomena jumped up and put her arms around him. They hugged one another and he kissed her again, refraining from the exuberant four kisses with which the French greet relatives.

'Daddy! *Here* you are! How *lovely* to see you!'

'Darling Phills, I'm late. I'm so sorry.'

'Never mind. I've been working and' – she indicated her glass – 'I got myself a drink.'

Oliver ordered a gin and tonic and they scanned the menu, whose prices seemed unjustifiably high. He raised his eyebrows and Philomena, watching him, said, 'It's not *that* expensive, Daddy. You're out of touch with London prices.'

'I don't mind what it costs,' he said expansively. 'Do you want champagne? I'll order champagne. Anything!'

'Are you mad? This is my one statutory glass of white wine; it's mineral water from now on or I shan't be able to work.'

Oliver thought, good heavens. In my working years, when I was back at base and not out in the field, we thought nothing of sharing two bottles of wine over lunch, with port or brandy afterwards. Your secretary would screen out callers if you weren't quite up to it when you got back to the office. *'I'm afraid Mr Gaunt will be tied up in a meeting for the rest of the afternoon.'* It was a code that everyone understood.

'Poor old thing,' he said sympathetically. 'Do they really work you that hard?'

'Daddy, *everyone* works "that hard". *You* on the other hand have obviously been taking it easy. You look marvellous – so brown and fit! Much younger than sixty.' Oliver was pleased by her flattery. For the first time in years he wanted to look young, brown and fit. But he said deprecatingly, 'It's the summer we've had. Almost too much of a good thing. And your mother's visitors keep me on my toes. I'm a cross between the lord of the manor and the second under-footman. It's a constant struggle not to be caught out.'

They ordered the food and she leaned forward to engage his concentration. 'Has Jenny talked to you?'

63

'For a moment, in the car last night. Gather things aren't too good with Roderick.'

'Things are *terminal* with Roderick. Disastrous. At the moment she's saying she wants a divorce. One of the reasons she was keen that you should come to London was to break the news. She doesn't dare tell Mum. It's never been an easy marriage. She's felt pretty pissed off with him before now.'

'Hold on, what about the children . . .?' Oliver asked.

'Mandy was a mistake. Jenny wanted an abortion but chickened out at the last moment. She was more than four months gone by then; eighteen weeks or so. It's pretty late – not legally of course but gynaecologically, I gather. I mean, she adores them and she'll get custody, naturally – it's very rare for the father to be awarded custody except in cases where there's evidence of maternal alcoholism, drug addiction or habitual violence and even then only with a *bloody* good barrister – but the point is, she and Roderick have been at daggers drawn for years. He's such a coward, he had to wait for his father to die before he could even begin to *talk* about it. That old man was a tyrant, you know. No wonder his wife's such a miserable little mouse. Old whatsisname, George Capel, dominated them all. If Jenny had realized what a wimp Roderick was she'd never have married him in the first place.'

'Harriet didn't strike me as a miserable little mouse. Nor would I have thought Roderick a wimp. He holds down a tough job in the City and that's not a place for wimps these days,' Oliver said.

'Well, whatever, things have changed. Women aren't prepared to be at the beck and call of their lord and master any more. Harriet's a rotten role model.'

'Rather a good granny, I believe.'

'Daddy, *Harriet* is neither here nor there. It's *Jennifer's* happiness I'm talking about.'

'And the happiness of her three children? Doesn't that deserve a thought?'

'Received wisdom seems to be that they're better off with one calm, concerned parent than two fighting ones. I'll be her back-up; try and be more of a hands-on aunt. I'm sure Jenny would allow Roderick reasonable access. He doesn't

64

have to lose touch with them, though I daresay he'll marry and breed again – men always do. *Useless* without a woman to run their lives.'

'Steady on, Philly. You're talking like a barrister on behalf of her client. This is your *sister*. These are her *children*. Let's skip the legal generalizations. We are not just talking about Jenny's happiness – and even if we were, I wouldn't take it for granted that she would be happier as a *divorcée*. We're talking about a whole network of relationships, which is what family means. We are talking about at least three generations here. If Jenny and Roderick divorce, the children become children of a broken home but they also lose a devoted granny.'

'I don't see why. They could still spend summer holidays with you and Mum.'

'What about Harriet? Could you see Jenny letting them go down to Dorset to spend holidays with her, too?'

Philomena put down her knife and fork and looked at him. 'What's all this nonsense about *Harriet*? She's the *last* person I'm bothered about. I mean, apart from the fact that her sodding husband did us all the favour of having a heart attack.'

Careful, thought Oliver. Time to change the subject. 'I can see I'm going to spend a lot of time talking about Jenny this week. Now let's talk about *you*, Philly. How goes it in chambers?'

'Gradually getting better. I've had some fairly good briefs recently; won a couple of tricky cases. The money's still crap but it should improve from now on. Things are looking up for women at the Bar, slowly. Feminism ahoy, all the old liners steaming off in the opposite direction. Meaning judges, head clerks, that lot.'

'But for now you're working too hard?'

'I don't know about *too* hard – this is the Nineties, you know. Whole different world from yours.'

'Do you ever have time to *play*?'

'Is that a disguised way of asking me whether there's a man in my life?'

'No it isn't, as a matter of fact. If I want to ask you I'm capable of being direct.'

'Go on then.'

'You tell me.'

'No, Daddy, there is *not* a man in my life. But I own my flat in the Barbican; I run a two-year-old car; I shop at Harvey Nicks, I eat out twice a week – OK, usually with a woman friend – and go to the opera twice a year. That's my life and I'm not changing it. Nor does my twin sister's example offer any great inducement.'

'I thought Jenny was one of those women who're supposed to have everything . . . marriage, children, job, social life. Isn't that what your feminism is all about?'

'*Please*, Daddy, let's not get onto the subject of feminism. OK, OK, I started it. Well, now I'm stopping. How's my baby brother Patrick? Settling down?'

'Your *baby brother* Patrick is twenty-five, you know. Yes, he's calming down. Started work with an estate agent in Rodez. Being bi-lingual comes in handy. Lots of Brits buying property in France. You know he's left home? Shares a flat with a *copine*.'

'Good. High time. Now tell me about you and Mummy. Good season this year? Lots of bloated Yanks and twittering Japs?'

'Philomena Gaunt – you *racist*. You should be ashamed of yourself.'

'*Touchée*.'

They smiled at one another and he reached a hand across the table to enclose hers. My daughter, my first-born . . .

'Tell me more about Patrick.'

'Your brother Patrick is known as *Patrice* these days. He's become ninety-nine per cent French.'

'OK, how is *Patrice*? Do you like his new girlfriend?'

At two o'clock Philomena looked at her watch. 'Got to get back. One and a quarter hours is my max for lunch. Lovely seeing you, Daddy. See you again on Sunday at Hugo's birthday lunch.'

'I brought you something . . .' Oliver said uncertainly. 'Nothing very much.' He reached into his jacket pocket for the small Duty Free package.

'Ooh, look, goody! *Mystère*: my favourite. Well *done*. Mum always gets it wrong and brings me *Femme*. Now, if you don't mind, Daddy, I really ought to go . . .'

'Go, Philly darling. I'm at the Reform. If you get any spare time this week I'd love to take you to the theatre or something . . .'

'Mmm . . . this week's pretty hectic. Actually there *is* the new Joanna Lumley thing – terrific reviews – well, give you a buzz. Thanks anyway, lovely lunch. Great to see you. Honestly. Dear Daddy . . .'

He stood up, hugged her, watched her hurry through the restaurant, her slender back bent purposefully towards her destination. She did not turn to smile or flicker her fingers at him. My solemn child: what a fretful young woman you have become. He summoned the waiter, ordered a brandy, and leaned back as far as the unforgiving chair would allow to indulge the luxury of thinking about Harriet. Before they parted she had agreed to have dinner with him. Where should he take her? Rules? Boulestin? L'Escargot? Did they still exist, the restaurants from his past, or was the world he knew quite lost?

As she unlocked the front door with the key Jennifer had given her, Harriet looked forward to two hours' peace before the children got home from school. If I go down to the basement at three thirty, she calculated, I could still have a freshly baked cake in the oven in time to welcome them back. Climbing the stairs to her room at the top of the house, she heard Jennifer's voice from the first-floor bedroom. She was talking on the telephone, loudly and with great indignation. '. . . and then he *sodding* said, "I am not interested in your children, Jennifer, only in how well you do your *job*." So I said, "In that case, Thorwald, you can *stuff* your job. I am clear about the priorities in my life and Thorenson and Markworth is *not* the first!" '

Harriet's shoulders sagged at the prospect of being the next audience for Jennifer's drama. She crept past the closed door and went up to her own room, where she folded up the counterpane and lay down with her cheek against the cool pillow.

'I love you, Harriet,' Oliver said.

They were sitting side by side on a red velvet banquette

in a corner of Rules, from which they could survey the whole dining room. They had arrived late, having both lied in order to get away. Their presence here had the lure of the clandestine but, overwhelmingly, that of intimacy. At the end of a day spent listening to their joint yet separate and warring children, they were finally alone together. How astonished those children would be! Oliver felt no guilt, only exultation.

'Do you know what Octavio Paz says about love?'

'No. Tell me.'

'He says "love is our share of paradise".'

Oliver did not add that Paz meant erotic love. Harriet would be alarmed, he felt sure, by a blatant sexual overture. His own body was electrified. He could feel each throb of blood through his arteries. The arm and thigh closest to her burned with proximity. But Harriet had not yet declared herself, although he did not doubt she would. She said, 'I like that.'

'Very Mexican. He was a diplomat as well as a poet. You look beautiful, my darling; thoughtful and reflective. *You* are my share of paradise. I ought to be more discreet but it's a luxury to speak the words out loud: *I love you, Harriet!*'

'This is my best dress. I don't really know why I brought it. In case . . .'

'You brought it in order to have dinner with me.'

'This wine is . . . well, just wonderful. I don't have the right vocabulary for it.'

'Don't try. Really good wine needs no description but when you talk about other things it makes your imagination soar. Just enjoy it, my darling.'

She turned the bottle to look at the label, the date, and knew enough to know how greatly he was indulging her.

'What a pleasure this is . . . you can't imagine how long it is since I felt *pleasure*.'

'Good. Don't spoil it with guilt.'

'Doesn't that come later? I don't know. Oddly enough I'm not very used to guilt. I felt it after George died but . . . don't let's talk about that.'

He said, 'Tell me about you. What were you like as a child? Were you happy?'

'I was born soon after the beginning of the war. My father was wounded and then he became a prisoner of war. Mother said he was never the same again afterwards, though he never talked about it. He was a grim, stony-faced sort of man; very unhappy I think now, when I look back. I wish I had understood him better. I think he longed for tenderness.'

'All men do, in secret, but they're afraid it will expose them.'

'My mother was a strong character, not much good at tenderness. When she found out I was clever she insisted on sending me to a serious girls' boarding school; the sort of place founded by Victorian feminists whose own lives had been frustrated, and were determined to change things for other girls in future. I was only eight.'

'What were you good at?'

She laughs. 'Everything! Honestly: it's true. I don't know whether it's because we were so well-taught. I did a bit of Maths and Science as well as all the usual things – French, German, and English Literature. Even Latin. But even though I might have got pretty good A Levels . . .' she paused and laughed at herself, '. . . look at me, boasting about A Levels that I never even took nearly forty years ago!'

'You were a clever girl. *Clever* Harriet.'

'It wouldn't have made any difference to my father. He would still have refused to let me go to university and it wouldn't have crossed my mind to argue with him.'

'You must have married very young.'

'I did. I left school in July. First we spent a month in Scotland at our Blythgowrie cousins' house – that was the last summer before it was sold to be converted into a hotel—'

'Vivian Blythgowrie?'

'Yes! Him! Do you know him?'

'Not well. My daughter's in chambers with his son-in-law.'

'He's a dreadful man. He broke up the estate, sold off all the properties, and has done nothing but make money. He's been married three times. Still no heir. If I'd been a boy it might all have ended up on *my* plate!'

Oliver preferred to dwell on his image of the fledgling Harriet. 'Go on about you.'

'After that summer I was sent to a finishing school outside Paris. Then I did my Season – this was nineteen fifty-eight, when I was just eighteen. Right at the beginning of it I met George and we were married that Christmas. That's me done. Now you.'

Oliver laughed. 'Not enough. How, when, where did you meet? Did you fall in love with him at first sight? Tell me everything.'

Harriet was used to eliding the account of How We Met into a few polished phrases for the benefit of people who enquired out of politeness rather than any real interest. But Oliver was so seductively easy to talk to that she told him the whole story truthfully, for once. At thirty-five – almost twice her age – George Capel was no ordinary debs' delight. He had been a big capable man, square and solid of face and torso. She had liked the vigorous way he walked and danced and the fact that he spent more time out of doors than in an office or a regimental mess. He was not a boor, not a chinless wonder and not a fool, and these three negatives added up to something positive, though it was hardly love. But she was accustomed to doing what men told her so when George had said she ought to think about marrying him, she mentioned it to her mother. He was a reasonable 'catch'; the Capels were a well-established county family who had always farmed their own land. Most of her fellow-débutantes would have done exactly as she did: it was what they had been trained for. Six weeks later George made a formal proposal and she accepted.

'But were you in *love* with him?'

Perhaps she had thought at the time it was love – being flattered and pleasantly excited by the attention focused upon her by George and her parents as well as the complicity or envy of the other debs. It was nice to be an object of approval rather than mild exasperation.

Hard as it was to credit nowadays, girls in the Fifties were not expected to feel – and on the whole, *did* not feel – sexual desire. All the same, shortly before accepting George's proposal Harriet had said to her mother that she doubted whether she was really *in love*. Her mother had replied briskly, 'Much better *not*, my dear girl! That's the way to keep a husband on tenterhooks. Don't ever let him be sure of you. Then he'll go on loving *you* – which is what matters – and won't ever take you for granted. They get bored and look elsewhere otherwise. What do you want to be in *love* with him for? You like him, don't you? Thoroughly suitable match. I didn't think you'd have so much good sense.'

By the time the Season ended the two families were planning a winter wedding. Not that there was any hurry. Harriet, acting in accordance with docility and quite unconscious of any desire for George, remained virgo intacta until her wedding night.

She sighed; so many disclosures, so long ago. 'Now you, Oliver: I want to hear about you.'

Oliver wanted the meal to be over so that he could kiss her. He wanted to tell her again that he loved her, ask if she loved him. All his impulses were physical now; an erection had distracted him more than once. But Harriet's food was almost untouched so, if only to give her a chance to eat, he told his own tale.

'Languages were my strong point. Greek and Latin at school; then the Army gave me what nowadays is called a "total immersion course" in Russian. After eight weeks you're supposed to be able to speak it, more or less. I did some Russian conversation lessons after that and . . . well, anyway, I had French and German already, bit of Italian. After reading Languages at Oxford I joined the Firm.'

'You mean the Foreign Office?'

He assumed she did not understand and was relieved. From schoolboy secret societies to Intelligence cliques, Biggles and Raffles, John Buchan to John le Carré, all the nicknames and disguises, always saying one thing and meaning another – mendacity had governed his adult life and he was tired of it.

'More or less, yes. That's how I found myself working in Bulgaria and Yugoslavia, Romania, Albania, all round there. My stamping-ground was the bit they used to call Eastern Europe or' (he put on a rolling Germanic voice, to see her smile) '*Mittel-Europa.* Twenty years ago Clarissa and I bought a place in France. It made a base for the holidays, a fixed point for our boarding-school children whose home was never in the same place three years running. Later, when the political map began to change, I got offered early retirement. Took it.'

He had become too conspicuous; linked to a network of covert Eastern European malcontents stretching across the Balkans, their intricate cross-purposes involving him too closely. Unwilling to become the victim of a Serbian faction ranged against some Bosnian cell, or a mad Albanian at odds with everyone, he had told the Firm it was time for him to get out. He would stay on 'in an advisory capacity'. He knew all the fanatics' names, aliases and allegiances; his advice had been useful sometimes. They'd even asked him to look in this week at their new HQ, that ugly modern ziggurat beside the Thames. Might as well, if he had a moment; they gave him a generous pension. Would do no harm to be civil, keep the old links alive. Something to tell Clarissa.

After early retirement twelve years ago, Oliver had spent his days in the shade of a tree, a wineglass and a dog or two beside him, another expatriate taking easy refuge in the lush French countryside. Sometimes he scanned the English papers that guests left lying around, occasionally he glanced at the *Weekly Telegraph*, but he preferred *Sud-Ouest* or *Figaro.* He was kept idle deliberately by Clarissa, who liked to have him at her beck and call. He was – he realized with a sudden shock of rage and honesty – waiting to die. And now Harriet had arrived, galvanizing him with an emotional and physical response that he had not known for years; not since being holed-up in fear of his life in some over-crowded flat in Romania or Hungary, where suddenly one night he and the daughter of the house might find them-selves grappling on the sofa in silent frenzy . . . Oliver had not been entirely faithful to his wife, but his forays had been opportunistic and conducted with extreme discretion. Love had never entered into them.

'Your hair is grey,' he said.

'Why, does Clarissa dye hers?'

'Yes. Her coiffeur told her all women over thirty-five should colour their hair.'

'Should I?'

'*No.*'

There was a pause. Harriet was filled with apprehension, almost terror. She knew the next question could not be delayed much longer. She knew he was about to ask whether she loved him and she needed time to reflect on what was happening, what it signified. Was it just the un-accustomed luxury of good wine, plush surroundings, the waiter's flattering attentions; or was her long-neglected capacity for love itself awakening, yawning, stretching and flexing its limbs, after being dormant all her life, in response to this relative stranger beside her?

No, she thought, I am *old*; absurdly old to be starting now. I am a grandmother. I am grey-haired. I am invisible, as women over fifty tend to be. I am a widow. It would be unseemly. I am not available for passion. I will not let it happen. I dare not be what he wants. *I am afraid.* I will slip into motherly mode, deny myself, emasculate him.

'Are you having pudding?' she asked. 'George always loved his puddings. Men usually have a sweet tooth, don't they?'

'Why, do you want a pudding?'

'No, no really, thank you.'

'Cheese?'

'No – but what about you? You ought to have some.'

He ignored her change of tone. 'Harriet, I have to ask: do you love me?'

Her heart leapt as though she had been given an electric shock, bouncing into her throat, setting her arteries jangling. Surely he must have seen her jump?

'Oliver, don't go on. Please don't ask, I really can't . . .'

'I want to make love to you.'

'I am old. We have nowhere to go. I haven't made love for years. *I am afraid.*'

'You cannot possibly be afraid of me. I am older than you and I, too, have hardly made love for years. I had begun to think I might never make love again.' He reached across the

73

table for her hand. It was cool and small. 'What can we do except trust one another?'

'I am afraid. My heart is thundering.'

He placed his index finger against her wrist and smiled.

'So it is. I can feel it. Beat, beat, beat, beat.'

She placed her palm upright and he pressed his palm against hers, as prisoners do through a glass window. It was a promise of all the things to come . . . the touch of lip to lip, mouth to mouth, of lying full-length, body pressed against body.

She withdrew her hand as the waiter approached.

'Will you have dessert, cheese, liqueur, madam, sir?'

'Nothing for me—'

'Harriet, stop. I have said I will look after you. Bring us two coffees.'

As the waiter moved away Oliver said, 'First we have to talk about our children and their troubles. I refuse to quarrel with *you*, my love; we shall never quarrel.'

'Roddy says they might divorce.'

'Jennifer says so too.'

'It *cannot* happen. I refuse to let it happen. The children . . .'

'. . . You mean, the little ones . . .'

'The grandchildren I mean; yes. Oliver, *why* do people expect marriage to be plain sailing? One goes through such storms, dashes oneself against rocks, comes into calm water for a while and then it gets tempestuous again. It goes on like that throughout your whole *life*.'

'Yes.'

A spasm of jealousy leapt across the table.

'Does your wife – does Clarissa still, I mean – *love* you?'

'I'm afraid so, yes.'

Another obstacle, Harriet thought. They spring up like fields of swords. She could not bring herself to ask the next question and in any case Oliver would not answer. This she understood. Love, love – after a lifetime of marriage love has become involuntary; it *is*. Even when it is hate it is still a kind of love.

'Oliver, if the children – I mean, *our* children — were to find out?'

That, Harriet knew, was the true field of swords they had to negotiate. She was mother-in-law to his daughter; he was father-in-law to her son. They were linked not by blood but by a thousand other invisible ties. She did not care about their age, nor the possibility of guilt, nor his wife — but she could not ignore the fact that *their children*, one a Capel, the other a Gaunt, had married and made a family. Who could say that it was not the same impulse that had drawn Roddy to Jennifer which now drew Harriet towards Oliver; as though the genes were programmed to respond to some deep magnetic pull, one to the other. Yet he seemed unaware of any conflict. Men are less concerned with family connections. They leave that to women.

'We shall make certain that they don't,' Oliver said. 'Trust me, my darling. I will protect you.'

They left the restaurant and threaded through the narrow darkness of Maiden Lane. In the doorway of a bookshop he drew her against him and held her in his arms. For the first time, they kissed. They were crushed against one another, close enough to feel their hearts thudding, centimetres apart, separated by coats and clothes and breasts and skin and a thin carapace of bone inside which the blood pulsed wildly between them, keeping time. When they separated, breathless, wide-eyed, Harriet touched her fingers to her bruised mouth and said, 'I love you, Oliver.'

Chapter Five

It was midnight; Jennifer and Roderick were exhausted with arguing and quite drunk.

'Where the hell has your *mother* got to?' said Jennifer.

In actual fact she did not care where Harriet was. She had come home from an unsatisfactory meeting with her father at the Reform Club braced for supper with her mother-in-law. Instead, at quarter to nine, Harriet had set out in her best dress to have dinner with 'a friend'. Jennifer, assuming that a friend of Harriet's could only be female, imagined two old biddies going Dutch in some local trattoria, comparing family photographs and boasting about their grandchildren. The question had merely been designed to mollify Roderick so that she could steer him towards bed; maybe even sex. Violent confrontation always made Jennifer feel randy. She had told her mother-in-law but not yet her husband that she had been fired and was afraid of being interrupted by Harriet, who might blurt it out. Roderick ignored the overture and poured himself another glass of wine.

'How should *I* know where she is? She's got plenty of people to see in London.'

'She was tarted up to the nines. Actually she looked surprisingly good.'

'Don't be so fucking patronizing. My mother *is* a good-looking woman.'

'Not bad. For her age, that is. Look better if she coloured her hair.'

'For your age you look pretty raddled, in *spite* of spending a fortune on your hair.'

'Trying to run this house *and* hold down a job . . . precious little help from you . . . off before seven in the morning . . . never see you again till nine o'clock at night—'

'I am *trying* to earn enough *money* to pay for your extravagant notions of how we are entitled to live. I am sick to death of trying to meet your mother's expectations of the living standards of "people like us"' – Roderick mimicked Clarissa's nasal, patrician voice.

Jennifer, tired as well as drunk, had run out of insults. First Thorwald, now her husband. 'All this talk about the importance of the family – our kids see less of you than I did of my father and God knows I never saw much of *him*. Call yourself a New Man? Ha!'

'I don't. *You're* not so bloody liberated either. Your salary hardly covers the cost of Ulrike, Mrs Thing, and your clothes, let alone this nanny you're supposed to be hiring. Might be better if you stayed at home and looked after your own children instead of leaving them to a bunch of strangers.'

'*Do* I detect the dulcet tones of dear Harriet, mother superior and housewife extraordinary? I can always tell when you've been talking to her. Time for the Angel in the House lecture again. Why couldn't my mother-in-law have been the sort of woman who *did* something with her life, for Christ's sake?'

It was the old grievance and like a donkey on a treadmill, Jennifer reverted to it. Pointless sacrifice . . . beck and call of two sons and a tyrant . . . ruined them for any other woman . . . was *she, Jennifer*, supposed to pick up the pieces? . . . not bloody likely . . . The familiar litany rose to a crescendo of incoherent repetition and abuse.

Roderick's voice was chill with contempt. 'What do you suppose you've done with *your* life? Third editor from the left in the annual corporate photograph. Big deal. Not yet broken the forty thousand a year barrier. Go get a *real* life!'

'Like *your* mother, I suppose,' she retaliated. 'Running smaller and smaller circles round your selfish bully of a father and his ninety-year-old isn't-she-marvellous *nanny*! Is *that* all you think women are good for?'

'Better than yours. The illustrious Clarissa, behaving like

a superannuated *grande dame* for the benefit of snobbish and gullible *tourists* whom she charges a fortune for the "privilege" of dining at her table. I suppose that's where you get it from. *Very* gracious you were last night: "*So* glad you enjoyed it . . . *dear* Oliver, it *is* good to see him" – not letting on that the au pairs did it all. You didn't so much as mix the vinaigrette. What did you tip them, I wonder? Let me guess: a fiver each?'

Jennifer, who had given Ulrike and Victoria exactly that, was goaded into reckless disclosure. 'Well, sunshine, have *I* got news for *you!* I got *fired* today so you may just get what you've always wanted: a dear little stay-at-home wife. Oh *shit* . . .'

They heard Harriet's key in the door and Jennifer burst into tears.

Harriet had hoped they would be too preoccupied to notice that she was bright-eyed and pink-cheeked, that her lips were swollen and she did not look at all as though she had just enjoyed a quiet supper with an old friend. Hearing the staircase creak she glanced up and saw Hugo peering fearfully through the banisters. In the drawing-room Jennifer was sobbing noisily and Roddy was hissing, 'Shut *up*, for God's sake!' Harriet climbed the first flight of stairs to the landing.

'What are *you* doing up so late?' she whispered. 'Quick now – hurry off to bed before Mummy and Daddy find you.'

'Carry me, Granny.'

'I can't carry you. You're much too heavy.'

But Hugo twined his thin arms round her neck and held on tight. Harriet lifted him up, took him to his bedroom and put him gently on the dishevelled bed. He lay there like the victim of a fall with sprawled limbs and neck akimbo. In the splinter of light from the landing she saw his eyes fixed on hers.

'G-g-granny, why is Mummy c-c-crying?'

'Oh darling, I don't know. Grown-ups have grown-up things to worry about.'

'If I tell you a s-s-secret do you promise not to t-t-tell Em and Mandy?'

'That depends – well, yes, all right: what secret, darling?'

'D-d-daddy and M-mummy are g-g-get...' His stutter became almost insuperable. Harriet waited in anguish, stroking his soft extended leg. '...G-getting a d-d-div-*divorce*. They *are*, Granny. I heard them say so.'

He was imploring her reassurance, a denial, the firm statement that it could not possibly be true. Harriet could not give it. One must never lie to children.

'They say that when they're having a quarrel, Hugo. People say all sorts of things when they're cross. It doesn't always mean it will *happen*.'

He looked at her in silence. She stroked his temples with one finger and his heavy-lidded blue eyes began to droop.

'G-g-granny,' he murmured, 'can I sleep in your bed? Oh go on, please – *let* me sleep with you!'

'No darling. You're too big for that. How about if I sing you a little song instead?'

'Am I too big for "Sleep my baby"?'

Harriet lifted the blanket and Hugo scrambled underneath and curled into a foetal position. He fixed his eyes upon her face. She adapted the old lullaby for him:

> '*Sleep, my Hugo, sleep so softly,*
> *While thy Granny watches o'er thee.*
> *Nothing can affright or harm thee,*
> *Sleep, oh sleep, my child.*'

Within moments he was asleep. She stood looking down on him, his flushed face softened into infant curves, bone of her bone, flesh of her flesh – and bone and flesh of Oliver also.

When she was quite sure that Hugo would not wake again Harriet tiptoed up to her bedroom on the top floor. The sounds of lavatorial flushing and running water had subsided from the other bathroom and although she was still thoroughly alert, she too prepared for bed. Washed, brushed and in her dressing gown, she went down to the kitchen to wait for Oliver's call. He did not have to explain; she knew that when he got back to his room he would telephone Clarissa. When that was safely accomplished, he had promised to ring her. Sleep was hours away. Her face burned, her mouth throbbed, but those were minor afflictions beside her turbulent mind.

Harriet put the kettle on and sat down to wait. She placed her hands palm to palm against one another as she and Oliver had done not two hours ago, then laid them against the polished pine of the kitchen table. Blue veins rose above the smooth surface of her skin. Her nails were unvarnished. They were, she thought, regarding their familiar shape and surface, the hands of half a lifetime; neither young and sleek nor old and liver-spotted. The kettle turned itself off and as Harriet poured scalding water over a tea bag, the telephone rang. She snatched it up.

'Hallo?'

There was a sigh, in which she heard both relief and a smile.

'My *love* . . .'

She might have expected tender words, compliments, reminiscences – they had twelve hours of memories to analyse and gloat over – but Oliver launched almost at once into a vehement declaration.

'Love is blood, Harriet. I knew I had fallen in love at the very first sight of you through the window at Camberwell. My heart raced. When I saw you the blood drained from my face. Even Ben noticed. *Your* love for me beats through your pulse: you can't hide it.'

Harriet braced herself for a confrontation, not a love duet.

'If love is blood, as you say, it's not only our blood but Roddy and Jennifer's blood and above all, their children's blood. *They* are Capel and Gaunt, too. No – listen to *me*. When I got back tonight, Hugo was sitting on the stairs listening to his parents quarrel. They are savage towards one another. He was frightened. I put him to bed and stayed with him until he fell asleep. He worries that they will divorce. The tanks are trundling through his world, Oliver. What would happen to him and his sisters if you and I were to say . . .' Her voice faded. She had not yet thought this far.

'That we loved each other?' he prompted. 'That I was coming to live with you? They are children, my darling. To blossom, they need love, that's all.'

She was unexpectedly scornful. 'Love is sunshine now? A

minute ago it was blood. Must we behave like animals and be blindly carnal; do we *have* to follow our blood-lust? What about reason, unselfishness, the need to protect others?' Harriet had spent half a lifetime being unselfish and knew it was not necessarily the worst course of action. 'Think of my name. I am a Capel and so are your grandchildren. *That* is the obstacle. I can't believe you don't feel it as strongly as I do. Oliver – am I hearing right? Are you seriously saying that it wouldn't matter to Jenny or Hugo, if you and I were suddenly to announce that we have become lovers and intend to go off together? To me, it would fly in the face of every family rule and expectation. And – not that I give a fig for social opinion – it would outrage your friends and mine.'

'How well you argue! All the same, you are wrong. I have learned more about the compulsion behind love in the last twenty-four hours than I knew in a lifetime before. Love has overwhelmed us. Love beats in my blood, systole and diastole, unstoppable.'

'Your heart was beating perfectly well without me, Oliver. Nothing has changed.'

'Touch your mouth.'

Alone in the basement kitchen, festooned with the children's daubs carried home from school, proof for their parents that they were learning to handle a paint brush, Harriet obeyed him.

'Feel. Your mouth is swollen. So is mine. The palm of my hand remembers the feel of your palm against it, the curve of your breast, the rise of your pubic mound, its crease. We have already broken the rules of family life and civilized behaviour.'

She paused to steady her voice. 'Yes, we have. But there is still time to draw back. We have done nothing irreparable, made no commitment. They think of us as *old*. We are the pillars that hold up their world. If we fall in love, the walls will tumble down.'

'*Have* fallen in love. *Are* tumbling. Jenny told me this evening that she and Roderick are planning to go ahead with a divorce. She says they waited till George was dead because your sons were always afraid of their father.'

81

'I hear everything you say and we will talk about George some other time. I don't believe this divorce will happen. They have a strong marriage – strong in anger as well as other things. But what's certain to rock it even more would be our . . .' she hesitated, not knowing what word to use. Love? Adultery? Affair? Relationship? She let the pause supply the word. 'But in any case, that's not why I say no. Not because of our children, whose disapproval I could bear – because of *their* children. Oliver, *Oliver!* If you were any-one else I would leap into your arms; I would never be without you again, I would trample on Clarissa, ignore your daughters, I would probably even, God help me, think your unknown grandchildren were bound to get over it and ignore them too. But you are the grandfather of Hugo and Emily and Amanda. Because of *them*, this love is wicked. No, not even wicked, it's *impossible.*'

She heard his sigh down the phone.

'Why do you sigh?'

'Because of the way you said, "Oliver, *Oliver!*"'

Harriet grew more frantic. A foreboding seized her. He was going to overcome her arguments without even under-standing their force. She must try practical solutions.

'We can stop now. Not meet tomorrow. Stay on the far sides of the room on Sunday. You could ring Clarissa back, ring her *now*, tell her everyone is missing her, ask her to join us. We *can* still stop. We don't have to capitulate to love.'

He leapt upon her confession. 'You feel it as well. *You* are overwhelmed by love.'

'After a life spent being docile, supportive, invisible? Of *course* I feel it. But I also held Hugo in my arms tonight and I tell you, my heart beat for him, too. I am not saying I do not love you . . .' her voice threatened to collapse, '. . . but our relationship would be a black hole, drawing everyone in the family after us in to nothingness. At best we would be isolated. Would your daughters come and visit you, if you were living with the woman who took you from their mother?'

He said, 'I am looking over St James's Park. The lights are strung across it like a necklace. The leaves on top of the trees are golden in the light, as though the trees were

82

covered with ripe fruit. I have never seen it look like that before. You are not only in my blood, Harriet, you are in my imagination. You have given me back my life. Before, I was in, what do they call it, a near-death situation. I love you, and I won't let you go. I intend to marry you. That's not a proposal, it's a vow.'

There was nothing more to say. She had agreed to an assignation (the wicked word leapt unbidden to her mind) in the afternoon. Oliver would find somewhere private: 'Not, I promise you, a hotel!' He would not allow her to put the phone down until she agreed. When at last she did she saw from the clock on the wall that they had been talking for more than an hour. She felt tired but determined. By to-morrow they would have made love. She needed to muster her forces before it was too late.

Harriet spread her hands on the kitchen table and tried to think methodically. First we would have to tell our children. Then the grandchildren. The earth would split open under their feet. Then Clarissa. Distant rumblings. Then the lawyers: sage counsel, heads shaken, very great expense. Next, Oliver would have to disentangle his life and possessions from France and bring them to Dorset. By this time two or three years could have passed, the first fine frenzy would have subsided, and she would be nearly sixty. And as well as all that there was Dodo . . .

The time was half past one but Dodo, at ninety, slept lightly and day and night were much the same to her. She had a telephone beside her bed. Harriet dialled the number.

'Dodo . . . ?' she said, and at last she allowed her voice to tremble with fear and uncertainty. 'Dodo? It's me. How are you, Dodo? How is Mrs Peters? Is she looking after you?'

'My lamb, my ladybird! What time is it, Hattie dear?'

'Middle of the night. Quite late.'

She heard a rustling as Dodo sat up laboriously in bed and reached for her illuminated bedside clock. Then the quavering frail voice said indignantly, 'It certainly is. You have not telephoned me at this hour to ask about Mrs Peters. What is the matter, my duck?'

Dodo's voice might quaver but her mind was as clear as a bell.

'I think I have fallen in love, Dodo.'

' "Think"! You don't *think*! You either have or you haven't! Which is it, dear?'

'I have.'

'Well, you're still young. These things happen. Now that dear George has gone, it may turn out to be a very good thing. You haven't wasted much time. Who is he?'

'Oliver Gaunt.'

'Gaunt? Is he a relation of your daughter-in-law? Wasn't she a Gaunt?'

'Yes. He is her father.'

'Oh-ho.' There was a long silence. 'Well then it *won't* do, will it? You've made a simple choice – I mean, a stupid one. Or at any rate a complicated one. Much too complicated. You can't have him and that's all there is to it.'

'I was afraid you'd say that.'

'Make yourself a cup of cocoa, Hattie, and go to bed. Sleep. Tell yourself in the morning it's all over and you will avoid him in future. Firmness of purpose, that's what it takes. Good night, dear. Sweet dreams.'

'Are you all right, darling? Is Mrs Peters coming in every day?'

'Every day, dear. Good night, I said.'

Chapter Six

'Good to see you again, sir; very very good to see you again. What can we do for you this morning?'

'I thought, a shave and general tidy-up.' Oliver waved in the direction of his nose and ears.

'Of course, sir. Very very good.'

With a flourish the barber threw a warm towel around his shoulders, knotting it at the back of his neck like a giant bib. He adjusted the reclining headrest and tipped Oliver's head backwards.

'Comfortable like that, sir?'

An assistant wheeled across a stainless-steel bowl of hot water around which were ranged several surgical instruments and Oliver surrendered to the intense pleasure of being shaved. His eyebrows were trimmed and unruly hairs plucked, with a pause for him to appraise the result; then his ears and nostrils. The barber anointed his palms with a lotion that smelled of wood-smoke and water, applied it to Oliver's shining cheeks and jawline, and swept away the encircling towel. Together they inspected his face in the mirror: a trimmer, sleeker, less French, more English Oliver. He nodded approval.

'Will there be anything else, sir? No? Very good, sir; it's a pleasure to be of service to you.'

The barber's soft hand appeared at the very place where Oliver might wish to deposit a couple of coins. He paid at the till and strode into the crisp morning.

Three weeks ago Harriet had written to an old friend from

her Paris finishing school, someone she rarely saw because Emma lived in Hertfordshire and was married to a busy GP, to say that she would soon be spending a week in London and could they meet up? Emma had replied suggesting Tuesday morning: coffee and cakes at Fortnum's, followed by a quick dash around the Royal Academy? 'No idea what's on and no time to check the Listings but it'll give me something to tell Jack when I get home in the evening. Not that *you're* not of interest to him too but he *does* get a lot of *widows* these days ... Ooops! No offence meant – darling Hats, you *do* understand? – dear oh dear, you can tell I'm as tactless as ever!' The breathless rush of her letter recalled the breathless girlish Emma. Harriet felt she couldn't cancel their appointment at short notice, although Oliver had begged her to spend the morning with him. Her other tentative plans for the week might have to be reorganized, but this one was set in stone.

At ten o'clock Harriet was sitting in Jennifer's bedroom while her daughter-in-law paced up and down in a lace petticoat, trying to decide what to wear for a hastily arranged final lunch with her favourite colleagues. Half a dozen soft suits had been hung on the back of the wardrobe door to be held one by one against Jennifer's lanky frame, quizzically inspected and discarded. Finally Harriet said, 'The navy costume, with your camel-coloured silk shirt? It looks smart *and* unusual. I thought that suited you best.'

'You don't think the black? No – you're right. Black suggests I'm in mourning and I'm not. They can *stuff* their bloody job! Oh God, you know I don't mean that. Harriet, if you can just wait one more sec I'll put on the navy with the gold Chanel shirt for you to see the finished effect.'

Her jaw and fists clenched with impatience, Harriet sat with apparent unconcern on the end of Jennifer's unmade bed. Displaying her gleaming limbs and flat midriff, Jennifer buttoned and zipped herself into the chosen outfit. She smoothed the skirt over her hips, angling her body towards its most flattering reflection in the full-length mirror.

'Very chic,' Harriet said, thinking it looked exactly like all the others. 'That's wonderful, darling. A very good choice.'

'You chose it!' said Jennifer magnanimously. 'Now then,

what are we going to do with *you* this morning? I have to go and have my hair done next. We who are about to die and all that . . . Will you be all right here? You won't be bored without the children?'

'I thought I'd slip out now for an hour or two,' said Harriet casually. 'Meet an old girlfriend, have lunch with Jules, generally get a breath of London air. Don't worry if I'm late back, Jenny. I know you have a busy day ahead.'

'Oh you healthy country-dwellers!' Jennifer said, and yawned. 'So much *energy*! I suppose I *ought* to bash out a *résumé* or something.'

'Sorry darling: bash out what?'

'Same as a CV – *curriculum vitae* . . . summary of your career and education that you send out to prospective employers.'

Thinking to herself, good heavens, she inhabits a whole different *world*, Jennifer pitied rather than envied Harriet's simple certainties. She watched from her first floor bay window as her mother-in-law walked briskly along the wide tree-lined street. There was a jauntiness in her step and a swing to her old-fashioned box-pleated skirt. Plucky, that's what people call widows like her: a plucky little widow. Well, I'm damned if I'm going to settle down and be a plucky little wife.

A couple of hours later, all over London, Capels and Gaunts were having lunch. Furthest west was Harriet, going to meet her younger son in his flat on the outer fringes of Notting Hill Gate. Julian had been heavily influenced when buying it by the magic postcode, W11. He tried to avoid letting people see the flat itself, since the entrance was a dingy stairway between a greengrocer that smelled of over-ripe fruit and rotting veg and a betting shop that smelled of cheap cigarettes. Oliver, meanwhile, was lunching with his old friend Mark at *his* club – the Garrick – while a couple of streets away his daughter Jennifer was indulging herself during a ritual farewell in the embarrassed company of half a dozen former colleagues. Further east, in Limehouse, Roderick and Catriona were not eating lunch at all; instead, they were enjoying a rapid coupling in her converted flat close to their office which, conveniently, they could now reach in fifteen minutes thanks to the sex express – their private name for Docklands Light Railway.

Even so, this only allowed them half an hour in which to make love. Afterwards, her taut, well-exercised body sprawled across the futon, Catriona asked again, as casually as she could manage, 'How was it when you got back last night?'

Catriona tracked the state of her lover's domestic skirmishes with interest. At twenty-eight she was approaching the age at which, for a straightforward pregnancy, an easy birth and a healthy child, she needed to think about conceiving. The long hours she worked gave her no time to shop around for a suitable father but she only intended to have one child and Roderick would make a perfectly good first husband.

'Disastrous. She's been fired. Her boss evidently said she had too much else on her mind; didn't give enough time to her work.'

Catriona pricked up her ears.

'You don't think she's been unfaithful?'

'She's welcome. Probably has. She's always been highly sexed . . .' Conscious that this was going too far – Jennifer was, after all, still his wife and they had had a messy but surprisingly passionate reconciliation in the middle of the night – Roderick looked at the time-round-the-world alarm clock on the bedside table and exclaimed, 'Christ! Is it as late as that? Sweetheart, we must get back! I'll go first, OK?'

They made a point of leaving and returning separately, for form's sake, although in the hothouse in which they worked it was rarely possible to keep office affairs secret and Catriona would rather one or two people knew of this one. It could come in handy some day.

Jennifer's friends were not drinking more than one glass of wine each since they had an afternoon's work in prospect. Jennifer, who had promised to 'bash out a sensational resumé' when she got home, felt pleasantly reckless and unbound. Her hair had been newly streaked and looked so good that on emerging from the hairdresser she had window-shopped along St Christopher's Place and treated herself to a dramatic brooch to set off the austere navy of her jacket. She was beginning to feel that a new job could be an exciting challenge.

'I threatened him with an industrial tribunal,' she told them. 'Sexual discrimination – unfair to women with children – the lot. He went even whiter than usual, poor old bone-face. But then I thought, hey, spare yourself the bother, honey – what's five or ten thousand pounds? Even if you *do* win, the awards are *miserly*. I couldn't face putting together all the evidence and having to pester you lot for exact dates and quotes. It'll be good for the babes to see a bit more of me for the next few weeks . . . couple of months . . .'

She waited for an answering chorus but they seemed muted beside her own splendid exuberance.

Marjorie, the chief editor in her department, pushed her chair back and they all looked up at her.

'I'm not going to make a speech . . .' she began, 'but we can't let Jennifer go without saying what *fun* she's been to work with and how *much* she'll be missed. Jenny: we've had a ball! Thank you. And here, from all of us' – she reached in to her handbag – 'is a tiny token for you to remember us by.'

She took out a small box, wrapped in paper from the very shop Jennifer had just visited, and handed it to her across the table. They clapped raggedly. Jennifer opened the box, to find a smaller but otherwise identical version of the parrot brooch she was wearing and had just bought for herself. She recovered swiftly and pinned it on to her lapel.

'Brilliant!' she said. 'I hardly ever wear this one because it really needs the pair!'

They smiled in relief, stood up, kissed her on each perfumed cheek, urged her to ring, come for lunch, meet again, keep in touch. When the others had left Marjorie, who had stayed behind to deal with the bill, said kindly, 'If I can do anything to help, Jenny – a reference or perhaps just a phone call at the right moment – do let me know. Meanwhile you might like to do a bit of freelance proof-reading or manuscript-gutting?'

'Sweet of you but I think I'll be OK.'

'Publishing's gone nuclear at the moment. It may take a bit of time.'

On this unwelcome note of warning she paid, kissed Jennifer, twinkled her fingers and went back to the security of a job, an office and a monthly pay-cheque.

Jennifer's shoulders slumped. Damn the lot of them! At least I've got children, which is more than any of *them* can say. On impulse she decided to collect Hugo and Emily from school. She went to the Ladies, then to the telephone, to let Harriet and Ulrike know that they needn't pick up the children. Ulrike answered.

'No, Mrs Capel is not back yet. I don't know where she is. Thank you, Jennifer. They will be very pleased. Do you want to say hi! to Amanda? No, OK then. See you later. 'Bye!'

Halfway down the long communal table in the Garrick dining room, Oliver and Mark were roaring happily amid the masculine babel of a lunch that differed from school or college fare chiefly in the cost and quality of the wine. They had shared a bottle of club claret and were halfway through a second. Oliver, since he hoped to be seeing Harriet soon, declined port and brandy. In a modified shout he said into Mark's ear, 'Let's go to the other room and have a coffee. I need to ask a bit of a favour.'

A few men whom he half-recognized looked over their shoulders and waved as he passed. One extended a hand to wring his, bellowing, 'Good to see you, old boy!' before turning back to the general hubbub.

'Who was that?' Oliver asked.

'No idea,' Mark answered. 'Don't suppose he knows who you are, either.'

They climbed upstairs to the Morning Room, relaxing into deep armchairs under high, murky windows that were never cleaned. The room had a comfortably dusty atmosphere; even the sound of traffic from the street outside was muted. Under the brooding gaze of several theatrical portraits they drank tepid, over-stewed coffee.

Mark and Belinda lived in Suffolk but came down to London often to visit their family, go to the theatre or the

Proms. Oliver had always assumed they had a London pied-à-terre. Mentally he placed it in Bloomsbury; conveniently central, within walking distance of theatres and restaurants. He had spent the morning wondering where he could take Harriet, for he desperately and imminently wanted to make love to her. His room at the Reform was out of the question. So was a hotel; he could not subject her to the shame of turning up with a suitcase and signing the register under a false name . . . though he had no idea if these stratagems were still necessary nowadays. Of his three friends, Mark seemed the best bet for the loan of a flat, since Thomas lived in London by himself while Ben and Mona, with a house in Tunbridge Wells, were unlikely to need a London base as well. He would not, of course, tell Mark the reason for his request.

Before he could broach the subject, Mark said, 'Spot of bad news, old man. Thought I'd let you know. Get myself regularly checked-up on BUPA – paid by the Firm: you should get it done while you're here; doesn't take long – anyhow, latest one came as a bit of shock. Too early to know how far it's gone; had a lot of tests in the last two weeks. Amazing, modern medicine! Prognosis not good. Wanted to tell you myself. Straight from the horse's mouth.' He smiled wanly.

Oliver looked at Mark, noting the dark circles around his eyes, the pallor of his lips and the unhealthy, almost bluish tinge to his skin. The deep lines scored from nose to chin seemed to sink even deeper as Mark, having delivered his news, leaned back in the comfortably sagging leather armchair. Oliver groaned sympathetically.

'Bloody rotten luck. Sorry to hear it. Take it this is serious?'

'Terminal. Not as deep as a well nor so wide as a church door, but it's enough,' Mark confirmed. 'You know that medical bookshop off the Euston Road, up towards Gower Street? Went along myself to check it out. Consultants never tell you anything. Wrap it up in jargon and look on the bright side. I wrote down the long words mine had bandied over my head and looked them up. Cancer of the colon's the layman's diagnosis. Six months, perhaps a year? After that I'm a grave man.'

91

He grimaced. Oliver leaned forward to pat him vaguely on the knee. What could he say? Women would embrace, burst into tears, profess devoted friendship, promise bedside care, send flowers. Men exchange a wry look.

'Belinda's been wonderful,' Mark said. 'Right. That's that. Roll on the Grim Reaper! Now I could do with a brandy. You join me?'

Oliver could hardly decline. A club servant brought a couple of huge brandy balloons, smoking with the power of the fiery liquor. In silence they hummed, sniffed, swirled and swallowed reverently.

'Aaahhh . . .' said Mark, on a long exhalation of breath. 'Now: what's this favour?'

Julian's flat welcomed Harriet with delicious cooking smells: something obscurely piquant; not spicy and thus not Indian, but definitely exotic.

'Thai,' said Julian. 'Coconut milk and garlic, that's what you can smell. And long slow simmering.'

'My darling!' Harriet was touched. 'How delicious. And how sweet of you to take so much trouble.'

'All I cook. Moment, that is. Shops round here are brilliant. Get anything.'

How like his father he was! Harriet recalled with a piercing dart of sorrow that George, when he was nervous, talked in those same abrupt, clipped sentences. 'Your kitchen looks marvellous!' she said, to reassure her son. 'You hadn't finished doing it up last time I was here.'

She remembered that last time she and George had visited their younger son – more than a year ago, on their way back from holiday in Turkey. Julian had still been employed. Now he had joined the band of dispirited young graduates living on the dole and whatever odds and ends they could conjure up by barter and mutual favours. When possible they would – preferably for cash – do what was vaguely referred to as 'a spot of freelancing'. Yet Julian had a good English degree from Bristol and had done a further year at a teacher training college. He had found jobs easily enough after that, but whether in a London comprehensive school or a spartan Yorkshire public school, had been miserably unhappy. Harriet never asked why, exactly, and Julian had not volunteered. She had sometimes wondered whether he had fallen in love with a too-beautiful adolescent but Julian's fierce scowl discouraged questions. He spent the next few years trying first to get into publishing, then working in Waterstone's. Gradually, inexorably, he sank past the level of most of his contemporaries from school and university until he was barely clinging to the fringes of the literate middle classes. He resented any help, although he had grudgingly accepted his father's offer of a cash downpayment to enable him to get a mortgage on this flat. Once installed, he had thrown his energies and a good deal of hitherto unsuspected creative talent into converting his dingy living quarters.

Her son's flat consisted of three narrow and gloomy rooms which Julian had metamorphosed with scumbled paint and worn Oriental rugs into a setting of faded magnificence. The dining-room walls were a deep ox-blood red and had been aged, using some painstaking decorator's technique, to the texture of a sun-baked Italian palazzo faded and cracked by the sun. The tiny entrance hall was pine green and this too had been scrubbed and flaked. Tall spiralling cast-iron candlesticks stood on the dining table; his table-linen was crisp and spotless, its ironed creases as sharp as those in an Old Master painting. Thus, gallantly, her hard-up son maintained the outward fabric of his life.

The kitchen had been transformed into a high-tech food factory, with doors and cupboards of bleached wood, a matt black rubber floor and gleaming stainless-steel hob-cover. Brilliantly coloured pottery bowls relieved the monochrome, filled with brilliantly coloured piles of fruit and vegetables. Julian was stirring a pan, from which puffs of pungent steam escaped.

'It must have cost you a fortune,' she said, adding swiftly, 'but *worth* it.'

'Not really. Buy most things at cost. You hungry? Be another ten minutes.'

'That's fine. I brought a bottle.'

Harriet withdrew from its plastic bag a bottle of what his father would have called 'rather decent burgundy'. Julian looked round, read the label and said, 'Won't go with what we're eating. Thanks, Mother. Jolly decent burgundy. Might have it tonight.'

'Yes: how *is* Fonzi?' she asked, thinking, damn! *That's* why he's so touchy. I should have asked straightaway.

Julian lived with a Spaniard called Alfonso whom he had met on holiday three years ago. Julian had fallen immediately, violently in love. The love was presumably mutual – his mother hoped very much that it was mutual – since a few months later, Alfonso had joined him in London. Julian referred to him defiantly as 'my lover'. Harriet modified this to the blessedly ambiguous 'partner'; not that this had made any difference when she had said, 'Julian, darling, could you come to Daddy's funeral *without* your partner?' Julian had come alone but had scowled at everyone and been surly to elderly relatives. Only Dodo, the symbol of childhood to all three of them, could coax him back into the sweet, loving boy she had lost. With Dodo, Julian was tender and considerate.

Dodo herself on the day of the funeral had wiped her moist eyes, squared her shoulders and been stoical about the death of her first and favourite charge.

'I never thought to see him go first!' she kept saying. 'He was nearly twenty years younger than me. Eighteen, to be exact. I'd just had my eighteenth birthday. I was nursery nurse to old Nanny Capel. He would only have been seventy-three in August and look at me – ninety! I *never* thought dear George would go before me.'

'Of course you didn't, Dodo dear,' Julian had soothed. 'One never does.'

Their thoughts must have been running along similar lines for Julian said, 'Fonzi's fine; got a job at the moment, been here otherwise. You OK without Dad? Bit sudden, wasn't it? Must miss him. Still in the wooden stage or is sensation returning to the nerve ends?'

Harriet wondered from what private reservoir of experience this accuracy sprang. Julian was the only person to have enquired after George; everyone else avoiding the subject as though six months were time enough to recover from the loss of the person who had accompanied you

94

through every day for the last thirty-seven years. The image of herself clasped in Oliver's arms, kissing ravenously, gasping for breath, clouded her face for a second and Julian, misunderstanding, laid a hand briefly on her arm.

'I'm managing – Dodo and I keep going between us. I look after her and she looks after me. We talk about him a lot. Daddy would have hated to decline into senility. He went with all his powers intact.'

More or less, she thought. George was never 100 per cent intact but no-one knew that except Dodo and me.

'Lunch is ready,' Julian said. 'You want beer to drink, or mineral water? Come and sit down.'

He carried in a tureen of lumpy mustard-yellow soup. Despite its colour it did not taste of mustard and the lumps dissolved deliciously in her mouth. The next course was chicken in a coconut sauce. That, too, was delicious. With it Julian served charred scraps of things mixed into whiplash egg noodles.

'*Darling!*' said his mother. 'How original!'

Gamely and with growing pleasure, she tucked in.

'Jules, I *miss* you. I wish you would bring Fonzi down to Dorset for a weekend occasionally. Dodo would so love to see you both.' (*Both* might not be strictly accurate, she thought, but to the pure in heart all things are pure and no heart is purer than Dodo's.) 'It would do you *good* to relax.'

'*When*', he answered scathingly, 'did I ever *relax*? And Fonzi has to work at weekends.'

Harriet subsided humbly. Julian was thirty. How hard it is to talk to the ultra-sensitive. She had nothing to offer him except her home, her loving welcome, his old bedroom. If this was not what he wanted – he was grown-up; his mother must accept his absence and not insist on filial duty.

She could not keep Oliver out of her mind

'I went to a marvellous exhibition yesterday,' she said. 'Young British portrait painters . . .'

They were back on safe ground.

Afterwards Julian, declining her help, made coffee, cleared the table and stacked their dirty plates and cutlery in a dishwasher hidden behind one of the bleached false doors. ('Got it out of a skip,' he said, with far more pride than if he had bought it at Peter Jones.) His mother asked if she might use the phone: she needed to check whether her next appointment with a friend was still on. Of course, he said, preoccupied with his own thoughts. He did not bother to listen to her conversation and even if he had, would have heard only her steady voice saying, 'Extension twenty-three, please,' and after a pause, 'I'm just checking whether we're still meeting this afternoon? Yes? Could you let me have the address? Fine. I should be there in about three-quarters of an hour. Right. Till then. Bye.'

Had he glanced through the door that led into the drawing room, however, Julian would have seen that the colour had left his mother's face and she was holding on to the edge of the table with both hands to keep her balance. But why should he look? She was his mother, for whom he had just prepared his second-best Thai menu. He already knew exactly what she looked like and she had never surprised him in his life . . . apart perhaps from the time when she had decided to learn Russian. And even that was only done to spur Roddy on.

He hoped she would soon leave, so that he could ring Fonzi on some pretext to check that he was spending his afternoon break in the restaurant's staffroom and not . . . elsewhere. Julian had sex on his mind, now as always, and unless he was actually alone in a room with Fonzi, sex meant jealousy. He did not know that, in this respect, he resembled his father as precisely as his bone-structure and features resembled those of his mother.

Capels and Gaunts returned from lunch: back to their offices, home to meet their children or, in Oliver's case, to his club, to wait for Harriet's phone call. Julian, Roddy and Jennifer were preoccupied with their own problems, taking for granted that their lives had an energy and momentum their parents had long ago left behind. Her sons, if asked, would have suggested that their mother was strolling through a park or a department store; Jennifer or Philomena would have said with just the same tone of indulgent, affectionate certainty that their father was back at his club having a snooze. ('A zizz. He always calls it a zizz.') Out of context and entirely out of character, Oliver and Harriet were hurrying towards their second clandestine meeting.

Oliver arrived first at the flat that Mark had lent him (with a quizzical look but 'no questions asked, old man') and turned the key in the unfamiliar lock. The place was dim and musty. He pulled back the curtains and threw windows open to let in fresh air – fresher, even from the streets of Pimlico, than the stale air trapped inside. He was laden with roses. In the kitchen he slammed doors open and shut in search of vases. There were none big enough for his extravagant offerings. He thrust them into a couple of buckets, placing one at the foot of the bed and the other on the bedside table on what he already thought of as 'Harriet's side'. Before he had a chance to search for clean sheets, the doorbell rang. Oliver's heart pounded. Despite Harriet's earlier telephone call he had not till this moment been certain that she would come and now that she had, he was still not sure whether they would go to bed. She said she had not made love for years.

He opened the door. Tentatively, speechlessly, she proffered a plastic bag from a wine merchant. Oliver found himself overwhelmed by her shyness and courage.

'Oh my darling!'

He drew her inside, closed the front door and took her in his arms.

'*Harriet*, you're *here!*'

'The rain has stopped,' she said. 'The sun was coming out as I walked along the street.' She pointed at the sky, visible through the drawing-room windows. 'Look how blue it is. Yes, I'm here. I couldn't help it. I don't feel guilty. I knew I'd come. Though I don't suppose that's anything to be proud of.'

Oliver saw that she was trying to postpone the moment when she walked into the bedroom. He drew the curtains and shrouded the room before turning to her.

'Roses. Look – bucketfuls. For you. Lift up your arms, Harriet. Let me take this off.'

Harriet retreated to the bathroom, emerging naked. Oliver, naked too, drew her close to him, feeling the chill of her

97

skin, her trembling. He wrapped her in his arms, pressing his warm body against her till his own flesh trembled and reared in response.

Oliver thought, how long is it since I fucked a woman I love? How can I reassure this dear, fearful person that she has nothing to be afraid of; that I will look after her? Is pleasure the way? Is she, at fifty-five, still able to enjoy fucking? What will I do then? How do I awaken her? Suppose her timidity makes me impotent? Nothing wrong with my erection now but will it last while I arouse her? Being a man is never more of a responsibility than at this moment. Tenderness always comes to my rescue. Long after I ceased to feel any desire for Clarissa, it was tenderness towards her own fierce desire that hardened my cock. Tenderness for the thin Balkan girls in their shabby rooms gave me the ability to fuck them silently and ferociously, as they so badly wanted. Tenderness will carry me through this first ordeal with Harriet and make it all right. Fucking is about generosity in the beginning, and again at the end.

Harriet thought, what if the sight of my old body kills his desire? Will he stop loving me then; will we part in shame and embarrassment? He is being so gentle, and I feel as timid as a virgin. I didn't hate sex with George but I can remember separately, one by one, the times when I actively enjoyed it. I could never have told George that; it would have meant admitting that all the other times – hundreds and hundreds, a lifetime of other times – were no more than a set of gymnastic exercises because, to him, it mattered so much. His entire well-being depended on how often we made love. Now what am I supposed to do? Why am I here? Oliver feels and smells entirely different. Best to kiss him. If I close my eyes I can pretend it isn't happening, let my body take over and hope . . . What if I can't come? When shall I pretend to come? I could always fool George but I don't know the rhythm of Oliver's build-up, the signs of his readiness, the moment when he has to spill.

They moved towards the bed and Oliver pulled the cold sheets over them. They lay together shyly, sensing each other's contours, mouth pressed against open mouth, hands at last touching more than hands. Minutes, half an hour, more, she had lost track of time, it could have been an hour later, surely not, at any rate, unmistakably *now* – she became what she had not been since her children were born . . . a tunnel of flesh, stretched then for parturition, now for pleasure. Harriet heard as though from a long way off the accelerating breath, harsh panting, and final animal howls of what sounded like birth but was in fact her own climax. When her breathing had subsided she turned to Oliver with a smile of delight and gratitude, but he was already asleep. How long since she had had an orgasm? Fifteen years? Twenty? She had forgotten its intensity and the utter sweetness that followed.

She did not look at her watch and had no idea how long it was before Oliver said, 'I know I have to let you go. I wish I hadn't. I want to lie beside you now and talk. Isn't post-coitus the best time to talk? Or I want to watch you sleep the sleep of gratified desire.'

'I know,' she said, 'but you are right. I shall have to go soon.'

Harriet propped herself up on one elbow and looked down into his face. She smiled, and touched her mouth.

'Why do they call love tender? It is rough.'

'*Was* I rough? Too rough? *I'll smooth that rough touch with a tender kiss.*'

'Yes my love, you were rough, but not *too*: and I am proud of every bruise. I can hardly believe what we have just done. That was Shakespeare?'

'Of course. *Did my heart love till now?*'

'Oliver, we have started something serious. It won't be easy to stop. Will you regret it? Should we call a halt now, while we still can?'

'*No!*'

She asked, 'Can we meet here again, tomorrow?'

'You know we will.'

Still she could not move, not yet. She thought, here I am in bed beside another man, for the first time in my life, brazenly showing him my breasts, unconcerned that they are not young and firm, that the nipples are reddened by his mouth; proud to display these trophies of rough love-making. I don't think I have ever experienced such violent pleasure. She shuddered slightly at the memory and Oliver pulled her down into his arms.

'My love! Amazing, astonishing, passionate Harriet! To think I was afraid of making love to you . . .'

'. . . So was I.'

He drew back to look into her face and laughed. 'How smug we both look!'

'*You* do. Do I?'

Harriet had promised to be back for the children; to bath Amanda and help Hugo with his homework; to read more poems to Emily, listen to Jennifer's plans for her next job. Darkness had fallen by the time they went their separate ways.

Chapter Seven

She rang the doorbell to let them know she was back and after a moment the children came careering down the hall, the girls shrieking with excitement.

'Granny, Granny!'

'You don't know if it's G-G-Granny. It might be someone else,' she heard Hugo say cautiously. They wrenched open the front door and gazed joyously up at her.

'It *is* Granny! Granny, you said you'd bath me!'

Amanda was naked, her small body wriggling with excitement. Ulrike descended the stairs from the bathroom, an extended towel in her hands.

'Mandy, come here. Granny looks tired. Anyway, you've already had your bath.'

'I haven't! I want another! Carry me, Granny.'

Harriet was exhausted; she longed to lie down and fall into unthinking, uncaring sleep. But she took off her jacket and allowed herself to be led by Amanda's hot damp hand upstairs to the children's bathroom. There she knelt beside the bath and blew bubbles through their facecloths, the way she used to do for Jules and Roderick, so that a great froth of soap appeared like magic on the other side of the flannel. The sheen on the girls' wet bodies was like crystal, glittering with rainbow colours. Their skin had the texture of egg-shells. Long damp tendrils of hair clung to their shoulders. I would *die* for them, Harriet thought. Would I die for Oliver?

'I'll go and make ready their supper,' Ulrike said from the doorway.

'Where is their mother?'

'Mummy's in her room, working. She p-p-picked us up from *school*. Now she said we mustn't b-b-b-bother her.'

'Hugo,' Harriet said tactfully, knowing the innate modesty of small boys, 'would you like to get undressed while I dry the girls and put them into their nighties? Then you could have a quick bath by yourself or I'll bath you, if you prefer.'

'I can do it.'

She wrapped a towel round Emily's shoulders, scooped up Amanda in the deep folds of another, and took them to their bedroom. There was an ache, a soreness between her legs, stiffness in her thighs and a flush around her mouth: but this, the only outward and visible sign of their love-making, would be attributed to the exertion of bath-time. Harriet thought again, I am so *tired*. She sat on a low chair in Emily's room and they clustered round, leaning against her. Amanda complained that the book had no pictures and when Hugo arrived he complained that poetry was boring, yet within moments they were absorbed by the rhythm of the words and the soft rise and fall of her voice.

There were pencil drawings in some of the margins and on the endpapers a castellated fort, a rain of arrows flying through the air, a few odd, angular people who were presumably bowmen. She showed these to Hugo.

'Look: your daddy drew this when he was a little boy – probably the same age as you are now.'

Hugo could not connect the inexpert pictures with his giant, omniscient father.

'I'm going to be *ten* on S-S-Saturday,' he said proudly.

'I know, darling; that's why we're here, to help you cele-brate – Grandy and me.'

She could not help linking their two names.

'Is Grandy your husband?' Emily asked.

'Sssh!' said Hugo, old enough to be embarrassed for her. 'You *mustn't* say that. Granny's husband was Grandpa *George*.'

'Where's Grandpa George, then? Why isn't he here too?'

Hugo avoided Harriet's eyes. He leaned forward and hissed into Emily's ear: 'Because he's *dead*, stupid!'

Jennifer appeared, urging them towards bed. She had

changed from the earlier power-suited sharpness into a long shirt and soft leggings. Harriet admitted to herself for the second time that day that while her daughter-in-law was a beautiful young woman she was also monstrously self-obsessed. Jennifer excused a good deal of behaviour that might otherwise have been put down to plain ordinary self-ishness by reference to women's rights. Harriet, who had spent most of her life suppressing her own wishes and desires in favour of her husband's and her sons', envied this single-mindedness. I wish Jenny could bring herself to think of the children's needs more often, she added mentally; I don't see how feminism can object to *that*.

The children abandoned her to crowd round their mother, reaching up to be hugged. 'Will you sing to them, Harriet?' she asked.

'Yes! Yes! Sing us Greensleeves!'

Harriet said, 'I will sing to these mice *only* if they *promise* to go *straight* to sleep!'

'Promise,' they chorused. 'We *promise*, Granny.'

Harriet drew a deep breath and tried not to let her voice tremble in the last verses:

'Greensleeves, now farewell, adieu!
God I pray to prosper thee;
For I am still thy lover true.
Come once again and love me.

Greensleeves was all my joy,
Greensleeves was my delight;
Greensleeves was my heart of gold,
And who but my lady Greensleeves.'

Jennifer, leaning against the door frame, watched them all with a complicated expression. Harriet looked up at her.

'Roddy adored that song when he was little.'

'Still does,' Jennifer replied.

It was eight o'clock. Her son and his wife were in the kitchen sharing the cooking and a bottle of wine. At last Harriet could, if not sleep – her mind was racing and her

103

body too agitated for sleep – spend some time on her own. She had undressed and washed. Lying on the bed in her dressing-gown, she traced the rise and fall of her bruised thighs. She remembered how with her own hands she had spread them as wide for him as for the midwife three decades ago, so that Julian's blind, purple, slippery new-born head could force its way out.

Oliver was only the second lover of her life. In a single afternoon she had learned more about her body's carnal responses than George had been able to teach her throughout their marriage. She was proud but also appalled that her parents' and her own lifelong moral principles, carefully inculcated and sincerely held, could be so easily smashed. Passion in novels, plays and operas had seemed far-fetched and exaggerated and she had been dismissive when people declared that it explained the most unlikely relationships and was the only justification for infidelity. *Passion* to Harriet had always denoted loss of self-control . . . a passion of anger meant someone unable to govern their temper . . . and she believed that adults should have learned self-control. She was humiliated now by the memory of past intolerance.

Her mind returned to Oliver. She tried to conjure up his face, and could not; only his gestures – his fingers nervously twisting his hair, the rapid rhythm with which he got dressed, tucking his shirt into his trousers and buckling his belt – small gestures that he performed automatically, yet quite unlike the way George had performed them. She felt that now she knew Oliver's most intimate physical secrets and had, without shame or guilt, offered him hers.

An hour later she went down to the kitchen.

'Dinner'll be ready in twenty minutes,' said Jennifer.

'Drink, Mother?' asked Roderick. 'What have you done to your mouth?'

Harriet pretended to cross to the mirror to look, although she knew already that her mouth was so rough and swollen that it could not be disguised by lipstick. She had prepared her reply.

'I blew soap bubbles for the children in the bath. I must be allergic to that soap. It's swollen up since then.'

Jennifer was quick and kind. She offered soothing creams and lotions or witch-hazel to bring down the swelling. Harriet made light of it.

'Don't worry; it'll be fine in the morning. Yes, darling, I'd love a small gin and tonic. How was your day?'

They had dinner at the big table in the basement kitchen. Ulrike had gone out; it was just the three of them. Roderick told her about an ordinary day in the life of the bank – without referring to Catriona – while Jennifer gave an elaborate account of the events of her farewell lunch.

'What about you, Mother – what have you been up to?' her son asked eventually.

'I had lunch with Julian. He cooked a delicious Thai meal.'

'He gets weirder by the day,' Roderick said dismissively. No room for amateur gourmet cooks in a banker's world.

'Jules isn't weird. He's extremely creative. His flat is amazing. Quite transformed. Have you seen it lately?'

'Gay men can *do* that sort of thing . . .' said Jennifer. 'They don't have children to occupy their time and money, they can afford to indulge themselves.'

Harriet was sharply reminded of Clarissa whose simplistic views, despite having kept the two sides of this family apart for more than a decade, were echoed in Jennifer's condescension towards her brother-in-law.

'Jenny dear, I don't think that's quite fair. He has time because he's temporarily out of work. Anyhow, whatever the reason dear old Jules was immensely kind. We talked about George.'

'Ah yes, death is another thing gay men have become good at.'

'I don't suppose', Roddy said coolly, 'that *death* is something anyone becomes "good at".'

Bravo, thought his mother. Hasn't she learned *yet* that none of us has ever tolerated criticism of Julian for being gay?

Harriet knew they would not enquire further into what she had done for the rest of the afternoon, assuming that some dull, grandmotherly activity had occupied the time.

How could her soft, creased limbs have been passionately entwined, her greying head have rolled wildly from side to side in pursuit of flesh or kisses? This was the best protection: that no-one would believe it could possibly have happened.

'Bless you, darling ... no coffee for me,' she said when the meal was over. 'Let me stack the dishwasher and then I'll take myself to bed. I must just make two quick phone calls – you go on up.'

They took their coffee to the drawing room and as soon as they were alone Jennifer said, '*There*, darling: wasn't I *good*?'

Roderick suppressed his irritation. They had had a reasonably amiable evening; best not to spoil it. He felt vestigial guilt about Catriona and for this reason decided to overlook Jennifer's smugness, her assumption that merely being civil to his mother entitled her to praise.

'It was fine,' he said neutrally. Jennifer pushed her luck.

'I mean, about her mouth and everything.'

'Yes you were *wonderful*. Sweetness and light. End of discussion.'

The emphasis in his voice was ominous. Jennifer, now that she had pushed him to the verge of a flare-up, thought it best to lower the emotional temperature.

'Do you want to watch *Newsnight*?'

He laid down *The Economist*.

'I don't mind. If you want to.'

Side by side they watched as Lib-Dem politicians, expansive after the euphoria of their annual conference, trotted out their well-rehearsed optimism. Roderick paid attention when the subject of Nick Leeson and Barings came up; Jennifer when atrocity pictures from Bosnia filled the screen.

'Jammy bastard!' he said. 'Bloody nearly got away with it, too.'

'Oh, Roderick look – isn't that ghastly? Look, look, how *appalling*! Christ, why doesn't John Major *do* something?' She paused. 'I wonder if that frightfully handsome blue beret chap, that UN peace-keeping force soldier, *you* know, forgotten his name, oh come on, you *do* know, the one who fell in love with the Bosnian Red Cross worker, *him*, whether he'd do a book about it? Call it *A Most UNlikely Love* and it would sell like hot cakes. I must see if I can track him down. He wouldn't have to actually write it himself. Get someone to ghost it. Make a terrific package for next year's Frankfurt. Oh Jesus, what are they doing *now*?'

'Good idea,' said Roderick non-committally.

After she had cleared the table and left the kitchen tidy, Harriet dialled the Reform Club and left a message; then settled down for her daily conversation with Dodo. Dodo was her diary, her recording angel, her comforter, her normality; Dodo the keeper of family memories, still centre of her turning world.

'I sat at my window this afternoon and watched the sun chasing shadows across the hills,' Dodo said serenely. 'The colours change, you know. I could watch them for hours, racing up and down the hillsides.'

'Did you, Dodo?' Harriet was soothed by her old, untroubled voice. Nothing would shake Dodo ever again, not even death, for which she had already waited a decade or more.

'But I am tired, my duck. What did you do? Tell me.'

Harriet told. Dodo knew everything, blamed nobody, accepted all, and Harriet could speak to her without explanation or excuse, simply in wonder.

'Well,' Dodo answered finally. 'You have made a choice, probably a foolish one. Now we shall see if you are allowed to get away with it. He always seemed a gentleman, this Mr Gaunt. I never cared for his wife, much. Poor Julian! I'll pray for you all. Did you have supper at home with Roddy and Jennifer? How nice for you. And the babies? Tell me about *them*. All that matters in the end is that they don't suffer from all this. *Is* it foolish? Well, since you ask me – yes, I think so. It sounds very violent and those sort of things often end badly.'

Harriet put the phone down and turned at the sound of footsteps on the stairs. It was Roderick, his legs white and bony under the short towelling dressing-gown. His hair was boyishly awry but his face looked more like that of a man in late middle age than one of thirty-six. Oh God, she thought; did he *hear*? No – I was telling her about the children, not Oliver.

'Mother! You're still up. Thought you might have gone to bed.'

'Let me make you a cup of tea, darling. Or hot chocolate?'

'Wouldn't go with Scotch – or Pepsodent.'

So, she thought, he did come down to talk to me. She seated herself at the kitchen table, smoothing her palms across it with a rhythmical, swishing movement, and waited for him to begin.

He prowled round the kitchen, fiddling with the alphabet magnets stuck onto the fridge and picking up a wipe-clean plastic pad called **Shopping List**. (It said: *coriander, tomatoes, watercress, Jif, fish fingers, chips, coffee, Penguin biscuits, 6 pts milk, cereal.*) He crossed out the Penguins ('Not as good as they used to be') and wrote *chocolate digestive* instead. Still he remained silent, looking at the children's drawings pinned to the cork board or sellotaped to cupboard doors. His mother said nothing. Men don't like to be questioned. You have to wait. Finally he said, half-apologetically, half-defiantly,

'It isn't *easy* you know. It's much harder for me than it was for D-D-Daddy.'

When trying to draw someone out there's only one thing to say and Harriet said it. 'What do you mean?'

'All this New Man stuff. *That.* The workaholic *Nineties.* The culture of the *bank. Laddishness* after work . . .'

'What's "laddishness"?'

'Getting plastered. Talking shop and football. Male bonding. Discover who your allies are. *And* enemies.'

'And then?'

''S fine for the bachelors. They can go home and chill out with a six-pack in front of a video, or take someone out to dinner. But *I'm* expected to come home and be a hands-on dad between eight and nine p.m., intellectually challenging from nine fifteen to eleven fifteen and a thrilling lover till God knows when.'

'It does sound demanding.'

'It's impossible. I *cannot* make her understand that

108

keeping up to speed at the bank takes all I've got. There's nothing *left* by the time I get home. She seems to think I deliberately neglect her and the children, don't pull my weight. But I've nothing left to give.'

'Does it *have* to be like that?'

Roderick stopped pacing up and down and came to sit at the table opposite her. Harriet stretched across and put one hand over his. He laid his head on it and she stroked his hair.

'I just want to be ordinary,' he said, his voice muffled. 'Just an *ordinary*, dopey dad. I don't want to go skiing, or rent a villa with two other couples in Tuscany. I don't give a fart for all that. I just want to muck about with my kids at weekends.'

'But you don't want to be like Daddy, either . . .?'

'Head-of-household. D-d-domestic dictator. No. Not *that*.'

'What does Jenny think?'

'She thinks I'm having it off with someone at work.'

'Well, is she right?'

He rolled his head to and fro across his knuckles.

'Yes, actually.' He lowered his voice. Harriet glanced up at the staircase leading from the kitchen. 'It's OK,' she said.

'I am. But it isn't an *affair*. It's just a way of coping with the stress. Some people snort coke – cocaine. Others get drunk as skunks every night. I take this, colleague, woman, from the bank, back to her flat and – you know—'

'Fuck her?' his mother said.

He looked up in surprise. 'Yes. That's precisely what I do. I *fuck* her. I don't *make love* to her – I don't love her in the least. I simply fuck her to get rid of the tension. It's probably why *she* fucks me. I hope so.'

'Why not make love to your wife?'

'I do that as well. When I have the energy.'

Marriage, thought Harriet – how complicated and changeable it is. From the outside it looks like a shelter, enclosing and safeguarding domestic bliss. From inside it can feel like a prison or a haven. It never stays the same for long. There are layers and layers to explore before you reach bedrock: who you are, who the other is, and what you have made together.

'Worthwhile, all the same. Marriage,' she said.

'You're right. I'm sure you're right. I don't have the time or effort to think about it, let alone enjoy it. Time flies past and I think, there goes my *life*.'

'And the children?'

'I would *die* to protect them. I would roll lorries off their prostrate bodies, chase away thieves and rapists, haul them back from cliff-tops. But *read* to them for half an hour in the evening? Can't do it. Too tired.'

'This is probably the worst time of all – if that's any consolation. It gets better from now on. They grow up and become less demanding. Work gets easier. Jenny will become wiser, recognize how lucky she is.'

'Get real,' he grinned.

'What does that mean?'

'Never mind. Good to have talked. Thanks.'

'My *darling* . . .' she said. 'Poor old Roddy. So *hard* to be a man.'

'Does everyone find that?'

'Expect so. Daddy certainly did.'

His jaw clenched.

'No,' she said hastily, 'we are *not* going to talk about *Daddy*.'

'What about *you*, Mother?' he asked. '*You* having a good time?'

'I'm fine,' she said. 'But tired. Like you. Bedtime, d'you think?'

She walked round the table to stroke his tangled hair – for the first time she noticed streaks of grey – but he stood up and embraced her awkwardly. She understood. The gesture was that of a little boy who wants to bury his head in Mummy's tummy or between her breasts, to feel warmly encircled and safe. But she was short and slight and he a strong young male more than six feet tall.

'I'm too big for that!' he said with a deprecating laugh.

'I know! I can't *cuddle* you any more.'

She reached up to stroke his jaw and he bent down to kiss her cheek.

'How's your mouth?' he asked solicitously.

'Better now.'

110

* * *

Meanwhile, Oliver too had his ordinary life to pursue and commitments to keep. The first was to his wife, whom he had promised to telephone at six o'clock. It was nearly eight by the time he woke from the deep sleep into which he fell the instant he returned to his room but that he could explain away by the vagaries of British Summer Time. Clarissa must have been waiting near the phone for she snatched it up eagerly on the second ring.

'*Yes*?'

'Clarissa. It's me.'

'I *knew* it would be. Hallo Olls. *Darling*. Mmm!' (Girlish squeak of expectation.) 'Tell me everything; I want to know *exactly* what you've been doing. Start at the beginning.'

She was like a child who wanted to be told a story; she would like him to begin, 'Once upon a time . . .' But she would not forgive today's story so he would give the truth as far as he could. Oliver knew from long experience that if the details were spelled out, the wider pattern was often overlooked.

'Well, first of all I gave myself a treat. I went to be shaved.'

'Oh darling, what *fun*! At Trumper's?'

No, but why disappoint her? One shave was very like another.

'Yes.'

'Olly, *did* you? Is Mr Cyril still there?'

'I don't think so. No, he can't be.'

'I suppose not. It must be years since Daddy went. Did you tell them you were Mr Sullivan's son-in-law?'

'No, Clarissa, I didn't.'

'I suppose it might have sounded like bragging. So silly. It's *years* ago.'

How she dwells upon past glories, Oliver reflected. Her father had been dead for thirteen years; had not visited Trumper's for ten before that, yet she still believed they would leap to attention at the mention of his name.

'Go on, Ol. Do you look' (her voice dropped to a flirtatious coo) '*handsome* . . .?'

'Not for me to say.' Mock-modest rumble.

'I bet you *do*.'

111

Brief silence.

'Any guests tonight?' he enquired. Clarissa perked up. She loved criticizing their guests.

'Only two. Deadly dull titchy Japanese couple. They've got a *nerve*, coming to Europe *now* of all times, when we've just had the fiftieth anniversary of VE Day. *Daddy* would have had them *horse*-whipped.' She giggled. It was an old joke. The late Mr Sullivan advocated horse-whipping for most people other than his own kind. Oliver snorted dutifully. 'Anyway, I left the kitchen girls taking care of them. Don't worry, I've got plenty of time to chat.'

'After the barber I went back to the exhibition I saw yesterday. The portraits.'

'*Really*?' Disbelief. Exhibitions were not Clarissa's 'thing' and in her view, going to the same one twice was close to eccentricity.

'It's right by the Garrick where I was meeting Mark and I had a spot of time to kill. Entrance was free.'

'Oh I *see*.' That explained it. Clarissa had her share of upper-class meanness. She took over with an account of her day. 'I saw Patrick today. So sweet of him. He came over for lunch to make sure I was all right *on my own*.' Faint guilt-inducing inflection.

'How is he?'

'Oh, you know, fine. Says it's been a rotten summer for property.'

I am not, Oliver thought, making this long-distance telephone call in order to discuss the French housing market. 'Same everywhere,' he said with finality.

Now he must tell a ripe and polished anecdote about lunch at the Garrick with which Clarissa could regale local English friends. He must break the news of poor old Mark's cancer. Above all, he must convincingly elide the hours after that, leaving his wife to assume that, such was his shock, he hardly remembered what he had done next. Clarissa's lifelong jealousy had given her needle-sharp antennae. Oliver picked his words with care, modified his voice, and was rescued by the appearance at her side of Mr titchy Japanese. He heard her irritation.

'Olly, I've *got* to *go*. Mr Ozugichi, would you *mind* giving me a *moment* to say goodbye to my *husband*? Thank you *so* much. Darling, I'll talk to you tomorrow. Same time? DYLM?' *Sotto voce* coo for the benefit of the Japanese guest, evidently still hovering. 'ILYT. *By*-ee!'

'Bye, Clarissa.'

It was quarter past eight. Oliver was due to meet Ben and Mona soon. He was giving them dinner, together with their unmarried son. Matthew was in his mid-thirties and it had occurred to both sets of parents that he might be encouraged to meet up with Philly again. He and the twins had known each other long ago, when all three used to join their parents from their respective boarding schools for the holidays – holidays during which they felt aimless and superfluous, 'home' being a government-issue flat in a circle of expatriates with no time for moody adolescents. Matthew and Philly might have eyed one another at Christmas parties for the Embassy children, or later on at cocktail parties. This would give them a shared starting point, if they could be persuaded to make contact again. A dynastic marriage, or simply a solution to the loneliness of their offspring, in a London driven by ambition and insecurity, would delight them all. Meanwhile, Oliver had quarter of an hour to kill and he badly needed a drink.

He went downstairs and immediately bumped into a man whose name he had forgotten but whom he recognized although the intervening two or three decades had laid a fine crazing over the youthful tautness of the face he had once known. His hand was warmly grasped.

'I say, what a coincidence! No, hang on a tick, don't tell me – got it, got it, it's coming – yes! It's Gaunt, isn't it? Captain Gaunt? Horsfall, Peregrine – Perry – must remember me?'

'Course I do!' Thank God for the regimental tie. 'We were on the same Russian course, surely . . . Aldershot, 'fifty-six? *Captain Gaunt's* been "Oliver" ever since then.'

'Russian, of course. I say, what a memory! Envy you that. Mine's like a sieve nowadays. What've you been doing with yourself since those days?'

'Oh, usual thing: FO and so on. Retired now, live in France most of the time. How about you?'

113

They launched into reminiscences that bore only a passing resemblance to the truth of both their lives. As they drank their double Scotches, Oliver functioned on automatic pilot. His mind was preoccupied with Harriet, her astonishingly passionate response and his own almost miraculous arousal. He and Clarissa had maintained some sort of sexual relationship but he had thought himself largely indifferent to sex for several years. He could, and did, caress his wife and bring her to satisfactory orgasm, but her elephantine playfulness failed to evoke a similar response in him. Harriet, however, her modesty and ultimate surrender to abandon, had restored a potency he did not dream he still possessed. Even now, talking to old Horsfall in the club Smoking Room, he felt an erection thicken at the image of Harriet, naked and spread wide for him.

'You still married?' he asked, to distract himself.

'Divorced,' Perry said glumly. 'Biggest mistake I ever made. Grass is greener and all that. She married again within a couple of years. I thought popsies were two a penny. Not any longer. Crusty old bachelor. Ah well – you coming to eat?'

'Can't old boy; terribly sorry. Dining out. Ought to be on my way.'

'Good to see you. Keep in touch. Let me know next time you're over. Toodle-pip.'

Poor old Perry, Oliver thought as he headed into the growing dusk towards good friends, good company and a good dinner; now I come to think of it, he never did pass the Russian course.

He arrived at Wheeler's to find Ben and Mona already installed at a corner table. Oliver could still remember their first sight of one another. He and Ben had been sauntering along one summer's afternoon, each with an essay to finish and neither giving a damn.

'Look at that! Over there . . . all legs and lipstick! Bags I!' Ben had said suddenly, and rushing across the High he had swept off his boater and laid it at Mona's feet.

'Trample on me,' he had implored her. 'Grind my head beneath your heel, or let me take you to the Trout and there, over a Pimm's, gaze into your peerless eyes.'

Mona had giggled, and brushing aside her full skirts, bent to retrieve his hat.

'The Trout it had better be, then!' she had said. The incident became famous, constantly cited as the perfect way to pick up a pretty girl.

For a moment in the restaurant Oliver had the advantage, watching them before they became aware of him. They both looked stout and flaccid; little sign now of the popular pair who had laughed and danced at college parties. Yet as he joined them their faces lit up with such warmth that Oliver reproached himself for his churlish thoughts.

They had ordered their food by the time Matthew finally arrived, whirling in with a gust of energy and charm very like his father's when young.

'*Sorry!*' he said. 'Rehearsals! They never end – and when they do, some actor in therapy wants a one-to-one brainstorming session to decide whether his character would have been a smoker or a non-smoker. Which I wouldn't mind, except that this is Restoration comedy. Hallo – I'm Matthew, the spotty adolescent who escorted Philly and Jenny through the perils of BEA when we were all about thirteen!'

'I know,' said Oliver. 'I can see you now, straggling through Customs with chalk marks on your suitcases . . . Very good to see you made it.'

Matthew was a director in fringe theatre with some well-received experimental shows to his credit. From university drama groups he had progressed via the Edinburgh Fringe to provincial repertory, what was left of it, before migrating down to the London fringe, the most competitive of all. Perhaps it was his work in the theatre that had given him an attractive openness, maybe he had always had it, but Oliver found him a thoroughly likeable young man and suspected that Philomena might too. Spurred by this inspiration, towards the end of the meal he said on impulse, 'The new *Carmen* at the Coliseum got rave reviews. Shall I try and get tickets for Saturday?'

'They're gold dust,' Matthew said, shaking his head. 'Sold out long before the reviews. I know someone who works in the ENO press office, though – let me know how many

115

you'd like and I'll give her a ring; see if I can wangle some.'

'Four possible, do you think? We could all go.'

Ben and Mona shook their heads. 'Can't do Saturday – it's sacred to bridge. You two go and' – Mona added, as though on a spontaneous inspiration – 'why don't you see if you could get Philly to come along as well? She and Matthew can't have seen each other since they were both about seventeen!'

'Bit more recent than that. Jenny's wedding was the last time,' Matthew said. 'Wow, they were good-lookers! How old would the girls have been then?'

'Twenty,' Oliver told him. 'Jenny married at twenty. Tell you what, if you *could* manage four tickets, I'll get Roderick's mother along to make up the numbers. She and old George Capel used to be tremendous opera-lovers.'

Had he got away with it? Ben and Mona seemed to have noticed nothing.

'Leave it to me,' Matthew said smilingly. 'See what I can do. No promises. There are lots of other shows. Have you seen *Steward of Christendom* at the Royal Court? Amazing piece of work. *Acting*? Wicked!'

'Wicked?' asked Mona doubtfully.

'Jargon, Mother. Like "smashing". Language being teased to mean its opposite.'

Yes, Oliver thought: Philly would definitely like Matthew.

He felt exultant. An evening with Harriet in the huge darkness of the Coliseum, or even the smaller, more intimate darkness of the Royal Court Theatre, would mark the culmination of their week, while with Philly and Matthew as chaperones their presence together would seem quite natural. On top of that, who knows? the young pair might hit it off.

Ben and Mona left the restaurant early to drive back to Tunbridge Wells and Oliver invited Matthew back to the club for a brandy. Right, he thought, I have done my bit for my daughter. The rest will depend on that lightning flash of sexual electricity without which all the parental plotting in the world brings only misery and the best intentions fizzle out in boredom. How capricious is the biological imperative, yet half our happiness depends on it.

Chapter Eight

Oliver woke next morning feeling like a small boy on his birthday, filled with excitement and dozy well-being. He basked in this happy expectation for a few seconds and then remembered – Christ! Harriet! Of course . . . yesterday they had . . . and today they would again . . . and he had lasted for ages and she, Harriet . . . his hand stole down to his swelling cock. I need a slash, thought Oliver.

Tea next, and the newspaper. Siamese twins had been born, joined at the liver. Not much hope for them, poor little beasts. The UN had entered Bosnia. That'll put an end to the dream of Greater Serbia, he reckoned. The Lib-Dems at their posturing annual conference wanted to reform the House of Lords. Didn't everyone, until they were made a life peer? Not much heard from old Grimond once he got the scarlet and ermine; just like those stocky, belligerent little trade unionists. Rabble-rousing one minute; next you heard they were Lord This of That: good as gold, deciding on their titles and quarterings. The OJ Simpson trial filled the headlines but it meant nothing to Oliver. He knew it was happening – you would have had to spend the last few months in the deep-freeze not to know, like the chap's poor bloody wife no doubt. His eyes grazed the front page. What day is it, anyway? Wednesday – time was rushing past.

Four days to spend with Harriet and then we'll have to face the families – how? Somehow. And Clarissa. For the time being his imagination evaded the details of telling Clarissa. But after that, a lifetime with Harriet. Extraordinary, he thought: this calm certainty. I have no

117

doubt at all that however many years are left, they will be spent with Harriet. That's what love does: it obliterates everything else. I loved when I was a boy of twenty, he thought, and now as a man – almost an old man – of sixty, I love again.

Oliver shaved in the serviceable old-fashioned bathroom at the end of the top corridor. Clarissa, with an eye on what she archly called 'the purse-strings', had suggested that he would save £20 a night by taking a single room without a bathroom. He had not demurred. As he studied his face in the mirror, the razor skiing through shaving foam down the angular slopes of his jaw and throat, shaving repeatedly so as to achieve a smooth surface that would not abrade Harriet's delicate skin, he thought about his daughter Philly. Fitfully, in the early hours of the night, Oliver had dreamed about a ceremony. This morning he could remember only its formality; the sense of being dressed up and on best behaviour. As though watching someone else he had seen himself, best-suited, long-faced and grave, conscious of his responsibilities. It must have been a wedding – presumably Philomena's. Wishful thinking, he had heard, accounted for 50 per cent of all dreams. Be good to see young Phil settled.

He recalled the concerned parental conversation over dinner last night. Ben and Mona had obviously been longing to ask their son why he didn't find a nice girl, get married, settle down, have babies; but even they, out of touch as they were, knew that you did not put such direct questions to a man in his thirties. Oliver had tried an oblique approach.

'Talking to Philly the other day I got the impression your generation hasn't much time for anything except work. Flirting and fun's pretty well taboo these days.'

'Between political correctness and the work ethic, there's not a lot of choice,' Matthew had agreed. 'It's become a very competitive world. Nobody keeps regular hours any more even if they work in an office, and in my game you go on till after midnight and start again at eight. Dead lucky to be working at all.'

Oliver and Harriet were due to meet at eleven in the Pimlico flat, this being the soonest she could get away without arousing suspicion, now that Jennifer was at home all day. Oliver arrived half an hour early. Ten minutes later he heard a key turning in the door. It was Mark. As he entered he too looked startled at the sight of Oliver.

'Didn't think you'd be here so soon, old man! Not bothering you, am I? Just thought I'd collect a couple of things, make sure the place was shipshape. Well, since you are here, how about a coffee? I have to go home and wait for the result of the last series of tests – shan't be around for the rest of the week. Must get on with clearing the orchard. Been meaning to do it for years. Might be my last chance.'

'There's no milk,' Oliver said, afraid that Mark would go in search of milk and find the bottle of white wine that had been cooling in the fridge since yesterday.

'Not to worry: have it black! Let me show you the kitchen, all the business.'

'No, honestly – find my own way . . .'

Neither moved. They were overcome with awkwardness. Oliver was thinking, what the hell did you *think* I wanted the flat for? Mark resented his oldest friend's apparent reluctance to spare half an hour of his – in Oliver's case, unlimited – time.

'Very well – since you're in a hurry . . .' he began, just as Oliver said, 'Quite right: have it black!'

As they went into the kitchen the door bell rang.

'Must be the postman,' Mark said. 'Lucky I was here.'

Oliver stood stock-still in the kitchen with racing heart, made aware for the first time of the public enormity of what they were doing. Harriet, my gentle girl: I am sorry to confront you with this! His mind framed sentences, whole paragraphs of apology and justification in the few seconds it took Mark to reach and open the front door. Oliver imagined, but did not step out to see, the smile fall from Harriet's face. There was a brief astonished silence; then her clear voice: 'Mark! I am here to meet Oliver. I came because . . . You see, we have fallen in love.'

'Ah. Well, gracious, you *have* surprised me. Come in, please, do come in . . .'

'Look, I brought some milk and some good coffee. Let's

119

have a coffee together. I think he should be here soon. I hope you have time?'

'I should like that very much. Thank you, Harriet. Oliver and I—'

Oliver emerged from the kitchen like a man from whose shoulders a great burden had fallen. Her face lit up as she saw him.

'Oliver! You're already here! My darling, how wonderful!'

She found mugs and five minutes later brought in a pot of coffee, real coffee, one of the best flavours in the world. As they drank it, Mark said, 'Now that I am going to die soon I find my chief regret is that I don't seem to have gone much for *happiness* in life. I've had plenty of other things – a good career, a lifelong marriage, decent children who have not been a disappointment to me. I do not complain. All the same, I feel I have lacked happiness. People don't talk much about it, do they? Not at our age. They talk about duty instead.'

'George, my husband, felt all his life that the important thing was to do one's duty. He felt that very strongly. George died unexpectedly – to himself, and the rest of us. He had no time to prepare. Yet his will and all his affairs were in perfect order.'

'Perhaps it is arrogant of me to feel that I have done my duty, more or less,' Mark said. 'But what I missed out on is happiness. Well, I hope you two are finding it. It doesn't always start at the church door. Now I must go. Thank you for the excellent coffee.'

Harriet stretched a hand out for his mug and said, 'Dear Mark – you do us a great favour by letting us use your flat. It allows us to meet without subterfuge or lies.'

Oliver was conscious that he had said almost nothing.

'You shame me, old man, with your generosity. I thought you'd be shocked! Live and learn, eh?'

'When a man has six months, more or less, to live, it concentrates his mind wonderfully. I am, as they say, worms' meat soon. No point in surgery. Waste of time. I am glad to see you both happy. I always thought Clarissa a splendid woman too, you know.'

'Goodbye, Mark.' Harriet said. 'I feel I want to give you a hug. Can I hug you?'

'All hugs particularly welcome!' He grinned at her. 'I say, I wish I'd had time to get to know you a bit better!'

They embraced warmly and as they separated, Oliver saw tears on her cheeks. Her emotion shamed him and he stepped forward, saying, 'Never done this in our lives before, I don't think, but a manly handshake doesn't seem adequate in the circs.'

He put his arms round Mark, patting him awkwardly on the back, feeling the thinness of the rib-cage, the resonance in his wasting body.

'Thanks, old boy. Better be going. Can't have Belinda fretting. Said I'd try and be back for lunch. Much joy to you both.' He gave them a steady look. 'Goodbye.'

They watched from the window as Mark got into his car and drove away. When he was out of sight, Harriet said, 'Hold me, Oliver . . . oh my love!'

He enfolded her in his arms and felt her shake with tears.

'Come and sit down,' he said. 'My darling. What a shock. I am so sorry. I had no idea.'

'He was so sweet about it. So generous and decent. He even praised your wife, as though to include her as well in his last affection. Oh Oliver, poor old Mark . . .' Her voice broke down and she wept again.

When she had regained control she said, 'I'm going to have another coffee first. You don't mind, do you, if I talk about George for a moment? You mustn't think I feel guilty about him because I don't but I do still think about him a lot. He was a very demanding presence. He won't let me go as easily as all that.

'George was jealous of everyone, even Roddy and Julian. He would rather we hadn't had them. He would have been happiest of all living with just me and Dodo. (Dodo was his nanny when he was little, and later on she nannied our boys too.) He would have bossed us both until everything was utterly predictable and ran like clockwork. *Then* he would have felt safe. George hated the unexpected. It terrified him. I'm glad he didn't know he was going to die; it would have been too much of an ordeal. Yet I can't help wishing he had been given the chance to get closer to his sons. They never really knew him and so, unfairly, they resented him.

121

You see, he – no, not now. I can't go on. I want to kiss you so much, my darling, that *that* supplants the words.'

'Talk, my love; talk as much as you like.'

'Not now. Take me in your arms. I am *aching* for you.'

Together they pulled back the bedcover and lay entwined between the sheets. Yesterday's roses had already dropped a few heavy petals. She picked one up and stroked her fingertip along its smooth, glossy surface; then lifted it to her nose and sniffed.

'Nothing,' she said. 'Commercially grown. Only *garden* roses retain their smell.'

Harriet wore no make-up or scent and Oliver stroked the nape of her bent neck and inhaled the natural odour of her skin and hair. Clarissa, a big woman, had a faintly sour tang no matter how often she washed or how much expensive scent she wore, but Harriet's skin smelled fresh and transparent. Her body was slight and trim, her hands and feet beautifully formed; she was altogether neat in her nakedness.

For a while she allowed him to scrutinize her, unself-conscious and shameless; then her body curved towards him, drawn to his warmth and his erection. In a gesture of unconscious surrender, she tipped her head languorously backwards and presented him with her throat, the bride to the vampire. He thought of the Transylvanian girls who were often, as though from centuries of inbreeding, impossibly long-necked, their bodies rank, hair tangled, the very antithesis of the hygienic, deodorized West. Their animal odours had once excited him. The prostitutes in Tirgu Mures had catered for men with Dracula fantasies but quite apart from the fact that they were obviously spies, Oliver had always preferred reality. Harriet, here and now, was palpably real.

'If only you could see it,' she said, straightening her head so as to look directly at him, 'I have a sort of very precisely focused ache that craves to be touched. I've felt hollow for so long – oh, for years. I never thought sex would mean anything to me and I tried not to disapprove of people who still indulged, but secretly I felt it was unnatural, once they could no longer have children. Sometimes old people can be so harsh and judgemental. It's because they have forgotten what making love can be like . . . or never knew. After yesterday, I shall never forget again. Popes and bishops should all have been great lovers in youth. It should be a requirement. Oh, I feel like one of Boucher's nudes. I may not look like one, but it's how I feel – all pink and dishevelled and lascivious!'

She smiled. Oliver could see the finely engraved lines radiating from the corners of her eyes and tiny flakes of dried salt left by her tears. Her face lost focus as he came close enough to kiss her opening mouth.

When they had made love they both plummeted into sleep, lying as though transfixed in their final position, the sweat gradually drying as their bodies cooled. Harriet's hair formed damp tendrils on her neck and temples. Oliver was utterly relaxed, his face unlined, all tension discharged, limbs loosely sprawled in the carelessness that followed physical abandonment.

She was the first to wake. Easing herself cautiously out of bed she went to the bathroom and showered, enjoying the jets of hot water that rained over her body. When she was clean she stood before the mirror and brutally appraised her nakedness. Her breasts had dropped, belly rounded, pubic hair gone grey, knees sagged. There were stretch marks across her abdomen and an old puckered appendix scar showed up whitely. Her skin was paler and greyer, the veins thicker and bluer since the last time she had looked at herself properly. It was a body marked by child-bearing; beyond the menopause, but not yet into the collapse of old age. She had not expected any man — other than a doctor — ever to look at it again, let alone find her sexually desirable. And now there was Oliver.

While he slept, Harriet went out in search of a delicatessen to buy their lunch. She struck lucky: a local Polish shop with a curved glass counter offered an assortment of cold meats, home-prepared dishes and good fresh cheese. These, with bread and fruit, would provide picnic food for the next two or three days. Further than that she dare not think. The present was luxury enough; she would not tempt fate by extending it into the future.

Onion tart, cold. Tomato salad, fresh, with garlic and basil. Pungent smoked Polish sausage, garlic sausage, rye bread, blue cheese. One of the two bottles of Burgundy that Oliver had purchased from the Reform Club's cellar. Coffee. While they ate they talked, exchanging as yet unknown details of their past lives.

'You have a degree in *Russian*?' Oliver asked. 'How simply extraordinary. Have you ever *been* to Russia? There is such a lot I don't know about you!'

'And such a lot you *do*. You know things nobody else knows. No, I've never been to Russia. And you've been dozens of times. Because you were a spy.'

'How did you think I earned my living?'

'I thought – I couldn't say why; it was more intuition than anything – but I *thought* you were a spy. I never told George, he would have thought me ridiculous. He said you were in the Foreign Office and when people asked we always said you were a diplomat.'

'My darling, how clever you are at picking up signals! And you never let on either. Eastern Europe was my patch, not Russia.'

'Oliver, when you first met me what did *you* think, can you remember?'

'I thought, isn't George's wife *small*, compared with Clarissa? She looked like a giantess next to you. She is a big woman – but,' he added hastily, loyally, 'not fat. Just *big*. Big bones. The Joan Hunter-Dunn type.'

'What else?'

'I thought how quiet you and I were and how much George and Clarissa talked. Was he always so loud?'

'Only when he was nervous. At home, when he didn't feel threatened, George could be subtle and observant. He hated to feel judged and meeting one's prospective in-laws is a very judgemental situation. He was roaring to warn you off.'

'Worked.'

'Would you like another coffee? Would you mind if I told you more about George? It doesn't matter now he's dead, but he was such a major part of my life that I am incomplete unless you know about him too.'

Harriet settled down on the floor, her head against

Oliver's knees. Sometimes he stroked her hair and sometimes she turned to look into his face for emphasis or
reassurance. It was a long-hidden story and she had never
told it before.

George had been born in 1923, into the generation that
grew up after the First World War, overshadowed by the
heroism of their dead uncles and cousins: those heroes in
brown photographs standing forever in pride of place on the
mantelpiece. The army that never grew up. It was a heavy
legacy for a little boy. George's ambition was to go into the
Army; he hated it when people said there'd never be
another war; that 1914–18 had been the war to end all wars.
He *wanted* a war to show that he too had courage enough to
die for his King and country. In 1939 he got one.

Having been a member of the Cadet Corps at school,
George automatically became a junior officer when he
joined up in 1941. By 'forty-three he was in Africa, but it
wasn't at all what he had expected. Nothing could have prepared him for the terror of daily, hourly uncertainty. George
was the sort of man who needed life to proceed along tram-
lines of predictability according to clearly laid-down rules.
In such a situation he behaved well; he would be disci-
plined, courteous, dependable. In arid dust and scorching
heat, with only administrative efficiency to stave off chaos
and slow ineffectual ceiling fans to stave off heat, he had no
way of knowing how hard other people found it to be brave.
For his own part, mastering his shaking limbs and bringing
his voice under control took superhuman effort. George was
terrified, above all of being found out. He became more and
more terse; his movements minimal; his gestures stifled. He
no longer laughed and began avoiding the beer and banter
of the Mess.

After a year George Capel had a nervous breakdown,
which was felt by all concerned to be a deep disgrace. In
those days it was described, scarcely more kindly, as
neurasthenia. George's medical officer confirmed that he
was not 'shamming' – as well he might, since by that time
George could not physically propel his limbs over the side
of his bed. He was the victim of psychosomatic, almost total
paralysis, brought on by deep depression. It seemed as

though his entire life had been moving towards this moment of helplessness and humiliation. George was then just twenty-two.

He was invalided out of the army and sent home. George's father had survived the Great War. 'Ought to be shot for desertion,' he growled when his pallid, shaking, sleepless son came back. His mother, after her first gratitude for his survival, soon realized that the body of her son might have survived but his mind was damaged. Only his nanny seemed to grasp that the tragedy that had overtaken him would leave a lifelong mark so that George would never be the same again; for Dodo was almost the same generation as the young men who had fought on the Somme and had seen its long-term effects on them, even the bravest.

For the first few months George's speech rarely rose above a whisper and when he did speak it was almost completely incoherent. He was unable to meet anyone's eyes; his own fluttered, half-closed. A twitch in his jaw flickered every few seconds. George was, in the cruel phrase of the time, 'a nervous wreck'.

After the war ended, he was transferred to what his father called 'a lunatic asylum'. It was in fact a humane and liberal establishment which, according to the current practice of those days, treated patients with the so-called miracle-cure methods of ECT: electroconvulsive therapy. And in fact, after a dozen treatments ECT had improved George's mental state considerably. Transmitting electrical charges to his head while his body was restrained by nurses did seem to clear some of the depressed brain pathways. Unfortunately, one side-effect was to slow his memory down for some time afterwards. But gradually this improved, until after six months in hospital, six months of ECT treatments and perhaps more importantly, tender and dedicated nursing care, George was ready to go home.

Having been invalided out of the Army without apparent stigma or disgrace, George could take advantage of the regulations that made it easy for ex-servicemen to go to university. He chose to read Greats at Oxford. Latin and Greek was an obvious choice. Alexander had been a boyhood hero and the classics master at school one of his mentors. As his special subject in his final year he opted for the military campaigns of Alexander the Great.

'That's why he married quite late. When I met George in nineteen fifty-eight he had only been out of university for five years, although he was thirty-five. It was true of lots of ex-service men; no-one jumped to conclusions or asked questions. After his degree he went home to help his father on the estate. (It *was* still an estate in those days. After the old man died we had to sell off so many acres to cover death duties that it became little more than a modest farm. Just as well, or it'd certainly be up for sale by now.) Five years after starting that he met me. I daresay one of the reasons I appealed was that I was young and biddable. And I was quite clever, not that he noticed at first, but he couldn't have been married to a fool. And pretty, I suppose. Nowadays I think almost all young women are pretty so there was nothing remarkable about that. But I *was* pretty. We married within less than a year of meeting.

'We were lucky, in a way, that his father died of a heart attack at the age of sixty-nine. It meant that not long after getting married we had the house more or less to ourselves. Well, there was my mother-in-law, of course, and Dodo. But his father was no longer there, not just disapproving of George but me too, and in due course poor little Roddy as well. I was glad when he died. So was George, though he never let on.

'After that fewer and fewer people knew about his Army record. Dodo told me first and I bearded George and made him tell me himself. I had to promise him that I would never tell the boys and they still don't know. The war had been over for more than twenty years by the time they were old enough to ask and they weren't really interested. So, you see, George wasn't the appalling bully he seemed to others. He did well to lead an outwardly normal life. People had no idea how hard it was for him. It wore him out. And sometimes he took it out on me.'

Oliver asked, 'Did he ever hit you?'

'Yes. Not often. Only when he couldn't help it.'

'Why did you let him?'

127

'Because he couldn't help it. He was so afraid of not being brave.'

'It's not *brave* to hit a woman!'

'No. But it's brave to hit a man. And brave to kill one. In wartime anyway. And George never had.'

'How often?'

'What?'

'Did he hit you?'

'Not very. And when he did, I understood. He couldn't help it.'

'So you forgave him?'

'Yes.' There was a silence. Harriet added, almost pleadingly, 'What else could I do? He couldn't help himself. First he would beat the dogs, to try and ward off his demons, and a few days after that, me. If it hadn't been me it would have been the boys. *What else could I do* except bear it in silence? Or divorce him. And that was never an option.'

Oliver leaned forward to put his arms round her and Harriet leaned back to rest her head on his knee. Her neck was exposed, the line of her jaw lengthened by the gesture into a clean curve.

'You mustn't think I was a passive victim. I had power too. It meant that he needed me very much. He needed my secrecy and my forgiveness but he knew I wasn't passive and he *never* took me for granted. I've seen wives who were part of the furniture. I had a sort of remote cousin called Reggie – his wife, Mary, might as well have been an automaton. She was a sweet woman, by no means a fool. For the last twenty years of their marriage I don't think he ever looked at her. She died a few years ago, poor old Mary, and Reggie only lasted eighteen months after that. He'd been totally dependent upon a woman he never so much as looked at! That, thank God, was never *my* fate. It's a mixed blessing. Now, are you going to tell me about Clarissa?'

'Not now,' Oliver said. 'That Burgundy has fired me up. We are going to make love again.'

Harriet's nipples tightened as he spoke. It's as though they can hear, she thought.

'It's as though they could *hear*!' she said.

'What?'

'When you said that, my . . . breasts . . . sort of . . . contracted, and . . .'

His hands moved up from her waist to cup her breasts. His fingers rubbed across their sharp tips.

'So they have!'

Through the soft wool of her sweater he ran his hands slowly up and down, teasing the nipples into excruciating sensitivity. Harriet's head lay back on his knee, her eyes closed, and as her breathing quickened Oliver said, 'I believe I could make you come just by doing this!'

'Yes,' she gasped, 'I think you probably could.'

His palms moved gently, then harder, until, excited himself by the sounds of her desire he lifted the folds of her sweater and loosened her constricting bra so that he could touch her heavy breasts. Harriet reached one hand upwards, tucking it between his legs.

'No,' Oliver said. 'No, this is just for you.'

'But if I . . . come now . . . then I won't be able to . . . come again . . . with you . . .'

'We shall see. If you can't, never mind. You have ways of making me come.'

He held her nipples between his fingers, rolling them gently to and fro. Harriet's eyes were closed, a flush rising in her cheeks.

'Touch me!' she said urgently. 'Now!'

He reached down, parting the elastic of her chaste white cotton pants to curl his fingertips into the folds of her flesh and watched her face as, urged on by his rapid abrasive rhythm, Harriet accelerated towards orgasm.

Jennifer had watched her mother-in-law leave the house with something like regret. She was not used to having time on her hands, time to kill, and what she thought of as highly desirable when she was employed had very quickly become a burden now that she was jobless. The thing to do, she decided, pulling herself together, was to draw up a plan of action, make some phone calls, set about looking for work. Maybe she could telephone some male colleagues, dig out the cards she'd been given at recent Book Fairs, persuade people to give her lunch and mine them for contacts and ideas. She ought to buy the *Bookseller* and *TLS* and look through the job vacancies. Right: first thing was to have a shower, get dressed, made up, start ringing round. She called down the stairs, 'Ulrike! Will you bring me a coffee in the drawing room at eleven? And make one for yourself at the same time.'

'OK, Jennifer. Do you want to have Mandy for a bit?'

'Not right now. I'm about to have a shower and then I must work.'

'OK!' shouted Ulrike cheerfully, but Amanda began to whine, 'Mummy! Wanna go 'n see my *Mummy*!' Jennifer pulled a face and going quickly into the bathroom, locked the door behind her and let the shower gush and steam, blotting out all external sounds.

It took her longer than planned to get going. Over coffee she read *Vogue* and *Tatler*, which lengthened a quarter to three-quarters of an hour. She found an article about women literary agents, however, which enabled her to classify the time as job-hunting. She tore it out and started a file which she labelled *Job-hunting*. By noon she had made a list of possible approaches drawn from her diary, Filofax and memory. Suspended between bravado and foreboding, she decided to start her telephone calls with Timothy Macleod. Although she hadn't seen him for months, she had always had the impression that he rather fancied her.

Jennifer dialled the number of the publishing conglomerate where Timothy worked. By allowing the intervening phalanx of personal assistants to assume that she was still at Thorensen and Markworth she was eventually put through to him.

'Hello, sweetie,' he said, friendly but brisk. 'How's tricks?'

'Give me lunch and I'll tell you,' she said, playing it at his speed.

'How're you placed – let's see – week beginning October sixteenth?'

'Not till *then*?' Jennifer said, then cursed herself for over-reacting. 'My, my, we *have* become important!'

'Frankfurt Book Fair . . . you can't have forgotten?'

Jennifer cursed again.

'*Squeeze* me in, Timothy – go on, you know you can!' she said coquettishly.

'It'll mean cancelling somebody if I do. Better be worth my while!'

They settled on Thursday week. 'Have to make it short though,' he said.

'Short?' said Jennifer. 'I wouldn't have thought that was your style . . .'

Feminism is all very well, Jennifer reflected, but there's nothing like plain old-fashioned sexual manipulation for getting your way with people – not people: *men*. By the end of the morning she had two firm lunch-dates and two disconcerting brush-offs. Publishing was a village and news of her dismissal had travelled fast. Her professional self-confidence was somewhat punctured. When in need of a morale boost she always turned to her old friend Marion. Jennifer dialled.

'Take my advice, sweetheart,' Marion said after listening to her story, 'do nothing until Frankfurt's over. They're all dashing towards it like lemmings. Sit tight, enjoy your children (lucky you) and give it a month. Answer a few ads if you like, just to keep your hand in, but don't run after contacts. OK? Now, how soon can you meet *me* for lunch?'

'Marion, you're an *angel*,' Jennifer said. 'Tomorrow? I really need a heart to heart.'

'I'll cancel an author who's been pestering me about his raised gold lettering airport rubbish. If *he* can't turn them into best-sellers why should he expect *me* to? Tomorrow's Thursday isn't it? Groucho's?'

Groucho's was a big favour, as Jennifer knew very well. It is the oasis of the media, its tribal members and their guests famous in the pages of *Private Eye* and the gossip columns. Here the lions and lionesses of publishing stalk their prey, the vulnerable, thirsty writers, desperate for a chance at the watering-hole. Lunching at Groucho's showed her face around, kept her in touch with the gossip.

'That would be *brilliant*. One o'clock. *Thanks*.'

She went down to the basement to find Ulrike spooning yoghurt into Mandy's baby-bird mouth.

'*Who's* Mummy's very good girl?' she said. 'And who's

coming to the *park* after lunch to feed the *ducks*?'

'Me, me, me, me!' said the ecstatic Amanda. She was sitting in an old-fashioned high chair with an abacus across the front and she sent the coloured wooden balls whizzing to and fro in her delight. They clicked and clacked against each other: a sound Jennifer remembered from her own childhood.

'Good girl,' Ulrike said. 'Eaten up all her lunch!'

'Duckies, duckies!' shouted Amanda.

Jennifer thought, I love my children so much that I would die for them but oh, how they bore me! Brimming with guilt and need, she picked Mandy up and buried her face in the plump pearly flesh, inhaling the smell of yoghurt and soap.

An hour later she stood beside her daughter in Battersea Park.

'Squirls!' Mandy shouted delightedly. 'Come here squirls! Come an' eat my nice nuts! Look squirls!'

How can mothers *stand* it all day long, Jennifer thought. The *boredom*, the endless repetition. If a man came along and tried to snatch her I'd fight like a tiger. But listening all day to her babble and squeak – *that* is beyond my power. She never says anything interesting.

'Mandy,' she asked her daughter, crouching down so as to look at the world through Amanda's eyes, at Amanda's level, 'what can you see, honey-baby?'

Amanda considered. 'No squirls,' she answered dejectedly. 'Not any squirls at all.'

Jenny heaved a deep sigh. 'Never mind. Do you love your Mummy?'

Amanda turned her head to look into her mother's large black-fringed eyes. 'I love you Mummy,' she answered, '. . . but I don't *like* you.'

'Mandy! That's a *wicked* thing to say! *Why* don't you like your poor Mummy?'

''Cos you've got spiders round your eyes.'

'Silly baby! Course I haven't! Why else don't you like me?'

'*Not* a baby. 'Cos you make Mandy sad an' poor 'Uge sad.'

'Mummy *has* to go to her office, you know that, Mandy. Doesn't it make Emily sad too?'

132

'Em'ly *never* sad.'

Quite true, Jennifer reflected. Tough as nails, young Em.

'Well, Mummy's here with you *now*, isn't she?'

'Wanna go an' feed duckies with silly old squirlses' nuts.'

Jennifer straightened up and, holding Amanda's hand, they made their way towards the water's edge.

The end of the day in the City is usually marked by a visit to one of its wine bars. After hours of mental and financial tightrope-walking it is a relief to let the brain and emotions go slack, the raucous anarchy of alcohol replacing the high tension of work. These bars are rigidly hierarchical. There are cellars with sawdust on the floor, three-legged stools and hand-chalked menus on the blackboard: low dives for the lowly where, in a beery smell of Dickensian conviviality, they drink as much, as fast and as cheaply as possible while cursing their superiors. The next level up from this might be a long bar attached to a restaurant offering the latest food fad, perhaps sun-dried Mediterranean vegetarian cooking or pale Oriental morsels. Here the house wine is marginally better and much pricier, but since whatever is consumed will come back in the form of expenses, it hardly matters. These customers like to be recognized and greeted by name, responding with exaggerated bonhomie. Finally, as superior to these as fine wines to house plonk, there are discreet temples reserved for those with the nerve and skill to negotiate the City's sheer drops and invisible hand-holds. These are dark, mirrored, mysterious shrines for the privileged acolytes of money.

Music is the other clue. The sawdust cellars play the latest pop music – Blur or Oasis – followed later in the evening, especially on Fridays, by the thump of House music – music for people looking for a sexual encounter, often in vain. The modish bars rely heavily on degraded classics: Vivaldi's *Four Seasons* or Albinoni's *Adagio*. This is music for discreet yet predatory flirting conducted in parallel with business conversations. Only the cool subterranean temples favour silence. Here, the most appropriate music would be Beethoven's *Missa Solemnis* or Brahms' *Requiem*, for money alone is worshipped here, and with religious fervour. This is no place for the intrusion of sex or any impropriety except the financial kind.

Roddy was having just such an end-of-day drink with three colleagues, downstairs in a bar of the halogen-spotlit temple variety. He knew Catriona had heard them arranging this and hoped she would not follow 'accidentally'. Lately there had been a couple of significant glances, pointed remarks, and he was beginning to feel uncomfortable. Office affairs were frowned upon, even between single colleagues, and the photograph on his work-area of two shining blond children left no-one in any doubt that he was married.

The barman eased the cork silently from a bottle of the house champagne (only the low dives liked to hear it pop and see the foam explode) and poured the golden bubbles into tall glasses. Guy placed a fifty-pound note on the bar, looking away as he did so to indicate that real money, *paper* money, was trivial. The bottle was soon finished.

'Bollinger . . .' said Roddy casually. 'Put it on my account, Fred, would you?'

This upped the stakes. Now, nothing less than Krug would do. He had done well to buy the second bottle. After the third it was acceptable to leave.

Soon they were halfway through the third bottle. (The third man had chickened out: it was not Krug. Black mark to Alastair.) Hunched at one end of the bar they were discussing the day's dealings when Roderick spotted a pair of slender and all-too-recognizable legs descending the staircase. 'Gotta have a slash . . .' he murmured as he made his escape. He waited as long as possible, hoping Catriona would assume he had already left, but as he emerged from the Gents she came swinging through the door of the Ladies.

'*Darling!*' she said on a sliding note and he knew at once that she was drunk. 'Where've you *been*? God, I need a fuck! Mmm . . .One more drink and let's *go* . . .'

'I can't,' he said, striving to keep his voice low and even. 'I have to get back. My mother's staying. Have to be home for dinner.'

'Home to Mummy for *din-dins*?' she mocked.

'Catriona, *please*, OK? Talk to you tomorrow. Might even be able to slip away at lunchtime,' he bargained.

'Wanna fuck *now*!' she insisted and he thought, she's just like my three year old. When Amanda wants something she wants it *now*.

'Sweetheart, listen, no can do. Scouts' honour. Not now.'

Catriona swirled away from him and marched over to the bar. So far the other three had noticed nothing.

'Whassa *matter* with you guys?' she demanded. 'Why does *nobody* round here wanna have *fun*?'

She had been drinking already, that was obvious, and by the sound of it had already been rejected once. The black jacket she had worn in the office all day was now un-buttoned to reveal a clinging velvet top. She braced both arms to slip the jacket off just as Roderick, following behind, took her elbow. He glanced complicitly at the others.

'Come along: let's get you a taxi, OK?'

'Wanna buy a bottl'f *champers*. Stand my round. One of the boys.'

'Not to worry. Not your turn. Come on, Catriona, time to head home.'

Catriona wrenched her elbow out of his grasp and swung round to face the others. This was suicide, personal and professional, and deep in the sane and sober vestiges of her brain she knew it. Go for broke, urged the drink. You *tell* 'em, sweetheart!

'This *fucker* here: yeah *you*, Roderick Capel. Tell, can't you – look at him – *shit*-scared! Well this cunt fucked me on Monday but now, *oh* no! Just wants me outa his way so he can go home to din-dins with his *mummy*! You're all the same, *wankers*. Doesn' matter what *I* want. Gotta be *your* cock that dictates. *Stuff* your jobs and your bonus and your share options and mobile phones and your *very own* car-park space for the new BMW and all the other sodding big boys' toys, the *lot* of you. As for *you* Roddy, *you're . . .*'

Roderick did not wait to hear what he was. With the help of the barman, who had slipped out from his mirrored haven to stand beside him, they lifted Catriona, her heels flailing a few inches above the ground, and carried her up the stairs until she was outside on the street, still clamped firmly between them. On her right, the barman extended an urgent arm towards an oncoming cab. On her left, Roderick stepped forward a pace, gave the taxi-driver her address and handed over a £10 note. They slid her into the back of the cab, the barman slammed the door, and in less than a minute from start to finish, Catriona was borne away out of sight.

They stood on the pavement, metaphorically dusting off their palms. The barman said, 'Sorry about that, sir. I assure you the lady had not been drinking on *our* premises.'

'Not to worry,' said Roddy. He slipped the man a fiver to buy his silence, and together they went back to a group that, despite bright spots of excitement in their eyes and on their cheeks, appeared suddenly muted. Nobody met his glance. There was a pause of several crucial seconds before they all spoke at once.

Guy said, 'Trouble with women, they just can't stand the pace . . .'

Alastair said, 'Well, chaps, now that the fat lady's sung I'll be on my way.'

Martin muttered, 'Anyone for another bottle?'

Roddy said, 'She's right about one thing: I *am* supposed to be having dinner with my mother.'

They drained their glasses and went their separate ways.

Chapter Nine

Jennifer and her mother-in-law, still in dressing gowns, sat over cold toast and tepid coffee. Ulrike had taken the children to school.

'I sometimes think it would be easier to *die* for those three than listen to them,' Jennifer said. 'Then I feel so *guilty*. Harriet, hey, be honest: did *you* ever feel that?'

Harriet picked her words carefully. Jennifer was not in the habit of confiding in her, and only did so now because she had been feeling insecure since losing her job. Jennifer had seen more of her children than usual in the last couple of days and may have realized that they were closer to – not fonder of, but certainly closer to – Ulrike the au pair, even their Granny, than to Jennifer herself. All three offered their mother rapturous affection yet were obviously uneasy with her. Hugo's stutter was worse in her presence and worse still when Roddy was at home.

'Remember, I had Dodo to help me. She taught me a lot. When Roddy was born she was fifty-four — almost exactly the same age as I am now, come to think of it – *gosh*, and she seemed so old! – but it's the ideal age to be looking after children. You've still got plenty of energy but have learned to be patient. Lovely Dodo. She had a long memory for games and stories, but a short one for naughtiness. And she never harped on about how much better-behaved children *used* to be.'

'Roddy still adores her,' Jenny said.

'Everyone loves Dodo. She's the saintliest human being I've ever met. You're right: small children *are* boring.

The trick is not to expect them to talk like adults.'

'Oh! Try making them get to the end of a story – it's *impossible*!'

'What is touching is that they're transparent. They have no guile. There's usually some grievance to get off their chest – children are terrific sticklers for fairness – and then of course the fibbing. Don't think these three are specially bad. All children tell fibs.'

'Such *obvious* liars.'

'Adults lie too. They just get better at disguising it.'

'Oh yes? Not Roderick.'

Harriet filed this away for a later conversation and went on with the present one: 'Children often try to say what *they* think *you* will think is interesting.'

Jennifer thought, she's got nicer since the appalling George died. She was *dull* with him around – so mute and subservient – how ever did she put *up* with him for nearly forty years? Come to think of it, she looks good too: here we are at nine fifteen, she's wearing no make-up, still in her dressing gown, and she positively glows.

'Harriet you *are* looking terrific!' she said. 'Perhaps one isn't meant to say this to someone who's just been widowed but hey, you look great.'

Harriet, who had looked in her mirror this morning, knew that she was lit by a quite unseemly radiance.

'How do you do it?' Jennifer persisted. 'If it's out of a bottle I *want* some!'

'Jenny, you exaggerate. I'm glad to be with you all. London's very stimulating.'

'Is it? I'm always so *busy*. What are your plans for today?'

Harriet was meeting Oliver at the Pimlico flat. He had wanted to make it ten o'clock in the morning but, conscious of having disappeared every day so far, Harriet had insisted on spending some time with Jennifer first.

'Why couldn't I invite myself over too, for coffee with you both?' he had asked.

'Because, my love, you give yourself away each time you look at me – and so do I. It's too much of a risk.'

'Jennifer is far too self-absorbed to notice. I must give her lunch one day, talk to her about Roderick and the marriage and their problems. It would be terrible if they split up. She was always "Daddy's girl" of the twins. She might listen to me; at any rate I ought to find out if things are as bad as Philly says. Not that I flatter myself she'll take my advice. The trouble is, I begrudge every hour away from you.'

Oliver was right about Jennifer's self-absorption yet the possibility of being found out by any one of their children obsessed Harriet. Their awkward encounter at the flat with Mark would be trivial by comparison. As long as their meetings remained secret, Harriet could still tell herself that she and Oliver were hurting no-one, but if Roderick and Jenny knew their parents had become lovers they would be appalled, and as for the effect on the grandchildren – she could not bear to imagine it. If that marriage broke up (though Harriet still thought this unlikely) Hugo, Emmy and Mandy would need their grandparents more than ever. If she and Oliver lived openly together, Clarissa would fight to deny them access to the grandchildren and Jennifer would no doubt side with her.

Harriet assumed that, apart from jealousy and revenge, the incest taboo was the true reason for their revulsion. This – the first and deepest taboo – is then to protect the genes and the young; to prevent fathers and daughters, uncles and nieces, cousins and aunts, from interbreeding. In this it coincides with the Church of England's Table of Kindred and Affinity. Married love is sanctioned by the church, the state and the advertising industry; adolescent sex is tolerated as a necessary spur to marriage; but post-menopausal sex is offensive and generally ignored, as though making it invisible meant it didn't happen.

Harriet was aware that if the passion between Oliver and herself were revealed, the family would be up in arms. It would be intolerably embarrassing. She could, after a decent interval, marry an elderly widower; *this* her sons would permit. They might even be relieved: 'Nice that Mum's got someone to look after her.' But marry *Oliver*? Never.

She turned to Jennifer, flicking half-heartedly through the *Daily Mail*. 'If you'd *like* to do something – we could go to the Tate, for example, see the Turners – I'd happily look at them again. Why don't we go this morning?'

Jennifer had very little desire to see the Turners, which she imagined she knew quite well enough.

'Darling – it's a sweet idea – but I *daren't* at the moment. I really must get down to serious job-hunting. You heard Roderick banging on last night: "If we don't have your salary coming in we can't afford Ulrike." I must bung off some more résumés – CVs. After that – it *is* Thursday today, isn't it? – I'm meeting a friend for lunch at . . .' (tiny pause, whose significance was lost on Harriet) '*Groucho's.*'

'All right: I'll leave you in peace and take myself out somewhere.'

'Will you be OK? I am *sorry* . . .'

Harriet thought: she can be ungracious at times. I thought she was interested in my plans for today, instead of which she merely wanted to know how soon I'd be out of her hair.

'More coffee?' Jennifer asked desultorily.

'Bless you – no. I'll go and get myself ready.' Harriet stood up.

'Ah, here's Ulrike! You're back! Listen, this morning I want you to . . .'

As Jennifer gave her orders Harriet heard the girl protesting that she was only supposed to work five hours a day, an objection that was smilingly overruled.

Roderick was having a difficult day at work. He knew the gossip about last night's encounter with Catriona would have spread fast but he had not expected to be summoned to his boss at nine o'clock in the morning. He emerged from an eight o'clock meeting to find an internal message in his personal computer file: *See me soonest. JPA.* John Paddy Arcachon was one of the few people in the bank who merited a secretary, a remarkably gorgeous young creature known for the sake of political correctness as his personal assistant. Roderick dialled her direct line.

'Sal? I gather JPA wants to see me. When could he fit me in?'

'Right away,' she said, as cryptic as her boss; and then, relenting, 'You've been a very naughty boy . . .'

'Not naughty enough. Never laid a finger on you, more's the pity.' Sally giggled. Roderick was tempted to be more specific but, remembering a recent sexual harassment case which had netted the victim several thousand pounds, he resisted.

'Tell JPA I'll be with him in two.'

He went to the gents, had a prophylactic leak, ran his fingers through his hair, twitched the knot in his tie and resisted the impulse to clean his teeth. *That'll do!* he told his reflection. As he strode towards JPA's glass and leather office, Guy beckoned.

'On your way to see the Big Cheese? He's done me and Mart and Alastair already. We said she'd been emotionally distraught and chucked a lot of wild accusations about. She must have gone to see him first thing this morning. Bitch!'

'Has she resigned?' Roderick asked.

'I don't know. If she doesn't jump she'll be pushed.'

'Christ! Hope he doesn't push me as well.'

'He won't. He can't. He needs you.'

'Thanks,' Roderick said fervently and he threaded his way through the wired-up office landscape towards JPA's very public sanctum.

'May I have your own version of what happened yesterday evening,' JPA began.

Roderick answered with no apparent pause for thought, candid and direct: 'As I believe you know, four of us went for a drink after work. Must have been about eight-thirty, nine o'clock. When we'd been there for three-quarters of an hour Catriona Stevenson arrived. I guessed that she'd been drinking already. She was a tad offended because we wouldn't let her buy another bottle of champagne. We told her we were on the point of leaving, which was true. She . . . lost her rag . . . raved on at us, until the barman and I escorted her out and put her in a black cab. That's it.'

'This scene occurred in a wine bar patronized not only by staff from this bank but also by many of our clients?'

'I don't remember seeing anyone else there that I knew.'

'You do not, I believe, know all our clients personally.'

'No, sir.'

'Catriona evidently made certain personal remarks

141

directed at you.'

'She did.'

'Were they true?'

Roddy looked JPA directly in the eyes. 'They were. The relationship is over.'

'The bank cannot forbid members of staff to associate with one another, socially or otherwise. But any institution founded upon the highest principles of personal and financial probity discourages affairs between members of staff, particularly if one or both of them is married.'

'Yes, sir.'

JPA smiled thinly, for the first time, at Roderick. 'Go thou, and sin no more.'

Roderick thought, *sanctimonious prick*! but let his shoulders slump with relief. He smiled back, aiming at a boyish, irrepressible, Hugh Grant sort of grin.

'Sorry, JPA.'

'I might add that Catriona has, shall we say, offered her resignation and I have accepted it. She has already cleared her desk and been escorted out of the building. Run a quick check on your secret files. Bugs, trespass, code-changes, deletions. That's off the record. I do not think she will risk suing either the bank or you personally for sexual harassment. In fact I have made sure that she won't. It's been, all in all, quite a costly affair. I do not expect to pay for another.'

The threat was unmistakable. Roddy imagined himself snapping a junior to commanding officer salute, a trick he used to make his facial expression suitably firm yet humble. One thing his father taught him was how to handle authority. Defer, defer, and defer again.

'Absolutely *not*. Thank you, JPA. I appreciate what you've done. I won't let you down.'

He went back to his desk and on impulse telephoned his wife.

'Hi. It's me. I can get off at a reasonable hour tonight – fancy a film? Dinner? Or both? No my darling, I am *not* going to take you to *The Bridges of Madison County*. Geriatric passion is not my scene. How about *Usual Suspects*? Check out when it starts and meet me seven-

142

thirty at Café P. My mother still with you? Right, OK, I'll talk to her later, make nice about leaving her on her own for the evening. No, I *haven't* got a rise. Just you keep looking for that job. 'Bye.'

'Don't get up,' Oliver begged, seeing Harriet wake. 'Stay in bed a bit longer.'

'My darling, I have to wash, tidy up, all those boring orderly things.'

'No, lie here with me. Let me be your *disorder*, let me be chaos. What am I?'

'My love, my passion, and my joy.'

'Poetic Harriet! When I think of *you*, words march in procession through my mind, flags and pomp and panoply in praise of you. Sensations flash all over my body. On guard! Prepare to attack boarders! Oh, all right then, *welcome* boarders . . .' He laughed, a lazy, languid sound, and Harriet joined in.

'I'm so glad we can laugh. Oh Oliver, you are such a delight to me, as well as – God *knows* – a source of the most frightful guilt.'

'We said we wouldn't talk about guilt.'

'We did. We won't.'

Showered, dressed, hair folded back into a French pleat, nose powdered, once again the image of decorum, Harriet said, 'I brought my car today. We could *go* somewhere.'

'It's a beautiful afternoon. We could, if I had the strength to walk.'

She laughed. 'You have the strength of ten men!'

'My knees feel weak and my arms are exhausted. Have you ever thought about the muscles a man needs when making love? Mine had atrophied for lack of use.'

She laughed this time, a rich, jubilant sound. 'My thighs ache and my spine is sore. My breasts are inflamed. My mouth is swollen. I'm not complaining – oh, believe me, not. I feel wonderful!'

'You *look* wonderful,' he said. 'Doesn't everyone notice?'

'Jennifer did remark on it this morning.'

143

'Whatever she said, she understated.'

'We could go to Kew Gardens. I love Kew. Or Hampton Court. They're probably far enough away to be safe.'

'Safe from what?'

'Oh Oliver, how can you be so innocent? Safe from being spotted.'

'Is it such a danger? People would see us as two friendly in-laws. All right: Kew.'

Jennifer made a mock-modest entrance at Groucho's, knowing she looked spectacular. Lankily elegant in a light green suit and black high heels, her appearance compelled attention. Men sprawled in armchairs checking out the lunchtime edition of the *Evening Standard* glanced up and took notice. Marion, waiting at the bar, greeted her with a kiss on each scented cheek.

'Good for you!' she said. 'Zap it to 'em! D'you want a drink here first or shall we go through?'

'How long have you got?'

'I ought to be back in the office by three. Plenty of time.'

They perched on bar stools sipping dry white wine, checking out the assembled company. There were two people from her old office – *good*! thought Jennifer; I hope it gets back to Thorwald – and a powerful agent wooing a powerful author. As they made their way towards the dining room for lunch the agent stood up.

'Jennifer! Great to see you! You know . . .?' Mercifully, she did.

'Of course . . . hi, Ian. Your new book's out soon? Hey, I can't *wait* to read it.'

'I'll get my assistant to send you a copy. In fact . . . why don't I give you a buzz sometime. Are you tied up till after Frankfurt?' the agent asked her.

'For you . . .' Jennifer smiled, 'there's always time.' She took a card from her handbag. 'Take my home phone and fax. I am *not* linked up to e-mail. Be great to hear from you. Here's to the top of the best-seller list, Ian. 'Bye both!'

A kiss from each for Jennifer; no acknowledgement for Marion, beyond a vague smile. Except on the day of a book launch, marketing people are regarded by authors and agents as sitting below the salt.

Over lunch they discussed their career problems. Marion said, 'Right . . . that's the shop-talk done! How're things at home? Roderick behaving himself?'

'*Roderick*,' answered Jennifer heavily, 'has got a *mistress*.'

'Oh darling, don't be so old fashioned. Apart from anything else he couldn't possibly afford one. A mistress is a kept woman. A man sets her up in a flat and she waits for him to come and screw her.'

'All right then: my husband is sleeping with a woman from his office.'

'How do you know?'

'Because she rang up and told me.'

'Cow!'

'Isn't she? Apparently she thinks he's going to divorce me and marry her, and she wanted to chat through the chronology of this happy event.'

'When did this happen?'

'A couple of weeks ago. I haven't said anything to him yet. I'm biding my time. I was furious at first, then depressed.'

'Things still not good between you?'

'Not great – though oddly enough our sex life's fine. Always is.'

'Then stop the whingefest. Not many wives can say that.'

Marion was fast approaching forty. She had never married or had a child. In the watches of the night she yearned for both and would have been prepared to settle for either. She had long ago put her own family behind her, choosing to forget the Essex background, the good comprehensive school, the swotting for A Levels and the disappointment when she failed to get good enough grades for a decent university. This past was concealed from her colleagues. Beginning as a secretary in a small publishing house, Marion had hauled herself up to the point where she headed the marketing department of a large conglomerate, earned a hefty salary and owned a small flat in the heart of Chelsea. She had two Siamese cats who greeted her nightly home-coming with plangent cries. These cats were her surrogate children although she hardly saw them except at weekends, when she lavished affection and luxury cat-food on them. During the week she was seldom home before ten o'clock, after some literary party at which she had ensured that the key people met and remembered one another's names. She envied Jennifer from the bottom of her heart.

'Last week I would have said, "I'm going to divorce the bugger, the sooner the better!"' Jennifer admitted. '*This* week I'm not so sure. Don't spread it around, but I didn't jump ship at T and M – I was pushed. They've given me six months' money (not that I've told Roderick *that*: never know when I may need a nest-egg) but it's a lousy time to be adrift in a small boat on the stormy seas of publishing.'

'Work is not your number one problem. Listen to your Auntie Marion. A good man is hard to find. The opposite is true too: a hard man is good to find. Your man, it seems, is good *and* hard. Don't let him go, Jenny.'

Jenny laughed. 'Divorce only looks tempting from the outside,' Marion went on. 'I know plenty of divorced women, with or without kids, and take it from me they have a hard time. You think the world is peopled with spare men? *Ain't so!* You're looking stunning, Jenny; plenty of men would be more than happy to bed you—'

'Believe it or not, I've never yet been unfaithful to Roderick. But right now, if someone asked . . .'

'Lots of people will *ask*. But how many are prepared to take on you *plus* three children? *Plus* the aftermath of divorce, all those deadly conversations about what his lawyer said to your lawyer? In a nutshell: *think hard*. End of lecture.'

They discussed Marion's meagre love-life until quarter to three. Marion paid, tucked the bill in a Filofax envelope marked Expenses, embraced her friend and flagged down a taxi. As soon as it was out of sight Jennifer headed soberly towards Leicester Square tube station.

At four o'clock Oliver and Harriet were strolling down the pathways of Kew. Along every vista, the gardener's art triumphed over nature's wildness. It was a mild autumn afternoon, too mild for a coat. Harriet was wearing what George used to call 'your good jacket'; Oliver the 'foreign-looking' jacket his friends had made fun of. Kew was dotted with similar couples. Looking at the pair of them, any passer-by would have said, old-marrieds; relaxed with one another, no need to talk, boring but contented. They in turn watched other, less happy strollers: young people with the wariness of the reluctantly single, joggers, nutters, loners, grievers. They passed a sobbing young woman and a black youth – student? refugee? – wearing a mask of harrowing pain.

Harriet thought, why does anyone yearn for *youth*? Being young was the hardest stage of life – until, she supposed, extreme old age. Dodo was the only person she knew who had never complained about the misery of ageing, but then, Dodo never complained about anything. Most people said ominously, 'Don't ever grow *old*, Harriet,' as though she had a choice. It would be nice to grow old with Oliver. She took his hand to make him look at her, to soften the intrusive question.

'I want to know about Clarissa . . .'

'First tell me *your* impression of her?'

She laughed. 'I remember *George's* first reaction: "Now *there's* a fine figure of a woman!" He meant it as a compliment. He was a bit in awe of Clarissa but at that stage, at the beginning, he liked her.'

'Until she made that ghastly remark . . .'

'Which you didn't hear.'

'I was in the porch at the time, holding my daughter's arm, feeling her tremble with nerves. But I heard about it later.'

'I'm afraid George never forgave her for that.'

'Don't blame him. I think even Clarissa was ashamed afterwards. It was only said to reassure herself. She was nervous, needed a spot of sisterly solidarity.'

'Why couldn't she have criticized somebody's *hat* instead?'

'Oh, Clarissa'd never do that. Would have been bad manners. Rude.'

'So instead she . . .' Harriet felt the old anger rising, '. . . she called my son *queer* in front of the whole church. *That* wasn't bad manners?'

147

'She has regretted it a thousand times since.'

'Why didn't she apologize, then? Not even to *us*, necessarily. To Julian.'

'Sullivans never say sorry. It's one of their rules. It's because they can't accept that they're ever in the wrong.'

With an effort, Harriet controlled herself. She had no desire to quarrel with Oliver, least of all on this golden afternoon. Already it was Thursday. On Sunday they must . . . what? Part, or decide. She squeezed his hand, meaning, let's not quarrel.

They walked on in silence. Oliver recalled ardent images from the last time they had made love. Her vigour in bed astounded him. For a modest woman who could surely have had little or no sex for a few years, Harriet was violently uninhibited. It must be the release after years of being passive with her husband. Another image rose before his eyes: that of George — hefty, thickset George — hitting his wife. Oliver had never hit a woman but he had seen other men do it, and the action had always seemed cruel, ugly and petulant; like a child kicking a puppy. They do it because they *can*, he thought. He and Harriet walked a hundred yards in silence.

'Do you remember *your* first impressions of Clarissa?'

Harriet hesitated, looking for a safe form of words. Oliver would not have married frivolously, or stayed married for thirty-five years, unless his wife had fulfilled many of his needs; yet her initial perception of Clarissa as someone overbearing, and snobbish had been reinforced by every subsequent encounter.

'I think Clarissa very much wants and needs to be liked, but if she can't be liked she would settle for being looked up to. She is a bit . . . élitist, perhaps?'

He laughed. 'How delicately you skirt round saying she's a snob! Don't worry: Clarissa *is* snobbish, and proud of it. She would call it "maintaining standards" or "behaving *properly*" but they're just different words for snobbery. It's her father's fault: he taught her respect for a world that hardly even outlived him.'

Fathers again; the awesome power of fathers. George's nature had been distorted by his father but when it was his

148

turn to be a father he had behaved in the same way to his sons, as though small boys needed to be heated up and hammered into shape, forged like horseshoes. Yet he was proud of them both and deeply loyal: which was why he had never forgiven Clarissa her gibe in church. Harriet sighed. 'Men of that generation! They did so much damage. What *did* he respect?'

'A world in which "everyone knew their place". A proper social order in which money was only earned by people who knew how to make use of it. *Spending* money was vulgar but looking after and hanging on to what one inherited was different; *that* he saw as a responsibility. He hated paying taxes – avoided it wherever he could – and was *splenetic* about death duties. Good manners mattered enormously. It was almost more important to maintain the façade than actually to behave well. Clarissa is a snob *and* prejudiced *and* philistine. But it is possible – though not many people would agree nowadays – it *is* possible to be kind and considerate in spite of these faults: especially if you happen to live in a beautiful old house in a rather feudal French village.'

Harriet said, 'I don't detect those attitudes in your daughters – what about Patrick? I hardly know your son. Don't even know what he looks like. Is he like you?'

'Nope – takes after Clarissa. All the same, credit me with *some* mitigating influence! Both my daughters are more intelligent than their mother, so their view of life is more complex than hers. But traces remain . . . have you noticed what lovely table manners they both have? Clarissa used to bang on endlessly. "Philomena, elbows off!"' He mimicked Clarissa's patrician bark so accurately that Harriet had to laugh, yet the question remained at the back of her mind: if she is an unintelligent snob, *why did you marry her*? Oliver heard the unspoken query.

'When I first met Clarissa she was about twenty and I was a year older – this was nineteen fifty-seven, to be exact. I'd done my stint of National Service, learned Russian; by then I was up at Oxford.'

'Reading Languages.'

'Yes, that's right. Clarissa, like most of the girls around

149

college in those days, was somebody's sister. Used to hang about during Eights Week, watch cricket in the Parks, that sort of thing. Big, gawky: like a young Labrador, hadn't yet worked out what to do with all four limbs. Terrifically hearty. A classic type: Miss Joan Hunter-Dunn. That summer my partner for the Commem Ball developed flu at the last minute. I'd paid five guineas for a double ticket, wasn't going to waste it, so I asked Clarissa. She must have known she was a substitute but she accepted anyway.'

Harriet thought, George and I met a year later, so no miracle could have brought me together with Oliver at a time when we were both still free.

Back in the late Fifties most girls were gawky and naïve, not like the sophisticated young women of today, disconcertingly knowing, with shrewd eyes and a hostile vocabulary. The world of her own and Clarissa's adolescence had been restricted and drab but at least everything had *worked*. Trains and buses ran on time. Prices were printed on the packets because they stayed unchanged for years. People bought houses and lived in them for life – often kept the same job for life, too. Rationing had ended but people didn't chuck their money around the way they do today. Until she was sixteen or seventeen, Harriet remembered, she had used her pocket money to buy National Savings stamps with pictures of bubbly haired Princess Anne on the sixpennies and a solemn little Prince Charles on the more expensive ones. Departing uncles would tip her half a crown, murmuring, 'Now young lady, *mind* you don't spend it all at once!' and she didn't. She would buy a Prince Charles stamp at the post office and stick it in a buff savings book.

It had been a time of innocence. None of the girls she had known at school or even any of the debs in her year had lost their virginity before getting married – or not as far as she knew. Men were decent, society had seemed decent. The sanctions of propriety and austerity still governed polite behaviour. She recognized the sort of girl he was describing as he talked about Clarissa. They'd all been Labrador puppies, more or less.

Oliver and Harriet pushed open a door and entered the

Palm House. The warm air held drops of water from circular sprinklers projecting a fine mist of spray. The leaves on the palm trees sweated tropical moisture. Harriet slipped off her jacket and trailed it over one shoulder. Above their heads arched the great cast-iron roof with hundreds of curved panes. The palm trees were heavy with fruit or brilliant blooms whose fallen petals lay on the ground. Oliver went on:

'Clarissa turned up for the Commem in a long dress with her mother's fur stole round her shoulders, although it was a hot summer evening. No make-up, hair all over the place. But she was an energetic dancer and we gallumphed away happily together. Supper at midnight – champagne flowing like water – until suddenly I realized how drunk she was. I don't suppose she'd have had more than a glass or two of sherry in her life before and she hadn't realized the effect of alcohol. She was bright-eyed and over-excited and rather amorous. That was OK by me. We kissed a bit – her first time, probably – and I took her to one of the "sitting-out rooms". It happened to be empty. I daresay my whole life might have been different otherwise. I wedged a chair under the door so that no-one else could come in.

'Before I knew it her dress and bra were round her waist and she was saying she loved me, had done for ages, always would. People took that kind of thing seriously then and to Clarissa it meant commitment.

'Well, after that I got her dressed and poured coffee into her and we walked round the gardens in the cool till she began to sober up. I hoped by the morning she'd have forgotten what had happened.'

'They never do,' Harriet murmured.

'Clarissa didn't. Next day she was overcome with embarrassment and remorse; accused herself of having behaved like a loose woman – her phrase – and said she'd perfectly understand if I never wanted to set eyes on her again. I couldn't let her think she was a loose woman so I told her that of course I wanted to see her again; and she cried.'

'That was it?'

There was a pause while they negotiated a narrow spiral

staircase in single file, climbing to the walkway overlooking the lush vegetation beneath.

'That, in retrospect, was already the moment of no return.' Oliver concurred. 'We went on seeing each other intermittently for the next two years. I kept hoping she'd fall in love with someone else, or that I would. Instead of which people, especially her parents, began to treat us like a couple. We started being invited to things together. She was obviously in love with me, which was flattering. Sexually she was very ardent, and eventually the inevitable happened . . .'

'She got pregnant?'

'Not *pregnant*: God no! That would have been unthinkable. But she was twenty-three by then and after two years of increasingly passionate groping and – whatever it was called in those days: *necking* – Clarissa was bursting with sexual frustration. We started sleeping together. No backing out after that. Both lots of parents were keen on the idea of an engagement; hints were dropped; people thought we made a handsome couple. At the age of twenty-four – as I was – I couldn't imagine – you can't imagine being with one person for thirty or forty years, let alone my whole life. You don't stop to consider how you might change. In those days it was easiest to do what everyone seemed to expect. If you didn't you were a cad or a heel. I'm amazed how young men nowadays can apparently live with a girl, sleep with her, be serviced by her – and after a few years say, no, thanks very much: and *nobody minds*. Nobody thinks they've done anything wrong.

'I had no idea what I was taking on but I couldn't see any honourable way to escape. We got engaged and at the end of nineteen fifty-nine Clarissa had her dream wedding. The county; flowers in the village church; table with a display of presents from Harrods and Peter Jones: the works. I'd joined the Firm by then and they were relieved to have me safely fixed up. Less risk of blackmail. Two months later we went abroad. Our married life kicked off in a tiny flat rented for us by the British Legation in Tito's Yugoslavia. I still have smatterings of Serbo-Croat.' While Oliver had been talking they had reached the topmost walkway overlooking the leafy canopy of palm trees.

'I am not saying I was trapped into marrying Clarissa, nor that she manipulated me,' Oliver said finally. 'But there was never at any stage a moment when I said to myself: *I choose this woman.*'

Roderick worked straight through lunch, grabbing a sandwich and a soft drink from the trolley as it circled the floor at one o'clock. He flashed from one turquoise screen to another, comparing and analysing figures, totting up the noughts, computing currency values, balancing comparative interest rates between capital cities and stock exchanges. He spoke to colleagues in Rome, New York, Chicago and Oslo. At six he tapped out a memo for his immediate boss, Patricia. She liked to have everything compressed into a single page and most of his time was spent condensing his original three-page draft into one, but by quarter past seven it was finished. He logged off, made a quick call to his mother to say he would be late, and waved a cheerful farewell to Sal, JPA's assistant, who winked back and gave him a double thumbs-up. Jubilantly, Roderick displayed his security smart card to the red eye beside the double exit doors. It flashed green. He took the express lift down eighteen floors, strode across the marble foyer with its inlaid corporate logo and swung through the twelve-foot-tall revolving glass door. Catriona was perched on the buffed steel balustrade surrounding the bank's forecourt and ornamental garden. She twinkled her fingers at him and smiled demurely. Roderick swore, silently but fervently. Tosser! He had been outwitted and outmanoeuvred. He should have anticipated this and left through the underground car park. *Jerk!*

'You're early,' she said smugly. 'Good. More time to buy me a drink. Two.'

'Catriona, sweetheart, I'm sorry. I really am. It was nothing to do with me. JPA saw me this morning; gave me a bloody hard time. I gathered from him that you'd resigned.'

'Come on. We'll discuss this over a drink,' Catriona said grimly.

'Some other time, Cat, please. I honestly can't now.'

'Oh, why not? Don't say you're meeting your wife? Little celebration, hm, to mark your new-found uxoriousness, lucky escape, all that?'

He was reminded how bright she was, and how intuitive. Catriona had held her job at the bank not least because she had always been able to anticipate a client's next move. She went on, 'Let me guess. You're on your way to meet her for a drink, right? Right. Then you'll go – not, I think, to the theatre – bit over the top for you – a *film*. Something nice and escapist. Spot of violence, spot of sex. See: don't I know you well? We have after all been fucking one another for a good eighteen months. Good, did I say? Let it pass. Now then, where are we going for that drink?'

Roderick bowed to the inevitable and gave her one of his best rueful grins. 'Remind me never to underestimate you. Come on: you're making me late but we could have half an hour.'

'We shall *have*, my dear Rodders, as long as it *takes*.'

An hour later he emerged alone from a cellar bar, angry and chastened. Catriona had talked. JPA knew all about them. Roderick felt bruised, exposed and – worst of all – foolish. He would now be more than an hour late meeting his wife. He phoned a message to the Café P and dived into a black cab.

An opalescent sky lingered over Kew Gardens. The gates shut at sunset. Oliver and Harriet, drawn by the magnet of closing time, hurried through darkening pathways between shrubs that had lost their leafy detail and colour and become solid clumps of yew-dark green. Oliver felt that he had told Harriet too much about Clarissa and not heard enough about her. He still had to convince her that they had a future together. London, where they were under constant threat of observation and discovery, made that difficult. He had to shift territory; go somewhere they could be sure of anonymity.

'I shall take you to Paris one day soon. We shall stay in the prettiest hotel room in the whole city. It is on the top floor of an eighteenth-century building and from its window you

154

look across to the Place de la Concorde. It's octagonal, high up above the rooftops. You can see down into other people's balconies and window-boxes. It also has the prettiest bathroom in Paris, with dark blue tiles and two basins. I shall watch you get ready for bed and slip my soapy fingers between your legs and wash you. We will draw the curtains, turn on the bedside lights and roll back the bedcover . . .'

'Have you stayed there often?'

'Not often.'

'Have you stayed there with Clarissa?'

'No, my love, I have not. I wouldn't take you to a room that had memories of Clarissa.'

'Or . . . *sorry*, darling! I'm sorry. I have no right.'

'Or with anyone else. I have only ever slept there alone.'

Chapter Ten

Jennifer, getting ready to go out for the evening with her husband, selected her clothes carefully. He liked her to look sexy yet discreet. She chose an electric-blue suit. Its clinging jacket zipped up to the neck above a short skirt whose narrowness outlined her legs at every stride. She dried her hair into an elaborately artless style and on an impulse, shrugged naked into the silk-lined jacket, zipping it up carefully between her breasts. She squirted zephyrs of Chanel No.5 around her throat and down the front of her jacket, blew kisses to the clamouring children and was out of the front door before they could detain her.

'Taxi!' she called.

Harriet got back to Camberwell just before seven to find her daughter-in-law gone and a note on the hall table. I'll read that later, she thought; first I must lie down for ten minutes to summon up enough energy to help Ulrike get the children to bed. She tucked the note in her jacket pocket and tried to tiptoe past the bathroom but they heard her.

'Granny! Granny! Come and blow us soap bubbles!' She put her head round the door. Ulrike, nearly as flushed and soapy as the children, said, 'Jennifer has gone out for the evening. She said to tell you they would be late. She is very sorry. She said there are lots of Marks' dishes in the freezer for you to choose from.'

Three extra hours, at least, to spend with Oliver: oh, the luxury. He might suggest she came to the Reform for a drink or a meal with him, after which perhaps they could stroll

156

through evening London pointing out their private milestones, filling in the gaps in their lives. She would ring him in a moment; meanwhile the children's pleas could not be ignored. Harriet slung her jacket over the back of the landing chair and went into the bathroom.

After reading a story and singing a song and observing the routine of good night kisses for teddy and dolly and donkey and koala bear; after hugging their warm, pliant (in Hugo's case, tense) small bodies and settling them under duvets, it was eight o'clock before Harriet was free to ring Oliver. The operator at the Reform Club tried his room and said his extension was engaged.

'I will call again in ten minutes,' she said.

When Oliver had returned to the club at the end of the afternoon he was intercepted by the porter, who handed him two notes. One said, '*Matthew Vulliamy rang to say he had four tickets for Saturday. Please call him back on . . .*' The other: '*Your wife telephoned from France at 6 and 6.30 p.m. Please ring her. P.S. Mrs Gaunt rang again at 7 and says it's urgent.*' All in good time, he thought irritably, as though Clarissa's domineering voice were in the room. First I need a drink.

After two stiff whiskies he braced himself and dialled his home number in France. With luck there would be guests; they would be about to go in for dinner and she would have to be brief.

'Clarissa . . . hello darling, it's—'

'*Olly!* At *last*! Where have you *been*? I've been ringing and ringing. I was getting *worried*.'

'I was downstairs having a drink at the Club. I've only just got your message. They don't page you here. Is anything wrong?'

'Nothing's wrong with *me* – but what about you?'

'I'm fine, fine.'

'Have you seen the girls again? How are they?'

'I'm having lunch with Jenny tomorrow – she wasn't free today; some business lunch – and Philly and I are going to the opera on Saturday.'

'To the *opera*? That's not like you. Why the *opera*?'

157

'Remember last time we spoke I was going to have dinner with Ben and Mona: on Tuesday? Yes, well, they brought along their son Matthew. Used to fly out with the girls for school holidays sometimes?'

'He must be grown up by now? Goodness, let me see . . .'

'Middle thirties, thereabouts. Seemed a nice chap; crossed my mind he might cheer Philly up. He was talking about some new production of *Carmen* so on the spur of the moment I suggested he might care to come along if I could get tickets – make up a foursome . . .'

It was out. Oliver cursed himself. Clarissa pounced.

'A *foursome*, Olly? *Foursome*? With *who*?'

'Occurred to me it might be a kindness to ask Harriet Capel. She's been on her own a lot in the last six months. Stuck in the country. Vaguely remembered she and George had been keen on opera . . .'

There was a pause; then Clarissa said archly, '*Olly* . . . you *fancy* her, don't you? Go on: *admit* it.'

He ought to have said, 'Come on darling: don't be *absurd*,' but he could not bring himself to deny his love. Instead, with long experience of his wife's jealousy, an area in which she displayed startling intuition, he scolded, 'Clarissa, that's not like you. She was *widowed* less than six months ago.'

He heard over the long-distance line the sound of Clarissa counting under her breath on her fingers: 'April – May . . . *September*. It's *exactly* six months,' she announced triumphantly.

Best not to argue. Change the subject. Safe ground. 'How are the dogs?'

'They *miss* you, Olly. They're mooning all over the place, looking for Master.'

'Give them my love.'

'They're right here beside me. I'll put the phone down to Poppy's ear and you can talk to her. Hang on a minute. There! *Now!*'

Feeling a fool, Oliver cooed, 'Hallo Poppy, how are you? Do you miss your Master, hmm?' – mainly in case Clarissa had cheated and was listening in. There was a pause and then her voice, triumphant: 'There! Did you hear *that*?'

'What?'

'Thump thump and a little whine. That's her tail on the floor. Go on Pops, wag tailies again for Master . . .'

Oliver uttered a sentimental moan somewhere between pleasure and sympathy and changed the subject briskly before she could repeat the performance with Mindy. A telephone conversation with Clarissa was like a game of chess. You needed to be two or three remarks ahead.

'What should I say to Jennifer at lunch tomorrow? I gather she's pretty strung up about Roderick at the moment. Seems to feel he's neglecting her. Has to work so hard he's practically never at home.'

'Jenny's like me,' Clarissa said, settling down happily to comparison and advice. 'She's the sort of girl who needs lots of *attention*. It's not *her* you ought to be talking to, poor *darling*, but her husband. How *dare* he neglect her? She's so busy with her job and everything . . . she *needs* a bit of a fuss made when she gets home in the evenings. And then she has the *children* on top of all that. *How* she manages with just *one* au pair girl I can't *imagine*! She doesn't even have a *femme de ménage*, does she?'

'She does in fact have a cleaner, yes. In any case I can hardly put all the blame on Roderick,' Oliver protested. 'They've been rowing a lot lately. Takes two. Serious, Philly thinks.'

'You're *not* – oh, darling – you *don't* mean . . .' she lowered her voice to indicate an appropriately scandalized reaction, '. . . *divorce*? Oh, they *couldn't*! The *disgrace*! There's never been a divorce in our family, *never*.'

'Clarissa, divorce isn't quite the same ostracizing disaster that it used to be. I believe they even let them into the Royal Enclosure nowadays – how else could the Queen have her family there?' He grinned like a schoolboy as Clarissa ticked him off.

'Oliver, that is *not funny*.'

'Sorry. *Definitely* not funny. Poor Queen.' He went on, 'The real question is what effect their break-up might have on the children? I don't mean Jenny and Roderick – I mean Hugo, Emily, that lot.'

'Oh, they're *young*. They'd get over it. Children do. I don't

159

care *what* you say, Oliver, you must have a *serious* talk with them both: Jenny of course but Roderick, *too*. Tell him . . .' and Clarissa was off, Harriet forgotten, as she re-enacted word for word the conversation *she* would have had with her son-in-law. Obligations – responsibilities – lifetime commitment – a woman's needs – happily rehearsing it all for his benefit. In the midst of his irritation at this performance, Oliver reflected that his wife could be more acute than he sometimes gave her credit for. The lecture, in his present situation, could apply equally well to himself.

Clarissa reached the climax of her peroration: 'They stood side by side, in church,' she pronounced, '"in the eyes of God and this congregation", and they promised "to love and cherish till *Death them did part*!" *That's* what they have to remember.'

Eventually he wound her down. Yes, he assured her again, *yes,* he missed her, *yes*, he looked forward to coming home; *no*, the weather was not as nice in London as it evidently was in France . . . until, mollified, Clarissa at last hung up.

As soon as his line was clear the operator rang with a message. 'A Mrs Capel rang you, sir, at eight o'clock; she would like you to call her back on this number . . .' Instantly he dialled the Camberwell house but the line was engaged. To fill time he tried Philomena's home number. It was almost half past eight, but all he got was a clipped recorded message: '*This is Philomena Gaunt. I cannot talk to you right now but if you will leave your number and the time of your call I will ring back as soon as possible. If it's urgent, my mobile phone number is: . . . If it is a query about evidence or a document you may prefer to fax me on* this *number . . . Thank you. Goodbye.*'

Oliver was stabbed with pity for his clever, conscientious daughter whose life seemed to consist of too much duty and too little joy. He began to leave a message but within a few seconds she picked up the phone.

'Philly – oh good, you *are* there,' he said. 'It's Daddy.'

'Hallo,' she said wearily. 'Sorry I haven't thanked you for lunch. It was Monday, wasn't it, and this is Thursday already! Time goes so fast. Didn't mean to be rude. It was a lovely lunch. I've been hectic ever since then.'

'You do sound tired. Are you working now?'

'Yup, 'fraid so.'

'I won't keep you long. I've got hold of some tickets for the Coliseum on Saturday for *Carmen*: the new Jonathan Miller production. Are you free? Like to come?'

'How did you do that?' She was impressed. 'They're gold dust.'

He explained about Matthew and Matthew's friend in the press office and that Matthew – remember him? – would be coming too. And, he added cautiously, Harriet Capel.

'Jenny's ma-in-law? Oh? Why *her*?'

'She's up in London this week for Hugo's birthday – I saw her at Jenny's on Sunday evening; she and poor old George used to be keen on opera.'

Philomena was not interested. 'What's Matthew like these days? I remember him as a spotty teenager.'

'*I* thought him rather likeable – but judge for yourself. You will come, then?'

'I shouldn't, I'm bowed down under files and pink string, but what the hell – you're not often in London and *I* don't get to the opera much – thank you, I'd love to come.'

'Good! Meet you in the foyer at seven fifteen? Excellent. Mummy sends her love by the way: I've just been talking to her. Oh, *you* know her, but she sounds all right. Made me talk to the dogs, usual nonsense.' They smiled together at Clarissa's foibles.

'Daddy, sorry, but if I'm to make it on Saturday, I must . . .'

'I know, darling. 'Bye.'

Harriet, having twice tried to get through to Oliver and found his line engaged – she did not speculate as to whom he might be ringing – made herself a cup of tea and helped Ulrike tidy the kitchen after the children. Ulrike asked, 'Are you in for the rest of the evening, Mrs Capel? I would like to go round to my friend, but I am baby-sitting. If *you* were here . . :'

'I'm not certain. Could you nip round for an hour or so, in case I go out later?'

'Of course,' Ulrike said obligingly, and Harriet thought, that girl is a godsend. I hope Jennifer knows how lucky she is.

'Why don't you give me a quick ring at nine and I can let you know my plans?'

'That would be fine. Thank you. The children are quiet; I think they are all asleep.'

When she had gone, Harriet tried Oliver again, but his extension was still engaged. She dialled her own number in Dorset but at the first sound of Dodo's calm, untroubled voice the day's emotions overwhelmed her.

'Oh Dodo, why is life so complicated?' she said before she could stop herself.

'Harriet, calm yourself, dear. Life is not at all complicated. If anything it is too predictable. What time is it?'

'Just after half past eight.'

'Well, that's an improvement, anyway. Not the middle of the night. What is the matter? You sound quite discombobulated.'

'Dodo, I know you don't think it right but I can't help it. I am irretrievably, I mean *fatally* in love with Oliver Gaunt.'

'Jennifer's father. Roddy's father-in-law.'

Harriet sighed, '*Yes*,' and paused to marshal her thoughts. If she could make Dodo understand, if she had Dodo on her side, all would be well. 'You know I've never been impulsive. I've never made a habit of falling in love with people.'

'You were always a very *steady* wife to dear George.'

'But now I am – quite unlike myself – I feel – washed over by new feelings about life, how it should be lived. Yes: *washed*. As though a great wave had bowled me over and I was bruised and buffeted but clean and exhilarated, too.'

'Baptism by total immersion?'

Harriet laughed. 'Dodo, I beg of you, *listen*. I need you to hear me think it through.'

'Go on . . . I will listen and not interrupt until you have finished. Or make jokes.'

'Thank you. Dodo, now I understand what people mean who say lovers are two halves of a whole. He completes me mentally and . . . physically. We have been kept apart by the old quarrel in our family, which of course is the *same* family. Neither of us has had entirely happy marriages but we have both been good spouses. I was faithful, as you know, and I believe Oliver had been too, at least on the whole. Men make exceptions. Now that George is dead, poor George, it makes no odds to *him*. I don't want Oliver to divorce his wife. I shan't deprive her of her status or home or his money. We could go away or stay and live in Dorset with you, Dodo. We are prepared to do whatever our families want: see them or not see them, marry or not marry, *but they must let us be together*. We will "behave well"; we won't flaunt ourselves or embarrass anybody. We have the chance of – I don't know, twenty years? more? – of happiness together. I am determined to take it. I want him to be with me for the rest of my life and *I shall die* if I can't have him.'

There was a pause. She heard Dodo's breathing down the line. She was wheezing very gently, like a kitten sleeping.

'That's all,' Harriet concluded.

'My dear child,' Dodo began. 'I am not entirely ignorant about love. I even know a bit about physical love, which is the explanation for the feeling that presently overwhelms you. Yes it is. When I was a girl I fell in love twice. The first boy was killed; the second went away in the end and found somebody else. No matter. I know much more about loving children, who must always be put first because they depend on us grown-ups and they are innocent. It gave me great happiness for nearly forty years, to watch George loving you – love was so *difficult* for George – and you bringing up the dear boys and loving him. You *did* love him, didn't you? – if not in the beginning, at any rate by the end?'

'Yes,' Harriet recognized the truth. 'Yes, I did.'

'The beginning of love is such a small part of it, quite different from the whole span. You love a baby for its helplessness and when it's a three-year-old, for being headstrong and bold and inquisitive. And so on. The nature of love changes throughout a long marriage or friendship. Love is stamina, tolerance, unselfishness. All those old-fashioned qualities which people nowadays call boring. They aren't boring; they are fascinating. But they *are* difficult.'

163

'Oh don't be so Christian! Let me have some *joy*!' Harriet implored.

'Hattie, dear, *that* doesn't sound like you! I don't much care for that word "joy". I always think it's rather a *hysterical* word. But you want this, *joy*, at the expense of both your sons' and your grandchildren's happiness?'

'*Must* it be at their expense? Would they really care all that much? Yes, for a few months, probably – but not for long. Whereas it's the whole of the rest of my *life. Please*, Dodo,' Harriet begged, '*let* me have this happiness.'

'You will take what you want and do what you want, people always do when they are infatuated. But don't ask me to give you permission.'

Harriet balked at the word 'infatuated'; but although she herself had never had much Christian faith she knew about stoicism and endurance and besides, Dodo was, always had been, the voice of her conscience.

'I am tired, dear,' Dodo concluded. 'I'm no more use to you now. We'll talk again tomorrow. Now, take something to help you sleep. Vervain, or dill.'

'Sleep well, Dodo. I will always love you, whatever you tell me. Good night.'

Oliver, who had made several attempts to ring Harriet, tried again.

The instant Harriet put the telephone down it rang. She snatched it up.

'Hello?' she asked eagerly.

'Mrs Capel? This is Ulrike. Do you know yet if you will be going out?'

Harriet expelled a breath of disappointment. 'Sorry, not yet. Leave me your number, could you, and I'll ring you?'

She could hear the girl's disappointment. 'We – were hoping to go for a drink . . .'

The habit of self-effacement was too strong. 'Of course: go. You've had a long day. You deserve to relax. I'll watch over the children.'

'Are they asleep?'

'Not a sound.'

'Good,' said Ulrike. 'Thank you very much, Mrs Capel. It is very kind. I shall not be late.'

Oliver had evidently given up. It was over an hour since she had left the message and her line had been almost continuously engaged. Meanwhile, remorsefully, Harriet had remembered that as yet she had only seen Julian once. Her son had cooked her a delicious meal, gone to much trouble on her behalf and she had not even thanked him. She was seldom in London; they ought to meet again. She would like to find out if he was happy with Fonzi. She would listen out for the babes and then make herself a sandwich. She dialled the number of his flat.

'Yes?' came Julian's familiar, still vulnerable voice. She could tell at once that he was waiting for another call.

'Jules dear, it's Mother. I never thanked you for that delicious, *fascinating* lunch . . .'

'Fascinating?' he interrupted. 'Don't patronize me, Mother. What do you mean, *fascinating*?'

Oh God, she thought; now I have put his back up. It did not occur to Harriet that a young man whose lover worked every evening but who himself tried to be faithful, probably spent the evenings in a haze of dope and second-rate television. Having no knowledge of his culture or the way he filled his time, she assumed her tactlessness must have offended him.

'Darling – I meant it was a really *interesting* meal. Really unusual flavours. I *loved* it, that's all. Don't be offended, please.'

He was mollified.

'OK, Ma, no need to go over the top.'

'Julian, you are coming to Hugo's birthday lunch on Sunday aren't you?'

'If I'm wanted.'

'You are *of course* wanted. But as the whole family will be there I may not get much chance to talk to you. Are you free for lunch tomorrow? Or dinner?'

'Which?'

Harriet knew that Oliver was lunching with Jennifer, but had not asked about his plans for the evening. 'Lunch,' she said.

165

'Friday. Yes, right, I'm free. Where do you want to meet?'

'You know London restaurants, I don't. Tell me where you'd like to go.'

'Blueprint Café. Next to the Pont de la Tour.'

'Sounds fine. I'll book a table. Shall we meet there at one?'

Julian relented. 'It's wildly expensive, Mother. We could go somewhere else. More your sort of place.'

'No: if you like the Blueprint Café we'll go there. It's not that very modish place run by an architect's wife, is it?'

'Nearly but not quite. You're thinking of The River Café. Very *au courant*. This is a new place. Only opened recently.'

'How exciting. I shall, as far as my wardrobe allows, dress so as not to embarrass you.'

'Come as you are. I'm not easily embarrassed.' She heard him smile and smiled back down the phone. 'The restaurant's down beside Tower Bridge. Tell the taxi to go to the Design Museum. Or do you want me to pick you up from Camberwell?'

'I'll manage to find my own way. One o'clock? Till then, darling.'

She pondered this conversation, not knowing whether to be touched by his image of her as an ageing woman who needed to be guided around London, or bitter that her son should still harbour such resentment.

Love often harbours resentment. It can also harbour boredom, irritation and misunderstanding, though by then it is hard to recognize it as love. Jenny, waiting for Roderick in the café in St Martin's Lane, felt all these emotions. In addition, the overheated atmosphere was making her uncomfortable, since she could not lower the zip on her jacket by more than a couple of inches.

Had she been honest she would also have admitted that she was enjoying the attention focused on her, a good-looking woman alone in a bar. She had drunk three glasses of wine, one of which was sent over by an older man a few seats away, to whom she had smilingly tipped the glass but whose company and conversation she did not encourage. She had read the evening paper. She had been to the Ladies twice to renew her lipstick. They had definitely missed the beginning of the film and she was getting increasingly cross. Determined not to watch the door, she had her back to it when her husband finally arrived, an hour and a half late. He kissed her neck and murmured,

'Darling, I am truly *truly* sorry. It wasn't my fault. You look amazing. Could we cut the film and just have dinner?'

'Not much choice, have we?' Jennifer said, not prepared to be won round too quickly. 'It started half an hour ago. What were you *doing*?'

'I got held up at the bank. One of my colleagues has just got the sack; wanted a spot of advice on future tactics.'

'Oh, who?' said Jennifer, not really interested.

'One of the usual suspects,' he said wryly. 'Come on.'

'No go on, *who*?'

'Woman I work with. Catriona Stevenson.

'*Catriona*! Really? Why was she sacked?'

'Come on darling, you don't want to hear about Catriona Stevenson's problems. Let's eat. Here, or somewhere else?'

'Wanna bet? Not here: the pianist is too loud. Let's go round the corner.'

She levered herself off the bar stool, he gave the barman a ten-pound note and took her arm. They made a striking couple – tall, close, even in their present ill humour – and more than one solitary drinker watched them go with envy. The older man who had been on the point of sending Jennifer his card and a glass of champagne, thought to himself, '*My* wife and I were like that once and I let her go. Bloody fool.'

They walked the few hundred yards to a favourite restaurant. Jennifer entered graciously; not spreading waves of animosity, not letting her anger lap around the other diners and alarm the waiters. One is either a sulker or one is not, and Jennifer was not. She sat down smilingly, chose from the menu vivaciously, sipped the chosen wine voluptuously, and then said dangerously: 'She rang me, you know.'

'Who rang you?'

'That friend at the office.'

Roderick, caught off-guard, steadied himself for the

167

onslaught. He made his voice casual, indifferent. 'Which friend?'

'Oh for *Christ's* sake, Roderick, don't give me that "Which friend?" crap. *Catriona Stevenson* rang me.'

Apprehension deepened. Stay cool. Smile now.

'She *did*? When?'

'Hmm ... now ... let me see: two, maybe three weeks ago.'

'What did she say?'

'Seems she had some career problem; wanted advice about future tactics.'

'Don't play games with me, Jennifer,' Roderick said, furious with Catriona for not telling him of this conversation. 'What are you getting at?'

'You want the punch-line or the whole build-up? Punchline is: I want a divorce. Definite. Decided. Finished.'

The waiter brought a fragrant fish soup and set some *rouille*, grated cheese and a cairn of croûtons in the centre of the table. This gave Roderick ninety seconds of silence during which his mind raced. Did he want a divorce? No. Best to confess or deny? Confess. He prolonged the silence while his wife helped herself, waited for her to dip her spoon in the soup, and only then said, 'We did have an affair, of sorts. That is true and I regret it. But it's *over*, Jennifer, I swear.'

Jennifer flinched from the venom of sexual jealousy, although she had known for nearly three weeks, ever since Catriona's insidious voice susurrated down the telephone at work one placid afternoon ... '*Is this Mrs Capel? It is? Oh good. I think you should know that your husband and I are in love. Oh yes, I'm serious all right. In fact I think we'll probably get married.*'

Jennifer looked at Roderick with distaste. A yellow strand of cheese was suspended from his lower lip. 'Wipe your mouth!' she said, and returned to the attack. He wiped his mouth. The strand hung on tenaciously.

'You heard me: a divorce. Catriona's not your first affair and won't be the last.'

'How dare you say that? I don't suppose *you've* been driven snow. Huh?'

'Funnily enough, I *have* been up till now. Often wondered why I bothered. We haven't been happy for years.'

'More fool me, then, mooning away in my own private illusion.'

'Yeah, *more fool you*.'

'Jennifer,' he said, dangerously intense, 'what do you *want* of me?'

What did she want? What did any wife want? The impossible and the mundane, Mr Everything-rolled-into-one, lover, provider, knight errant, confidant, father and friend. How could he or any man be all these in two or three exhausted hours at the end of the day? It was years since she and Roddy had shared anything but rushed early mornings and sometimes – not always – a meal together in the evening. In these distracted snatches of time, how were they meant to care for their children and each other, unravel the tensions of work and remain a loving, mutually supportive couple? It was impossible. Her needs and her indignation were so great, she could not name them. Jealousy made her banal.

'I want a *husband*, who *talks* to me and puts me first, not some tart in the office; who plays with his children instead of endlessly snapping at them because he's so stressed-out.' A recent incident flashed into her mind. 'I *don't* want the sort of man who calls his son's stutter a problem-solving challenge situation.'

'If I did I was joking.'

'That's the tragic thing – you *weren't*.'

'Don't tell me I use that pyscho-babble business-speak about my children. I don't even use it at work. Just don't tell me. Because it's *bullshit*.' He spat out the word, finally dislodging the shred of cheese. 'What sort of word is "*stressed-out*" anyway? What's wrong with tired . . . exhausted . . . *knackered*?'

'Oh? Do I have to record you and present the evidence on playback?'

'Jennifer, if you don't stop these ludicrous accusations I shall walk out.'

'Leave your credit card behind when you go. *I'm* not paying for this meal.'

169

'That's it in a nutshell. That's all I am! A credit card for you and three hangers-on. *And* the au pair *and* your cleaner and laundry bills and travel agent and . . .'

'Hangers-on, is that what your children are? *Hangers-on*? You're sick, Roderick, *sick*. I want a husband, not some automaton at the beck and call of his boss, the oh-so-trendily-named John, Paddy, Arcachon!'

The waiter, half-listening from the swing door beside the kitchen, scented a pause on both sides to gather forces and in that pause removed their plates. Despite the ferocity of the argument, they had finished their *soupe de poissons*. I must tell the chef, he thought. Myself, if I was so mad I wouldn't be able to eat nothing.

They sipped the wine in silence, avoiding each other's eyes until the next course arrived. Roderick resumed. 'It's true about Catriona and I'm sorry. But I didn't love her, I *fucked* her, the way other people take coke or booze – to get away from the pressures of the bloody office. I earn a small fortune so that you lot can enjoy the lifestyle *I* seem to exist solely to provide! *You* know how tough it is out there: you've just been fired because you couldn't stand the pace. I do stand the pace: but at a cost.'

'Yeah – the cost of our marriage.' Despite her self-pity, Jennifer felt a twinge of sympathy for Roderick, who was well into his stride.

'What do you want – a three-bed semi in the suburbs and a couple of weeks in Cornwall? *You* lower your demands and *I'll* be a tame husband. But since you insist on a big house, three holidays a year and two cars, *I* have to slave my guts out. I'd *love* to work an eight-hour day and catch the six eighteen from London Bridge. *Evening Standard* crossword as far as Lewisham; home in time for supper with the kids: great! Make up your mind – cosy suburban life or exciting London one? *Radio Times* or *Tatler*?'

'I was talking about *Catriona*. Your *mistress*. Don't change the subject.'

'Don't be melodramatic. A *mistress* is something else I couldn't afford. Catriona, to be brutal, was an occasional fuck. Nothing more.'

'How often?'

'I didn't count.' Roderick knew she was calming down and risked a lie. 'Twice – three times – at *most* four. It wasn't important.'

'I bet it was four.'

Roderick remembered how his wife had looked as he entered the bar earlier in the evening; her outward composure, her long legs as she preceded him to the revolving door, the envious glance of another man who must have been hoping for a pick-up. He decided it was time to placate her.

'Jenny, hey, listen sweetheart – where did all the love go? Remember how crazy we were about each other? We used to make love three times a *day* at weekends. Look, even if I agree on four, do *four* indifferent fucks make it worth your while calling in the divorce lawyer, the estate agent and the child therapist?'

'*Were* they indifferent?'

'Catriona may not have thought so. I did.'

He was winning her round. A glance at the waiter, then the empty bottle, brought a replacement. Their glasses were filled. Jennifer, in retreat, made a last foray for her pride's sake.

'I *hate* it when you talk about us all in terms of crisis management or problem solving strategy . . .'

'I wasn't aware that I did. I'll try not to.'

They ate in silence for a while, sipping their wine and enjoying the food. She recalled past evenings they had spent here, feet pushing against each other under the table, hands held. Once she had given him such an urgent erection that he'd been forced to go to the Gents to relieve it. She would have gone with him but for the risk that someone might interrupt them. Jennifer smiled to herself. I can handle my husband! Her cheeks and eyes glowing, she felt sexy and female and imagined that Roderick, to make up for his confession, would call her wonderful and say how lucky he was to have her. She pulled the zip of her jacket down a few inches and leaned forward so that he could see that she was naked underneath.

'Now, darling,' she cooed, 'tell me what bugs you about *me*?'

This was an unwise question, but Jenny was drunk. She had not expected him to return to the attack.

'I *hate* it when you show off to our friends, pretending to be posher than you are. I hate that affected voice you put on, especially down the phone. You sound ridiculous when you're trying to be grand. Leave that to your mother. It makes me wild when you buy stupid clothes with meaningless labels and flog them off a month later because they don't suit you.'

'Like what?'

'Like that ghastly pink outfit. It made you look like a thirteen-year-old. And *don't* tell me what it cost because I *don't want to know.*'

'I bought it out of *my* money.'

'Christ almighty, Jennifer, you *still* don't understand! There's no such thing as "*your*" money. It's *our* money: what you waste on clothes has to be made up by me to pay the mortgage and sodding Sainsburys!' He sighed and looked for the waiter. 'Do you want pudding? Coffee? Or shall we go?'

She knew she'd been wrong-footed. She *did* spend too much on clothes. Time to get out of the argument? Confrontation would escalate it. Capitulation was the answer . . . not too obviously. Simpering, Jennifer risked her little girl voice. 'I wan' *puddin*'!'

OK, he thought; argument over, now she wants to wind me down so we'll fuck tonight. Yes? No? 'It's after eleven. What about my mother?'

'She'll have gone to bed long ago. But first I wan' some *puddin*' . . .'

Roderick felt the familiar desire to be cruel; to ignore Jennifer's flirtatiousness and petulance; the nearest she could get to asking directly for a fuck. Should he escalate the argument? No, he concluded as her fork scraped round the plate for the last remaining flakes of *tarte tatin*; the truth was, domestic stability suited him. His wife was a powerfully intelligent, temperamental woman with her mother's overbearing manner but she had her father's acute brain. He didn't want a docile wife and he didn't really want an easy marriage; much less one that shoved all its problems under the carpet. Jennifer never sulked, was never disloyal – and she was still, after thirteen years, better in bed than Catriona. Time to make peace. In any case he could not humiliate his wife by abandoning her now, half-drunk and half-naked, to the hostility of a restaurant suddenly full of strangers. He looked up. 'Waiter!' He made a C with his finger and thumb for coffee.

'I've been a naughty boy, haven't I?' he said. 'And you've been a good girl?'

'I have, as a matter of fact. You may not believe me but it's true.'

Roderick extended a cautious hand from his lap onto the tablecloth. She covered it with hers.

'You are a *bastard*, you know. You and that bloody woman.'

'Not really. It was never serious. She just took the pressure off me at times. She's not half as good as you are in bed. I'm pissed off that she rang you. She knew she was losing me. Anyway she got fired today. Out of the building as fast as the security men could carry her. Feet never touched the ground. I'm not really a bastard, am I? Not deep down.'

'What are you deep down?'

'You know what I am deep down. *Randy.* Just like you. Drink up your coffee and let's go home . . .'

It was after eleven before Harriet and Oliver finally managed to get through to one another on the phone.

'Oh my darling . . .' he said, and she heard a long exhalation of relief.

'My *dearest* love . . .'

'What are you doing?'

'Talking to you.'

'You've been on the phone for *hours.*'

'So have you.'

'Sorry.'

'I forgive you. I always will.'

'I am a mighty hunter with an elk slung over my shoulder.' (How strange, he thought for a moment, that habit is so strong that I find myself using the private language of my marriage to Clarissa when I talk to Harriet! But she doesn't know and in time we'll invent our own private language.)

'You're *what*?'

'Saturday evening . . . treat for us.'

'Tell me?'

'*Carmen*. At the Coliseum. I've managed to get tickets.'

'Darling, how *wonderful*!'

As the day ended, Capels and Gaunts all over London were talking to their lovers, trying to jump across the gaps in their relationships. Julian, reunited with his Fonzi, was trying to find out what Fonzi had got up to in his waiter's afternoon between three-thirty and six-thirty, those dangerous hours when he hardly ever came home and about which he volunteered no information. Alone in her austere flat, gleaming hair pulled tightly back, a Tizio lamp shedding white light across the desk, with Gregorian plainchant to underline her concentration, Philomena tried to unpick the vulnerable clauses in a tenancy dispute. In the back of the cab ('*Thank you for not smoking*') Roderick slipped one hand inside his wife's electric-blue jacket to cradle her breast, his fingers teasing and cajoling. She threw her head back and he pressed his mouth against the deep vee of revealed flesh. The cabbie, glancing covertly at them through his rear-view mirror, thought, Never know, do you? I'd got those two down for married and look at them now! Jennifer cursed silently. Why did she always let her husband get round her? She wanted a *divorce*, didn't she? Well, *didn't* she?

And in France, in the shuttered bedroom of an old stone manor house in the Aveyron, Clarissa lay awake, music from the evening's rehearsal running through her head. Rain beat against the closed shutters making a soft and doleful sound. The two dogs had been allowed into the bedroom – a treat that was only permitted when Oliver was away – and lay like heraldic beasts on the floor beside the bed nearest the door. Clarissa was trying to read herself to sleep. The Japanese couple had gone. Because of the two concerts

174

coming up on Saturday and Sunday and Oliver's absence she had refused bookings for the weekend. For a moment she considered ringing her husband, but she knew it would only annoy him. They had, after all, talked earlier that evening.

'Do you miss *Master* then?' she asked out loud, and the dogs beat their tails sleepily against the polished floorboards.

'*Mummy* misses him.' Clarissa went on. 'Poor Mummy's *lonely* all by herself.'

She pulled open her bedside table drawer. Inside was a bundle of special letters from the twins; an album of family photographs – she dwelled lovingly on the one of herself and Oliver in Paris, on the Pont de la Concorde, taken by a street photographer on their tenth wedding anniversary: entwined, trusting, and so completely happy – her passport ('Her Britannic Majesty's Secretary of State Requests and requires . . .': *those* were the days!) and the cheque book for her private account with Coutts in the Strand. There was also a slim volume of sonnets that Oliver had given her the day they got engaged. She knew the inscription by heart but she turned to look at it again. His handwriting had changed over the years, becoming smaller and scrawlier, but it was still recognizably his. 'To Clarissa Sullivan, <u>my fiancée</u>, with pride and joy, forever yours, Oliver'. Hidden in the back was a scrap torn from a paper table napkin on which was written in blotchy ink, YES I DO LOVE YOU! It was signed meaningfully, ME.

She turned back to her book, a Dorothy Sayers mystery that she had read before, a long time ago. It failed to hold her attention. The top right-hand corner of the fly-leaf was inscribed in faded blue ink, 'Clarissa Sullivan, wishing her a very happy Christmas, from her Godfather' and below that, firmly underlined, 'Christmas 1951'. She would have been – let's see – fifteen then. It seemed so recent, yet it was nearly forty-four years ago. In another forty-four years she would be . . . best not to think about that. Dead, said a sepulchral voice in her head. '*Dead.*' Either that or over a hundred. Dead was probably better.

She opened the drawer on the other side of the bed.

Oliver's drawer. It wasn't private. They had no secrets from one another. Oliver wouldn't mind. It held a small black Bible with India paper that she had given him on their wedding day. She knew that inscription by heart as well. 'To my adored husband on our Wedding Day, August 23rd, 1959, I am yours eternally, Clarissa <u>Gaunt</u>'. He used to take that Bible with him whenever he went off on his missions. She had often unpacked it from his suitcase and slipped it back into its usual place. Sometimes she would find one of her own letters tucked inside, forwarded By Favour of Diplomatic Bag. She looked. No letters remained now. Also in the drawer was a collection of odd buttons and cuff-links, a few old visiting cards, an empty envelope, a theatre programme, couple of bills, discarded leather wallet that he had carried for more than ten years and presumably couldn't bear to throw away and right at the back of the drawer, wrapped in an old pair of socks, his pistol. The pistol was vaguely reassuring.

'I wish *Master* was here,' said Clarissa, and peered over the side of the bed. Poppy lifted her muzzle from the floor to look at her sleepily.

'Do you want to come and sleep with Mummy? Come on then. Onto the bed – hup! *Naughty* Mummy. *Bad* Pops.'

Clarissa buried her nose in glossy black fur and the dog whined softly.

The telephone rang, making them both jump. At this hour – one o'clock in the morning – it could only be Olly. How clever of him to know she was missing him at that very moment! She snatched up the receiver.

'Darling! Hallo!' she said eagerly.

'Clarissa?' said a voice she did not at once recognize. 'It's me. Mark. Mark Ellacott. Am I ringing too late? I had to wait until Belinda had gone to bed. What time is it there?'

'Mark!' she said. 'Good heavens! It's nearly one o'clock, but it couldn't matter less. I was wide awake. How *are* you? Olly said he'd seen you and you'd told him your bad news. I am most frightfully sorry. *Désolée*. I was going to write.'

'Yes, I'm afraid the outlook on the health front isn't good. Oliver and I had lunch on Tuesday. Took him to my club. No, the Garrick. Pretty decent grub. Not that I have much appetite these days. Yes, yes it is I'm afraid. Well, they can't say exactly. Not long. Oh, I'm bound to see you before then. Old times' sake and all that. Dear Clarry . . .'

'*Dear* Mark. I *say*, what rotten luck! *Gosh* I'm so sorry! How's Belinda taking it?'

'Bearing up. But that's not really why I'm ringing. I'm ringing about Oliver.'

'Why? Has something happened to him? Quick, quick!'

'Yes, but not what you think. He hasn't had an accident. Clarissa my dear, I've thought about this for days before deciding to tell you. I hope I'm not doing the wrong thing, but . . .'

As the taxi negotiated the one-way streets towards the tall Camberwell house; as Fonzi at last relented and slid into Julian's arms; as Philomena rubbed her itching eyes and folded away her papers; at that same moment, Oliver and Harriet were about to put down the telephone, smiling at their last exchange of endearments.

'There's something almost masochistic in the pleasure of ending this phone call!' Harriet said. 'But now we have to say goodbye until tomorrow.'

They hung up, glanced at their watches – midnight – and prepared to go to their separate beds.

Harriet did not hear her son and his wife return, nor did their noisy love-making disturb her. Marriages under threat of break-up often have a resurgence of sexual activity, as though biology were making a last stand; like societies on the verge of collapse undergoing violent riots, the last flicker of energy before burn-out.

Chapter Eleven

Harriet's first thought when she woke on Friday morning was, I have forgotten what George looked like! How could Oliver have superseded him so completely? I can remember George's clothes – his old jacket with leather elbow patches, still so moulded to the shape of his body after he died that I couldn't bear to touch it and had to get one of the boys to throw it away. I remember his hats and his brogues, deeply creased across the front where he rose on the balls of his feet for the next step. I could describe every single one of his shirts, including the short-sleeved ones he wore in a heat-wave (George would never have worn T-shirts) *but I cannot remember his face*.

She picked up the photograph that Jennifer had placed on the bedside table: George grinning with Christmas spirit, a green tissue-paper crown sliding rakishly down his fore-head. The camera has stolen his face, Harriet thought. The photographs I have stuck into albums over the years, from the earliest deckle-edged black and white ones down to the final polaroids, glossy and technicoloured, which fade any-way in a matter of years – those and this are all I have left; a long line of diminishing smiles before the last twisted grin, one liver-spotted hand raised to obstruct the camera. George was always a vain man.

He got so haggard towards the end that his cheek and jaw were grey and creased like a ploughed field, his skin bristly because he could no longer see well enough to shave fastidiously. In any case by then his hand shook so much that he couldn't hold the razor steady, yet he hated me to shave him. But his eyes: what colour were they? And his hair ... when did it turn from bushy brown to iron grey to white, in fact, did it ever go white at all?

She began to panic. Could George's still-hovering spirit somehow view her with Oliver – like a sort of aerial eavesdropper? She blushed and a heady wave of rising blood made the sweat prickle on her forehead as she remembered Oliver saying, 'Love is blood, Harriet.'

One floor down she heard a door open and a panicky childish wail, 'Mummy, come quick, there's blood on my pillow!'

Harriet sighed, got out of bed and tightened the dressing gown cord around her waist. 'Granny's coming, darling!' she called, and heard Jennifer's voice, thick with sleep and laziness: 'Granny will see to it, Emmy. There's a good girl. Sorry, Harriet. I'm *knackered*!'

'Sweetheart,' said Harriet soothingly as she entered the small room where the two girls slept in bunk beds. 'What is it? Show Granny!'

Emily was sitting in the top bunk, her face distraught, pointing to a tiny spot of blood on the pillow.

'My tooth's come out, Granny!' she said. 'Am I bleeding to death?'

'Of course not, darling. Let me see. So it has! What a funny face! I'll get a mirror and show you.'

'It hu-urts . . .' Emily wailed.

'No it doesn't,' Harriet said sensibly. 'Where is it? Have you got the tooth to put under your pillow for the tooth fairy?'

Emily brandished a pearl with a pointed pink root. 'Will the tooth fairy give me a pound like last time?'

A *pound*? Harriet thought. We used to get a silver sixpence.

'If you're a good brave girl . . . now come to the bathroom with Granny and you can admire the gap in the mirror and we'll wash your face.'

'Ganny?' said a voice from the lower bunk.

'Look Mandy, my tooth!' Emily announced.

Amanda scrambled out of bed squeaking, 'Toofy's out! Toofy's out!'

179

'Shush,' said Harriet. 'Your mummy's trying to get some *sleep*.'

Hugo stumbled into the bathroom to find his sister grimacing at her reflection.

'Is it t-t-time for school?' he asked anxiously. 'Must I g-g-get up?'

'It's ten to seven darling,' said Harriet. 'Not just yet. Shall we have a little read, all of us?'

Emily bounced up and down, blond hair flying like spaniels' ears. 'Yes! Yes! Read to us, Granny!'

'Will you make up a st-st-st – *story*?' Hugo pleaded. 'Out of your head?'

'Let's all go upstairs to my room, so we don't disturb Mummy and Daddy. We won't have a story though. I'll test your memories instead.'

She settled them in an expectant circle on her bed and began.

'Do you remember, when you came to see Granny at Easter—'

'Was Grandpa George there too?'

'Yes, that was the last time you all saw Grandpa George, just before he died. One morning Dodo showed you her garden? Now, think hard: what did she *grow* in it?'

'Flowers?' asked Emily.

Hugo's stutter was almost more than he could bear. His body heaved and his face struggled to eject the word. Finally he forced it out. '*Herbs!*' he said triumphantly.

'Hugo's right. She grows herbs. Who knows what they're for?'

'Put in the cooking!' said Emily.

'Making people better!' said Hugo.

Amanda snuggled closer to Harriet and put her thumb into her mouth.

'*Good*, children. You're both right. Plants and herbs are powerful things. They can make you better, or they can be bad for you – poisonous, even. Remember the deadly night-shade I warned you never to pick? And those mushrooms we looked up in a book? Those are bad plants.'

'Could they k-k-kill you?' Hugo said, round-eyed.

'If you ate an awful lot they might. But probably they'd

just give you a bad tummy-ache. Let's talk about good herbs. Emily's tooth came out this morning, didn't it?' Emily opened her mouth in an exaggerated yawn to reveal a shining pink cavern, sweet and fresh, with one crater. She pointed at it proudly.

'Bugger off!' said Hugo.

'Hugo! You are *not* to use words like that. I *mean* it. Don't ever let me hear you say that again. Promise? Good boy. No, I'm not cross. Now, there's a special plant medicine that's awfully good for sore mouths, called cloves. It doesn't taste nice – it's very bitter – but it works. When I was a little girl my mother used to give me oil of cloves till my pain had gone. Emmy, have you got toothache now, darling?'

Emily weighed the bitterness of cloves against her desire for sympathy. 'No,' she admitted grudgingly, annoyed at having the spotlight taken away from her tooth.

'Have you all heard of the *Narnia* books?' They shook their heads. 'Well, I brought one with me specially. If I leave it behind you can ask Mummy or Daddy to read you it. Daddy will remember because I read it out loud to him and Julian when *they* were little. Who can tell me what it's called?'

'*The L-L-Lion, the Witch and the W-W-Wardrobe,*' said Hugo.

'I knew too, *schtoopid*!' Emily scoffed.

When she was about their age, only more docile, unseen and unheard than these three, Harriet often used to read secretly in bed or crouched behind the drawing-room curtains. She identified with the four children in the *Narnia* books. Best of all she loved the thrilling fight when Aslan, the Lion, had led them into battle against the Witch. After their victory there had been a great feast and after the feast, Aslan had crowned the children. They were all enthroned and acclaimed: 'Long live King Peter! Long live Queen Susan!' She would whisper to herself, 'Long live Queen Harriet!' comforted by this affirmation of her worth.

At the time of the Queen's coronation in 1953 she and her parents had camped out in The Mall for two days to watch the new Elizabethan monarch – as the papers called her – pass by in her golden coach. Harriet remembered hearing the coronation service broadcast through loudspeakers from Westminster Abbey to the attentive crowds lining the London streets. When the culminating moment came and the Queen was crowned to a roar of acclamation, Harriet had been reminded of *The Lion, the Witch and the Wardrobe*. 'Long live the Queen!' the congregation in the Abbey and the crowds along The Mall had shouted; 'Long live the Queen!' to which her thirteen-year-old mind had echoed, 'Long live King Peter! Long live Queen Susan!' She meant, but dared not add, 'Long live Queen Harriet! Long live *me*!'

She opened the book and in a steady voice began: 'Once there were four children . . .'

Harriet read on until she heard Ulrike entering the girls' bedroom, calling their names.

'Off you go, mice!' she said. 'Give Granny a quick kiss. It's time for Ulrike to dress you both.' They tumbled down the stairs and she turned to Hugo.

'Granny, can I ask you s-s-something?' said Hugo, and he frowned. 'Except it's rather *private*.'

'What is it, darling?'

'Where is Grandpa George n-n-*now*?' he asked.

'You were at his funeral, all of you. Don't you remember what happened after that?' Harriet was disturbed by his question. Hugo was a strangely melancholy little boy. She did not want to make him morbid.

'The box he was in . . .' Hugo continued.

'. . . his coffin, yes?'

'. . . that *thing*. It went behind some curtains. Then they played music and we went outside and looked at the flowers people had sent him. But where did *Grandpa* go?'

In his earnestness, Harriet noted, he had quite forgotten to stutter. He was right to be earnest. It was a deeply serious question and she must do it justice. He had probably been brooding over it for months.

'Hugo darling, I'll explain if you really want me to. You know Granny always tells you the truth. But why are you asking?'

'Ulrike's friend Victoria says he's in heaven watching over me.'

'Do you like to think of him watching you?'

'Yes. No. I d-d-don't know. But is it *true*?'

'Victoria thinks it's true.'

'But do *you*, Granny?'

'Well, Hugo darling, not really. Do you *mind* very much that Grandpa George is dead?'

'Yes.'

'He was quite old. And you didn't see him very often.'

'I liked to know he was *there*. Granny 'Rissa's big and strong,' added Hugo fervently. 'She says she can frighten my ogres away.'

Harriet was surprised. She would not have expected this delicate boy to expose his demons to Clarissa.

'When we went to stay in France for our holidays,' Hugo went on, 'with Ulrike. We swam. And we met Victoria and she came back with us. Emily saw a snake. I didn't.' Harriet noticed that he had already acquired the male Capels' mode of speech: clipped, staccato, non-committal. George had had it, so did Roddy, and now Hugo as well. 'But Granny 'Rissa didn't let me be scared. Of the snake.'

'Did you like it in France?' she enquired, treacherously.

'Yes.' Unexpectedly, Hugo grinned. 'Grandpa Oliver and Granny 'Rissa are funny. They make the dogs walk on their back legs and they hold their front feet and then they say, look at Poppy dancing!'

Harriet wanted no more insights into Oliver's domestic life. She reverted to their previous conversation. 'Well, that must be funny. Now Hugo, will you stop worrying?'

His smile faded instantly and the scared look came back. '*You* won't die, will you Granny?'

'No darling, not for a long time.'

'Or Grandpa Olly?'

'Hugo, look at me. I don't think any of us are going to die soon. Probably not till you're grown up.'

'But Grandpa George *did* die. If he isn't there now, or in heaven, where is he?'

Harriet drew a deep sigh and gathered his thin body close. 'When he went behind the curtains, darling, the coffin went into some flames. And it burned. All of it.'

'With Grandpa George inside as well?'

'Yes, Hugo, Grandpa George as well.'

Hugo started to hiccup and shudder and clutched his arms tightly round her. Together, Harriet and her grandson cried for the man they had lost.

When Ulrike had been given the day's instructions, Jennifer – 'as a *very special treat*' – took the children to school herself. After breakfast Harriet had described the conversation with Hugo, indicating that he might want to ask his mother a few questions. Jennifer had herded the three of them into the car and drove off with Hugo next to her in the front.

Harriet lingered at the kitchen table over a third cup of coffee, absent-mindedly watching Ulrike load the washing machine.

'Did you have a nice time with your friend last night?' she asked.

The girl raised one elbow to push a long blonde strand of hair from her forehead. 'Yes, very nice,' she said. 'But I'm tired this morning.'

'You *do* seem to work very hard . . .' Harriet said, and immediately regretted it, for Ulrike said with extraordinary vehemence, 'Do you know, Mrs Capel, how many hours au pair girls are supposed to work in this country?'

'No . . .' Harriet answered. 'I thought it was a matter to be decided between individuals.'

'An au pair girl must not do more than five hours child-care or housework a day. She must have also her weekends free, and as well three or four evenings a week. And she must be told by her employer where she can do English lessons to improve her knowledge of the language. Jennifer does not give me any of these things. I am her nanny and cook and cleaner and baby-sitter. For this I earn forty pounds a week. It is not fair!'

'Jennifer works very hard . . .' Harriet said soothingly.

'So do I!' Ulrike replied. 'I do it only for the children, because they are so nice and sweet.'

Harriet heard the unspoken accusation, and responded to that. 'They are dear children,' she soothed, 'and very very fond of you. It is difficult for career women nowadays, who have a job as well as a young family. And

Jenny is *trying* to get another nanny.'

'She must try harder. She is saving money by having only me. But I am not trained to look after little children.'

'Perhaps not, but you do it beautifully.' Harriet soothed.

'Their mummy should do it, especially now she is at home all day. In Sweden where I come from, every mother has *two years* off, paid by the state and her employer, after her baby is born to her.'

'Yes, well, your country is much more advanced than we are in these matters.'

'I do not want to leave those children. I love them and they are very loving with me. But I am really tired and I have only been here three months. I came at the beginning of July because the family were going to France for their holidays and I had never been to France. I am to stay nearly one year more, I promised Jennifer, but I cannot. My friend Victoria, who I met in France – Jennifer fixed up for her an au pair job in London – *she* gets more money and does not have so long hours.'

'Do you want me to have a word with Jennifer?'

'No, thank you very much. And now I must go upstairs, please excuse me . . .'

Harriet thought, I don't blame her, poor girl. It isn't physical tiredness she's suffering from – a strong healthy nineteen-year-old can cope with children and housework. It's carrying the burden of the children's unhappiness and their parents' conflict that is tiring. Hugo needs his mother's attention, yet both parents are too self-absorbed to notice his problems so this girl from a Swedish village tries to compensate for their neglect.

I dare not stir things up by saying anything to Roddy, while as for *Jenny* . . . She felt cowardly for keeping silent. Harriet had been brought up to believe, and did believe, that family life can only flourish if men and children come first. Women have to be resigned to this and accept second place. The security of children and the domestic comfort of men depends on the docility of women. What went wrong was that the strength such docility demands was mistaken for weakness; women's sacrifice was read as women's helplessness, and women were taken for

185

granted rather than being treasured above rubies.

Every household needs one person who will be an invariable fount of tenderness, competence, sympathy, observation. Women have to work hardest, demand least, get up first, eat last, care for others, and let men have the last word. Only then can everyone else thrive. This Angel in the House – in Virginia Woolf's dismissive phrase – need not be the wife and mother. Maiden aunt, nanny, older sister, servant, or grandmother . . . any of these will do. It can even be a man, though this rarely happens. Whatever the *Guardian* may say, Harriet reflected, I have never come across such self-effacement in a male.

Throughout my marriage *I* was the self-sacrificing woman, with Dodo's support and advice. Ulrike, rather than Jennifer, plays that role in this family; but is Jennifer any happier as a result? She seems sullenly dissatisfied. What compensations has she? A foothold in the world of work – though not, apparently, a very steady one – but at least she earns her own money, which gives her some claim to equality with Roddy. She certainly doesn't behave like his chattel. She wears beautiful clothes and moves through life as an autonomous adult. But does all this make her *happy*?

Duty, not happiness, was George's goal in life, Harriet decided, and after thirty-seven years it has become mine too. What chance is there, after such a long indoctrination, that I can allow myself to be happy with Oliver at everyone else's expense? She tidied away her cup and saucer and went up to the bathroom. Is it just an imagined happiness we'll both get from this encounter? She sighed, shrugged, and spread toothpaste along the brush.

Oliver and Harriet had both arranged to have lunch with their children but planned to meet first at Mark's flat, at eleven. On her way Harriet stopped at the Polish delicatessen for fresh milk. On impulse she pointed to a tray of dark sweet-smelling biscuits. The woman serving her beamed.

'These I bake myself,' she said. 'Rye flour and black sugar. Polish recipe. Very old. Very good.'

Moments later Harriet rang the intercom doorbell and heard Oliver's eager voice.

'Yes?'

'It's me.'

'Come *up.*'

He was standing in the hallway of the flat as she came up the stairs. He closed the door behind them and pulled her into his arms. 'Oh my darling . . . a whole evening wasted, when we could have spent it together!'

They kissed wholeheartedly, the way new lovers kiss, mouth into mouth, melding bodies that rejoin like liquid. Harriet thought, we have less than three days left. By Sunday evening I have promised to be back home with Dodo and on Monday morning Oliver is booked on Eurostar. Are we to reverse the whole course of our lives in the next three days?

'Why are you frowning?' he asked.

'There is still so much to talk about.'

'How we tell them. When we tell them. What we do next. Do I go over to France and tell Clarissa face to face? I think I must. How long do I stay? Do I clear out my stuff immediately? Join you in Dorset, or find somewhere else to stay while things settle down? My darling – I know. All this we need to discuss. But the big decision is made. We shall be together for the rest of our lives.'

'Will we, Oliver? I am frightened both ways. Frightened of being without you; frightened of the chaos that will follow if we decide to be together. I have never done anything so destructive before.'

'My love . . . have you had a sleepless night? It looks like it.'

'Almost, yes.'

He drew her to the sofa and said, 'Never mind coffee. Listen to me, Harriet. I told you: the big decision is made. I am coming to live with you in a few weeks' time; in less than a month. I shall tell my wife and my lawyers and the bank that I want a divorce. I have already thought it through. I can't anticipate what Clarissa will do but her father left her quite a bit of money; I shall make her an allowance; she will not go short. She will be upset, of course, but she'll have to come to terms with it. She will. She's tough – a survivor. I don't think she'll want to live in

England; she'll stay in France, where she has her friends, her son, a life.

'I will be with you and Dodo, a suitcase in each hand, by the end of October at the latest. I promise. Look at me: *I promise*. Does that put your mind at rest? Kiss me. My wonderful Harriet. This is not a game, not a fantasy, it is a certainty. I am talking about the rest of our lives. I'm giving Jenny lunch today: do you want me to start preparing the ground?'

'*No!*' Harriet said, remembering the morning's conversation with Hugo.

'All right – don't look so anxious – I will do whatever you want. Perhaps it's best if we tell them together. On Sunday evening, do you think, when the birthday lunch is over? Jenny and Roderick, Philly and your Julian – they'll all be there. That's our opportunity.'

'*No!*' Harriet said, and she began to weep. 'Oliver – it's an impossible situation. I love you. I love them. I love those three little ones. How can we chuck a firecracker into their lives?'

'*Small explosion in Camberwell: none dead.*' he said. 'Oh darling . . . smile at me, please smile.'

She lowered her head mutely, thinking, I cannot persuade him because I cannot persuade *myself*. After a while he said,

'Come to bed.'

Harriet lifted a reddened distraught face. 'I can't, Oliver. Not now. I'm a coward. I don't know if I can face the consequences of loving you. How come *you* are so brave and resolute?'

'I will go and make coffee while you tidy yourself up. And then I will tell you a story. It is a secret. I have never told anyone before.'

He stood up and extended both hands. Harriet took them and he pulled her to her feet. He kissed her face gently. 'Bathroom,' he said.

Oliver prepared to open a door in his memory which he deliberately and habitually kept shut. It was true that he had never hitherto disclosed this story to anyone; but that did not mean no-one knew. He put the kettle on and measured four large spoonfuls of coffee into an inverted triangular filter.

He had met Nina in 1954, when he was an energetic and impatient virgin of nineteen and she – it had seemed to him then – a middle-aged woman of thirty-four. She was therefore almost exactly the same age as his twin daughters now. He winced at this belated realization of her youth. By this time he had already completed the twelve-week immersion course in Russian that the Army organized for young officers who showed linguistic promise. Passing out top, it was suggested that he might take further lessons, perhaps in conversation and Russian history, if he wanted to use it as a professional qualification. He would be well advised to do so; fluent Russian speakers were few and far between in the Fifties, many fewer than were needed. The Army instructor clenched his lips and arched his eyebrows to indicate name-less career opportunities, excitement and mystery.

Entirely by chance, reading the *New Statesman* that week — not a magazine he normally took — Oliver had scanned the classified advertisements at the back. A single insertion leapt out at him: 'Native Russian speaker living W. London offers conversation lessons. Small classes 2/6d an hour; individual tuition, 4/-.' On impulse he rang the number and a deep contralto voice, absurdly foreign, answered.

'I want to enquire about Russian conversation lessons,' Oliver said.

She replied in liquid Russian, asking him what standard he had reached, how long he had studied, what was his objective. Haltingly, he told her, intermediate; twelve weeks; pleasure, and after that professional competence.

'You want class or individual tuition?'

His decision was instantaneous. He would not share the rolling flow of that glorious voice with anyone. 'Individual,' said Oliver.

She rented a poky room in North Acton, sharing the bath-room with her son and two other lodgers. There was linoleum on the floor, a primitive Ascot to supply hot water and a gas fire that devoured shillings in its rapacious (and surely tampered with) meter, returning them as a series of tiny blue flames that hissed and popped sullenly in front of

189

the blocked-up fireplace. Oliver had never known anyone live in such humiliating discomfort. Twice a week he travelled by Underground along the Central Line to pay four shillings for a Russian lesson. She gave good value for money. After the first month he had learned her life history. By then they were already lovers.

Her parents had fled a few years after the Revolution, taking the infant Nina and her older sister by long risky stages down to the Black Sea, escaping from there across to Turkey, and finally coming to rest in London. The four of them lodged in twenty-three different places in the nineteen years after fleeing Kiev. They suffered the émigré descent through layers of increasingly remote family and friends until in the end they had to rely on the kindness and eventually endure the hostility of strangers.

When she was twenty, Nina had been raped by one such stranger, their then-landlord. For months he had fumbled at Nina and her sister on the stairs, his hands clutching at their soft breasts and haunches, exploiting their terror of saying anything lest they should be forced to move on yet again. The rape happened at the outbreak of the war and her parents, desperate to secure a foothold in England and protect themselves against possible internment, persuaded Nina that it was best to marry the squat, bullying landlord more than twice her age, and to bear his child. The marriage meant that she, though not the rest of her family, acquired British nationality.

As soon as war ended she left her husband, taking with her the child – a boy now five years old. She was twenty-five; she had nothing to sell except her beautiful, fluent, *ancien-régime* Russian tongue and the universal female skills of cleaning, mending, dressmaking, and childcare. On these she survived. She refused to return to her husband (which meant, her parents as well) and he refused her a divorce. Nine years later, Nina existed in limbo, and Oliver came to understand that limbo was worse than hell. It was a nothingness.

'She was the most tragic and the most interesting person I had ever met,' he told Harriet. 'Nothing could have been more romantic. Of course, I adored her. We spent the afternoons together until her son got home from school. He was a lout, took after his father, had nothing of her . . .' Nothing, he remembered, except her delicate Russian eyes – pale as grey glass and haunted. Nina taught Oliver to speak her own marvellous, flexible, cultured Russian, read Pushkin's poetry out loud to him and urged him to discover Turgenev and Chekhov for himself: those melancholy Russians whose voices echoed her own.

'How long did it go on?' Harriet asked, curiosity overcoming the jealousy that stabbed her, forty years after the events he was retelling.

'Six months.'

'Is that all? You make it sound like years!'

'It would have been – should have been. But I was only just twenty, and about to go up to Oxford. I couldn't have lived a half and half life, weekdays in college, weekends with her, that great boy hanging around, spying on us. Besides, she was still married and her husband refused to divorce her. I couldn't have let my parents meet her. I was twenty. It was more than I could cope with. Soon her overpowering love for me became oppressive. I think I was the only good and happy thing in her life. She wanted us to stay together for ever, somehow, she didn't care how.'

'What happened?'

'I loved her, we made love hundreds of times, I became a man under her hands, I learned fluent Russian, I left her, went up to Oxford, became an undergraduate, wrote her a letter, thanked her, said sorry and goodbye. So she killed herself.'

Harriet could not suppress a gasp of horror.

'*Love is blood*, Harriet. You think it's just a turn of phrase? The first I knew of it was a phone call from her husband. The son had come home from school – it was a Thursday – to find his mother behind a locked door with her throat cut.'

How often Oliver had imagined that single fierce slash with the knife sharpened for that purpose.

'I was lucky; the college and my tutor extricated me without it getting into the newspapers. They paid off the boy. I never heard from him again. I don't even know where Nina is buried; or if they buried her at all.

191

Cremated, probably. I never saw her body, but the image of her white throat . . . slack, raw, bubbling . . . love is blood, Harriet. Believe me, I know.

'After that Clarissa fell in love with me and uttered melodramatic schoolgirl threats about what she'd do if I ever left her. I couldn't risk it. Perhaps if I'd loved someone else the way I loved Nina, but I never let myself. Never again. Until you.'

'Yet you're prepared to risk leaving Clarissa now, when she's nearly sixty years old?'

'Odd thing, people are much more likely to commit suicide when they're young. Clarissa won't kill herself: never would have done, but how was I to know that?'

Harriet thinks, does he fear that I will? Oliver's face is ashen and she sees that he is not thinking of her, but of a young woman in lonely exile from a country she had never known with a husband she had never loved, who died forty years ago. It is her turn to hold and comfort him.

Chapter Twelve

Julian was already waiting when Harriet arrived at the restaurant. She had assumed that the journey from Pimlico to Tower Bridge would involve a quick scenic ride along the Embankment. It could hardly take more than a quarter of an hour. She had therefore allowed a prudent twenty minutes and prudent again (a mother's needs always come second), had insisted on leaving Mark's flat at twelve-thirty. She and Oliver had parted on the pavement, where he flagged down a black cab for her before catching another to take him to his club to give his daughter lunch.

Harriet's taxi sat clogged in a solid line of traffic crawling past the Tate Gallery, the Houses of Parliament, the earthworks by Westminster tube station and all points east through the City, round the massy pile of the Tower of London to the far side of Tower Bridge. She turned her attention away from Oliver and his harrowing tale of the young Russian woman's life and death towards the two problems that should have been in the forefront of her mind. Hugo was the first; the feud the second. Whatever might happen between herself and Oliver (and she still had no idea how their future would resolve itself), for the children's sake, the quarrel must be repaired.

It had occurred to her, brilliantly, after her conversation with Hugo that the member of the family whom he seemed most to resemble was not Roderick but Julian. Why not therefore consult her son about this sensitive, fearful boy? After that – having, as she hoped, softened him up – she could talk to Julian about ending the feud. Since he had been the person insulted, he should be the first to decide whether the time had come to forgive and lay the cruel words to rest.

The Blueprint Café was spacious and cool. Along one wall, vast picture windows looked out across the river traffic of the Thames. They had opened a museum on the ground floor of the building and the restaurant too had something of the self-conscious air of a museum. It felt as though designed to be looked at. These, it proclaimed, are the Nineties and this is the spirit of the times. The same sense of muted self-regard extended to the people who served or sat at impeccable tables devoted to Nineties food. Waiters and diners were almost indistinguishable. True, the waiters wore long white aprons over spotless T-shirts with inky-black trousers; yet this austere uniform did not seem like the badge of their trade but more like some ineffably elegant rig that each individual had chosen to emphasize their smooth-faced, reverent calm.

Julian rose from the chair to greet her and they kissed like social acquaintances, since she dared not hug him in public. He smelled of something entirely in keeping with the setting; faint, herbal, monastic. She touched her lips briefly to each close-shaven cheek.

'I'm sorry I'm late. London traffic . . . I can't get used to it. I thought there must be a march or demonstration or something.'

'Traffic in central London moves at roughly eight miles an hour,' he told her. 'Demos were the Eighties. Not now.'

A beautiful young man, raven-haired and black-eyed, came and stood beside their table with raised eyebrows.

'Will you have something to drink while you study the menu?' he enquired.

'Jules?' asked his mother.

'A glass of white wine for me. House.'

'I'll have the same,' Harriet said, and smiled at the impassive young man. He sketched a faint bow and an infinitesimal smile in return.

Mother and son bent their heads to look at the menu. It was indeed, as Julian had warned, expensive. Harriet was aghast at the vertiginous prices. Lunch would cost nearly a

194

hundred pounds. She and Dodo could eat for three weeks for a hundred pounds. She kept her head down and said nothing.

'Cheers,' said Julian, tipping a tall, pale glass towards her.

'Cheers my darling,' she said. 'Goodness, it all looks delicious!'

'They've got good Australian and New Zealand wines here.'

'The only wine I know anything at all about is Burgundy, because of Daddy. He'd have had a fit at the thought of drinking *Australian* wine.'

Mother and son grinned at each other.

'Convicts . . .' murmured Julian.

'*Common prostitutes* . . .' said Harriet.

'God, he could be appalling at times! Poor old Pa.'

'Will you choose a bottle?' Harriet asked. 'Or get the waiter to suggest something.'

'I think I could find us an acceptable wine,' Julian assured her silkily. 'What sort of price? Ten? Twenty? Thirty?'

'Is there anything nice under twenty?' she said, studiously non-committal. 'Round about that price range?'

'Not a lot,' he said. 'But don't worry. I know their list. I'll find us something drinkable.'

All this, Harriet understood very well, was merely preliminary skirmishing. He was assessing her generosity and aplomb while displaying his own expertise. She must defer to his urban sophistication in this alien environment. She might claim maternal privileges but should not act like an ignoramus. She knew she walked a tightrope and that at the slightest wobble, her difficult son would clam up.

Their first course arrived, exquisitely arranged, exquisite-tasting. Harriet praised it; knew better than to add salt. The waiter proffered the wine bottle. Julian tasted; approved; smiled; nodded. Their glasses were filled to halfway. *Now*, she thought.

'I talked to Hugo this morning, on his own, before Jennifer was up. Roddy had already gone to work. He leaves the house around half past six every morning.' No comment. Julian was after all currently unemployed.

'I think he's a very susceptible little boy, if you know what I mean. And already quite *deep*. He had obviously

195

been worrying a lot about your father . . . About where he had *gone*. It hadn't occurred to me before to explain about cremation.'

'And have you now?'

'Yes,' Harriet said. 'Poor little Hugo. He cried. We both did.'

'What a touching scene!' said Julian; but Harriet, knowing very well that he was being sarcastic only to protect himself from a public display of emotion, let it pass.

'You know Hugo stutters quite badly? I don't think Jennifer or Roddy have done anything about it yet. But childhood stuttering can be cured. It's much harder if you wait until they're grown up. I don't know whether to suggest they take him to a speech therapist, or . . . darling what I'm trying to say, if you would stop glaring at me like that, is that perhaps *you* could talk to him. Take a bit of trouble over him.'

Julian took a deep draught of wine, held it in his mouth for a moment, then swallowed. He looked directly into his mother's eyes.

'The only thing wrong with Hugo — if *wrong* is the word — is that he's queer. Gay. Hu-go is a ho-mo-sex-ual. *He* may not know it yet, but I spotted it long ago.'

Harriet flinched, and instantly concealed the flinch. Careful now. 'Darling, do you think so?' (*Not* 'poor little Hugo'.) 'How do you know?'

'Takes one to know one,' said Julian.

(Laugh? Smile? How to react?) 'Don't be flippant, Julian. I'm asking your advice.'

'Hugo is "deep" and "sensitive" and altogether different, and possibly even stutters as well, because he's gay. And while the implications of this may not dawn upon him for another couple of years, he *senses* that he's different. Also, being a beautiful child, he may have been approached already. *Pederasts —*' he put a savage emphasis on the word — '*pederasts* have an unerring instinct. This will have troubled him and, given Hugo's parents, he probably hasn't told anyone about it. Plenty there to worry a small boy, without having to try and work out where his grandfather's body has gone, don't you think?'

The waiter arrived with their next course and Julian fell silent. Their glasses were topped up, again only as far as the halfway mark. They each took a sip; then a mouthful of food. I will not change the subject now, Harriet thought. This is my only chance. The silence prolonged itself. All around, noise from the other tables was increasing.

'Terrible, wasn't it, those bombs on the Paris Metro yesterday . . .' a young woman said shrilly. 'Mad Algerians. Or was it the Muslims?'

'No difference really, is there?' said her languid companion.

'Seen the new MGF they launched today?' a voice from another table asked.

'Nice-looking motor. Not a patch on the classic MG. Cashing in on nostalgia . . .'

'Only give the IRA ideas . . .'

'. . . but there's a *cease*-fire . . .'

Still his mother held her peace.

'There isn't a lot they *can* do,' Julian said at last. 'Not send him to a single-sex public school, where he'll get buggered by the masters. On the other hand he may be lucky and find someone his own age to initiate him. Or to the Boy Scouts. But he'll find out for himself soon enough.' Another pause. Stoically, Harriet ate on. Silence is the hardest thing. 'Are you suggesting that *I* should talk to him?'

At last! His mother raised her head.

'Not about being gay, Julian. I think it may still be a bit too soon for that. But if you were to *befriend* him; make a point of seeing him, taking him to things on his own – Roddy doesn't have the time – I think *that* would be a very good idea.'

'All right. I will. And when Fonzi's free, Fonzi will come with us. That a problem?'

'Not in the least.'

'Right. I promise, then. How d'you like the food?'

'I think it's *absolutely wonderful*,' Harriet said with relief.

Conversation flowed more easily after this. She told Julian she was going to the Coliseum to see the Jonathan Miller production of *Carmen*, and he was impressed. He told her he'd got an interview coming up, for freelance

197

work. He'd sent some sample book reviews to *Time Out* and they'd liked them. Harriet was impressed. He confided – made expansive by the wine, the setting, and their unaccustomed ease together – that he had started writing a novel. It was about a sex tourist in Thailand, he said. A metaphor for modern sleaze.

'Is that fair?' she asked, paying him the compliment of taking his view of the world seriously, although it was so much more bitter than her own. '*Are* most people sleazy? Don't you think it's just the media that makes them seem so? Can you really equate the sale and corruption of small boys with the sex-lives of ordinary people?'

'Buying and buggering little brown children isn't about *sex*, Mother,' he said vehemently. 'It's about power, it's about consumption, about novelty. They do it because they can. A fat ugly German or Dutchman or Australian – *or Brit* – feels better about his own grossness because he has the power to indulge his fantasies on the body of a helpless, if alas far from innocent, child.'

'But are people's sexual relationships normally based on power? Aren't they based on love? It is possible that just a few of these men – not all of whom can be fat – may *love* these children?'

'The love is used as an excuse to justify the power, don't you think? How often do you come across a relationship between equals? One loves, the other *is* loved. One stays out of love; but both are trapped. One pays, the other is bought. A nine-year-old Burmese or Thai or Vietnamese kid doesn't have much equality or any say in the matter.' He started to outline the plot of his novel.

The sleek olive-skinned waiter materialized beside them.

'Would you like to see the dessert menu?' he asked. Julian flashed him a conspiratorial smile and Harriet thought – *no, darling, don't!* He turned to her.

'Mother?'

'No, you say. I'll have whatever you have.'

'I could manage a light pudding,' he said. They ordered two puddings; two coffees. Harriet braced herself. That would add another twenty quid to the bill. Was this the right moment to broach the subject of the feud?

Oliver, giving his daughter Jennifer lunch at his club – both relishing the clichéd situation – watched as a club servant escorted her to his table in the Morning Room and a number of heads turned surreptitiously to follow her progress. Jenny had her mother's legs – always Clarissa's best feature – but she moved with a classy confidence that showed them off better than Clarissa's schoolgirlish bounce. She beamed as he stood up and kissed him warmly.

'Get a whiff of *that*! Go on, Daddy: inhale ... Chanel No.5. You *gave* me it!'

'What'll you have to drink?' her father asked, steering her towards the drinks trolley to one side of the marble-columned ground floor.

'Do I look all right? Do you credit?'

'Still fishing for compliments!' he grinned. 'My dear Jennifer, you look elegant enough to shatter a sherry glass at thirty paces. You make an old man very proud. All right? Now then, club claret? Or would you prefer white?'

When Jenny had left him – more bounce than glide after one glass of white wine, three of red, and a final glass of a particularly delicious Sauternes – Oliver went upstairs to ring Clarissa. Best to get his account of the lunch over and done with now; then he need not phone her later but could devote the entire afternoon and evening to Harriet.

Jennifer's high heels clicked across the splendid marble floor of the Reform Club on her way to the Ladies Room before heading home. She had been counting on this lunch to provide sympathy for her predicament, righteous paternal indignation about Thorensen and Markworth, soothing male advice about how to handle her husband, in short: a morale-boost. Instead she had received a lecture about being spoiled and irresponsible. God! she said to herself, what I need's a *lover*! Roll on lunch with Timothy!

From the phone beside his narrow single bed Oliver dialled his home number and heard his wife's patrician Anglo-French.

''*Allo, oui*? Maison des Glycines.'

'Clarissa,' said Oliver. 'It's me. How are things?'

'Oh, fine. I'm fine. You?'

'Rehearsals going well?'

'Fine. All set for tomorrow evening.'

'How many performances are you doing, remind me?'

'There were to have been two – one on Saturday and another on Sunday – but we decided we might not get enough of an audience for both, so now it's just tomorrow evening's one.'

'Not disappointed, are you?'

'*Au contraire,* it's quite handy. Gives me a free day. How about you, Oliver? What have you been up to?'

'Just had a splendid lunch with Jennifer . . .'

'With *Jennifer*? How nice. *Do* tell.'

Oliver, intent on a fast getaway, failed to notice her uncharacteristically cryptic replies or the reserve in her voice. 'We met here – at the club – at one. She came to the Morning Room first for a drink.'

'How did she *look*?'

'Credit to us all. Madly elegant. Got your legs. Turned every head in the saloon . . .'

'The *what*?'

'Saloon, Clarissa. You know: that downstairs bit where you get drinks from the trolley.'

Clarissa, satisfied that she had not caught him out, murmured assent.

'Then we went into the Coffee Room for lunch.'

'Anyone there we know?'

'Nope. Oh, apart from poor old Perry Horsfall. Hangs around the place nowadays. Club bore. Steered her well away from *him*.'

'What did you have to eat?'

'Usual sort of grub. Dish of the day, I think. Wine was good. Drinks committee have improved standards no end. Thoroughly decent Bordeaux, less than ten quid a bottle.'

'Ten *pounds*! That's about eighty francs! You should have gone for the house red. Never mind: tell me what Jenny said. I'm *extremely* concerned about her.'

'We *did* drink the house red, Clarissa. Please stop bullying me and listen.'

Oliver detected a faint snort but she did not interrupt.

'Appears that Jenny isn't happy about the way things are

200

going with her and Roderick. It all sounds pretty normal to me, but she seems to think she's unhappily married. She's muttering about a divorce – not very convincingly, but still. By a piece of bad timing she's also just lost her job.'

'*Don't* say she's been *sacked*?'

'I think they call it "voluntary redundancy" these days and pay you to go away but yes – that's more or less it. Any rate her self-confidence has been shaken. I think it would be best if *you* talked to her. Put a bit of backbone into her. Sake of the children, look to the future, no fun being divorced – *woman's* point of view.'

'It doesn't sound as though *you* were much help, poor little Jenny.'

'*Poor little Jenny* is thirty-three years old and the mother of three children, Clarissa. Don't pander to her or let her feel sorry for herself. Roderick's not a bad husband and he works like a dog for them all. She mustn't have unreasonable expectations. That women's lib rubbish has put ideas into her head. She thinks he ought to treat her like an equal, share the housework, all that sort of nonsense. Wants to know why he doesn't stack the dishwasher in the evenings or put the infants to bed.' Clarissa, as he knew very well, would have none of this.

'That's absurd! When he's been at the bank all day long. Can't be expected to come home and put on an *apron*.'

'Quite. You tell her that. Remind her of her responsibilities.'

'*Responsibilities!* That's a bit rich, Oliver!'

This was disconcerting, but Oliver had no time now to investigate what she meant by it. He turned instead to those perennial peacemakers, the dogs.

'How's Pops? And old Mindy? Keeping an eye on you? Been walkies yet today?'

'It's a bit wet here. Very misty first thing. Took them out early and went through the woods. Picked a whole basketful of gorgeous mushrooms. *Cèpes, girolles*, I even found a few *trompettes-des-morts*. Dogs came home sopping. Been drying out in front of the boiler ever since. Oh look, here's Mindy! *Come* on then, old girl. There's a good dog! *Who* loves her Mummy then? *Yes! Mindy* does!'

Oliver heard harrumphing sounds as Clarissa rubbed her nose against the old dog's fur and Mindy growled with pleasure.

'Must go then. Oh, Clarissa!' he called out down the phone. '. . .There is one other thing. Are you still there?'

'I'm here,' she said.

'Listen, I don't want you to get cross. It's about the feud.'

He heard an undog-like snort. How well he knew the expression that accompanied it. Clarissa's chin would go up, her mouth tighten, eyes narrow, creating an aggressive bulldog front that masked her dislike of confrontation and exposure. If he persisted she might use her other weapon and burst into noisy sobs. Regardless, Oliver persisted. 'It's thirteen years ago now, all that business. Time it was over and forgotten. *I* know, I know: there was wrong on both sides. I'm not arguing that. But old Capel is dead, meanwhile the children are growing up – Hugo'll be ten on Saturday – yes I've got your present for him. Clarissa *will* you shut up for a moment and *listen*. It's high time to forgive and forget. Clarissa? Are you there? Don't you agree?'

'Forgive and forget *what*?'

'Now you are being ridiculous. It's the Sullivan pride. I've seen it too often. "Never say sorry". I'm not *asking* you to say sorry; I'm only saying all that ancient history should be laid to rest. Clarissa? I've said my bit. You talk it over with Jennifer. Maybe *she* can make you see sense. I give up.'

Their conversation ended without any of the ritual questions and cooing endearments by which Clarissa usually had to be wound down and detached from the instrument.

'Well, if you're going to be like *that*,' she said, 'it's probably better to ring off and let you cool your heels.'

'Fine by me,' said Oliver. 'Don't forget to talk to Jenny. I'll give you a call tomorrow,' he added, 'when we've both calmed down. Tell you how Hugo liked his present. Goodbye, Clarissa.'

He glanced across the park at Big Ben. Half past three. They had hoped to be together by half past three. He looked at his face in the glass above the chest of drawers, and saw that anger had made him high-coloured. He changed into a

202

clean shirt, patted cologne on his cheeks – no time to shave again – and set off for Pimlico.

At the same moment Harriet, her impatience perfectly concealed, had at last persuaded the beautiful waiter to bring the bill. They were almost the only people left in the restaurant. Presumably all the other diners had jobs or offices to return to. One other table in the corner was still occupied. She paid in cash, counting out eight tenners and adding ten per cent for a tip. Ninety pounds!

Julian noticed. 'It's usually twelve and a half per cent,' he said. 'Some people give fifteen.'

'Daddy never gave more than ten per cent,' she said, 'and sixpence to taxi drivers. That never changed, no matter how much fares went up. Once I remember a chap actually handed it back. "If you're that hard up, guv, you need it more than I do." Daddy took it without a qualm.'

'He would!' Julian agreed.

The waiter glided back to stand beside them, proffering the change she had left. She smiled up at him.

'No no – that's for you,' she said. 'It was a delicious lunch. Thank you.'

'Mother,' Julian said: 'this is Alfonso Aurelio. Fonzi – meet my mother, Harriet Capel. At long last.'

Should I have guessed? Harriet asked herself. How could I have known? The three of them had left the Blueprint Café and crossed to a nearby restaurant – rustic Tuscan this time – where she ordered coffee and made her escape to the Ladies. She rinsed her face with cold water, let the tap run over her wrists – an old trick, the theory being that cold blood then coursed all round the body, cooling the rest of you – and combed her hair ineffectually. She tucked a few strands back into the French pleat. He should have told me! She stood back from the mirror to survey her image. Next to Fonzi's startling saturnine beauty she paled into insignificance, but so would most people. She looked around for a telephone to warn Oliver she would be late – Mark's number could presumably be had from Directory Enquiries – but seeing none, went back to the table where the two young men awaited her.

'My mother wants me to make a point of looking after my

203

nephew Hugo; which will no doubt mean that in due course I shall have to explain to him about being gay,' Julian said to Fonzi when she had sat down. 'He is only nine now and she thinks he's a bit young. When would you tell him? And what would you say?'

'Not just yet, but soon,' said Fonzi, 'I would tell him that he is in a special group of one or two in every ten people who will love stronger and feel more and suffer more than ordinary people. He is lucky. His life will not be easy but it will not ever be boring.'

'I think he already finds life more difficult,' Harriet said, addressing herself directly to Fonzi.

'I should like to meet him,' Fonzi said, 'but Julian is afraid to introduce me to his brother.'

'I'm not afraid!' Julian expostulated. 'I just . . .'

'Just what, darling?' Harriet asked. 'Whether or not you are lucky to be gay I'm not the person to judge. But in one way you *are* lucky, which is that nobody in our family (I do not, *of course*, count Clarissa Gaunt) has ever thought any differently, let alone any the worse of you for it.' She turned and addressed herself directly to Fonzi. 'George, my late husband – Julian's father – was a difficult man in many ways. He could be a bully. I expect Julian has told you. But his own experiences in life made him very sensitive to other people's pain, especially the pain of being in a minority. He knew what it was like to be persecuted.' Julian was looking at her with astonishment.

'He *did*? My *father*?'

'Yes, Julian,' said Harriet. 'Your *father*.' She looked back at Fonzi. 'My husband recognized before I did – perhaps even before Julian himself – what our son was and upheld his right to be gay with *passionate* loyalty. Always. In a stick-in-the-mud farming community that was not easy.'

She turned to Julian again. 'Roddy, George, Dodo, me – *none* of us ever felt sorry for you, or tried to tell you that you'd change or that it was a phase. We totally accepted you. Didn't we?'

'It's true,' Julian admitted.

'Then you were very lucky!' Fonzi said wryly. 'My mother, my father, my grandmother, my sisters, my teachers

– everyone except the priest refused to believe I was not going to find a beautiful pure girl and fall in love and marry her and give them all lots and lots of babies.'

'Are you the only boy in the family? I mean man?' Harriet asked.

'Yes. Five sisters, and at last: Alfonso! His own name! My father was so happy! My mother and all the aunts and sisters were happy. At last, a male Aurelio.' He made a rapid chopping gesture with his hand to indicate aggressive masculinity. Julian stretched his own hand across the aluminium tabletop and enclosed Fonzi's slender brown one.

'*I*,' he said, with deep emphasis, 'am *very happy* that you are a man!'

'And so am I,' Fonzi responded.

Harriet said unexpectedly, 'I think we should celebrate. Will they let us have champagne at this hour?'

Julian turned a radiant face towards her. 'Mother! How wonderful! Of course they will. Let Fonzi arrange it.'

Fonzi stood up and walked confidently over to the waiter, whom he engaged in urgent conversation.

'Oh Mother – you *like* him!' Julian said.

'Darling, I think he's just about the most beautiful human being I've ever set eyes on. And while you're with him, you are transformed. I've no idea what will happen to you both in future: but nobody ever knows that. Yes, I'm happy for you. *And* I like him.'

Fonzi returned beaming proudly. 'Champagne is on its way!' he said. 'Mrs Capel, I am proud to have met you. For two years I have been begging Julian to introduce me. Never would.'

'Please call me Harriet. Please come and visit us in Dorset as soon as possible – both of you. It's high time.'

And who do I mean by 'us', she thought. Me and Dodo? Or Oliver and me? What would Julian think? For a moment she was tempted to match his revelation with her own, but it was more important to use his present sweet vulnerability to talk about the feud. In the presence of Fonzi he would surely agree to make peace. The waiter approached bearing a bucket. Down its sides ran transparent silver drops of

205

condensation. Behind him came a second waiter with three tall glasses on a tray. Harriet thought, I have never seen Julian look like this. And the time is quarter past four and I cannot get away for at least another half hour . . . oh, *Oliver!* Golden bubbles foamed in her glass as she tipped it towards the pair of them. '*Santé!*' said Harriet, adding recklessly, 'Let's drink to love!'

Had Julian asked at that moment, '*Love, Mother? What's all this?*' she would have told him everything, made bold by his pride and joy in Fonzi. But he did not, of course; he thought of his mother as a grey-haired little widow in late middle age; love was not her game. Instead, she braced herself to tackle the matter of the feud.

She talked for ten minutes, encouraged by Fonzi's smiles, and finally Julian capitulated.

'I give in: no more feud.'

'Word never mentioned again? No recriminations? No frowns, no snide remarks?'

'Promise,' Julian conceded. 'But that's our side – what about them? The Gaunts?'

'Leave that to me,' Harriet said.

'And now, Mother, if you don't mind, I think Fonzi and I might . . .'

She thought, what an idiot I am: they're desperate to go home and make love! 'Of course, darling,' she said. 'Don't let me keep you. I'll stay and settle the bill.'

'It is all taken care of, Harriet,' Fonzi said. He bent and kissed her on both cheeks. 'I am so happy we have met. I will make Julian bring me to your home very soon.'

The two young men strode away and she thought, poor them, they can't even hold hands in public, let alone touch or kiss. Neither can Oliver and I. The world is very particular about who is permitted to be in love. It does not approve if you are too young or too old, too ugly or too fat, the same sex or far apart in age. Above all you must not be members of the same family. Poor Julian, poor Harriet! Both of us so unsuitably in love, as the world judges. Suppose I had told my son, *I am madly in love with Oliver Gaunt and as soon as we have said goodbye I am going to our borrowed flat where he is waiting impatiently for me and we shall make love for hours.* How would Julian have reacted? With disbelief, disgust – or understanding?

Individuals must be very strong if they are to defy society's stereotypes and one of the most rigid and unquestioned of these lays down that a woman is old from the moment she becomes a widow. In the eighteenth century she was called a 'relict', a leftover from her dead husband, like cold pudding. Even today that stigma remains. At the instant of George's death – Harriet reflected – I was transformed from his (useful, socially acceptable, properly coupled) wife into his (embarrassing, superfluous) widow. Only if your husband should die before you are forty are you a 'young widow' – and the phrase is uttered with a raised eyebrow and a smutty implication. Another stereotype, this time implying ravenous sexual availability. Either way, a widow is a woman without a man. She can never simply be a person in her own right.

But old widows are not expected to want a sex life. Old widows, like old women generally, are sexless creatures. When does this perception begin? With the menopause, probably. Once a woman can no longer bear children her sexuality becomes redundant. Society finds something gross in the notion of a woman over about the age of fifty making love and not merely because of the incest taboo. Yet – Harriet remembered with a stab of guilt – I knew a woman who was widowed when she was seventy-three and her husband seventy-six – 'sweet old couple', everyone had thought placidly. She was tormented by the loss of her sex life. 'We last made love two days before he died,' she told anyone who would listen, 'and I *miss* it so!' People could hardly repress a shudder of distaste.

Youth, beauty, sex and reproduction are inextricably entwined – the very metaphor is erotic – just as age and ugliness and sexlessness go together. Falling in love is less indecent but a good deal of pity and ridicule goes with it. 'Poor old girl, she's gone a bit loopy since he died. Keeps falling for the most unsuitable people. Beautiful young men, mostly. Pathetic isn't it – frightfully undignified.' The world is ignorant and judgemental, Harriet thought; *why* should we feel obliged to conform to the dictates of this blundering oaf?

* * *

On the grimy, claustrophobic platform of Bank underground station, as they stood waiting for the train to Notting
Hill Gate, Julian whispered to Fonzi, 'What would my
mother say if she knew we were going home to make love?'

Fonzi replied, 'I think she knows perfectly well. She is
happy if you are happy, like all good mothers.'

Harriet drained her champagne glass and set off in search of
a cab along streets dwarfed by Tower Bridge.

Chapter Thirteen

Not long after George died, Harriet had stood mesmerized one afternoon in the downstairs loo, watching a wasp trying to escape from a spider's web. The web was only visible when its gleaming strands were caught in a shaft of light through the dusty windowpane. The wasp, dazed by the first hot day of summer, vibrated furiously in its attempts to shake the sticky substance off its legs and wings. After several minutes the spider risked emerging from its hiding place and raced down one fine strand to gloat over its prey. At its approach the wasp made a final effort, and actually succeeded in shaking itself free. It crawled onto the stone alcove next to the window and crouched there motionless recovering its strength before using its long front legs to scrape the deadly glue from its antennae and its golden wings. The spider, furious at having lost its lunch, tried to drag the wasp back into its web but the wasp buzzed so vigorously that it eventually scuttled away. Harriet felt as though she had just witnessed a titanic battle; the forces of life and death, kill or be killed, no less epic for the miniature size of the protagonists. The struggle to maintain life is life's first imperative. Did George struggle in his dying seconds, she wondered? Did he realize with a cold pang of terror that the moment of his death had come, or was it all over while he slept? I wish I had been there.

Life's second imperative is love ... or rather, reproduction. Here am I, Harriet thought, poised between the two: imperatives, the urge to survive and the urge to reproduce, having achieved both. Is *this* why I have fallen so hectically in love – because at last I have the leisure and the freedom to do so? If Oliver had not come along would it have been someone else? Or did some unique and special bond draw us irresistibly towards each other? Julian loves Fonzi for his beauty; that seems obvious – but perhaps he has a sweet nature as well. I hope so, poor Jules: he's had bad luck with his lovers. Fonzi loves Julian (*if* he does) for saving him from a lifetime of hypocrisy; for springing him from the trap of his female family and his Spanish tourist village to the great wen of London. But maybe, oh I do hope so, he loves him for being *my Julian*: shy, clever, diffident, creative, loving, proud, touchy, and in many ways so like his father!

Her taxi drew up outside the anonymous terraced house in Pimlico which had been the magnet of her thoughts and desires for the last four days. She got out, paid the driver, and glanced up at the first floor window – to see Oliver looking down at her with an expression of the utmost concern, relief and adoration. He turned away and by the time she had pressed the doorbell, was already at the front door to let her in.

Inside the flat, for the first time, he looked almost old.

'Come to bed,' he said. 'Don't say anything – I know it's idiotic – for the last hour I was sure you'd been killed. Now that you're here, alive, I have to hold you naked in my arms.'

He pulled her inside and began hurriedly, roughly to undress her. She smelled the alcohol on his breath but he did not seem drunk. His distress overwhelmed her.

'Oliver,' she tried to explain, 'I'm so sorry – it was just that Julian—'

'Don't!' he said, putting his hand across her mouth. 'Don't speak! I don't *care* why! You're here! Kiss me. *Christ*, Harriet . . .'

She had never known him so frantic. He pulled off his clothes, pulled back the bedspread, pulled her towards him, all with a clumsy awkwardness that made him seem more like a rapist than a lover. To her astonishment she realized he was sobbing. She took his head between her hands and made him look directly at her.

210

'*Oliver!*' she said. 'What's happened? Was it Jenny? My darling – whatever is the matter?'

'I thought you'd died,' he said. 'For half an hour I have been paralysed by the conviction that you were dead. Knocked over in a car accident, knifed by a maniac – doesn't matter – I thought you were dead and I'd never hold you again. Harriet, my darling, I hadn't realized how much I need you. You won't slip away at the end of this week, will you? Try and pretend nothing's happened, for the sake of the children? *We* are what matters – do you promise, Harriet? Do you *swear*?'

The sound of a man crying is terrible. Oliver's sobs lurched from his throat in gasps that sounded like the last spasms of passion. He clutched her to him, still half-undressed, not yet properly naked, and groaned. They staggered towards the bed, fell across it, struggled out of their underwear and kicked it on the floor. They clutched one another like drowning creatures. Oliver's hands and mouth fumbled and groped like some blind thing. Harriet grew hot and slippery. She howled, not tender loving words but old meaningless sounds. They grunted and gasped for breath. He was frantic, desperate. Without subtlety or self-control he thrust into her, she received him with a gush, they arched and groaned aloud as he came.

She was the first to wake. She eased herself silently out of bed, showered, washed her hair, dressed, and made a pot of tea. Entering the bedroom where Oliver was still sleeping, she picked up his clothes from the floor and laid them neatly across an armchair. Oliver's arm trailed from under the edge of the sheet, his hand slumped on the carpet, fingers curled with utter relaxation. His breathing quickened for a moment before resuming its steady rhythm. Harriet looked at him tenderly, with an acceptance of all that he was, his needs, his demands, his physical flaws and secret weaknesses, such as she had not known since her sons were little. She thought, you are the man of my life and I cannot let you go!

She sat down on the bed and stroked his arm, murmuring to wake him gently, 'Oliver, my love, my angel . . . I've brought you a cup of tea.'

211

He muttered sleepily, like a child, "Rissa, C'rissa, want to kiss her . . .'

An old marital joke, no doubt. Every couple accumulates them. Oliver opened his eyes and looked straight into Harriet's.

'Mmmph!' he snorted vigorously. 'What's the time? Have I been asleep? For long? God, I am sorry. What a waste. Harriet. *Tea.* Bliss. Wonderful woman.'

'It's getting on for seven,' she said steadily. 'I had an hour's sleep. You've had a bit more. I thought probably a cup of tea was advisable before we started on the wine. Then we might decide what to do with this evening?'

He sat up abruptly, tousled his hair and stretched, flexing his arms to the fingertips. His skin was dry and ridged rather than smooth but the muscles still ran strongly beneath its surface. All males wake in the same way, Harriet thought. They check their readiness for fight or flight, check the proximity of woman and food, and then they want to pee.

'Must go the bathroom . . .' Oliver said. 'Why do you smile?'

'All men say that . . .'

'Women, too. Especially after making love. That was a wonderful fuck. *God*, I needed it! Lean over, my darling, and let me kiss you. How sweet and fresh you smell. All cool. I can't concentrate until I've emptied my bladder.'

Jennifer was bathing her daughters while Hugo sat on the side of the bidet and watched, smiling at their ecstatic giggles. He was happy because they had their mother all to themselves, with no Ulrike to shoo him upstairs to get into his pyjamas, or Granny Harriet, who smelled peculiar, sort of sweet and sour, and not even Daddy, stern and strong and enviable, to remind him that he was still only a stupid little boy. Mummy looked wonderful, all red in the face and laughing, with soapy water right up the sides of her arms and her hair gone sticky round her cheeks. Mandy was being silly and going too far, screaming and splashing a lot, and Hugo was afraid Mummy would soon get cross and stop.

'Shall I t-t-take Mandy out?' he asked, coming forward with a towel.

'Darling! You *are* a good, helpful boy!'

'No!' shrieked Mandy, '*No no no no . . .*'

'Amanda, *yes.*'

'*I'm* having another five minutes 'cos I was good about my tooth *all day,*' Emily announced.

'That's what *you* think, Miss Muffet!' and Jennifer scooped Emily out of the bath in one tall movement and turned her upside down in the towel so that she couldn't escape. Hugo gasped with admiration. She's so strong, he thought. It's easy for them. He struggled to confine the wriggling thrashing form of Amanda. At that moment the telephone rang downstairs in the hall. Don't let Mummy hear it, he prayed; don't let her, no, please God not.

'Mummmeee! Pho – one!' said Emily.

Jennifer put her down, said – 'Keep an eye, Huge, there's a good boy!' – and lithe, glorious and majestic, walked out of his sight.

'Jenny darling,' said Harriet's voice. 'I've met an old friend and we're going to see a film and maybe have dinner afterwards. So don't count me in for supper. Is that all right? Doesn't put you out, I hope?'

'No, that's fine. What are you going to see?'

'We haven't decided yet. Anything you recommend?'

'Roddy and I tried to get to *Usual Suspects* the other evening – never made it actually – but I don't suppose that's your kind of film. How about *Bridges of Madison County*? Meryl Streep and Clint Eastwood. Damn: Hugo's yelling something at me, hang on – Hugo will you *shut up*, I'm on the *phone*! – must go, Harriet. Have fun.'

'Give them my love and a hug . . .'

'I'll do that. By-yee!'

Why should I give a *damn* what she's doing, thought Jennifer, her and her boring middle-aged friend? Apart from the fact that it might be quite *nice* if she were here to give a hand with her *grand*children so that I could have perhaps *fifteen* minutes to myself. *Shit*, why couldn't it have been

Timothy? Returning to the hot and steamy bathroom she said, 'Will you *behave*, all of you! Hugo, *stop whingeing.* Get to your rooms and put your nighties on. Or I'll tell Daddy when he gets home. Amanda shut up NOW! Sorry, kids. Mummy needs a break, OK?'

Hugo tried to mollify his mother. She'll be nice if I ask about my birthday. I won't say has she got my present because that would be greedy and I mustn't be greedy. 'Is it still my birthday tomorrow, Mummy? Am I having a party?'

'Hugo, you're nearly *ten years old*! Of *course* it's your birthday and *yes* we have fourteen of your little friends from school coming here for tea and God *help* me, a conjuror. Now *will* you get upstairs!'

She leaned over the bath to let the plug out and thought, I love them, I love them – but do *they* know that? I will read them all a story for at *least* twenty minutes and I won't say shut up once. Does *everyone* find motherhood this hard?

'Well, did she ask?' said Oliver.

'You know she didn't.'

'I knew she *wouldn't.* In all probability my daughter envisages you and a stout middle-aged lady sipping a couple of sherries at the Victoria station hotel before setting off, arm in arm for – wait, I know—'

'*The Bridges of Madison County*,' they said in unison.

'What should your daughter-in-law's father, who is utterly besotted, physically rampant and madly in love with you, suggest instead? Apart from taking you back to bed?'

'Take me back to bed,' said Harriet. 'The last time was over so soon. Can we do it again, *slowly . . . ?*'

This time it was Harriet who slept while Oliver got up, dressed, and went out onto the streets of Pimlico in search of a newsagent and a wine merchant, returning quarter of an hour later to find Harriet still asleep. He put the champagne in the freezer, poured himself a glass of burgundy and settled down to read the *Evening Standard* until she awoke. His groin and his thigh muscles ached but he felt replete with physical well-being. Harriet's gentleness, subtlety, and intelligence delighted him as much as her sexual quickening. Not since Nina – pale Nina, forty years

214

gone and still a wound upon his conscience – had he felt both love and desire for a woman. I must hear Harriet speak Russian, he thought idly, his earlier terrors forgotten.

By the time they were ready to leave the flat it was too late for a film *and* dinner. Oliver booked a table at an Italian restaurant and they set off. It was dark and the streets were almost empty. The workers had gone home, City people were still in their offices, small children in bed, older children intent on television or magnetized by a computer game. It had rained and a filmy glaze covered the streets. Overhead sodium lights picked out the flotsam and jetsam of discarded fast-food cartons, cigarette packets, dog shit, plastic bags and the gutter slush of dead leaves, casting a jaundiced sheen across the equally discarded humans – drug addicts, beggars, the homeless and superfluous – crouching in shop doorways under a grimy blanket or sleeping bag. Sharp misery had worn them to the bone. Their faces were gaunt, cupped hands haggard. They could beg, starve, even die in the streets. Society would say it was all their own fault.

A young man lurched towards them. He wore a hooded anorak, baggy track suit trousers, dirty trainers with slug-like soles, and a look of aggressive hopelessness. Oliver quelled his imminent request with a basilisk glance and the youth lurched past, muttering to himself.

Oliver was astonished by the detritus that had accumulated on the streets of the capital in the course of the last, supposedly so prosperous, decade. Doorways, parks, tube stations, tents, underpasses – any urban cave that might offer shelter was home to whey-faced human beings living in the malodorous nooks and crannies of society.

'How long has it been like this?' he asked.

Harriet turned a shining face up at him and smiled. 'Has what been like what?' she said, and he realized that the squalor and the scruffy youth had passed quite unnoticed in her present euphoria. A cab with its yellow sign illuminated approached and Oliver said, 'Nothing – doesn't matter – TAXI!'

By the time they had climbed into it she had forgotten the question.

'Covent Garden,' said Oliver, 'Floral Street,' and he slid the glass partition across between them and the driver so that, like lovestruck adolescents, they could kiss in the back of the taxi. Only after they had stepped out and he had paid the driver did he strike his forehead and exclaim,

'Oh *blast* . . .!'

'*What?*'

'I've left a bottle of champagne in the freezer!'

Harriet shrugged.

'Never mind. It'll probably crack the fridge and we may have to buy him a new one, but I'm *not* going to worry about it now.'

Their faces alight with passion and laughter, they entered the restaurant.

One or two heads turned as they walked through . . . an ordinary enough middle-aged woman in turquoise and grey, transfigured by, what? 'I'll have whatever she's had,' quoted one woman to her companion as Harriet threaded past their table. From a table at the back of the room, a few steps raised above the rest, they overlooked the other diners. As she sat down and scanned the menu, Harriet felt her ecstatic mood ebb, conscious of the gravity of their imminent decision.

'I'll have to talk to Dodo tonight, after I get back.'

Ah yes, Dodo, Oliver thought grimly: the Mrs Danvers to her Rebecca. She'll be jealous but surely she won't offer more than passive resistance.

'Bit late? Won't get you home till after midnight.'

'Dodo never *really* sleeps. She dozes at intervals throughout the twenty-four hours. She's often quite sprightly around midnight.'

'What if she says she won't have me in the house?'

'Darling, she wouldn't say no. She accepts everything. She may not – be honest: *does* not – approve, but she won't refuse.'

Dodo will not refuse, Harriet thought, she will even be polite towards him but she will withdraw herself. Even the house will resist Oliver's intruding presence. It has never, as far as I know, been headed by a male who was not a Capel.

Capel Farm House, a sturdy, practical red brick building,

216

had been occupied by Capels for at least the previous four generations; perhaps longer. Roddy and Julian; George; George's father Archie and *his* father, old George, had all been born and reared there. Clearing up after Archie's death, George and Harriet had come across a suitcase full of cheques and accounts. The accounts were written in slanting copperplate; the cheques were the size of the old Bank of England five pound notes: large and serious, as befitted the days when five pounds was a large and serious sum of money.

'My father hated throwing anything away,' George had said, and as a lifetime of records emerged from trunks stored in the attic and outhouses it became obvious that this was literally true. They spent weeks sorting through bills, scrawled receipts recording the price paid for a prize bull, for cattle feed, milk churns, veterinary treatment, a pedigree Airedale . . . written evidence of the transactions that marked Archie's passage through life.

In another box she found an optical instrument, one end shaped like a pair of binoculars and widening out at the other into two windows like a double slide-viewer. Its function became clear when she opened one of the yellowing envelopes stored with it. Each had a printed title and a dozen numbered images: Arctic Explorers' Heroic Feats, dated 1914; panoramic scenes of Yellowstone Park, Niagara Falls, New York City, 1906. Inside the envelopes were stiff cards with matching stereoscopic pictures, the left very slightly different from the right. When slotted into the viewer and looked at through the lenses, they produced a three-dimensional image. George had greeted the box with boyish glee. '*I* remember these!' he said – 'Look, New York at the turn of the century. Look at all the horses-and-carts. Amazing! I must have spent *hours* looking at these! It was my father's when *he* was a child. Fantastic! What was it called, this thing . . . kaleidoscope – stethoscope – *stereoscope*! That's it: a stereoscope. Put it away, Hattie, I don't want anyone playing about with it. They'd only wreck it.' It gave, Harriet remembered thinking, a very married view of life. You both looked at the same scene from slightly different angles but together your joint view created a solid

217

object. You could not describe the differences since they were infinitesimal, yet they *were* different and only when combined did they create a whole. She tried to express this idea to George but he had stroked the back of her neck and said, 'Clever girl!' without really bothering to try and understand.

Their marriage had created two sons, after which they had agreed to stop. Harriet did not find pregnancy or childbirth easy. George was not the sort of man to yearn for a daughter. Two boys growing up on a farm, healthy little animals living the outdoor life, suited him fine. Yet neither Roddy nor in due course Julian was allowed the fun their father and grandfather had had with the stereoscope. They had games like L'Attaque and Monopoly and Nine Men's Morris to keep them occupied on rainy days and television, strictly rationed, instead. Bill and Ben the Flower-pot Men.

George had been distressed by the reappearance of his father's old riding boots, Coke hat and above all by his First World War officer's coat.

'How old was he when that war started?' Harriet had asked, to break the tension.

'He was born in eighteen ninety,' George had said, 'so he'd have been twenty-four. Prime officer material. Actually he didn't join up till nineteen sixteen, after the Somme. It was because of the farm. Needed here.'

'So,' Harriet had risked, 'not *that* brave and patriotic then?'

George had glared coldly at her without answering.

Later on, when her mother-in-law Elizabeth had finally died – eighty-two and quite gaga – Harriet came across her vanity case containing a sepia photograph of Archie as a young officer, rigid with apprehension and duty, and a slim bundle of handwritten letters. She felt she ought to show them to George. He turned them over and over in his large hands until Harriet put them firmly back into the case. She locked it and threw the case away a few days later without reopening it.

These were only the Capels within living memory. There were other, more distant Capels revealed in careful journals

218

of the weather ('31 January 1857: cold again, hard frost, east wind.'), in cheerless crinolined wedding portraits, school-books, first in pencil and then ink-blotted handwriting, the child's name carefully inscribed on the front. Gilbert Capel, George Capel; she even came across a copperplate *Julian Capel, 1846.* Children love writing their names on books. It proves they exist and that something belongs to them. In a trunk full of mildew she had found nursery rhymes and stories; *The Boy's Book of Soldiers*; *Scouting for Boys*; and a French book entitled *Peau d'Ane.* On the cover an angelic-faced little girl draped in an ass's skin crouched beside a pool while in the background, black turkeycocks extended dark red necks and gobbled at her. It was a terrifyingly sexual image, bizarre and threatening. Naïve pre-Freudian days!

'Were there *no* daughters in your family?' Harriet had asked George.

'Can't have been many,' he conceded, 'or maybe they all died young. My father had two brothers . . .'

'What happened to them?'

'. . . died in the War. My grandfather had a brother, Great Uncle Gilbert. And of course they all had wives. But I can't think of many Capel girls, no.'

Were they lonely, all those Capel wives, she used to wonder. As lonely as I am? Or were they solid, unimaginative women content with their role at home and in the village, doing good works, raising sons to be buried in due course in foreign fields until finally they themselves lay under tombstones, commemorated as Beloved Wife of . . . Devoted Mother of . . . ?

Harriet slept between monogrammed sheets their hands had embroidered, ate with silver cutlery that they, or their maids, had polished, sat at tables burnished down the years with beeswax melted and mixed to their recipes. Could she invade this sacred territory with another man? The Capel family had a blameless matrimonial record: no divorces, naturally; not even very many early deaths in childbirth, thereby enabling grieving widowers to marry blooming young second wives to look after the first one's motherless litter. Capels took care to marry healthy stock. If she introduced Oliver to Capel Farm House the old ghosts would be scandalized, the very air would shrink from giving this interloper breath.

Oliver's voice broke in on her thoughts.

'When shall we tell the rest? My girls – and your two?'

'I've been thinking about that. Sunday seems to me the wrong time. And the wrong order. First has to be Clarissa. You surely owe it to her to tell her first. Then you might come back to London – more likely *she'll* come over for a few days to see the girls while you clear out your stuff . . . oh Oliver, *I* don't know when we'll tell them. I dread it. I suppose I'll have to take Roddy out to lunch and Julian to dinner or vice versa, and break it to them. Or even together. Now that I've met Julian's Fonzi I don't think Jules'll be that upset. Roddy's the conventional character. But *that's* not the point. The *point* is the little ones.'

Oliver inwardly disagreed, but said nothing except, 'I've hardly seen anything of them this week – feel bad about that – so I don't know them as well as you do. *Are* they going to mind all that much? I'm far more worried about Clarissa. She's likely to retaliate by being extremely bloody and naturally Jennifer will take her side . . .'

'The children *will* mind, but that's not the worst thing. It's the upheaval in their lives – rows and arguments . . .' Harriet stopped while the waitress put a plate in front of her, topped up their glasses, fetched their salad, and smilingly checked that everything was all right.

'Everything's wonderful!' Harriet said, returning the smile.

She resumed, 'It's going to be awful for them. I can hardly bear to talk about it, let alone *do* it.'

'Harriet, don't say that. They're absorbed in their own lives. They'll get over it. May make a fuss and a drama for a month or two, refuse to talk to us – but they'll settle down. *We'll* still be there, still be grandparents. I hardly give a fuck about Clarissa, to be brutal. She's had thirty-five years. I care more about Jenny and Phills, but they're big grown-up girls. As for Patrick – I don't know – an odd fish, my son. Remote from me. But he's twenty-five. A man.'

'The *children*, though? You can't just dismiss the *children*. Already they see far too much of their parents' quarrels. Now we're going to add to that . . . Oliver, it's . . . don't you see? . . . No.'

'Darling, to me those children are like three little – mice, as you call them – or dolls, or teddies, anything small and cuddly. I can't think of them as *real people*. I'm more concerned to sort out the practical side. Divide the money – fifty/fifty to me and Clarissa, or should she have more? Or less? Those are the things that interest me. I accept your fears but I'm sure you exaggerate.'

Harriet picked at the bright shreds and curls of food on her plate. Emotion, physical exhaustion and the elaborate lunch earlier that day had taken away her appetite. In the last week she had eaten once at home with Roddy and Julian had cooked her one lunch in his flat. Most other meals seemed to have involved paying huge sums of money for food she didn't want.

'Listen to me,' Oliver was saying urgently. He took his glass and ticked it against hers to compel her attention. 'This may be our last chance to talk. Tomorrow we'll be at the opera and afterwards Philly or Matthew – or both – may join us at dinner. Sunday it's the big family lunch. We *must* sort out the logistics now. For instance: how will we communicate once I'm back in France?'

'I can't ring you? No, I suppose not. I'll write to you every day. Can I? I'd enjoy that.'

'We have a fax. You can send me a coded fax, as if from a guest, and that'll be my signal to . . .'

'But I haven't got a fax machine. I've never used one. I hate the idea. It all sounds so underhand.'

'I know!' he said eagerly. 'You can phone me in Russian!'

'And if *she* answers?'

'She's used to that sort of thing. She'll fetch me.'

'Oliver, it sounds so sordid and clandestine!'

'Not for more than a couple of weeks. I'll write to you too – love-letters, my darling – every day as well. I'll soon be with you.'

'And if Clarissa – talks of suicide . . .?'

'She won't. I know her. Harriet, suddenly you don't

221

sound sure. Do you love me? Are you backing out?'

'I love you, Oliver. I adore you. Don't ever doubt it. Only I'm not used to inflicting pain on other people, least of all on the small and helpless – who happen also to be my grandchildren.'

His foot slid against hers under the table and a tiny shock leaped up her nerves, as though her flesh sizzled. Her eyes widened and he saw the reaction. He grinned and drained his glass.

'Another bottle!'

'Not for me – I've drunk far too much today. I'm not used to . . .'

The waitress had already spotted his upraised hand. Oliver held the bottle aloft and she went to fetch another. Tiredness threatened to overcome Harriet. She shook herself, sat upright, and said with as much energy as she could manage, 'Tell me about your lunch with Jenny. Did you broach the feud?'

It was after midnight when their taxi stopped, diesel engine turning over, outside the house in Camberwell. Jennifer and Roddy had just gone to bed.

'There's a taxi now – *must* be her. Look through the curtains, Roddy: is it her?'

'I'm not bloody spying on my mother. *You* look, if you're so curious.'

Jennifer hopped out of bed and, parting the curtains a fraction, peered through. She saw Harriet step out; then a dark shape leaned through the open door of the cab and kissed her. The shape was almost definitely male; the kiss, disappointingly, a brief touch of lips against cheek.

Harriet, unheard by her daughter-in-law, said tenderly, 'We have to say goodbye, until tomorrow.'

'Quick, Rods!' Jennifer hissed. 'I'm pretty sure it *is* a man! Come and see!'

'I don't give a damn who it is. She can do what she likes. *Unlike me.*' With a masculine snort he turned away from the window and humped his shoulders against his wife. Suppressing a giggle, Jennifer looked away and said, '*Harriet*, with a *man* – I bet it *was* a man. Why should a

222

woman bother to see her home? What a surprise!'

'Your capacity for prurient speculation never ceases to amaze me,' said Roderick. 'Life to you is a soap-opera full of people behaving badly. Someone's probably dropping her off before taking the taxi on home. Why don't you mind your own business and come to bed?'

Harriet climbed the stairs with slow, deep weariness, took her dressing gown from the bedroom, went to the top floor bathroom and showered. She cleaned her teeth, put Nivea Creme on her face, loosened and combed her hair, then went to the telephone in the basement. Jenny was tempted to eavesdrop but she could tell by his breathing that her husband was still awake. Pity, she thought, and fell asleep.

'Dodo, the die is cast. I have decided.'

'Hallo, my lamb. I was waiting for you to ring. Don't tell me the time. It's pitch dark and pouring with rain outside. The curtains are blowing. I ought to shut the window, but I can't get out of bed again now. I'll catch my death with jumping up and down. What is this die you've cast?'

'Ring your buzzer for Mrs Peters.'

'I'd rather leave the window open than disturb her now.'

'Is she looking after you?'

'She is doing very well. She's a thoroughly good woman. Harriet, dear, what have you decided, you and Mr Gaunt?'

'Oliver is his name.'

There was a long silence. Dodo accepted it placidly.

'His name is Oliver,' said Harriet again. Eventually she drew a deep sigh.

'He is going to come and live with us, Dodo. You and me. Mainly me.'

'And what does his wife say about that?'

'She doesn't know yet.'

'His daughters, then?'

'They don't know either.'

'The two of you have decided, all on your own, to break up the family. No doubt you have your reasons.'

'Love. That's all. There are no other reasons. No excuses. Love.'

'At your age?'

223

'My love has grown to such excess I can't describe the half of it. I could say I love him madly or frantically or desperately, but those are hysterical words. I could say I love him very much, but that's a qualification. My love for him is an absolute. I can only measure it by saying that everything else dwindles beside it.'

'So you will bring him to live with you here, in Capel Farm House. You don't give a hoot for anyone else. Not even those three little children?'

'Yes, Dodo: if you force me to say it, I have to be honest – *not even those three little children.* I do give a hoot about them, of course, many hoots, but I won't let them stand between Oliver and me and our future.'

'What sort of love throws away the happiness of children?'

Quietly, holding the mouthpiece of the phone aside, trying not to let Dodo hear, Harriet began to weep. The day had been long and emotional. Julian's revelation, the agreement to end the feud that had split the family for thirteen years, the great decision that she and Oliver had made together, and now the remorseless probing of her dearest, oldest companion, loosened her self-control. She rested her forehead on the palm of her hand and felt rivulets trickling down her face and spilling onto her wrist.

'Are you snuffling, Harriet?'

'I'm tired out. I should be happy, but I'm utterly confused and exhausted.'

'Oh Harriet, I already know your grief.'

'Tell me then.'

'You are crying because you have to let him go. I believe you love him. But sometimes the world denies you the things you want or even deserve.'

'The *world* is a *blundering* oaf!'

'The world knows that cherishing young things is the measure of civilization. If their welfare is abandoned – by Hitler or Stalin or that Chow man in Rumania—'

'Ceaucescu.'

'I daresay that's him – and the butchers in Bosnia today, all monsters – when people destroy little children it is proof that the world's gone mad. Either *you* have gone

224

mad, Hattie, or you know you can't have what you want.'

'I never thought you'd refuse me this!'

'It isn't for me to say no. It's for you. As you will. That's why you're weeping now.'

There was another pause. Dodo breathed patiently down the line. She reached for the glass beside her bed and took a drink of water. The curtains of her room fluttered wildly in the wind. The weather was gathering its forces for a storm. Soon, she thought, there will be thunder. When Harriet puts the telephone down I shall have to get out and close the windows. Gradually she began to shift her legs, inch by inch, towards the side of the bed. She swivelled slightly on her bottom. It was going to be a long, slow process. She was stiff tonight. Poor little Hattie, Dodo thought, nothing like this has ever happened to her before. George was lucky. But he always knew the risks he ran. Her beauty and grace . . . plenty of people noticed. That's why he was so jealous. It made him cruelly dismissive of her at times. He tried to make her think she was nothing. Now she's quite unprepared; doesn't know how to deal with it. Love. Finally Dodo judged that the faint lurching gasps on the other end of the phone were coming to an end.

'Harriet, you've got my present for Hugo, haven't you? It's his birthday of course . . . today! It must be well past midnight.'

'Yes, Dodo, I've got it. I'll let you sleep. I'll let him talk to you tomorrow. Hugo, I mean.'

'Of course you mean Hugo, dear. Good night then. Remember I *also* love you, Harriet.'

On her way back to her bedroom, Harriet tiptoed in to look at Amanda and Emily – rosy and abandoned in sleep. How self-confident and relaxed the two girls were! She was reminded of the old soap advertisement: *preparing to be a beautiful lady*. They were preparing to be bossy Gaunt women. Hugo on the other hand lay hunched up, breathing hard, one hand cupped round his penis. He was a Capel male: diffident and sensitive. His face twitched in sleep. He muttered. He's having a nightmare, she thought, and laid a hand on his bony shoulder. He twitched it off, frowning.

'Shush, poppet, there there, shush. It's all right,' she murmured. 'Granny's here. It's all right. Only a dream. Settle down now. Settle down. Good boy.'

She rearranged his sleeping limbs and stood watching over him until his breathing slowed down and he slept calmly at last.

Chapter Fourteen

Hugo sat on his bed surrounded by a heap of opened presents. He'd got an Airfix kit which Daddy had promised to show him how to put together.

'*You* remember, Mother, when I was his age my room at home was full of dusty balsa wood aeroplanes suspended on string from the ceiling? I used to spend hours painting them and sticking them together with that special Airfix glue.' Roderick had taken the small tube of glue from Hugo's kit, unscrewed its top and sniffed the nozzle. 'God, how that smell brings it all back. Ships I made, too. Model soldiers. Painted them, by hand, one by one. These kids can't be bothered to concentrate on anything for long. Me and Julian were endlessly fighting the battle of Waterloo. Do you remember?'

Hugo had waited patiently until his father had finished. Then he said, '*When* will you show me, Daddy?'

'Oh Huge, I don't know. There won't be time this morning. This afternoon's your party and tomorrow you've got another party. Lucky little sod, aren't you?'

'Roderick! I'd rather you *didn't* say "sod" in front of the children,' Mummy had said in her snake voice. But Daddy often said it. Probably she meant not in front of Granny.

Amanda danced around after that singing, 'Sod – soddy – silly sod! Silly old sod-a-sod,' until Mummy told her to shut up so that he could get on with opening his presents. But the magical mood had gone. Hugo tried to work out which ones were from Granny Harriet and Dodo but he got it wrong and had to unwrap the great big one from Granny

227

'Rissa first and be pleased with that, so by the time he finally got to Granny Harriet's present his pleased face was getting tired.

Ulrike had come in with lots of little packages wrapped up in material, not paper. Inside each parcel was a painted wooden horse, starting from quite a big one and going down to a tiny baby horse. Hugo thought these were wonderful but he didn't want to hurt anyone's feelings by being too keen, so he'd just given Ulrike a kiss and whispered, 'It's my best!' quickly when nobody else could hear.

Now the six Swedish horses, shiny red and yellow with brightly coloured manes and tails and tiny leather saddles, stood in a row on his windowsill looking out into the street. On the chair beside his bed he had folded up the shirt from Granny and the Lion King T-shirt from Mummy, with the matching trainers that had lion cubs on the toes. He piled the other things on the bed and opened the first of the books. *The Dorling Kindersley Boys' Book of Classic Cars*, it was called, from Grandpa Oliver. He settled down to read. '*In 1896 . . .*' Hugo sighed.

As the rest of the family left the kitchen, after Hugo had opened his cards and presents, after Harriet had folded the paper up tidily for re-use and Jennifer had stuffed it quickly out of sight into the rubbish bin, she said to no-one in particular, 'I'm not cooking a proper lunch today. Ulrike's not prepared to since a) she's supposed to get weekends off and b) she's helping with the party. Roderick says he has to go in to the bank – thanks a *bunch*, Rods – so it'll just be bread and cheese and fruit. Harriet, does that suit you?'

'That's fine.'

'Kids? No cooked lunch, OK. I'm warning you now. I don't want any whingeing later.'

'But Mummy what if we're *hun-gry*?' asked Emily.

'All the more appetite for the party this afternoon. Harriet, were you planning to stick around and give a hand with that? You don't have to.'

Harriet had been wondering whether she might have a spare hour or two to get her hair done before the opera.

'It's more than twenty years since I was at a children's

228

birthday tea but of course, if I can help, Jenny darling. Just tell me what needs doing and I'll . . .'

The doorbell shrilled in the hall and shrilled again down in the kitchen.

'Me me me *me me*!' shouted Amanda, and she and Emily raced upstairs.

'Morning girls!' came Oliver's voice from the hall. 'Mummy about? Most important of all, where is young *Hugo*?'

Ulrike emerged from the dining room, where she had been sorting out party plates and paper napkins and wrapping each child's going-away present.

'He is in his bedroom, Mr Gaunt,' she said. 'Will you that I bring him down?'

Harriet, alone in the kitchen with Jennifer, heard Oliver's voice and a deep blush spread across her face and neck. She bent down and pretended to have dropped something under the table.

'Daddy! I'm in here! Come on down!' shouted Jennifer.

'Just going to say hello to the birthday boy!'

Harriet straightened up. 'Can't find it,' she muttered.

'Whatever were you – you're all red in the face. What have you dropped?'

'Nothing. Just thought I . . .'

At that moment Roderick clattered down the stairs. 'Right! I'm off! Back by six, latest.'

He sketched a kiss in the direction of his wife and mother, ran upstairs, called out, 'Sorry I can't stop, Oliver — see you later!' and the front door slammed.

'Why does he have to go into the bloody bank on his son's *birthday*?' Jennifer complained.

'So as not to have to go in tomorrow, perhaps?' Harriet suggested.

'And why for that matter does he have to work at weekends at *all*?'

Jennifer began an incoherent complaint about her husband's hours and dedication to his job, unfavourably contrasted with his indifference to his son's tenth birthday and the demands this placed on his wife. Her father's arrival cut it short.

229

'*Because*,' said Oliver, catching the tail-end of her tirade, 'or at least so Philly would have me believe, you lot work longer and harder and higher and faster than anyone of my generation can even begin to imagine. Hallo, Jenny. Morning, Harriet.'

'Oliver! How nice! What a surprise,' said Harriet, relieved that her voice sounded normal. 'Jenny, why don't you take your father upstairs and I'll bring you both a cup of coffee in a minute? He must be longing to see the children.'

'OK, that'd be good,' said Jennifer. 'Thanks Harriet. Come on up, Daddy. Amanda, *no*! We're just *coming*.'

Had she turned back and said, 'And bring a cup for yourself and join us!' – she would have caught sight of Harriet's longing expression, her face once again suffused in a blush. But second thoughts, let alone second sight, were not Jennifer's style so she missed the clues that her mother-in-law was quite unable to hide.

The telephone rang in the bedroom, the hall, the drawing room and the kitchen. Jennifer called out,

'Harriet – be an *angel*, would you? *Say* I'm not here!'

Harriet picked up the telephone.

'Oh, hallo, who's that?' asked an unfamiliar voice.

'This is Harriet Capel, Roderick's mother,' she replied.

'Harriet! Good gracious. Yes of course, I'd quite forgotten. Clarissa here. Good morning. How are you? I wonder, *could* I have a word with my daughter?'

'Hallo, Clarissa. Such a busy morning we're having! Hugo loved your present. Hold on, would you like to talk to him while I see if I can find Jenny?'

Her heart thundering again, Harriet went upstairs. She looked into the drawing room to see Oliver with a granddaughter on each knee and Jennifer apparently midway through some lengthy explanation. The children were fidgeting.

'Excuse me,' said Harriet. 'Sorry to interrupt, Jenny, but your mother's on the telephone. I haven't said you're here yet – do you want to speak to her now? Or shall I call Hugo to thank her for his present? Or perhaps . . .' she looked directly at Oliver for the first time, '*you'd* like a word with your wife?'

Jennifer jumped up, clutching her hands into fists and shaking them melodramatically to and fro, lips clenched. 'Oh *fuck*, I ought to have rung her earlier! She bought him that *fantastic* Bagatelle table! It must have cost the earth. *I'll* go and talk to her first. Thanks, Harriet. D'you want a word with her after me, Daddy?'

'Not to bother . . . I'll talk to her later. Tell her I'm trapped in my seat by two great big heavy bouncing girls,' he said.

Jennifer ran down the stairs to the kitchen. The two little girls knelt on Oliver's lap and made him pull funny faces, tugging at his lower lip and pushing up his eyebrows. This was obviously an old and favourite game. Above their hands he looked mutely across at Harriet.

'Come *on* Grandy, be a fierce tiger!' said Emily.

'No, no, growly bear!' shrieked Amanda.

'Shall we ask Granny Harriet what *she* wants me to be?' said Oliver, leaning his head backwards to free himself from their clutching fingers. 'What do you think I should be, Harriet?'

Be my love, she thought, and the old song came into her head unbidden, *for no-one else can end this yearning, this every sweet desire, that you alone inspire . . .*

'I think Hugo should decide. It's *his* birthday after all. I'll go and get him,' she said.

'Tiger tiger tiger . . .' shouted Emily.

'Bear, bear bearbearbear!' insisted Amanda.

Hugo was sitting on his unmade bed surrounded by birthday presents.

'Darling!' said Harriet. 'All alone? You know Grandpa Oliver's here?'

'Does he know how to do Airfix k-k-kits?' asked Hugo, frowning.

'I'm sure he does. Let's bring the box downstairs and ask him.'

She helped Hugo to pick up the flat pieces of plastic and complicated sheets of instructions and put them all back in the box. He carried it downstairs to Oliver.

Minutes later, Jennifer came into the drawing room where all five of them were kneeling on the carpet with pieces of

231

Airfix kit set out tidily in order of assembly.

'*Hugo!*' she said, contorting her face with annoyance. 'Ulrike has hoovered this room *once* already! Will you *please* put that junk away . . .'

'Hey, hey, hold on, Jenny. It was my suggestion. We're working out how to make a Messerschmidt 109,' her father said evenly.

'Mum's on the phone. She wants a word,' said Jennifer sullenly. 'You first, then Hugo.'

'Come on, old chap,' said Oliver, standing up and pulling Hugo to his feet. 'Let's go and talk to your other granny.'

As he passed Jennifer, Hugo said, 'I'm s-s-sorry, Mummy, honestly. I'll pick them up in a minute, promise.'

Jennifer's shoulders slumped. 'Never mind, Huge,' she said. 'Shouldn't have shouted at you on your birthday.'

That's the trouble, Harriet thought; she thinks that if she apologizes, it makes everything all right. Now I can't say anything either. She is an *impossible* young woman.

Hugo dangled his feet on a three-legged stool in the kitchen thinking, *We were all having fun and Grandpa was explaining and the girls were watching too and I hadn't done anything wrong and—*

'You-know-who's being fairly bloody this morning,' his grandfather said down the telephone. 'I don't give a damn whether it's PMT; she ought to control herself. Poor little bloke.'

I know who you-know-who is, but what's bloke? It must mean me. Is it good or bad?

'I don't know if he did; I wasn't there. I've been to Sandersons already, getting your curtain material. Yes, that William Morris stuff. They hadn't got it in olive green so I took the yellow; is that OK? Twelve metres.'

What did Granny 'Rissa give me? I've forgotten. Oh help!

'Clarissa don't, please, shout at me. You sound exactly like your daughter. I didn't know it *had* to be green. Look you'd better have a word with . . .'

But Hugo had levered himself off the stool and raced upstairs to look at his presents and try and remember which one his grandmother had given him.

232

'He'll be back in a minute. It's just an ordinary sort of yellow. Not lemon yellow. More sort of corn-coloured. Clarissa, if you speak to me like that I shall put the phone down. Hugo's coming back now. Talk to him.'

He handed the telephone to Hugo and marched out of the kitchen. The sooner the better, he thought; the sooner the better. God, I could do with a stiff drink.

'Thank you Granny 'Rissa for my lovely shirt,' said Hugo breathlessly. 'I like it very mu-mu-*much*. I'll wear it t-t-today for my *party*. It's very nice. Thank you.' He ended the conversation politely, said how sorry he was that she couldn't be here for his birthday like Grandpa Oliver and Granny Harriet, who were having a lovely time, said good-bye after one last thank-you and went upstairs to the drawing room.

'Did you thank Granny 'Rissa for that *wonderful* Bagatelle game?' asked his mother, and Hugo thought fervently, *Oh, bugger it!* He smiled ingratiatingly at her. *Please God remember it's my birthday, God.* 'Yuh-yuh-yes,' he said. 'I did.'

Jennifer was in the hall at three to greet the arriving children, propelled forward clutching birthday presents for Hugo by parents for whom a £9.99 video, an Action-Man uniform (duplicate of one already received last Christmas) or even a £49.99 interactive CD-Rom was not too high a price to pay for getting rid of their offspring on Saturday afternoon. She planned to be there again between half past five and six to offer the returning parents a glass of wine ('Red or white? And do have a Kettle Chip – no, children, *down*!'). During much of Hugo's party she was preoccupied elsewhere. Returning from these mysterious tasks, she would put her head round the door of the drawing room or kitchen to say with a teasing smile,

'How's it all going? Everyone happy? Huge, darling, birth-day boy? Ulrike, is he being a good host? Harriet, you are a *brick*!'

Then she would be glorious; glamorous, funny and play-ful, every boy's dream mother, so that the other children gazed at her admiringly. Jennifer could never keep it up for long, however, and soon she would ruffle Hugo's blond hair and disappear again.

Probably just as well, Harriet thought. He's desperately tense when she's around, it makes him worse. He's so anxious to please that he invariably gets it wrong. With us it was George the boys always tried to humour, yet Hugo is quite relaxed with his father. Not that Roddy is around much: not even this afternoon. Work, bank, CVs or résumés as she calls them, letters, phone calls. The children don't figure high enough on their list of priorities. Come to that, how high do they figure on *mine*?

The conjuror had been and gone, speeded on his way by a gracious Jennifer and a hefty cheque. Tea was degenerating into a rout, Hugo looked dangerously bright-eyed and flushed and Amanda had been escorted upstairs in tears on account of the bigger, rougher boys. Emily held her own, Harriet observed, partly because she had already acquired her mother's patrician manner.

'You're just being *schtoo*-pid,' she would say witheringly. 'I think you're idi*otic*,' and big rough boys would wilt and skulk. If ridicule failed, she swore at them. '*Bugger* it, Damian, why don't you just *bugger* off?' she shrilled. The first time this happened, Ulrike looked across and caught Harriet's eye. Harriet shrugged, raised her eyebrows, and they smiled at one another. *Not* the moment, the smiles said.

Boys and girls sucked Coca-Cola up their straws and blew it over one another, ducking, shrieking and giggling, until Harriet decided enough was enough. With a firmness that surprised her, she announced to the over-excited children in precisely the tones Dodo would have used – or Joyce Grenfell: 'Right, everyone! Best behaviour for the last half hour. Can't have your parents arriving to find a full-scale riot going on. We're going to sing Happy Birthday to Hugo and then we shall go upstairs and everyone will sit round quietly while I tell you a story. No, not a video: a proper made-up out of my head never before told once in a lifetime bargain story. Charmian, you can spend a penny in a *minute*. All right? Sorry, *Rosie* then. Here we go . . . not you, Hugo, but everyone else:

> *Happy Birthday to you!*
> *Happy Birthday to* you*!*
> *Happy* birthday *dear . . .'*

which is what Oliver saw and heard as he walked through the kitchen door.

He had spent the previous couple of hours at John Lewis, trying to find everything on Clarissa's lengthy shopping list. Dismayed by his earlier failure to grasp that curtain fabric printed with a William Morris grapes-and-vine-leaves design in green was immeasurably superior to the identical pattern in yellow, Oliver had insisted on buying precisely what was specified on his wife's list. It had been an arduous and not entirely successful afternoon. The goods were now stacked in dark green striped carrier bags back in his room. He had changed for the opera and was hoping to slip away for an hour alone with Harriet before meeting Matthew and Philly at the Coliseum. *No* chance, as his daughter would have said. Where, come to think of it, was she?

'Where is Hugo's mother?' Oliver said to Ulrike, when the singing ended.

'I believe Jennifer is in her room,' the girl said with an undertone of contempt.

'Then she damned well shouldn't be!' he answered. 'It's her son's birthday party.'

'I must take this child to the toilet,' the au pair said. 'Excuse me, please. After that I clear the tea and tidy up the kitchen and after that I shall give her my notice.'

Oliver said grimly, 'I can't blame you.'

Harriet said, 'Ulrike, *no*! Please, can we have a word first?'

Hugo burst into tears.

There is something dark, velvety and palpably erotic about an opera house. An atmosphere of expectancy grips the audience as they display themselves and survey everyone else. On this particular Saturday in late September there was the added satisfaction of knowing that tickets for this production of *Carmen* were almost impossible to obtain. '*Wonderful* reviews!' people were saying, and '*Dear*

Jonathan Miller's always *so* good, isn't he?' and 'This new Carmen is supposed to be absolutely *dazzling*.' With an air of self-congratulation they started to drift towards the auditorium in search of their seats. All good children deserve a treat.

Harriet and Oliver had gone out of the house together leaving in their wake Jennifer, tight-lipped, Roderick, seething, Hugo, gulping bravely; and two over-strung little girls. Ulrike, clearing up after the birthday party, had not yet delivered her news. Amid all this their departure went almost unnoticed other than a brief, 'Envy you both! Mother, you look a knock-out – doesn't she, Oliver?' from Roddy. The fervour of Oliver's '*Yes!*' was also unremarked.

Matthew was already waiting in the teeming foyer of the Coliseum. Philomena arrived in a flurry of apologies. A short black dress set off her good legs, high heels elongated them further, and her dark hair was loosely pinned up on top of her head. She wore, and needed, no make-up other than red lipstick. Oliver, glancing at Matthew, could see that he was impressed. He introduced Harriet and Matthew, watched with approval as Philly leaned forward and kissed Harriet's cheek as if there had never been a feud, and went off to order interval drinks, leaving them studying the programme. The expectant buzz in the air and the electricity between the four of them boded well.

At the two-minute call he ushered them into place, having worked out the seating order in advance. First Matthew, then Philly, then Oliver himself and finally Harriet threaded their way past earlier sets of knees. They were in the centre of the stalls. Oliver leaned across his daughter (she smelled delicious) as the house lights went down and whispered, 'Don't know how you managed this, Matthew! *Marvellous* seats!'

'Reserved for critics or celebs who don't show up. Usual thing: mutual favours . . .' Matthew grinned, and Oliver saw that he too was buoyed up by the presence of the woman beside him.

An hour later, Oliver and his party drank champagne in the interval. He checked, since this was his main reason for having ordered champagne, and once again Harriet delicately inserted her tongue so that the bubbles prickled and burst against its tip.

A couple of miles to the south-east, the household in Camberwell contained almost as much flouncing passion and melodrama as the cigarette factory on stage.

'And where were *you*?' Jennifer was shouting. 'Not even in the *house*! And don't tell me *the bank, I was at the bank*—' (she mimicked a whining voice and cringing expression) 'I bet you were in the arms of that bloody *woman*!'

Roderick strode across the drawing room to pick up the telephone, practically tearing it from its socket. He thrust the instrument at his wife.

'Here!' he shouted. '*Dial!* You know my extension: five three seven two. *Dial that number.* Poor sodding Alastair's probably still there. He's holding the fort so that *I* could get home early. Ask him. You heard what I said Jennifer – *ask him.*'

Jennifer was afraid. She had evidently gone too far. She rallied. 'Oh yeah: men covering up for one another. You think I don't know? Can't fool me *that* easily.'

'I said *dial*, Jennifer,' he said evenly, 'or I swear I shall walk out *now* and tell Catriona that so far from having ended our affair – if an occasional screw can be dignified with that word – I am coming to live with her. She will welcome me with open arms and *you* can *whistle* for me, birthday or no birthday.'

'All right,' she subsided, 'all right, all right, needn't get so hot under the collar.' She walked across the room and put the telephone back, swinging her hips. She glanced at her husband over her shoulder and said in a wheedling voice, 'Drink?'

'*Oh* no, my dear wife, don't *you* think it's that easy, either! Where were you this afternoon? Couldn't even preside at our first-born's tenth birthday party? Ulrike and my mother did most of it!' Silence, while Jennifer poured herself a whisky. His voice became dangerously low.

'I asked you a question, Jennifer. I want to know' – it rose to a shout – '*where you were*?'

Jennifer could hardly confess the truth, which was that

237

she had spent much of the afternoon staring gloomily at her reflection, deploring her own inadequacy as a mother, a wife and a working woman. She had never admitted to Roderick how hopeless she felt with their son, that she had no interest in his school friends or his teachers, whose names she could never remember; least of all could she admit that she was infuriated by his mournful desire to please, his stutter, his moist hangdog eyes, his full pink mouth, and the timidity revealed in every ingratiating glance and gesture. Daughters, yes – she could manage the girls, above all Emily. Mandy was just a cuddly little bunny. But in Hugo she saw Julian, and Roddy in his weaker moments, and the self-effacing Harriet, and this proof that his genes were Capel genes rather than the splendid Gaunt genes was something she found hard to bear. Am I the *only* mother in the world, she thought in a panic, who finds it a struggle to like her child? Roll on public school and summer camp, staying with friends and adventure holidays and the whole damn shoot. Oh Lord, what can I say to Rods that'll wind him down?

She was saved by a knock on the door.

'Come in – oh Ulrike: you don't have to *knock*! You *are* an angel – thanks for holding the fort. You're free to go out now, if you like. *I'll* keep an ear open for the children. They must be *dead* to the world. Worn out, I should think!'

Roderick saw that Ulrike had a reason for knocking. Sensible, straightforward girls, these Swedes, no mucking about with hints and hypocrisy.

'What did you want to say?' he asked.

Ulrike addressed herself directly to Jennifer. 'I have come to give you my notice. I will work for the whole month if you say I must but I would like to go as soon as it's possible.'

Jennifer tried to assert her authority as an employer, failing to see that she had been wrong-footed.

'You can't *do* this to me, Ulrike. We agreed you'd stay for a year. That's why we paid your fare over here and gave you a holiday in France. You can't just *walk out* after less than two months. What's the *problem*, anyway? Don't you *like* the children?'

Ulrike straightened her shoulders and drew a deep breath. She looked at Jennifer hard and square. 'I love them, and I know they love me. But I cannot try to be their mummy when they want their proper mummy. I would not say this, except but you asked. It hurts me to see them every day be sad. Hugo loves you very much. He is being . . . in Sweden we say ruined, but it does not mean like spoiled.'

'Damaged?' put in Roderick grimly.

'Perhaps, yes. *Damaged*. I will stay one month if you insist. In that time I will prepare them for my to leave. I shall not go back to Sweden. There are many au pair agencies here. I will find me a job in London.'

'Don't think *I'll* give you a reference!' Jennifer said.

'I will make sure you have an *excellent* reference, Ulrike,' Roderick said; but Jennifer interrupted him and, confronting the white-faced nineteen-year-old, burst out, 'How *dare* you tell me what I should and should not do! You're just an ignorant high-minded typical humourless—'

'*Jennifer*,' said Roderick. He was breathing hard.

Ulrike caught the sound of a noise on the stairs. Unheard by his parents, drawn like a magnet by the sound of shouting, Hugo had overheard Ulrike's announcement and his mother's reaction. He turned and ran up to his room, heaving great snorts of misery.

'Hugo! I am coming!' called Ulrike, going to the door.

'It's all right, Huge darling,' said his mother, hissing at Ulrike. 'There, *see* what you've done to him now. On his *birthday*!'

'Oh Jesus Christ,' said Roderick, 'I *give up* . . .'

Setting her glass down with exaggerated care, Jennifer burst into tears.

Several hundred miles away, Clarissa Gaunt and the Cercle des Oiseaux Aveyronnais stood on an improvised stage in the Salle des Fêtes, surrounded by pots of blue hydrangeas. Round the walls hung photographs of local people displaying newly slaughtered trophies in the shape of deer and wild boar. The framed, laboriously autographed picture of their football team and its silver cup had pride of place. The audience was in their best clothes, the men holding hats in

239

their hands and looking forward to the free glasses of *vin du pays* included in the cost of the ticket, once the singing was over. The women watched the conductor's precisely swaying arms and tiptoeing fingers. Up on the dais, their husbands and daughters concentrated fiercely.

The conductor was another *émigré* from the England of the Seventies. His pretty daughters played the viola and cello respectively and in deference to its four English members, the Cercle was attempting two madrigals in English. Clarissa's clear diction soared above the choir's uncertainties. '*Tosse not my soule, O love, twixt hope and feare,*' she sang in a clipped yet passionate voice. '*Shew mee some ground where I may firmly stand.*'

Unobserved by the audience, unknown to other members of the choir, she brimmed with suppressed fury and hard-eyed determination. *Oh* no, Olly, she thought, you don't imagine you'll get away with *this*? You're my husband and no-one else's, least of all *that* colourless little mouse. Thinks she can get her claws into you the moment she's *widowed*, does she? Thank goodness for Mark – poor old Mark – though I'd probably have guessed. I know my husband pretty well by now. Ought to, after thirty-six years. I *thought* he'd been rather evasive the last few days. '*When once of ill the uttermost is knowne, The strength of sorrow quite is overthrowne.*' Wonder if the two of them have *done* it yet, or whether it's all dopey looks and snatched rendezvous? Poor susceptible Ols, trapped in *that* little spider's web! Hope Patrick remembers to feed the dogs while I'm away.

A new song was beginning. Time to pay attention; this one had a tricky beat and lots of counting. Clarissa threw her head back and in her strong voice sang:

> *Withowt dyscorde and bothe accorde now let us be,*
> *Bothe hart alone to set in one best semeyth me.*
> *For when one sole ys in the dole of lovers payne*
> *Then helpe must have hymself to save and love to*
>   *optaine.*

Ten minutes later the audience was beginning to shuffle and fidget. Old men ignored their wives' disapproving glances and settled their caps purposefully over bald heads. Clarissa prepared to count into the final song:

> *Then music with her silver sound*
> *With speedy help doth lend redress.*

Speedy help, she thought: *that's* what Oliver needs!

Two thousand three hundred people sat in five ascending tiers in the perfumed warmth of the Coliseum as Louise Winter, singing the role for the first time, defied Don José in music of haunting passion. The performance was almost over, her voice had held up magnificently and now, transfigured by the part and the gusts of attention that surged towards her from the spellbound audience, she sang with all the force of her throat, her lungs, her ribcage, her swelling diaphragm and her heart. Carmen sang for life and love, knowing that in doing so she willed her own death. Above her stood her fellow singer, eyes outlined with kohl and darkened with passion, heaving with emotional and vocal exhaustion, his legs trembling.

> *But promise you will never leave, Carmen!*
> *Remember how we said we'd never part!* he implored;
> *Not while I live! You'll never go!*
> *Carmen, I'll make you come with me!*

Moved by the hushed silence of the audience and the spiralling voices from the stage, Harriet too found herself trembling. It's spurious emotion, she told herself; pure artifice. Oliver and I are committed to being together and happy for the rest of our lives . . . She shivered nonetheless as the struggle between passion, freedom and death was played out before her eyes.

Under cover of the darkness and rapt concentration around them, Matthew took Philly's hand. With indrawn breath she half-turned to him, smiling. Oh good, she thought – oh, maybe – oh *good*! She focused on the stage again and prepared for the sonorous chords that heralded a death.

The bull-fight crowd surged onto the stage, their blood-lust excited by the fallen bull, to offer the matador his trophy. Vivid with exhilaration, they propelled him forward to claim Carmen. The music rose to a last crescendo as Escamillo recoiled from the sight of Carmen's spread-eagled body.

You can take me away for I'm the one who killed her! declared Don José. The dead woman is his for ever. His love for her justifies murder.

Oliver listened to the last act of *Carmen* thinking, *what have I done?* My gentle Harriet, I may have brought you up from Hades, out of the shades of darkness, but into what? Love is blood, as I have known since I was twenty. Why do I pretend that Clarissa will go quietly, settle down with her dogs and her visitors into a life of patrician decline and alcoholism? She will take revenge in whatever way she can – and she can be powerful and dangerous. Yet still I cannot give you up. Then he thought, don't be asinine, Gaunt! Infected by the melodrama on stage. Pull yourself together; any minute now you're going to have to play the urbane host. He squeezed Harriet's hand as the curtain fell, withdrew his own, and they joined in the rainstorm of applause that greeted the appearance of the panting, triumphant cast.

Jennifer and Roderick were in the kitchen eating scrambled eggs on toast, each pretending to read sections of the Saturday paper. After a while Jennifer said, 'The new serialisation of *Pride and Prejudice* starts tomorrow evening. Sounds good. Must watch.'

'Uh-huh?' was Roderick's response.

Non-committal, she thought; but at least it's broken the silence.

'What time's Harriet planning to set off?'

'I suggest you ask her.'

'I will.'

Add: been lovely having her with us? No, too ingratiating. Back to the paper. Why should I butter him up anyway? Bloody male. Soon talk Ulrike round. Extra fiver a week should do it. Ten if I must. Be a sod getting another au pair at this stage, and agencies charge £75 minimum. To say nothing of the drama Mandy'll kick up. Oh fuck it, just when I'm trying to find a new job too.

In the upstairs bedroom, Emily sat on her bed with Amanda curled into a sleepy lump in her lap. Hugo sat at the other end, his blanket round his shoulders, one thumb in his mouth, one forefinger twisting his hair into tendrils.

'Once upon a time, long long ago,' Emily intoned, 'there was an old man and an old woman and they were sad because no child had been born to them. How they both longed for a child. Next door, behind a high wall, there lived a wicked old witch.' Amanda snuggled more deeply into Emily's warm nightie. Hugo said,

'Does it end happily, Em'ly?'

'Course it does.'

''Cos when Granny Harriet tells it, it's sad.'

'Don't worry, I'll make everything be all right. Shut up and listen. In the old witch's garden there was lots of lovely salad, and the wife said, "Oh husband, husband, how I'd like some of that salad" . . .'

Hugo jammed his thumb more deeply into his mouth.

The audience, catharsis achieved, flowed down the broad steps of the Coliseum. Several stood in groups directly outside the double doors waiting for chauffeurs or waving at passing taxis, while others dispersed into the dark damp streets leading off St Martin's Lane. Oliver and Matthew were engaged in delicate negotiations, each pair by now anxious to go off alone, each man reluctant to say so.

'I wasn't sure whether to book a table . . .' Oliver began, deliberately ambiguous.

'If you two wouldn't think it rude, I was going to suggest a place I know . . .' Matthew said with equal ambiguity.

'*I* ought to be getting back,' said Harriet.

'Why don't I . . .?' Oliver offered.

'Matthew, could I contribute my share of the evening by buying you and me dinner?' asked Philomena, blessedly direct.

The other three turned towards her with smiles of relief.

'That'd be wonderful,' Matthew said. 'We've got a lot to catch up on.'

They said their goodbyes, Matthew took Philly's arm and the four of them melted into the crowded London nightscape.

Minutes later Oliver shouted, 'Taxi!' As they climbed inside, Harriet said, 'I didn't mean it about going back to Camberwell . . .'

'Of course you didn't, my love. We are *going*—' he gave the driver the address – 'back to Mark's flat, where I have prepared a surprise.'

They embraced each other as the taxi wove past crowds, past neon shopfronts, alongside passing buses, and stopped at traffic lights to let a ceaseless current of people flow in front of and around it. Amid the teeming energy of Saturday night, Oliver and Harriet kissed, almost as if they did not have ten thousand tomorrows.

Oliver preceded her into Mark's flat and switched on the table lamps in the drawing room. He had been determined to fill the place with colour and warmth for his last evening with Harriet before their brief and necessary separation and had been up early in order to do so. A flat in town used only as a pied-à-terre tends to be neglected, supplied with second-best china and cutlery, shabby furniture that is not quite bad enough to be thrown out; worn carpets and curtains that don't fit or hang properly. Despite Belinda's cleaner, 'Mrs Thing from four doors down', the London flat had never looked loved or lived in. In the course of the next year, after Mark's death, his widow would sell it for ten times the original purchase price.

Oliver wanted to give her a shining memory to set against Dodo's persuasiveness. He could only vaguely remember Dodo: a dim presiding figure, the *genius loci* of the Capel household. Now he felt her baleful influence braced like a shoulder against the opening door of their happiness.

Two vases of fresh flowers gave colour to the drab setting; the table was laid, glasses ready. He lit the gas fire and an artificial heap of coals glowed into life. Taking Harriet's coat he hung it in the hall, then gathered her into his arms and strained her body against him until her ribs cracked and she laughed and said, 'Oliver, help! Let me out!'

When he had seen her smile he went towards the kitchen saying as he went, 'Switch the oven on and half an hour later we can eat . . . so it says on the packet.'

He returned with a bottle of wine. As he was opening it, Harriet put her arms round him from behind and laid her head against his inclined back.

'My darling: when did you do all *this*?'

He turned. 'I was outside Marks and Spencer's at nine, stocked up, round here to do my under-butler stuff – had lots of practice, you know – scraped frozen champagne off the freezer – quick dash to Sandersons – before turning up to pay my respects to Hugo at noon.'

'Whatever were you doing at Sandersons?'

Blast! Oliver thought. Buying curtain material for Clarissa implies continuity although in two weeks' time . . . well, let it pass. He poured the wine and handed her a glass. He held up his own in a toast and said, 'Harriet, I love you. That means I choose you. Now, and for the rest of our lives.'

Harriet's mood of foreboding, induced by the ominous chords in the final scene of the opera and intensified by their violent climax on stage, would not be stilled. She recalled the first dinner at Rules before they had even touched or kissed, like a distant scene at the start of a journey already many miles long.

'*Love is blood*, Oliver,' she said. 'You told me that. Why don't we – oh, keep the memory of this week and leave it at that? Why try and prolong it? We are so lucky to have had it, and each other. I could almost settle for that.'

'I was wide awake last night, couldn't sleep. I drew up a timetable of our plans – did the arithmetic to show my lawyer – ran through the conversation with Clarissa in my mind. Finally, since my head was still spinning, I wrote a poem. Do you know how long it is, Harriet, since I felt like writing poetry? Forty years. Let's see if I remember . . . it begins with me on Eurostar:

Light at the end of the tunnel, a pinpoint through circles
*   of dark,*
A train howling close to its target; a laser slicing its mark,
My London and Paris, my axis, my magnetic star,
The world is contracted to Harriet, my love for all that
*   you are.*'

245

He stopped. 'It's not finished yet. The fourth line needs more work. It *was* the middle of the night . . .'

'Nobody,' she said, 'ever, has written me a poem. Don't change a word. Will you write it down and give it to me?'

Oliver tore a page from the back of his diary; XYZ of the address section. He unscrewed his fountain pen – it was, she noticed, cherishing every detail, a mottled green Conway-Stewart – and inscribed the poem from memory. At the top he wrote To Harriet, with pride and joy, for ever yours, Oliver and underlined <u>To Harriet</u>. He dated it at the foot: 23 September 1995.

'Now,' he said, 'while we eat we can discuss our timetable for the next two or three weeks. For a start, I'm staying here in London till Monday. I have to see my lawyer, get him to start drawing up a separation; then the bank manager to sort out the money.'

'I'm going back to Dorset tomorrow,' she said. 'I promised Dodo.'

'All right, if you must. But Harriet, can we – *please* – spend tonight here?'

She stretched a hand across the table to touch his – remembering the moment yesterday when Julian had reached across to grasp Fonzi's lean, smooth hand. Hers was veined, Oliver's speckled, yet the gesture was the same expression of love and trust.

'I *can't*. Roddy and Jennifer know we're together. There's no reason to suppose Philomena will pretend we had dinner in a foursome. My coming home so late will look pretty suspect as it is.'

'But my darling, we could tell them tomorrow?'

'No: you have to talk to Clarissa first. You'll be with her by Tuesday evening. After that we'll tell our children. Somehow.'

'Let's talk about practical details. The money. You ought to know what I propose to assign to Clarissa and how much I shall bring . . .'

I would love her less if she were less scrupulous, Oliver thought; yet I long for her recklessness to be as great as mine! Now we have to make love in a hurry, can't relax – so that she can get back to Camberwell. All this undermines the certainty she feels, I know she feels, when we're together. She doesn't know how to assert herself. I must hold her hard to our decision, not let her slip away. Harriet interrupted his train of thought.

'Oliver, I'm sure you've bought us something for pudding, but I can't wait any longer to be in bed with you. I ache, oh God how I ache. *Here*–' she pointed, '– and here.'

She got up and walked round the table. Leaning over so that her breasts brushed against him, Harriet pressed her mouth to Oliver's. They both tasted of wine and garlic. Her tongue pushed against his as they kissed, not *a* precise, separate kiss but kiss upon kiss, each kiss renewed with hardly an interval to draw breath. He paused to undo the buttons down the front of her dress. When it was open to the waist Harriet straightened up, pulled one breast free and held it to his lips. Her head fell back, she moaned with pleasure. Oliver stood up from the chair and with one supporting arm round her shoulders led her, stumbling, towards the bedroom.

At my age, breathed Harriet's inner voice, and for the first time, I am shuddering with lust. My body opens shamelessly and his entry brings such pleasure that I would sacrifice anything for it, which means, for him. If this is passion, the world's well lost. My skin darkens, my breasts are red, my face flushed. He makes me wait so long – I'm throbbing with the rhythm of desire. Faster, my love, don't slow down now! She disengaged herself from his entwining limbs to sit on top of him. His body strained towards her. She knelt upright and leaned forward to ease his cock deep inside herself. Oliver groaned with shock and pleasure. Harriet rode as though he were a galloping horse, keeping time with his movements, urging him on, 'Come *on*, I'm coming, quick, I'm coming, *now* . . .'

Together they howled aloud, like people in the throes of a terrible catastrophe.

Harriet thought, I have lived all my life and never fucked like this till now. I have not understood the half of it – until now.

Between midnight and 3 a.m. London is full of lovers. It is

a looser, more anarchic city and the tribe that roams the night streets is both more generous and more dangerous than that tucked up indoors. Oliver and Harriet leaned tiredly against one another as their taxi curved round Trafalgar Square, Nelson's phallic column silhouetted above them, flanked by a pride of lions.

'I've always wanted to sit on top of one of those,' Harriet murmured without lifting her head from his shoulder, 'On the way home from deb dances I used to look up and *long* to know how it would feel. I was far too well-behaved ever to *do* it.'

Oliver straightened up. 'Driver – drop us anywhere here,' he said.

The taxi slowed to a halt beside the pavement and they got out. Traffic swerved and parted to let them dash hand in hand through to the empty expanse of the Square. Nelson rampant above them, puddled York stone beneath their feet, a shallow pool to one side, they regarded the stone plinths crowned by four lions *couchant*.

Harriet said, 'I never realized they were quite that *high*.'

'Do you seriously want to sit on one?' Oliver asked. 'Shall I hoist you up?'

'I'd love to *try . . .*' she said, dubious now that they loomed so close. She put her handbag down, set one foot against the smooth side of the plinth and Oliver extended his flattened palm to support her other foot. She gave a half-hearted try and slumped back, defeated by the height and effort required.

'It was a nice idea . . .' Harriet said. 'Should have done it when I was young.'

A group of three drunks wove its undulating way towards them – benevolent, unsteady, playful as children.

'Big, innit?' said one of the young men.

'Enormous,' Harriet said. 'I wanted to sit on a lion but I've changed my mind.'

''Ere, missis, you wanna leg-up then?' asked another.

Again she placed one foot on the plinth about two feet up its smooth side and clumsily, powerfully, the young men hoisted her up, their hands supporting her buttocks, linked hands offering footholds. Harriet leaned back, trusted them, let them take her weight, lurched forward and swung high onto the flat surface. She almost toppled over, regained her balance and straightened up. The young men cheered.

'Darling, are you OK up there?' Oliver could see her standing on the plinth, outlined against scudding clouds and London's palely electrical night sky. Harriet inspected the huge rump and sinuous tail of the nearest lion.

'It's still quite a long way up,' she called out. 'And the rain's made it slippery.'

'Greg, give us shove,' said one young man.

'Blimey, not another one,' said his friend amiably; but he braced himself to take the straining weight and with the confident and fortuitous agility of the very drunk, the first man swung up to stand beside Harriet.

'*I'm the King of the Castle!*' he sang out, joyfully childish. '*You're the dirty rascals*! Hey, Sam, 's brilliant up 'ere! Greg, give us yer 'and.'

'Not bloody likely!' said the other two men. The youth beside her shrugged.

'What's your name, lady? – OK Harriet, stick your foot on its arse, lean back on me – don't worry, I won't let you go: one two three – *heave!*'

For a moment her feet scrabbled against the sloping black basalt and then she was on the lion's broad back, perched securely astride the pride of Empire, looking down into Oliver's anxious face.

'Darling, here I am! *All* my life I've . . . God, this is *wonderful*. I can see right down Whitehall to Big Ben.'

Her legs were wrenched wide apart and she felt between them the ache of their recent love-making. The young drunks grinned up at her.

'Looks like Mrs bleedin' Thatcher, doesn't she?' one said.

'Looks like the Queen of the Night!' Oliver said. 'She looks like *Cleopatra*.'

'Love don't half make 'im poetic – 'Ow long you two bin married?'

'We're not married,' Oliver said.

'At your age? Disgustin',' they teased. 'Way people carry on nowadays . . .'

The lion reminded Harriet of Aslan in the *Narnia* books.

249

He had the same imperturbable majesty, strength and grandeur. I am sitting astride Aslan, she thought, victorious at last! She remembered the old cry, 'Long live King Peter! Long live Queen Susan!' and wanted to cry out loud, 'Long live King Oliver! Long live Queen Harriet!' just as her younger self might have done had she been able to shed her decorum then. But even Oliver might have misunderstood and put it down to drunkenness and Harriet was not drunk but filled with exultation. This was the crowning moment of her life. Flinging her arms wide, leaning back until her throat was extended and her spine arched, Harriet repeated Aslan's noble pledge. She shouted it aloud to Big Ben, down the canyon of Whitehall, over the wide black plain of Trafalgar Square and up to the erect figure of Nelson overlooking the panorama of sleeping London. '*Once a king or queen in Narnia, always a king or queen!*'

Oliver laughed. 'Darling, you must be pissed!' She shook her head in vigorous denial. She wanted to yell at him and the young men below her, 'Look out, I'm going to jump – catch me!' but that too would have taken a young girl's recklessness. Soberly she remembered the words at the end of the book: 'In the name of Aslan, if ye will all have it so, let us go on and take the adventure that shall fall to us.'

She swivelled round to face the lion's tail and slid awkwardly down its backside until she could plant her feet on the plinth. Willing hands helped her back to earth.

Chapter Fifteen

What is love at first sight? Does it even exist? It did for Philomena and Matthew, both of whom would say to the end of their lives that it had happened to them.

Two people meet. They spend an increasingly light-headed evening together, glancing secretly at one another to confirm the tug of mutual attraction. Finally, hours later, they look deep into one another's eyes. That first scrutiny acknowledges the hope of much more to come – confessions, bed, love, commitment and perhaps a lifetime together. Nothing could be more vital – literally, life-giving – than the longed-for first stare.

With that mutual gaze the face of the other – the long-awaited, all-important Other – is absorbed into the brain, pumped through the bloodstream into the heart, lodged in the memory and deeper still in the unconscious, for this fierce looking must fix the image so securely that nothing can ever unseat it. Not rivals, nor the predatory and the envious; neither familiarity and boredom; not the pearly softness of a baby's face nor the blanched and wrinkled features of old age. Human relationships turn on this moment, love and children are born of it, genes transmitted, families welded, history made. This moment of imprinting is love at first sight.

After *Carmen*, that moment came in the restaurant Philly had chosen, when they had put their heads together over the menu and agreed that although not vegetarians, they tended to avoid red meat and both preferred roasted or char-grilled vegetables. Somehow the char-grilled vegetables seemed crucial. Into both their minds came a picture of sweet red peppers and ripe tomatoes, acrid fennel and purple aubergines, scored with parallel black lines from the searing grill, skins crisp and curling, giving off pungent herb aromas and conjuring Mediterranean memories of sun and heat. They smiled at one another. 'Yes!'

Next they scanned the wine list ('Let me at *least* pay for this?' offered Matthew. 'Next time,' said Philomena, bravely) and agreed on an Italian red. The waiter was given its number from the list and went to fetch it and at last there was no excuse for prevarication or distraction. They sat back in their seats and their eyes met, steadied, locked across the table; for a second or two; several seconds; half a minute, smiles fading, colour rising, heartbeat speeding.

Philomena was the first to tear her gaze away. She shook her head a couple of times and laughed. 'Wow!' she said, to cover her confusion. 'Is *that* what they teach you at drama school?'

'It's not acting, it's real,' he said.

The next significant moment comes the following morning. After the locked gaze the next stages are more or less inevitable ... heightened concentration, a growing confidence, recklessness, laughter, revelations; the first kiss. At this point optimism buoys the atmosphere as though a balloon had been inflated around the heart. A sense of breathless joy fills the senses. It doesn't matter that the words – 'Your place or mine?' – are banal. Expectation is so overwhelming that words become irrelevant.

They chose Philly's flat, for Matthew shared his with an actor and neither wanted to make love for the first time within earshot of someone else.

'We could walk there,' she said. 'It's only just down the road. I live in the Barbican. Cromwell Towers.'

'Why thou scheming wench, you planned this!'

'No, honestly – it's just – they know me here, at this restaurant, and—'

'Sweetheart, I'm *joking*!'

Sweetheart, she registered.

The lift shot towards the fourteenth floor ('There isn't a thirteenth,' said Philly with a grin) and they entered her calm

252

black and white flat, London's panorama glittering at their feet as though the stars in the sky were below and not above them. They tumbled together onto the voluptuous depths of her double bed. Afterwards they both slept like the innocent children they had been when they first met, twenty years ago.

But next morning, when the new lovers wake and break-fast together – this is a daunting moment. Each worries: how do I look? How do I smell? Is my breath sour? Should I clean my teeth straightaway? What did I say last night – was it all right – was she faking – did he mean it – *can it all be true?*

Philomena came into the bedroom in a short dressing gown carrying a tray with two cups of coffee, some milk and sugar.

'How do you normally spend Sunday mornings?' said Matthew.

'I don't usually go to bed with men on the first date,' she said simultaneously.

They both laughed.

'Say again?'

'No, you.'

'I said, I don't usually go to bed with a man I've only just met.'

'Twenty years seems a reasonably prudent interval.'

'In fact I don't usually go to bed with men full stop.'

'Good *God* what a waste! Why not?'

'Too busy. Too cautious. Don't go to bed with colleagues or clients and don't meet many other men.'

'What shall we do today?'

'I have to go to a family lunch organized by my sister. It's her oldest child Hugo's tenth birthday.'

'Will you be free by the evening?'

'Hope so.'

'Good. Do you want me to clean my teeth before we make love again?'

'Oh *good*! Yes please.'

'An honest woman is prized above rubies. Can I use your toothbrush?'

'If you don't I shall assume you carry your own every-where and be riven with doubts.'

Matthew laughed, threw back the bedclothes and,

resplendently naked, walked along the corridor to her bathroom.

The Camberwell house. In the basement kitchen a noisy breakfast was in progress. Roderick was trying to read the Sunday paper; Jennifer was absorbed in the colour supplement's fashion pages. The little girls were giggling and Amanda was about to throw Coco Pops at her sister.

Roderick looked up. 'Mandy . . . *no!*' he said. 'Em, don't tease her.'

The telephone rang.

'*I'll* take it,' said Jennifer (rather that than mop up the infants, all dribble and chocolate) and she picked up the receiver.

'Jenny, thank God it's *you*,' said an urgent, conspiratorial voice in her ear. 'Don't say anything. It's *me*. Mummy.'

'Oh, hallo. How are you? *Where* are you?'

'Gare du Nord. Paris. I'm going to surprise Hugo for his birthday lunch.'

'But I thought you . . . ?'

'Tell you later. *Quick*, I've only got twenty francs left on my Télécarte and they're ticking through like billyo. Where is it? Where should I come?'

'Pizza Express. It's the one in Clapham, forty-three Abbeville Road. Due south from Waterloo. Any cab driver'll know it. Couldn't be easier. OK? One o'clock. But . . . ?'

'Must dash. Next Eurostar goes in twenty minutes. Gets in at twelve-thirty. *Don't tell anyone*. It's a *surprise*. See you later. I'll come straight there, soon as I can get a taxi. Won't Huggy be *thrilled*! Bye darling! Remember it's secret. *Bye Bye!*'

'Bye . . .' said her bemused daughter.

'Who was that?' asked Roderick.

'. . . Daddy.'

'Doesn't he *know* where we're having lunch?'

'Must have forgotten.'

'The P-P-Pizza Express's my favourite p-p-place, Mummy,' said Hugo.

'*That's* why we *chose* it,' his mother told him, suppress-

254

ing with difficulty the penultimate word, 'obviously', and the last word of all, '. . . *idiot.*'

'I want a Pizza *Special*,' said Emily. 'And *two* ice-creams and a sundae.'

Harriet stood up. 'Upstairs with you, young lady. Time to clean those toothy-pegs and get you dressed.'

Harriet was beginning to long for privacy and the freedom to be on her own, make phone calls, come and go un-observed. She could not, except in the middle of the night, ring Dodo or the couple of friends – one in particular – she wanted to talk to. She badly needed – not advice, but to locate herself in the orderly world that had preceded this maelstrom. It was impossible. Every phone call could be overheard – since there were extensions all over the house – and any action might be interrupted by the arrival of clamorous children. Her small top-floor guest bedroom and the minute bathroom beside it felt as constricting as a ship's cabin. She needed the familiar spaces of her own home, where she could walk blindfold from room to room and know exactly how many paces it took to cross a floor and precisely where to place her hand so that it grasped the door-handle. Could she have that safety and predictability and Oliver too?

After making love they had stayed on at the flat for a further hour, making plans, working out a timetable of their future together. Tell Clarissa . . . the girls; tell her sons. Oliver leaves France, moves in with her; sets divorce in motion. Oliver to organize payments to Clarissa; arrange removal of furniture and personal effects. (Can it possibly be as smooth and simple as that? Harriet asked herself, and the muffled answer came back: No.) She was desperately short of sleep and the long muscles in her thighs ached. The little girls had come and bounced on her bed soon after seven o'clock and she looked as tired as she felt. When she came down to break-fast her son had commented on this.

'I know,' she had responded. 'That's what a week in London does to me!'

'What time did you get back?' Jenny had asked inquisi-tively.

'Goodness *knows*. Your father very kindly insisted on

255

giving me dinner after the opera. I should have refused. I'm worn out this morning.'

'Was it good?' asked Jennifer languidly, stretching and yawning.

'*Carmen* was marvellous. Very stirring. I couldn't eat much at dinner.'

Jennifer had turned back to her paper, curiosity satisfied. If only you knew, my girl, Harriet thought; if only you knew!

She made herself coffee and toast and ate breakfast in silence, her head throbbing. Ulrike had Sundays off and across the breakfast table the children waged their own anarchic battles, apparently below the level of their parents' attention.

'Emmie, *teeth*. Time to come upstairs with Granny. *And* you, Amanda – come along.'

As she left the room Harriet heard Jennifer saying sullenly to her husband,

'Hey, Rods, why don't you ever take *me* to the opera?' and his answer: 'Because you know nothing about music.'

Harriet washed both the girls' long blond hair, blow-drying it with Jenny's hairdryer until it gleamed like silk.

'There!' she said, holding up a hand-mirror so that they could admire themselves. 'Don't you both look like little princesses? Go and find Mummy. She'll dress you. Granny needs to get herself ready now.'

The truth – that she needed time to be alone – was not something the children could be expected to understand. Harriet locked the bedroom door and still in her dressing gown, stared sightlessly out of the window over the rooftops of Camberwell.

Her thoughts were urgent and haphazard. Now that I've discovered sex, its drumming crescendo and the extraordinary sweetness and calm afterwards, I can't go back to being an ageing celibate woman. These new sensations have nothing to do with what George and I did in bed. He had a need and I satisfied it, just often enough so that he wasn't unhappy. Frustration made him more log-like than ever. When we'd made love he was amiable and filled with well-being, until the need burdened him once more. George and I never named the parts out loud. He grunted and I would make little encouraging moans and call him 'Sweetheart' to hurry him up and reassure him. Now the short brutal exact words spring from my mouth as though I had always used them. Now that I've known Oliver I can't let him go.

His life story – that Russian girl, extraordinary. No wonder he says love is blood. His work – something secret – I don't care. He was evidently a spy: so what? I'm more interested to know his favourite food, what books he has read, his taste in music, where he goes on holiday; can he swim, is he a walker; does he believe in God? If we can't spend the rest of our lives together I shall wither away and become a little old woman with wandering thoughts and palsied hands, talking to myself. I am fifty-five and suddenly it all makes sense ... the lens clicks, human behaviour comes sharply into focus. I am ashamed to remember how disparaging I was in the past, when some poor woman had left her husband or scandalized the county with an affair. *Thoroughly undignified,* I would have thought to myself. *Ought to have had more sense. No self-control.* And worst of all: *at her age!*

I remember an old school friend of mine who rang me once, Constance King – forget her married name – utterly distraught with love. She had asked if she could bring the man down to stay. They badly needed to get out of London for a few days. I was embarrassed at the thought of a couple in their fifties mooning around and George was appalled at the prospect. 'Are you mad, Harriet? You haven't *seen* the woman for years. Why should they come here? No. Tell her *no.*' I put her off with some excuse, poor Constance. She never asked again. Whatever happened to her? I'd love to talk to her now.

How will the boys react? Jules will be startled at first and then pleased. Roderick? He is much more his father's son. He'll disapprove. It's not a good moment in his life to upset him. Jennifer plays him up but I've heard them making love a couple of times this week. I don't believe their marriage is on the point of breakdown. Losing her job will give her a breathing space; time to think. It's a bad patch but they'll weather it. *She'll* pretend to be shocked. She has a poison-ous tongue, like her mother. Oliver *is* her father, of course. Oh, God . . . oh *God*, what am I to do?

Are the babies young enough to take it in their stride? Girls probably will – tough little creatures; take after her. But Hugo – poor old Hugo, wan and insecure. Perhaps if Oliver and I had him down to stay with us on his own; bit of undivided attention, things like riding and – well, making Airfix kits. That might stiffen his spine. *Don't fool yourself, Harriet.* The children will suffer. So will Julian and Roderick.

She remembered George, sleeves rolled up to the elbow, brawny forearms flexing as he worked to repair an area of woodland near the house after the great storm of 1987. Several old and many-branched trees had been blown over by its force, leaving a gaping hole in the earth, exposing the twisting, earth-encumbered roots. What we propose is like uprooting an ancient oak. This is the family I came to mend.

And then there is Dodo. Well, can't be helped. I cannot order my life according to the whims and wishes of a ninety-year-old woman. Of course she will disapprove. Hate having him under our roof. Give him black looks. But we can't wait for Dodo to die. Might be another four or five years. Dodo is not necessarily right. I was a good wife, made George happy. Now it's my turn.

Clarissa is not my problem. Oliver can worry about her. Don't envy him that. She'll fight tooth and nail. The only one on his side I care about is Philomena. Nice girl. She and young Matthew ought to get something going. They all work too hard, poor young things. No time for love. Or sex. Sex – sex – I cannot give Oliver up! In the end it comes down to this simple fact: I cannot renounce him.

I shall ring Dodo later this afternoon and tell her. What? That I can't leave London while Oliver's still here. We might even stay a couple of nights in the flat. My only love. In all my life, just this one. That's it, then. Decided.

Nearly noon. Time to get dressed.

Oliver, browsing through the Sunday papers in the Morning Room at the Reform Club, had tried twice to ring his wife and got no reply. He'd come in too late to speak to her – almost 3 a.m. by the time he finally got back – but there had been no message. She seldom went out on Sunday mornings – called it her 'luxury time' – but it was just possible that she had gone to church. Praying for Hugo? Much more likely she hoped to bask in congratulations for the madrigal concert. Still, odd that she hadn't tried to ring. Sulking, probably. He went to his room, tried a third time and got an answer.

''*Allo, oui? Maison des Glycines.*'

'*Puis-je parler avec ma femme?*'

'Dad?'

'Patrick! Where's Mum? What are you doing there?'

'*Mah, bah, ouah* . . .' Patrick began, in the slovenly adolescents' French that had become fashionable and which Oliver deplored.

'Where *is* she?'

'Out somewhere – I dunno – be back soon, probably. Want me to give her a message? *Ils y'ont des problèmes?*'

'No problem . . . just wanted a chat. Did the concert go well, d'you know?'

'Sang *comme un rossignol*. Great success.'

'Good. OK, old boy – tell her I'll try again later. How's things with you? All well?'

'*Mah, bah – moi, je suis peinard, tu sais* . . . yeah, Dad, I'm fine.'

'All right. Good. Tell Mum I rang then. Be with her soon.'

'Right . . . cheers then.'

'Goodbye, Patrick.'

Why, thought Oliver as he put the phone down, does my son irritate me so? If only he would speak either English or French, instead of a bastard mixture of the two. In brooding on this he overlooked the more important question: where the blazes was Clarissa?

Oliver packed his case, got out his diary and tore a page from the small message pad at the back. On this he had calculated the money he would have to allow his wife and how much would be left for himself and Harriet. He was too fastidious to enquire after her finances but it seemed safe to assume that old Capel had left her adequately provided for.

259

His own pension – since he had opted for early retirement – was not quite £24,000 a year. Half of that should go to Clarissa. There was a dwindling trust fund left by his father which brought in roughly £5,000 a year and that he would keep for himself. The house in France was fully paid for. If she put the guests on a more professional footing; advertised properly, redecorated a couple of bedrooms, she ought to make a clear £8,000 a year profit. Even without old Sullivan's money – most of which was earmarked for the grandchildren's education – she should be able to get by on £20,000 a year. He'd have about £17,000. He jotted these figures down, looked at them, and added a row of question marks.

But first there was an expensive divorce to be negotiated, lawyers' fees – hers as well as his own, in all probability – and an ugly dividing up of their joint possessions. He was prepared to let Clarissa have almost, but not quite, everything and she'd fight to a standstill over the *not quite*. She was welcome to keep the photo albums, the silver and other family heirlooms – Gaunt as well as Sullivan – her jewellery: none of that mattered to him. But he wanted the best bottles of Eighties claret gathering dust in the cellar, waiting for their perfect moment. There were also a couple of fine old cognacs which he had often savoured in anticipation. Occasionally he would hold a bottle up to the dim cellar light and admire its deepening amber. Of course, he could simply help himself and wait for her to find out – she probably wouldn't even notice – but that would be clandestine and he didn't care to be shifty, not over this. How strange human nature is! He was prepared to lie about the week he had spent with Harriet, to be evasive with his son and daughters; but somehow it seemed a more ignoble deception to strip the wine cellar of its choicest vintages without telling her.

Daughters – another problem. Both the girls would be on her side, he supposed. It was only to be expected. What about Patrick? He'd certainly stay in France: might even move back in with her. Huge *manoir* . . . plenty of room for them to lead their own lives. The idea of Clarissa taking up with another man was hard to imagine. Bloody good thing if she did, of course. Tough little Frenchman, stand no non-sense. He pulled himself up short. Gaunt, stop thinking in clichés. She'll be bereft without you. His conscience echoed, bereft, bereft . . . bereft but not, he felt sure, inconsolable.

All the same, I have to tell Jenny and Phill, and the sooner the better. End of the afternoon perhaps, while that Swedish girl was putting the infants to bed. Somehow I must try and get them on their own . . . might suggest they came to the club for a drink? I've always found it best to break bad news in public; then people can't kick up too much of a fuss. Amazing how the English let themselves be constrained by social niceties. Then at last he would be free to go to Mark's flat, with Harriet. That fuck last night had been amazing. What an incredible woman. Bottle up sex for years and it's like uncorking the genie. He put a hand in his pocket to ease an erection. Cock swelled at the mere thought of her. And at sixty: just when he'd begun to think all that would soon be a thing of the past. Not only sex . . . *love*. Never have thought you could fall in love like a hot-blooded youth at this age.

An old Edwardian music hall song came to mind; one that his father – was it his father, or an uncle? never mind . . . *someone* used to sing, in an exaggeratedly theatrical voice with rolling eyes and a swooning expression. How did it go?

> *At seventeen*
> *He fell in love quite madly*
> *Eyes of deepest blue.*
> *At twenty-one*
> *He got it just as badly*
> *Eyes of a different hue.*
> *At thirty-four*
> *You'll find him flirting madly*
> *Two or three or more . . .*

The voice would swoop into tremulous sincerity:

> *When he thought he was just past love*
> *It was then he met his last love*
> *And he loved her as he'd ne-e-ever loved before!*

261

Oliver smiled to himself. Quite true.

Across the park came the sound of Big Ben striking twelve. Time to go down, pay his bill, dump his case with the porter and set off for this lunch. It was a shame that young Hugo was such a sissy. Still only ten of course. Plenty of time. Handsome boy. Hope to God he's not queer. Oliver grinned. That's not very politically correct. Still, it's a far cry nowadays from the 'bugger-hunting' that went on back in the Forties, right up to the Fifties, when drunken hearties would pursue terrified homosexuals through the West End on a Saturday evening.

Looking every inch the predictable, old-fashioned, courteous and correct English gentleman, Oliver slowly descended the carpeted and – for its final sweep – marble staircase to the ground floor of the Reform. Brace yourself, Gaunt: this is the big ordeal. Time for a couple of Scotches and by the end of this afternoon it'll all be over – the secrecy, the deception. Never been so sure of anything in my life.

Chapter Sixteen

'Might as well take both cars,' Roderick said when they were all assembled on the pavement at twelve-thirty, ready to leave. He's exactly like George, Harriet thought; obsessively punctual.

'Huge, which do you want to go in? Me and Mummy's, or Granny Harriet's?'

Hugo turned anguished eyes upon his father and Harriet made the decision for him. 'Hugo will go with you two,' she said firmly, 'by *himself,* and I'll take the girls.' Before they could protest she had bundled them into the back just as Ulrike appeared from the basement.

'Can I come with you too?' she asked.

'Goody goody *goody,* 'Rike's coming with u-us!' the girls sang triumphantly as Ulrike climbed in beside them.

They settled themselves round a large table in an order designed to give Hugo maximum prominence. Attentive waiters handed out large menus which named and described twenty or more different pizza toppings. The restaurant floor was tiled, the walls bright with modern pictures. On each table stood a vase of fresh flowers. It was brisk, welcoming and child-friendly.

'Bloody good marketing!' said Roderick approvingly.

'Bloody good!' said Hugo daringly, and got away with it.

'*Bloody* good!' said Emily, and was ticked off.

'*Buddy*-good, buddy-*good* . . .' said Amanda under her breath.

'Oh *will* you shut up, Mandy!' said Jennifer.

Hugo was flanked by his parents at a round table, in the seat giving the best view of the room. Next to Roderick was Emily, perkily confident; then Ulrike keeping an eye on Mandy. Harriet was on the other side of Amanda with her back to the entrance so that she would not see Oliver arrive. She hoped she would not start or blush. The two remaining places awaited Philly and Julian.

As she studied the menu, Harriet – perhaps because of the Italian names: Parmigiana, Veronese, Toscana – found herself vividly reminded of a holiday she and George had taken in Tuscany some fifteen years ago. It would have been the year Julian went up to Bristol. George had felt this was the beginning of their time together as a couple rather than as parents. It touched her now to remember that he should have thought this an event worth celebrating. It had been autumn; tourists were few, the weather still balmy. One evening they had gone out for dinner to a hill-top town near the farmhouse they had rented for two weeks. That, too, had had a tiled floor and dishes called Napoletana, Parmigiana or Veneziana.

They had strolled through the little town beforehand, under an indigo sky. She had been bare-armed, a cardigan slung round her shoulders, tied at her throat. She and George had held hands . . . not something they did in England. The timelessness of the town's scarred mediaeval walls and the people who had come out to stroll and chat peacefully as the day wound down put them into a benevolent humour. The restaurant they chose was in a basement and the few other diners were all Italian. They sat at a corner table under a barrel-vaulted ceiling, intimate and private, drinking a particularly delicious wine – its name flew back to her across the intervening fifteen years: Tignanello! A wonderful wine. They had made love at the end of the evening, and George had not been a log, nor she a passive receptacle. How disloyal I've been, Harriet thought: we were happy then and on many other occasions. I have betrayed George by belittling him and our happiness. I had not really forgotten; I have lied – to myself and to Oliver.

A man leaned over to greet her with a kiss on the cheek and she turned and rose smilingly, expecting Julian, but it was Oliver. By accident their lips touched and a deep blush flooded her face.

'Harriet – sorry – you shouldn't get up!' At the same moment she apologized too: 'Sorry, Oliver, I thought you were Julian, I don't know why!'

'Can I sit next to Granny Harriet?' he asked the little girls and they shrieked, 'Yes! Yes!' making it easy for him.

He sat beside her and smiled around the table.

'Hallo Huge! *Isn't* this a treat? *Hugo's birthday lunch*,' he said, emphasizing every word, and Hugo glowed.

Within a few moments Julian had arrived, dressed in black which emphasized his alabaster skin. He handed Hugo an elaborately wrapped box.

'Open it later, Huge!' said Roderick, but Julian over-ruled him as only a brother could, saying, 'Bollocks, Rods, don't be so pompous. Open it *now*, Hugo, or I shall sulk.'

Glancing nervously at his father, Hugo tore at the silk ribbon and ripped off the shiny wrapping paper. Inside was a miniature matador's outfit: a brilliantly embroidered jacket, black waistcoat and narrow white trousers. Hugo was speechless with delight. Jennifer said, 'Oh Julian, *really*. How unsuitable can you *get*, for Christ's sake.'

Julian ignored her. 'It's a real one, Hugo, all the way from Spain. My friend Alfonso sent for it. He's Spanish so he knows about these things. It's called a *traja de luces*.'

Hugo turned a radiant face towards his uncle. 'I think it's totally totally mega,' he said.

'*Good*! That's all that matters then, isn't it?'

Before the moment could be spoiled there was a stir around the table as two waiters and Philomena arrived at once. Harriet saw a wink cross from Julian to Hugo and, inexpertly, Hugo winked back.

'Huggy!' said Philomena as she bent over to kiss him. 'What's *that*? Isn't it *gorgeous*! Well, I've brought you something nearly as nice, I hope.' She handed him a large square rustling package, loosely wrapped, saying, 'Open it carefully. It squeaks.'

Hugo slipped off the string round the square brown parcel to reveal a wire cage. Inside, palpitating and as wide-eyed as

265

Hugo himself, sat a small guinea pig. Black-and-white whorls of fur swirled over its body.

'He's *beautiful*!' Hugo whispered. 'What's his name?'

'That's up to you. You can call him whatever you like,' said Philly.

There was a long moment of indecision. Philomena could see that the two little girls were bursting with ideas. She hushed them sternly while everyone looked expectantly at Hugo.

'I shall call him Mowgli,' he said finally; and putting his face to the bars of the cage, he murmured adoringly, 'Hello, Mowgli!'

'Don't think *I'm* going to clean out his cage, Huge,' his mother said crisply. 'That's *your* responsibility.' She turned to glare at Philomena, who grinned serenely back. 'Traitor!' Jennifer hissed at her twin.

'N-N-Nobody's *allowed* to c-c-clean it out except *me*,' Hugo said proudly.

'Right! Good! Now, put Mowgli on the floor under your seat,' his father said. 'He'll be quite safe there. I expect he'll go to sleep.'

Harriet, watching them all, keeping her eyes averted from Oliver, thought: this is a *happy* family. In spite of the rows, the threats, the problems, the stutter, these Capels and Gaunts have met and married and created a happy family. Oliver moved his knee fractionally so that his thigh pressed against hers, at the same time saying to Philomena, as she seated herself next to him, 'Darling Phills, you look – as one used to say of the Queen – radiant. Hope you enjoyed yesterday evening. Good chap, Matthew, isn't he?'

Before Philomena could reply Jennifer said, 'Course, Phills – *Matthew* . . . Matthew *Vulliamy*. You met up again didn't you? Harriet didn't mention *him*. I seem to remember he was rather sweet if a bit spotty. What's he like now?'

'*Utterly* dishy . . .'

'Lucky old you. Fingers crossed, then . . .'

The babble round the table diminished briefly as Roderick insisted that everyone chose their food and drink. Hugo gave his order first.

'Pizza Fiorentina.'

'Good choice,' said Julian. 'Same for me.'

'Wine for the grown-ups, Coke for the kids and *no whingeing*,' Roderick ordered.

'Am I grown-up or a kid?' asked Ulrike. Roderick grinned at her and said, 'A grown-up . . . *definitely*.'

He looked at the hovering waiter. 'I'll have Pizza Guineapiggiana,' he said. 'Here, Huge – pass the cage.'

'*No!*' said Hugo fiercely, and everyone laughed.

The drinks were poured and glasses raised to Hugo.

'What's it like being ten?' Philomena asked.

Hugo said, 'Don't know yet,' and they all laughed again.

Philomena began to talk to Julian; Ulrike calmed Emily and Amanda, who were already arguing with Hugo about the cage-cleaning rota, Roddy leant across to speak to Jenny and under cover of all this Oliver squeezed Harriet's hand under the table and said softly, 'You all right this morning? Tired?'

'No I'm fine,' she said, adding a bit too loudly, 'marvellous evening. The opera was great – didn't you think so?'

There is a pause when the tide is full, before it turns and flows the other way. In that moment time seems sluggish. It dawdles. The water gathers itself and waits. That pause precedes any momentous change and is recalled with nostalgia, like a lost Golden Age. Such were the final few summers before the Great War; the decades before the French Revolution; the glittering Court of the last Tsar, his virgin daughters dressed in white muslin like girls in a Russian fairytale – the seven daughters who were turned into swans, perhaps, flying high in the midsummer sky. Such too were the Kennedys' Camelot years. In this dream-like interval things happen separately, unhurriedly, deliberately, as though frames of film were being examined slowly, one by one, rather than flashing across the screen too quickly for single moments to be isolated. Oliver held Harriet's hand, Hugo, his two feet clamped firmly on either side of the cage underneath his chair, basked in the knowledge that he was the centre of attention, Julian and Philomena talked to each other for the first time since the feud had begun thirteen years ago, Roddy and his wife looked lovingly at their three handsome children and the two little girls sitting next to Ulrike trusted her never to leave them. A dreamlike interval; perfection achieved.

Then Jennifer and her sister, their attention distracted, turned to look towards the door. A triumphant figure bore down on them, one finger and both eyebrows raised to command silence. She swooped on the startled Hugo, announcing at the top of her voice: '*Yoo*-hoo! Sur*prise*, everyone! Happy *birthday*, Huggy!'

She enveloped him in a hot, tickly embrace smelling of fur, scent and perspiration.

Hugo looked up and said, 'Granny '*Rissa*!' Overwhelmed with emotion, he burst into tears.

In the Zaprudder film, seconds after Kennedy has been shot, the next frames show the panic-stricken figure of his wife trying to escape death by crawling across the long boot of the Presidential automobile. Her slender figure in the chic pink suit with which she had hoped to win over the good people of Dallas is intercepted by a Secret Service man riding on the rear bumper. Seconds later she is back in the car beside her dying husband, the pink suit splashed with bright red blood. It happens too fast for the eye to catch; but viewed frame by frame, the film reveals it. None of the hundreds of reporters who viewed the assassination reported this, perhaps out of sympathy with the distraught young widow; or perhaps because they literally did not see it, or if they did, could not believe their eyes.

In just the same way nobody saw Oliver, his eyes desperately locked onto hers, lift Harriet's hand and kiss it once, hard, before standing up to greet his wife. No-one saw the exasperated look that passed between Jenny and Philomena, or heard them sigh. No-one saw Julian clench his lips, half-rise, and slump back into his chair. No-one heard Roderick mutter, 'Oh fuck her, fuck her, *fuck* her!' The only thing anyone noticed was that Hugo, the star of the occasion, had burst into tears.

Clarissa had succeeded in astonishing them all. Gratified, she kissed her daughters and embraced her husband.

'*There*, Olly!' she said. 'I surprised you, didn't I?'

'Yes,' said Oliver, 'you certainly did.'

'You had no idea I was coming? Promise!'

'No idea at all.'

Julian stood up and Philomena took his place so that Clarissa could sit beside her husband while Julian went in search of another chair. Harriet too stood up and as she did so, Clarissa leaned across saying graciously, 'Harriet! My dear, I'm *so* sorry . . . I didn't *see* you tucked away there! No no, don't move. *Do* sit down again. I'm sure Roddy will . . .'

'It's all right, Julian already *is* . . .' Harriet said, thinking, so *this* is how it is to end.

Julian found a chair and the others shuffled closer together to make room. Hugo had stopped crying, but his eyes glittered and there was mucus round his nose. Julian took out a linen handkerchief and wiped Hugo's face with a flourish before sitting in the empty chair between the two sisters.

Oliver thought, Harriet on my left, Clarissa on my right. Why didn't I anticipate this when I rang Patrick this morning? My reactions must be slowing down. I've lost the ability to sense danger. Yet what could I have done? I *will not* let it all unravel. *Harriet is mine.*

Someone pushed a glass across to Clarissa, who was bright-eyed and triumphant. She took a sip, made a face, ('What *is* this? Petrol?') and said aloud to Oliver, 'Tell me honestly – you *hadn't* guessed, had you? Jenny didn't tell?'

'No, Clarissa, your secret was safe with her,' Oliver said. 'Now perhaps you'd better order, or you'll hold everyone up.'

'Oh, darling – I've no *idea* – what do they have here – is it *just* pizzas? Well then, I'll have the same as you. I'm sure that'll be *fine*. Doesn't *Huggy* look smart? Philly, you're looking *marvellous*. And Jenny too of course. Proud young mother . . . mmmm, darling? *Gosh* it seems ages since I've seen you all! Isn't this a *treat*?'

It *was*, thought Roderick, until you turned up. He whispered to Jenny, 'Did you know?' and she whispered back, 'Yes, but on pain of secrecy. She rang from the station in Paris only this morning – at breakfast – when I said it was Dad.'

'Too late to stop her by then,' he said.

'You can't stop *Mum*,' Jenny answered indignantly, and leaning across the table she addressed her mother: 'Clever *you*! So tell us how you came? You decided not to fly?'

'*Well*,' said Clarissa, 'I *could* have flown of course, but it would have meant hardly any sleep at *all* and poor Patrick driving me to Toulouse and *then* I'd have had to catch a seven-thirty flight which would have got me in to Heathrow at something like quarter to *nine* because of the time difference – so although I *could* have been with you by ten o'clock I'd have been *exhausted*. I decided *instead* to take the *night* train from Rodez after the concert – *up* to Paris . . .'

Philly interrupted before she could embark on a further timetable. 'How did it go, Mum? Your concert?'

'*Éclatant!* They *loved* it! So sweet, all the dear people in the *Salle des Fêtes*, listening with *such* concentration and clapping like *mad*. But I mustn't be selfish – that's quite enough about *me*: I want to hear *everyone's* news. Hugo first. How was your *party*, Huggy? Did you get nice *presents*?'

Harriet thought, yes, this is the beginning of the end. A life force such as hers brooks no opposition. She is like a hurricane, flattening everything in its path.

Sometimes, small children have a natural impulse to torment helpless things. It is not so much cruelty as curiosity. They tear the wings off insects simply to see what happens. The scientifically minded will tear off one left and one right wing from two flies and compare the results. They cannot imagine insects suffering pain, and perhaps they are right. Or they will trap a kitten or a puppy in a basement and torture it. Every so often – just as a cat does with a mouse – they'll stop to reassure it and when the young animal has been convinced by soft voices and beckoning hands and comes back trustingly to be petted, they torment it again. But the child is only trying out its power – because it *can*. Children are the playthings of even the most well-meaning adults and sometimes they want to see the tables turned. But in adults, cruelty is seldom accidental. When it is knowingly deliberate, as was the case now with Clarissa, it becomes sadism. Clarissa had many old scores to pay off and had rarely been offered such an ideal opportunity to exact revenge.

Clarissa said, '*Harriet*, my dear, I gather you've been having a *thrilling* week in London?'

'Yes, for a country mouse like me it's been quite a change.'

'Oh you mustn't say *that*! It makes *me* a country mouse too – as we say in France, *un rat des champs*.' Clarissa laughed indulgently. '*Do* tell me what you've been doing with yourself?'

'Not a great deal, really. I wanted to make the most of my time with the grandchildren. And Roddy and Julian, of course.' Harriet looked at her sons, hoping one would take the conversational cup from her.

'*Oliver* said you planned to go to the *opera*?'

'Yes – we did that last night. *Carmen.* A wonderful production. Wasn't it, Philly?'

'Really, Harriet? How *exciting* for you. And what else?'

'Well, as I say, not much. Jenny told me about a marvellous exhibition at the National Portrait Gallery so I went and saw that and loved it . . .'

'Did you? What a *coincidence*! It must have been the same one that Oliver went to! Or perhaps you went together?'

'No . . .' said Oliver.

'Yes . . .' said Harriet.

'We bumped into each other there,' said Oliver.

Clarissa beamed benevolently upon them both. 'Goodness! *What* a coincidence!' she said again.

Before she could go on – *What else have you been doing together? How nice that you, so to speak, found each other! Such a good thing the silly feud is over – don't you agree, Julian?* – all the remarks she had been turning over in her mind throughout the long train journey – Clarissa was interrupted by the arrival of two waiters carrying what looked like blood-bespattered pizzas. The first was set before Hugo. The waiters went round the table depositing a gory plate in front of each member of the family. Wine glasses were refilled ('*Could* I have water, do you think? Do you have *Badoit*?' asked Clarissa) and everyone began to eat. Harriet drew Amanda's plate towards herself and cut the food into bite-sized morsels.

'Here you are, Mandy darling. Birdy bits!' she said.

Her heart beat with a slow, measured heaviness. It's all over. Oliver cannot stand up to her. Why else would they still be married, after thirty-six years? Clarissa is a formidable adversary – I underestimated her – and she *knows*.

'Now, we must *all* drink to *Huggy*!' Clarissa announced. People put down their knives and forks and lifted their glasses. Clarissa's was empty.

'*Olly* won't mind – *do* you, darling?' she said and taking his glass, held it up. 'Now then: to *Hugo*! A very happy tenth birthday and a wonderful *wonderful* life!'

They all drank to Hugo.

'Later on,' Clarissa told him, 'you must make a little *speech*. Not yet. You need a bit of time to think what to *say*, don't you darling?'

Hugo, his lunch turned to misery (after the meal you may be asked to say a few words . . .) nodded speechlessly.

Oliver's glass, Harriet saw, was now smeared with cyclamen-red lipstick, as though by this mouth-to-mouth intimacy Clarissa were claiming him as her own. It was all Harriet could do not to seize the glass and wipe it between the folds of her table napkin until not a trace of the red stain remained.

Oliver thought, she is torturing my love and I am helpless to defend her. While everyone was preoccupied with the glutinous pizzas he whispered to his wife, 'What are you doing? What's the matter with you? Why so belligerent?'

'Mark rang me,' his wife said under her breath, turning to look deliberately into her husband's face. She watched him blanch. She held the suspense before continuing, 'Two – no, three nights ago. He told me about his illness. I thought I ought to come and see him one last time. After all, they're practically our oldest friends, him and Belinda. We met them back in the Bucharest days. And I was, you know, jolly *fond* of him once. I mean, I still *am*, of course.'

Oliver's antennae were on full alert. 'What are you trying to say? That you and Mark had an affair?'

'What makes you jump to that conclusion, I wonder? Even if I *had* it would have been an awful long time ago now. And at least,' she hissed in a furious whisper, '*I* would have been *discreet* about it.'

Oliver stood up, scraping his chair across the tiles. He said, 'Could you excuse us both? We won't be long. Hugo – *may* we leave you, please, just for a moment?'

'Course, Grandpa Oliver,' said Hugo.

Oliver took his wife's wrist in an iron grip, giving her no choice but to stand up. 'Poor Granny 'Rissa's not feeling too brilliant. She just needs a bit of a walk outside in the fresh air. Then she'll be fine. *Won't you*?'

Clarissa smiled glassily. 'Yes,' she said.

Oliver strode through the centre of the noisy Sunday lunchtime crowd, his wife clattering awkwardly behind him. A waiter held the door and they passed through it into the street. He walked a dozen paces before stopping to face her.

'Clarissa, *what is this*?'

Harriet was unable to eat. She lifted the fork to her mouth, looked at the vomitlike strands it had speared and put them back on her plate. Philomena leaned across the empty places vacated by her parents and asked kindly,

'Harriet? Are you all right?'

'Yes, bless you. Just don't seem to have much of an appetite.' In a desperate attempt at normality Harriet went on, 'He seemed tremendously nice, young Matthew. And it was brilliant of him to have got us such marvellous seats.'

Philomena's smile was eloquent reply. 'You mustn't let Mum upset you,' she said. 'She has this rather imperious manner. I don't think she realizes.'

'No,' Harriet answered.

Julian asked Hugo, 'What shall we do when lunch's over, have you decided?'

Hugo looked uncertainly at his mother.

'Nothing planned,' Jennifer said. 'Do you have any thoughts?'

'Tower of London. Museum of the Moving Image. Ice-skating.'

'You could take him off to any one of those, if you wanted. Not with Mowgli, though. We'll take him home,

273

Huge. He'll be waiting for you in your bedroom.'

'Granny 'Rissa said I've got to make a sp-sp-speech . . .' said Hugo in a desperate sibilant rush.

'And you don't want to?' asked his uncle.

'I don't know what to s-s-say.'

Julian turned to his brother. 'Rods, has this poor kid really got to stand up and make a speech?'

'Course not! Granny 'Rissa was only joking!'

'There you are, Hugo. Now you can relax, OK?'

The waiters came to clear their plates and offer ice-cream. Oliver and Clarissa had returned. Her colour was even higher than usual; his face set rigid with anger. Harriet glanced at him once. It's all over, she thought. She has won and I have lost him. But as he sat down Oliver squeezed her hand briefly, bringing hope leaping like a salmon. He pressed his foot re-assuringly against hers and Harriet was reminded of that first electric contact so long – nearly a week – ago. Clarissa was silent. Maybe not, Harriet thought – God in heaven, *maybe I have not lost*!

Tension was mounting as one by one it dawned upon Harriet's sons and Oliver's daughters that something momentous was occurring, though they did not grasp what it might be. The noisy banter of an hour ago had become a nervous display of good manners. Only the two little girls scoffed their ice-cream regardless. Ulrike suggested that she might walk them home, and Jennifer said significantly, 'You and I must have a *chat*, Ulrike . . . later.'

Before Ulrike could gather the children up, Oliver — his face granite-like in its solemnity – pushed his chair back and began to rise to his feet. 'I have something to say to all of you round this table,' he began. 'I wouldn't have chosen this precise moment, but . . .'

Puzzled, Roderick and Jennifer glanced at one another. Harriet's heart hammered like a fast metronome. Clarissa stood up too, her jaw clenched in a hysterical smile.

'What better moment could there be?' she cried gaily. 'We're all here – it's perfect! Come on now, everybody – I want you *all* to join in!'

The Capel and Gaunt family formed a tableau like those Victorian paintings showing three generations gathered

274

round the groaning board; paintings in which every gesture is recorded, every sentimental detail captured for posterity. This one could have been entitled The Young Master, or perhaps The Heart of the Family. In the centre sits the modest, good-looking lad with two rosy-cheeked little sisters; on either side, their indulgent parents. The artist has captured the matriarchal beam of one grandmother and the tremulous smile that illuminates the pale profile of the other. It is an eternal scene: the family united by love and blood.

Clarissa, vigorously conducting with both arms, sang in her strong soprano voice,

'Happy *Birthday* to you!

Happy Birthday to *you*!

Happy *birthday* dear . . .'

Interrupt her, Harriet prayed. Stop her. You have to tell them now or it will be too late. Be strong, my love, my only love. I can't do it for you. But nothing happened. Clarissa had seized the initiative, hijacked the moment, and Oliver was forced to concede.

They sang raggedly, looking at Hugo whose eyes were wide with apprehension and embarrassment. Encouraged by Clarissa and Jenny they went on to sing *For He's a Jolly Good Fellow!* and at the end Clarissa clapped and called out, 'Speech! *Speech*!'

'No,' said Julian firmly. 'Hugo has decided against making a speech, but he would like to thank you all very much for being here and for his lovely presents. Is that right, Hugo?'

'Yes,' said Hugo, smiling with radiant relief.

The official proceedings were over. The Pizza Express was almost empty. Waiters began hovering and Roderick snapped his fingers and scribbled in the air for them to bring the bill. Harriet sat paralysed. Time is running out, Oliver; you must do it *now*, or never. In case her absence might concentrate his mind or allow him to say something to Clarissa or his daughters, she stood up, saying, 'Excuse me, everyone . . . the Ladies . . . back in a minute.'

In the pristine white-tiled room Harriet stared at her spotlit reflection. She looked like a woman in a high fever. Her eyes glittered in the harsh light that bounced off the white walls into the expanse of mirror; her cheeks bore crimson highlights. She locked one of the cubicle doors and sat down. She could feel a soft, dull ache, a reminder of last night's frenzied love-making. Last night! An image of her ecstatic body mounted astride Oliver's flashed through her mind, and superimposed across it the image of a cowboy on a bucking bronco, one jubilant hand waving his hat in the air. As if viewed through a stereoscope, the two pictures became one and three-dimensional.

These images slid away and were replaced by a memory of herself a few days ago in Mark's flat: her head tipped back, eyes closed in rapture as Oliver fondled her breasts. Simultaneously Harriet saw Clarissa as a young girl in the sitting-out room at a Commem Ball. Her dress bunched around her waist, young breasts exposed, she sat at Oliver's feet leaning against his knees. That was it, thought Harriet, whether they knew it or not – that first virginal exposure was the moment when Clarissa and Oliver became shackled for life. Their fate was decided nearly forty years ago. They married because he was the first man to see her breasts – and because she had conceived a passion for him that he could not resist. Any force will overcome unless confronted by a greater force. Clarissa's force is greater than mine.

I had better go now. Drive home. No point hanging around.

She flushed the loo, splashed cold water over her face, tidied her hair and twitched her skirt straight. Then she returned to the restaurant.

'Well, darlings,' she said, addressing the general company, 'it's after three and I've got a long drive ahead. Would it be all right if I took myself off now? Hugo: you won't mind?'

She took her jacket from the back of the chair, shrugged it on, went to the head of the table and kissed Hugo and her sons Roddy and Julian, bending more briefly to kiss Jenny and Philomena as well. She gave the two little girls a hug and slipped five pounds covertly into Ulrike's hand as the girl stood up politely to say goodbye. She walked round to Oliver. He rose to his feet. Time stopped.

'*Good*bye, Clarissa,' said Harriet, dry-mouthed. 'Oliver . . .'

Don't let him lean forward and give me a social kiss, she prayed. It would be a Judas kiss.

'Good*bye*, Harriet dear,' gushed Clarissa triumphantly. 'You *must* come and *visit* us in *France*, now that you're on your own . . .'

Emily jumped up and ran round to stand beside her. 'Granny Harriet I *wish* you didn't have to *go*!' she said. 'I *liked* you reading to us.'

'So did I, Emmy darling,' Harriet said. She crouched down and the child's warm arms twined pleadingly round her neck.

'*Don't* go, Granny, don't *go* – you don't *have* to go! *Stay!*'

'No, Emily, I can't stay. Honestly. But remember, I love you very much. I shall think of you a lot. I've had a very happy week with you. Bye-bye now, darling' – she stood up – 'goodbye, everyone.'

She waved one hand and walked towards the door across an endless expanse of white squares outlined in red . . . white, red, white, red, hopscotch, one, two, one, two, one foot goes in front of the next, one, two, nearly there, one, two, don't turn, this is it, there's the door – *out*!

She had taken a dozen steps towards her car when she heard footsteps behind her. She did not look round. Oliver pulled at her hand, forcing her to stop.

'Do you really intend to leave me?' he asked. 'Or are you going somewhere to wait for me? You would have left a message at the club, wouldn't you? You could wait – I don't know – at the National Portrait Gallery?'

'No,' she said, not looking at him. 'I am going. Come with me *now*, if you are coming. But you won't. I understand that, having seen her. She has a grand passion for you. It is rare among wives. Clarissa won't let you go. Your only hope is to come with me now. You've got your jacket – don't look back – just *come*, Oliver.' She raised her eyes to look unflinchingly into his. '*Now*.'

'You heard me. I tried to say something. She prevented me. I can't humiliate her in front of everyone. It would be despicable. Harriet, I can't *live* without you. You haven't begun to understand how much I love you. I'll tell Clarissa tonight that I am leaving her and tomorrow I'll ring you

277

from Mark's flat. I'll be with you in a few days, perhaps by Tuesday. *Soon.* Believe me. *I cannot live without you.*'

'I believe that *you* believe it. Oliver: *my only love.* Goodbye.'

She released her hand from his grip. They did not kiss. He stood still, stock still on the pavement, watching her steadily walk away.

Chapter Seventeen

Harriet drove back to Camberwell, losing her way once or twice. Even so it didn't take long. On wet Sunday afternoons the streets of London are nearly deserted. She parked and climbed the seven steps up to the front door, glancing in through the window at her left to make sure the drawing room was empty and they hadn't somehow managed to get back before her. No, no-one there. She rummaged for the key Roddy had given her, thinking, I must remember to leave it on the hall table. Better do it now.

Packing took a few minutes. She always travelled light. She put the shoes at the bottom of her case, fetched her washing things from the bathroom and dressing gown from the hook on the back of the door – well done not to forget that! – took everything from the wardrobe and chest of drawers and closed the suitcase. Emptier than when she came. No presents, of course. She stripped her bed, folding the sheets and pillowcases tidily, and opened the window to air the room.

She carried her case downstairs. In the drawing room stood a small desk inside which she found sheets of headed writing paper . . . RODERICK AND JENNIFER CAPEL . . . and their address. She unscrewed the fountain pen from her handbag, sat with it poised for a few seconds and then scribbled:

Sunday, 3.30
Darlings,
Sorry to dash off like that – it's been a very intense and happy week but suddenly I felt exhausted. Dodo needs

me too. I didn't want to hurry anyone else so it was best to just go. I'd rather avoid the evening rush and not have to drive in the dark. Thank you all for giving me a wonderful reminder of the closeness and importance of family life. It matters more than anything, doesn't it? Whatever the ups and downs. I did love seeing you all although I couldn't help thinking about Daddy. I shall learn to live without him. So selfish to be inconsolable.

I'll ring when I get back – once again, lots of love and big hugs for Hugo, Emmie and Mandy – from Mother / Granny Harriet.

She put this letter in an envelope addressed to *R and J*, stuck it down and propped it on the hall table beside the key. Then she shut the front door firmly behind her and headed west, out of London, away from her children and grandchildren.

'Daddy?' said Jenny when her father returned ashen-faced after running out of the restaurant in pursuit of Harriet. 'What was all *that* about? What's going *on*?'

'Nothing,' said Oliver.

'*Nothing!*' said Clarissa. 'What do you *mean*, Jenny? *Nothing's* going on! Now darlings – *where* are you going to take Granny 'Rissa, who's come *all the way* from *France* to see you? Shall we go and visit Peter Pan in Kensington Gardens?'

'I must go,' said Philly. 'It's been brilliant, everyone – really good to see you all. Thanks so much, Rods. Be in touch!'

'Hey, Phills – where . . . ?' asked her sister.

'Philomena?' said her mother. 'You're not leaving *now*? You *can't!*'

''Fraid I can, Mum! Try and get together before you leave. Lunch tomorrow maybe, but it'll mean cancelling a client. Bye-bye, Huggy . . . *bye*, everyone.'

Julian set off with Hugo to the Museum of the Moving Image ('No, you *can't* come! We're going on our *own*!'). Jenny drove home with Ulrike in the car beside her, Mowgli in his cage on the back seat. Roderick set off with both his parents-in-law to walk the little girls into tiredness. With joyful noise and clatter the Capel and Gaunt family left the Pizza Express. It was after half past three and they were the last to go. The waiters sagged with relief. Worth it though. Nice to make people happy.

Harriet followed the signs for the south-west. Putney ... Richmond ... Sunbury. I must ring Dodo, she thought. I never phoned her last night and she may be worrying. I'll stop at the first service station on the M3. Could probably do with some petrol in any case. Mind blank. Plenty of time to think later.

George had said once, 'Hattie, you have a splinter of ice in your heart.' The remark had frightened her at the time but she thought now, yes, I have. I can hold back this bursting dyke of emotions, this brainstorm of memories and possibilities, until I choose to release them – perhaps never. I always thought people underestimated the benefits of self-control.

She glanced up through the windscreen at the lurid, darkening sky. There's going to be a storm. Good thing I left early. Traffic's building up. Weekend drivers. A nightmare. Be dark by seven. I'll be home by then. Supper with Dodo and after that I might sit with her and watch the new Jane Austen serial on the BBC. Wonderful to sleep in my own bed again. Pull up the drawbridge.

She stopped for petrol and bought a Sunday paper. She queued for a cup of turgid coffee and while she drank it, glanced at the paper. It was full of articles analysing the O.J. Simpson trial and the aftermath of the Lib-Dems' annual conference, neither of which interested her. She went in search of the public telephones.

'Dodo? Hello darling, it's Hattie. Are you all right?'

'I am, thank you dear. What about you?'

'I'm on my way. I should be home in a couple of hours. Expect me soon after six.'

'Are you alone?'

'Yes.'

There was a tranquil silence. Harriet knew Dodo wouldn't ask.

'I did what you said. I renounced him. He hasn't even realized it yet but I have. *Oh my God I hope you were right.*'

To Harriet's astonishment, tears gushed from her eyes and flowed down her face. The telephone booth splintered into a thousand pointed shards of light. She turned her back on the young woman waiting outside and spoke into the foul-smelling mouthpiece, rank with cigarette smoke. Her voice broke up, as though on a badly tuned radio. She had not spoken since leaving the Pizza Express an hour ago.

'I did it, Dodo – I walked away from him. *My only love.*'

'There there; poor lamb. There there. Don't dawdle, hurry straight back, drive carefully. Concentrate on the road. Don't think. You can think later.'

'He said to me, Dodo, his very last words were: "*I can't live without you.*" And I just walked away and left him standing there.'

'He'll survive, Harriet, and so will you. It's a nasty-looking black sky. Take care.'

'I'm not blaming you, Dodo. It wasn't your decision; hardly even mine. It was his wife. I'm on my way.'

She put the receiver down without saying goodbye lest her weeping became too blatant and upset Dodo. She rubbed the back of her hand across her eyes, squeezed them open and shut, shook her head and pushed open the sluggish door.

She longed to talk to someone. If only she could get hold of Constance King, the old school-friend who had been smitten by middle-aged passion. She took the tatty little leather-bound address book out of her handbag and by a miracle, it was there at the very top of the K column, indexed under K for King. (*M'd to Paul Liddell*) it said and after that, in pencil, (*divorced*). There was a London number. Harriet went back to the newsagent and paid for a second unwanted Sunday paper to get some change.

She went into another foetid phone booth, dialled the number and a vibrant young male voice answered instantly,

'Yes – hallo?'

'Sorry to bother you – could I speak to Constance, please?'

'She moved ages ago. We bought from the people after her.'

'Would you happen to have her new number?'

'I'll have a quick look . . .' She could hear the sounds of frantic rustling. Then his voice came back on the line: 'I can't find it and as a matter of fact my wife's just gone into labour. I thought you were the midwife ringing back. I ought to clear the line.'

'Of course,' Harriet said. 'I'm so sorry. Best of luck. Hope it goes well.'

'OK, cheers.'

'Goodbye.'

She had not even had the presence of mind to ask where Constance had moved to. Poor young man, he did sound frantic.

She climbed back into the car and continued down the M3. She'd cut out Salisbury and go via Southampton and then get onto the M27 and finally the A31. Longer mileage but shorter driving time. Dark clouds were piling up. The trees were silhouetted against the sky and fields were jagged shapes of green and brown like stained glass, unnaturally brilliant. Cows stood about in muted clumps. Music. That would distract her. She sorted through the tapes under the dashboard with one hand, glancing rapidly at them and up again at the road ahead. They were all what George called diddly-um-dee-dee music . . . Ravel, Debussy. She needed something more solid. She swerved violently to avoid a car overtaking too fast. She hadn't seen it coming. 'Look in your rear-view mirror every fifteen seconds,' George said. 'Constant vigilance.' He always said the same things. Oliver probably did too but she hadn't had time to find out.

Oliver! She thought she had pulled up the drawbridge in her mind that kept him out but his name had slipped through, agile as a lizard. Oliver. Just as I thought I was becoming used to living alone he shook up my carefully assembled routine like pieces in a kaleidoscope. Now they make a different pattern and I can't find my way through it.

It was five o'clock by the time Dodo rang the Camberwell number.

283

'Is that you, Roddy?' she asked and he thought, how old and quavery she's become.

'Yes, Dodo. It's me. Are you all right? Is Mother back?'

'No. I don't want to worry you, Roderick, but—'

'She couldn't have got to you yet. She didn't leave us till after three. Then she had to come back here and pack and it's nearly three hours' driving time.'

'It's not that. She rang me about half an hour ago. She seemed very upset about something. Roddy, I'm worried. Will you ring the police and tell them to look out for her car? Do you know its number?'

'Dodo, I'm sure that's not necessary. She was fine when she left us.'

'Roderick, *please* do as I ask. The police won't take me seriously. They'll think I'm just a silly old woman. It needs a man's voice.'

'Dodo . . .' he said, still uncertain.

'*Roderick*, now will you *please* do as I ask.'

'All right. Remind me of the number. It's a dark green Volvo . . . .?'

'J652 something . . .'

'I remember. She must be well on her way. She'll be there within the hour. But if it makes you feel better I'll ring the Dorset and Somerset traffic police.'

'It does, Roddy. Thank you. How was dear Hugo? Did he enjoy his day?'

'He's gone off with Jules for a treat, all by himself. Now *don't worry*. Let me know when she arrives.'

'I will. You are a good boy.'

Roderick smiled. 'Dear old Dodo. You still know how to order me about! Bye-bye.'

'Goodbye, Roddy.'

He hesitated for a moment, then got hold of the numbers for the south-west traffic police and left a message. 'Woman driver – on her own – very upset – if they could just keep an eye – sorry to bother them –Yes: the number to ring is 0171 . . .'

Jennifer, emerging from the kitchen after a long talk with Ulrike, said, 'Phew! She'll stay! I've had to give her a rise though. Ten pounds a week. God knows where I'll find it. What was all *that* about?'

'Dodo, worrying about Mother. Said she'd rung up and seemed very distressed. She was OK when she left, wasn't she? Pass me her note again.' He read it aloud. '*"I couldn't help thinking about Daddy. I shall learn to live without him. So selfish to be inconsolable."* Did *you* notice her missing him that much?'

'No. Though she did seem in a hell of a state after lunch. Poor old Harriet. It *is* only six months, I suppose. Marriage. It's such a strong and secret thing. I had no idea she was that devoted to him.'

'Are you that devoted to me?' Roderick asked.

'I must be or I wouldn't put up with you. Where are the girls?'

'Watching TV. Doesn't always *feel* like devotion.'

'Come here. Give me a kiss. Do you love *me*?'

'Yes, damn you, difficult woman that you are. I do. But you'd better hurry up and get yourself another job or it'll be love in a South London semi.'

Oliver and his wife made their way back to the Reform Club. The place was deserted, since on Sundays it did not provide anything to eat or drink. They moved to a different, double bedroom on the top floor, overlooking the same view of St James's. Clarissa peered out of the window and pressed hard on the bed, frowning critically. He knew she expected to make love later – his wife had always found hotel bedrooms stimulating – and knew he could not possibly accommodate her desire; not tonight and probably never again. The memory of Harriet's neat little body losing all modesty and neatness as she scaled hitherto unknown peaks of pleasure, suffused him with anguished lust.

Clarissa commandeered the bathroom, emerging after ten minutes freshly lipsticked and smelling of some orchidaceous scent.

'What a *treat*, Olly, a night *out* together in *London*! What shall we *do*? Do you suppose *Rules* is open on Sunday evenings? I haven't been there for *ages*!'

'We could be more adventurous than that,' Oliver said,

pierced by the recollection of dining there with Harriet a mere six days earlier.

'All right, darling,' Clarissa said. 'Whatever you suggest. Boulestins used to be *lovely*. Daddy took me there for my first grown-up dinner when I was seventeen. Or there's always Prunier's for fish. Or if you *want* to try somewhere modern we could ask the porter chappie? *He* must know plenty of restaurants.'

'It's not yet seven – bit early to eat now.'

'Oh darling, I'm *ravenous*! I could hardly eat a *thing* at lunch. We can wander a bit first, look at the shops in Regent's Street. How thrilling – it's *so* long since I was in London!'

Dusk was falling fast and Harriet was tired. Nearly home. Relief to be off the motorway. Hard to stay awake, with the monotonous road and its monotonous stream of monotonous cars. She glanced down and rummaged for more stimulating music. She took out a couple of tapes and peered at them in the light from the dash board. Ah! Perfect. Saint-Saëns' Organ Symphony. She slipped it in and with an electronic clatter and click the tape righted itself and began to play.

Above her head the sky was vivid with muscular streaks of grey and liver-coloured clouds. Half past six. Sunset and the imminent storm combined in a threatening palette. Have to concentrate harder on these narrow lanes. George's black spot coming up quite soon. She dropped her speed and pulled in ready for the coming right-hand bend. Were there lights ahead? It's the trickiest time of day, that half hour between dusk and darkness. At that moment there was a pause on the tape, the great pause that heralds the moment when the organ crashes in. Tossing her head, Harriet drew a deep inward breath in expectation of its familiar and tremendous sound. She concentrated joyously as the organ blared, its sonorous chords filling every corner of the car with strong, resounding music. For a fraction of a second, she lost her line. In that same split second, a blundering oaf in a sports car came round the corner at nearly fifty miles an hour, headlights full on, his passenger shrieking in panic,

'Slow *down*, for Christ's sake, there's something *coming*—'

Had Harriet's eyes been on the road an instant earlier, she might have had time to wrench the steering wheel round. Had the oaf been going ten miles an hour slower, he might have been able to avoid her. As it was, his long bonnet drove straight into the side of her car, crushing her through the window, through the strong Swedish-built door, in its headlong rush. For a millisecond the music of Saint-Saëns continued. Then the organ too stopped and very soon after that the screaming; the sound of splintering glass and metal stopped, the spinning wheels stopped and the country silence reasserted itself. The only sound was the spattering of raindrops on leaves arching over the lane. This was followed minutes later by a slower, thicker drip onto the surface of the road.

It took the police more than half an hour to find the scene of the accident. The blundering oaf was unconscious and his hysterical girlfriend couldn't get the mobile phone to work. But when they did arrive and radioed in to central traffic control, the police had a record of Roderick's earlier call and his telephone number. From that they were quickly able to trace his address. All the same, it was after seven o'clock when the local copper on the beat climbed the steps to the front door of the Camberwell house and rang the bell. Glancing sideways through the box window he could see Roderick and his wife enjoying a quiet glass of wine together. Poor sods, he thought. Hate doing this. Never get used to it. Poor bloody sods. He heard the scampering feet of children and dropped his eyes to knee level, meeting those of the small fair-haired girl pulling open the door.

'Hallo there!' he said. 'Could I have a word with your daddy?'

'*You're* a *policeman*,' she said, awestruck.

'Yes, I am,' he said, and taking off his helmet he stood there with it in his hand, smiling down at her. Looking sideways again, he saw Roderick rising to his feet. Already the expression on his face was stricken. Intuition, the young policeman thought. Amazing how often they know the moment they hear your voice. He straightened up and twitched his pocket as Roderick strode down the hall.

Julian, returning twenty minutes later with Hugo, found the house full of people with shocked faces and two little girls being unnaturally quiet and good. Hugo, impervious, ran upstairs in search of his guinea pig. Roderick led his brother into the drawing room, shut the door firmly, poured him a whisky and indicated the chair by the window. Julian, collapsing numbly into it, thought something terrible must have happened to Alfonso. His immediate reaction, therefore, was a split-second of relief when his brother said, 'Bad news, Jules. *Mother* was killed in a crash on the way home. No, absolutely none at all. Killed *instantly*, they said.'

With an odd explosive snort that sounded more like the beginning of a stutter or uncontrollable laughter, Roderick burst into tears. His face crumpled, becoming unrecognizable, ape-like, grotesque. His brother came and put his arms round him and the two men stood, heads bowed against one another's shoulders, shaking convulsively. They breathed each other's warmth, inhaling the young male smell recognizable from a thousand childhood fights: the smell of sweat, hair, skin, hiccuping breath and tears. Julian straightened up first. He stepped back and said, 'Be OK by you if *I* told Hugo?'

Roderick said, 'Do you realize we've got *no parents* now?'

Julian said, 'It *was* an accident, Rods? There's no *doubt* about that?'

'None at all. Cunt in a s-s-sports car. He's *alive*.'

'Have the Scotch. I don't want it. I'm going to find Hugo.'

'Jules – s-s-sorry but I *can't* tell Dodo.'

'Shouldn't tell her over the phone anyway. We'll have to go down together. You OK to drive? How much have you had?'

'This is my second.'

'Brew up some coffee while I talk to Hugo. Make it strong. Then we'll go. Be there by ten thirty. Oh *fuck* it, Rods, fuck this *whole* fucking *world*!'

Julian kissed his brother, ran the palm of his hand across the top of his head and, calling out to Hugo, left the room.

Jennifer tried to telephone her sister but Philomena,

gloriously entwined with Matthew, had left the answering machine on. She rang again, and again. At the fourth attempt Matthew lifted his burrowing head and said, 'D'you want to answer that?'

'No *way*!'

'*Good!*'

Philly's thighs were clasped round his ears so he did not hear the message that her sister left on the fifth call. Her own hands were cupped ecstatically around her face, so she couldn't hear it either. Life, you see, goes on. Birth, copulation and death.

Chapter Eighteen

April 1996

Clarissa got her way. Philomena and Matthew agreed to hold their wedding reception in France, under her hospitable roof. They had married quietly at a London register office in mid-April, with just Jennifer and Roderick as witnesses. Matthew was an only child and memories of Jenny's catastrophic wedding and Harriet's still-recent death, as well as Philly's obvious pregnancy, all militated against a big church event. Clarissa, in conceding, had stipulated that the two families – Gaunts and Vulliamys – should spend a long weekend at the Manoir des Glycines to celebrate this, their almost dynastic union.

It was heavenly weather, the wisteria at its most exuberant, pale blue flowers cascading like bunches of grapes down the soft stone walls of the house against a background of brilliant green foliage. The surrounding woods were filled with wild violets which Clarissa had risen early to pick and arrange in bowls placed round the *salon*, their tentative, sweet smell perfuming the air. These, she felt, along with creamy lilies of the valley, wisteria and the purple and blue spikes of early irises, made a thoroughly suitable colour scheme.

'White is *essential* for weddings, isn't it?' she could be heard repeating throughout the day, even to guests who had already smiled agreement; 'And *something blue* – well the irises do duty *there* – and I felt, for poor darling Roddy's sake, we ought to have' (she would drop her voice tactfully) 'a thoughtful little gesture in memory of his *mother*. Touches of mauve and purple seemed *appropriate* somehow.'

Thanks to the subtle persuasion of her neighbour, Madame Victorine, Clarissa wore a simple dress and jacket of Wedgwood blue rather than the tropical print she herself would have picked. Philomena billowed in cream. Matthew was narrow and elegant in black. Together they looked like a ship breasting the waves in an arc of spray. The three overexcited grandchildren, petted and admired by every French neighbour, bobbed up and down like colourful yachts in their wake. Madame Victorine's daughter Victoria, back home from Camberwell for the occasion, helped Ulrike serve champagne and food to the family and friends who, with a few legal and theatrical colleagues, had gathered to share the bridal couple's joy.

The first guests had arrived before noon. The day was in full swing. Clarissa basked in her triumph. It was the climax she had always dreamed of; an affirmation of family life, love and fecundity, the next generation like a magnet drawing everyone towards the future. She rode the gathering victoriously, Boadicea on her chariot. *I have survived!* she thought; despite every temptation and every rival I held on to him . . . despite the scheming girls he slept with when he was away who coveted my beautiful secretive husband. God *only* knows how many letters I intercepted, all pleading poverty, pregnancy or broken hearts. Why should I care? They may have been prettier and cleverer and had more sex appeal but I *loved* him best and their mucky little lusts were no match for my great and proper passion.

Last and wickedest of the lot, that woman *Harriet* thought she could take him from me – yet still I have survived as his wife. He's not very happy at the moment and he hasn't made love to me yet, not since *her*, but that will change in time. He's a man, still virile, he has his needs. So, God *knows*, do I! But I am patient. I will wait for as long as it takes. She looked across the room at Oliver, absorbed and unfathomable. *You* my darling, have been my life's work! In the end, being a wife is about holding firm. Hope *Philly* knows that, since she too seems to have married a

291

fascinating but rather a complicated man. All her modern feminist ideas vanished soon enough when she found herself expecting a baby. *Was* it an accident? Bet it wasn't! Love and children are the only real basis for women's lives.

Nothing but his daughter's joy, Oliver thought, made the occasion endurable. Harriet flitted, a discreet grey ghost, between the laughing, chattering figures of the guests. Her presence hovered near him, silent and invisible to everyone except himself. Sometimes he heard her murmur in his ear, 'Oliver: *my only love.*' Once he thought she whispered, 'If they love each other as much as we do, they'll be all right.' But on the whole she drifted quietly and attentively beside and slightly above him as he inclined courteously over the congratulations of his guests.

At dinner on the last evening of his week in London, the Sunday, after Hugo's party was over and they had all dispersed, Oliver had listened to Clarissa's first angry explosion in contemptuous silence. Dapper, gleaming Thai waiters stood unmoving against the walls of the restaurant, stepping forward from time to time to remove dish after tasteless dish from his place. Clarissa had sampled them all and he had listened to her chewing and swallowing and resuming her tirade. Finally she had smiled graciously and said to the waiter,
   '*Really* it was too much! But *so* delicious I simply *couldn't* resist!' When she sat back with a small sigh, satisfied that everything was now crystal clear, Oliver told her that he and Harriet loved each other. He proposed to leave her, Clarissa, and was still here only because he had stayed on in London to finalize arrangements with his lawyer and accountant the following day. He would be joining Harriet by the end of the week, at the very latest. He would make provision for her, Clarissa, and Patrick and hoped she would be civilized about the divorce, since he had dealt generously with them both. Clarissa's fury and pleading despair equally had been met with eyes like icicles and a face like stone, grey and hard. The Thai waiters had stood like temple gods until half past eleven, when at last he paid

the bill and they left. Clarissa smiled her final thanks, a rictus of a smile revealing bad teeth.

Back at the club they found a message left for Oliver, handed to him by the yawning porter. The man covered his mouth hastily and said, 'Beg pardon sir.' The message, like a tolling bell, read: 'Please ring your daughter, no matter how late you get back', and his heart had turned to marble in his ribs. At Jenny's first words the marble became colder still; skeletally cold.

'Daddy, something *ghastly's* happened.' (The words ricocheted like a figure running through a corridor of mirrors – *ghastly's* happened – ghastly's *happened* – swerving from side to side in their headlong rush – *ghastly,* ghastly, *ghastly*.) 'Harriet's car was in an accident on the way home. Roddy's gone to Dorset with Jules. He rang from the hospital just now. He had to identify the body, *poor* Rods.'

'Body?' he had repeated, in a voice like a robot. 'Body? Body? Body? What *body*?'

(*'What* body?' Clarissa echoed idiotically beside him.)

'*Harriet's* body,' said his daughter.

Harriet's body. Dear God, one last living memory. Harriet's palm curled sweetly against his lips as he kissed her hand in the restaurant. Harriet's foot, warm against his own as he pressed it under the table to reassure her. Harriet gloriously on high, astride the lion as earlier that evening (*yesterday* evening) she had been astride him. Harriet's legs, spread wide apart, Harriet's breasts bouncing as she rode towards the joyful certainty of orgasm. Harriet's body, crushed and motionless on a mortuary slab. Oliver had seen violent death and knew what it looked like. Butcher's meat.

'Dad?' said Jennifer's voice down the telephone urgently. '*Daddy* – are you still there?'

He had growled, a barely human noise. He wanted to tip his head back like a wolf and howl to the indifferent heavens. In the first moments after bad news, clichés are the only response.

'What hospital?' he managed to ask.

'Daddy, *you* don't have to go down. Both the boys have gone . . . they'll take care of the formalities.'

'*Tell me what hospital*, Jennifer?'

He heard the fear and puzzlement in her voice but she told him.

Leaving Clarissa without a word, Oliver had walked out of the club and summoning a taxi cruising down Pall Mall, ordered it to drive to Taunton. When he got there two hours later, he overwhelmed the sleepy, protective duty nurses with his authority and his need until they summoned a porter on night duty to escort him to the ice-cold basement mortuary. Only when he saw the body on its burnished steel trolley did he know for certain that Harriet was dead. Her clothes, bundled up and stuffed into a transparent plastic bag hooked over the end of the trolley, were more recognizable than she was. He did not look at the corpse for long but thanked the porter, tipped him a fiver, got into the waiting black cab and was driven back to London, arriving as dawn broke. After that the only question in Oliver's mind was, *when shall I die?*

Hardened by a lifetime of reticence, for the next six months, throughout the chill winter, Oliver concealed his obsessive thoughts behind a mask of imperturbability. Concern for Harriet's sons was one motive; the protection of her – *their* – beloved grandchildren another. Revulsion at the idea of his wife contaminating her name with reproaches or – worse still – mawkishness was also strong. He ordered Clarissa never to mention Harriet again. When once she forgot he almost hit her.

Roderick had shown him her last note and its words haunted him. '*A very intense and happy week ... I shall learn to live without him. So selfish to be inconsolable.*' She meant him, of course; her words had nothing to do with George. *Had* it been suicide? The conclusions of the inquest and the court hearing were unequivocal: death by misadventure. The judge was resolute despite the driver's appearance in a wheelchair. Dangerous driving while under the influence of alcohol. Three years.

Philomena, wearing a chaplet of lilies-of-the valley which bobbed and nodded in time with her laughter and gestures, was talking to her new parents-in-law. 'It's famous, you know, in my generation – the story of how you two met. It

294

makes *ours'* – she grinned at Matthew – 'seem positively *Victorian* by comparison! An evening at the opera chaperoned by my father – how old-fashioned can you *get*! Wait, I remember exactly. Ben: *you* saw *Mona* from the other side of Oxford High Street and you rushed across and said, "Grind my head beneath your feet or else let me take you to the Trout and gaze into your eyes over a glass of Pimm's." That it?'

Ben said, 'Not quite such a smoothie as *that* was I, dear?'

'Oh, he was wonderful,' Mona told Philomena. 'I'd never met anyone so sophisticated in all my life! You *were*, darling. Shut up and let *me* tell the story. He swept me off to this gorgeous riverside pub with peacocks shrieking beside a weir and we sat there half the afternoon and that evening I wrote to my mother – she kept the letter – saying, "Today I met the man I'm going to marry!" And I was *right*.'

'I knew pretty much straightaway, too,' Philly said. 'I think one does.'

It was getting late and the weekend was winding down. Local guests were beginning to wander away, taxis were arriving to ferry people to the station, lifts were being organized to Toulouse airport for the London contingent. Jennifer, with Hugo beside her, was talking to her mother. Clarissa basked in well-being, the knowledge of a big occasion flawlessly carried off. A buffet lunch on the terrace under a canopy of trees had enabled people to wander from table to table; French neighbours had revised their prejudices about the dowdiness of Englishwomen; the English had concluded that maybe the French were not so standoffish after all. Nobody had looked askance at Philomena's pregnancy.

'*Mais c'est* normal *aujourd'hui!*' their most prim and proper neighbour had said. '*Tout le monde vivent comme concubins. Même la fille du* Maire . . . *Les temps jadis sont disparus . . . heureusement, je trouve, moi!*'

'Look over there at Daddy,' Jenny was saying. 'He just doesn't seem *part* of it. He's absolutely sweet when you talk to him directly but the rest of the time he's – I don't know – in a *dream*. You don't suppose it's the onset of *Parkinson's*?'

'Your father's *fine*. Parkinson's? *Nonsense!* He's only sixty-one and still *very* vigorous.'

'Well good for *you*, Mum!'

They smiled conspiratorially, married women both, privy to the secrets of marriage.

'I hope you're as happy with Roddy as *we've* been, darling.' Clarissa said fondly.

'I hope so, too,' her daughter answered. 'He's not always easy but then I suppose it's *just* possible I'm not, either. I think marriage is a bit like a marathon. You have to go through the pain barrier. What *is* it, Huge?'

'What's P-P-*Parkinson's*?'

'It's an illness old people sometimes get but which Grandpa Oliver *has not got*!'

'Did Grandpa George have it?'

'No, he didn't have it either.'

'Did Gran-Gran-Grandma . . .' Hugo stopped. He had gathered, without knowing why, that her name was taboo. Jennifer bent down and looked into his eyes. 'Poor old Huge – *full* of terrors aren't you? No, Grandma Harriet didn't have Parkinson's either.'

'She had an accident?'

'That's right.'

'She p-p-promised me she wasn't going to die.'

'Hugo, sometimes people don't *know* what's going to happen to them. She would have kept her promise if she could. Now look, why don't you and me find the girls and all go and watch the fish swimming along in the shade of the trees? Shall we?'

Jennifer glanced at her mother and shrugged faintly as she walked away. I can't protect my children, she thought, above all not from death. I *can* protect them from divorce and the chaos it would make in their lives and that I have resolved to do.

Oliver stood at the wide door that opened onto the sweep of the drive, accepting the farewells and thanks of departing guests. Julian and Alfonso approached and Julian said, 'Oliver, can we drag you away from your duties for five minutes?'

296

Oliver beckoned his wife with an encircling sweep of one arm and a sideways inclination of his head and Clarissa hurried over.

'Can you do the honours for five minutes? Julian and Fonzi want to see the cellar.'

'Oh yes, we've got some *wonderful* wines . . .' Clarissa said eagerly. '*Do*, darling.'

It seemed as though the happy day would never end. This was the crowning moment of Clarissa's life and she would have liked it to go on for ever. If *only* her mother had been alive to see it! Even she would have been forced to admit that Clarissa's love for Oliver was not a grubby, shameful thing but real and lasting. After thirty-six years of marriage, she had proved herself worthy of the Sullivan name! Philly and Jenny were glowing, both now married to clever and devoted husbands; Patrick had been charmingly bi-lingual; the house and garden looked simply marvellous, the Sullivan silver and crystal shone, the linen tablecloths were crisp, everything sparkled. If only her mother could have witnessed it then surely she would have forgiven her daughter for not being a virgin on her wedding day.

Oliver led Julian and Alfonso down into the dank wine cellar, switching on a dim light. Against the walls, dozens of bottles lay in racks, their dark green and brown glass opaque with dust and spiders' webs. A torch lay on a stool nearby.

'I know about you and . . . Mother,' said Julian.

'*She* told you?'

'No, she didn't say anything. But we had lunch together, that last Friday. She met Fonzi then for the first and only time in her life and I knew from her response to him – us – that something must have happened to her as well. When I saw you together on the Sunday, I understood what.'

'Yes,' Oliver said.

'You kissed her hand when your wife arrived. Just for a second, but I saw.'

'Yes.'

'The palm of her hand. And after the accident, when they retrieved her handbag, it was passed on to me. I found a poem in the back of her diary. I've got it here. Do you want it?'

He handed a piece of paper to Oliver who, without glancing at it, tucked the folded scrap under an ancient wine bottle. Julian thought, he is afraid he will weep. He ought to. This rigidity will kill him. He persisted, 'Are you all right? You look as though you are suffering.'

'Yes.'

'All *right*, or *suffering*?'

'Both.'

Fonzi said, 'Forgive me for interrupting. Julian and I have lost a lot of the people we loved. They have died, sometimes very young. Can *we* do anything? – to help?'

'You are very kind. Thank you. No,' said Oliver.

'*I* have lost her *too*,' said Julian in desperation.

Oliver looked at him in silence. Julian's fine-boned face reminded him of Harriet's; his aquiline nose was identical to hers, almost as though her marble features were superimposed upon her son's warm, three-dimensional reality. All weekend he had managed to avoid Julian but now, standing beside him, he saw for the last time Harriet's unconquered beauty. Oliver had a powerful impulse to lean forward and kiss Julian on the lips, as though he would meet Harriet's pliant kiss. But even the distraught obey convention and for her sake he would not embarrass her son. Since he could not touch Julian it was intolerable to stand so close to him, here in the chilly atmosphere of the cellar. Oliver said, 'It does not ease with time. You have my profound sympathy. Now shall we go back upstairs?'

Jennifer and her sister were embracing before making their separate departures. Philly and Matthew planned to tour France for the last week in April; the others were on their way back to London.

'Feels funny, *you* having the great bump!' Jenny said. 'I'm so *thrilled*. Have you decided yet what to call it – what's the current favourite?'

'With a surname like Vulliamy you have to be jolly careful. I mean, *Philomena Vulliamy* – wow! They call me Philly Vully in the office, though I'm still Capel professionally. So we thought perhaps Kate for a girl and Tom if it's a boy.'

'Tom Vulliamy . . . hey, great! *Love* it!'

'Break it up, you two,' Roderick called out. 'We're going to miss that flight. Kids and Ulrike are waiting in the car.'

'Coming . . .' said Jennifer. 'Where's Dad? Oh there you are! *Darling* Daddy: thanks for a *brilliant* occasion. We got it *right* this time, didn't we?'

'Did we?' asked Oliver. 'Goodbye Jenny, Roderick. Safe journey home. Look after each other.'

One by one the guests and family smiled and kissed; two kisses, four kisses, soft perfume against soft cheeks. The men shook hands and murmured something gallant and everyone drifted away, glancing backwards as if reluctant to let the vision go. By half past six the house was empty. Clarissa lay back exhausted on a sofa in the salon surrounded by the débris of gifts, smeared wine glasses, crumbed plates and tiny cups with bitter coffee dregs. She was radiantly happy at last.

Oliver climbed the stairs to their bedroom. He pulled open his bedside drawer, found an old envelope and wrote on the back of it I AM INCONSOLABLE. He took out and unwrapped the pistol and without pausing for a second held it to his right temple and fired. It was precisely eight months, almost to the minute, since Harriet had died. Sometimes it is the man who loves most.

THE END

HUMAN CROQUET
Kate Atkinson

'VIVID AND INTRIGUING ... FIZZLES AND CRACKLES ALONG
... A COMPELLING STORY WITH EXCURSIONS INTO
FANTASY, EXPERIMENT AND OUTRAGEOUS GRAND
GUIGNOL ... A *TOUR DE FORCE*'
Penelope Lively, *Independent*

Once it had been the great forest of Lythe – a vast and impen-
etrable thicket of green with a mystery in the very heart of the
trees. And here, in the beginning, lived the Fairfaxes, grandly, at
Fairfax Manor, visited once by the great Gloriana herself.

But over the centuries the forest had been destroyed, replaced by
Streets of Trees. The Fairfaxes had dwindled too; now they lived
in 'Arden' at the end of Hawthorne Close and were hardly a
family at all.

There was Vinny (the Aunt from Hell) – with her cats and her
crab-apple face. And Gordon, who had forgotten them for seven
years and, when he remembered, came back with fat Debbie, who
shared her one brain cell with a poodle. And then there were
Charles and Isobel, the children. Charles, the acne-scarred Lost
Boy, passed his life awaiting visits from aliens and the return of
his mother. But it is Isobel to whom the story belongs – Isobel,
born on the Streets of Trees, who drops into pockets of time and
out again. Isobel is sixteen and she too is waiting for the return of
her mother – the thin, dangerous Eliza with her scent of nicotine,
Arpège and sex, whose disappearance is part of the mystery that
still remains at the heart of the forest.

'READS LIKE A DARKER SHENA MACKAY OR A FUNNIER,
MORE LITERARY BARBARA VINE. VIVID, RICHLY
IMAGINATIVE, HILARIOUS AND FRIGHTENING BY TURNS'
Cressida Connolly, *Observer*

0 552 99619 X

BLACK SWAN

EXIT, ORANGE & RED
Martyn Bedford

Blood is found smeared on the doors of Urbopark, a vast out-of-town shopping complex. Local reporter Constance Amory is assigned to cover the crime – an assignment which plunges her into the biggest story of her life. As one increasingly ferocious attack follows another, she becomes the point of contact with the saboteur whose identity is gradually revealed by a trail of cryptic clues which have more relevance to the past than the present.

Constance's investigations point towards her own family history, towards a Victorian era of industrial conflict. In a city renowned for its steel and cutlery, a saw grinder, Thomas Amory, works among the disenfranchised folk whose code of social justice is at violent odds with that of the employers, factory owners and lawmakers and whose life is to be overtaken by violent conflict.

Separated from Thomas by 130 years and seven generations, Constance can only watch as the past and present converge on a tragic and dramatic collision course...

'INGENIOUS AND INTRIGUING...MOVING, GRIPPING, ENTERTAINING...I WAS GENUINELY SORRY TO FINISH IT'
Lesley Glaister, *Independent*

'A CHALLENGING AND INTELLIGENT WRITER WHO IS TO BE ADMIRED FOR HIS BOLDNESS. BEDFORD'S IDEAS AND HIS EXECUTION OF THEM ARE STRIKINGLY ORIGINAL AND HIS SENSIBILITIES UNUSUAL'
Mary Loudon, *The Times*

0 552 99675 0

BLACK SWAN

IN A LAND OF PLENTY
Tim Pears

'IMPOSSIBLE TO RESIST . . . A GENEROSITY OF SPIRIT THAT
IS GENUINELY UPLIFTING. I COULD GO ON AND ON ABOUT
HOW WONDERFUL IT IS, BUT READ IT FOR YOURSELF'
Time Out

In a small town somewhere in the heart of England, the aftermath
of the Second World War brings change. For ambitious and
expansive industrialist Charles Freeman, it brings new
opportunities and marriage to Mary. He buys the big house on the
hill to cement their union and to nail his aspirations to the future.

In quick succession, three sons and a daughter bring life to the
big house and with it, the seeds of joy and tragedy. As his
children grow up, Charles' business expands in direct proportion
to his girth as Britain claws its way from the grey austerity of the
war years.

As times change, so do the family's fortunes for better and for
worse, ebbing and flowing with the years. Their stories create a
powerful and resonant epic, nothing less than the story of our
lives.

'ASTONISHING AND AMBITIOUS . . . EACH DETAIL IS
RESONANT, AND THE AUTHOR'S REALISM AND
COMPASSION IRRADIATES THE WRITING. A STORY ABOUT
PEOPLE – US – AND THEIR CONTEXT, WRITTEN WITH
AUTHORITY AND UNSHOWY GRACE. EARLY NINETEENTH-
CENTURY FRANCE HAD BALZAC, WE HAVE PEARS TO
TRACE OUR FORTUNES AND FOLLIES'
The Times

'A BIG BOOK WITH A BIG HEART. PEARS IS AN
UNASHAMEDLY MOVING WRITER AND THIS MARVELLOUS
BOOK WILL REDUCE MANY TO TEARS'
Punch

'HIS GENIUS LIES IN TELLING A TORY . . . AN OPERATIC
NOVEL FULL OF DEATH, SEX, BROTHERS, SISTERS, COUSINS
AND THROBBING HEARTS'
Daily Telegraph

0 552 99718 8

BLACK SWAN

THE SERPENTINE CAVE
Jill Paton Walsh

'AN ENTHRALLING NOVEL...HUGELY ENJOYABLE'
Mail on Sunday

When Marion's mother dies, she is left confronting the chaotic detritus of a life obsessively devoted to art. She has left it too late to ask the crucial questions about scenes confusedly remembered from her childhood, and above all about the identity of her own father. Out of the hundreds of paintings in her mother's studio, one, a portrait of a young man, is inscribed 'For Marion'. Is this her father? And who was he?

Marion's search takes her to St Ives. In the closeknit Cornish town where communities of fisherfolk and artists have coexisted for many years, she learns of a tragedy which is intrinsically tied up with her father's life. Over fifty years before, the St Ives lifeboat went down with all hands bar one. Marion must delve deep into the past to discover the identity of a man she never knew, and in so doing confront the demons which have tortured her own adult life.

'ANOTHER TRIUMPH WHICH WILL SURELY RANK AMONGST THE YEAR'S FINEST...A NOVEL THAT LIVES AND BREATHES BEYOND ITS EDGES...VIVID, WISE AND EMOTIONALLY SATISFYING'
Punch

'A NOVEL WHICH ENGAGES THE READER'S SYMPATHIES. IT IS INTELLIGENT AND PERCEPTIVE, THE KIND OF BOOK LIKELY TO STAY IN THE MEMORY...VERY GOOD INDEED'
Allan Massie, The Scotsman

'A COMPELLING TALE'
The Times

0 552 99720 X

BLACK SWAN

A SELECTED LIST OF FINE WRITING
AVAILABLE FROM BLACK SWAN

99313 1	**OF LOVE AND SHADOWS**	*Isabel Allende*	£6.99
99766 8	**EVERY GOOD GIRL**	*Judy Astley*	£6.99
99619 X	**HUMAN CROQUET**	*Kate Atkinson*	£6.99
99675 0	**EXIT, ORANGE & RED**	*Martyn Bedford*	£6.99
99715 3	**BEACHCOMBING FOR A SHIPWRECKED GOD**	*Joe Coomer*	£6.99
99669 6	**ARRANGED MARRIAGE**	*Chitra Banerjee Divakaruni*	£6.99
99624 6	**THE COUNTER-TENOR'S DAUGHTER**	*Elizabeth Falconer*	£6.99
99721 8	**BEFORE WOMAN HAD WINGS**	*Connie May Fowler*	£6.99
99599 1	**SEPARATION**	*Dan Franck*	£5.99
99656 4	**THE TEN O'CLOCK HORSES**	*Laurie Graham*	£5.99
99681 5	**A MAP OF THE WORLD**	*Jane Hamilton*	£6.99
99754 4	**CLOUD MUSIC**	*Karen Hayes*	£6.99
99771 4	**MALLINGFORD**	*Alison Love*	£6.99
99689 0	**WATERWINGS**	*Joan Marysmith*	£6.99
99718 8	**IN A LAND OF PLENTY**	*Tim Pears*	£6.99
99608 4	**LAURIE AND CLAIRE**	*Kathleen Rowntree*	£6.99
99777 3	**THE SPARROW**	*Mary Doria Russell*	£6.99
99671 8	**THAT AWKWARD AGE**	*Mary Selby*	£6.99
99753 6	**AN ACCIDENTAL LIFE**	*Titia Sutherland*	£6.99
99700 5	**NEXT OF KIN**	*Joanna Trollope*	£6.99
99720 X	**THE SERPENTINE CAVE**	*Jill Paton Walsh*	£6.99
99673 4	**DINA'S BOOK**	*Herbjørg Wassmo*	£6.99
99592 4	**AN IMAGINATIVE EXPERIENCE**	*Mary Wesley*	£5.99
99761 7	**THE GATECRASHER**	*Madeleine Wickham*	£6.99
99591 6	**A MISLAID MAGIC**	*Joyce Windsor*	£4.99